The Assa

Alan Bardos

© Alan Bardos 2016

Alan Bardos has asserted his rights under the Copyright, Design and Patents Act, 1988, to be identified as the author of this work.

First published in 2016 by Endeavour Press Ltd.

This Edition published in 2018 by Endeavour Media Ltd.

Table of Contents

Chapter 1	5
Chapter 2	10
Chapter 3	13
Chapter 4	18
Chapter 5	21
Chapter 6	24
Chapter 7	28
Chapter 8	35
Chapter 9	39
Chapter 10	43
Chapter 11	49
Chapter 12	55
Chapter 13	57
Chapter 14	61
Chapter 15	67
Chapter 16	74
Chapter 17	80
Chapter 18	91
Chapter 19	95
Chapter 20	106
Chapter 21	109
Chapter 22	113
Chapter 23	120
Chapter 24	127

Chapter 25	130
Chapter 26	137
Chapter 27	139
Chapter 28	146
Chapter 29	152
Chapter 30	154
Chapter 31	163
Chapter 32	173
Chapter 33	184
Chapter 34	195
Chapter 35	203
Chapter 36	214
Chapter 37	224
Chapter 38	234
Chapter 39	246
Chapter 40	250
Chapter 41	255
Chapter 42	261
Chapter 43	268
Chapter 44	275
Historical Notes	288

Chapter 1

14th May, 1914. Johnny Swift carefully signed and dated the note and was rewarded with another stack of chips. He was starting to think that he should have tried a more sophisticated strategy. He steadied himself and redoubled his bet on nineteen.

The croupier smirked at him and sent the ball spinning. Johnny gripped the roulette table, struggling to suppress his anxiety as the ball circled the wheel. He straightened his shoulders, trying to distance himself from the other wretched people around him. He wasn't done yet.

The ball started flicking about the pockets and Johnny caught his breath as it landed on nineteen. Then Fortuna grinned and the ball flicked straight out again.

The croupier swept away Johnny's chips and he redoubled his bet on nineteen. Statistically, he knew that his number would come up eventually. Doubling his bet ensured he'd win back everything he'd lost tonight and make a return equal to his first bet. However, he was finding that he could easily run out of money before that happened.

He'd never liked the public school ethos of the taking part being more important than the winning. It seemed particularly absurd now.

The ball mesmerized him as it whirled around the wheel, this time landing on zero without any preamble. Johnny choked. Zero was his usual number of choice, but as nineteen was his age, he'd thought it would be lucky. He persevered, redoubling his bet.

There was only enough money left for one more turn of the wheel. He considered trying to bamboozle another note. He was so deep in the abyss now that a few more hundred couldn't possibly make a difference. It was all about staying in the game, but that became increasingly unlikely as the ball plopped down on eight.

He crossed his arms in frustration, hugging himself in an effort not to smash the bloody contraption. As he did so, Johnny felt a sheet of paper crumple in his jacket pocket. It was a simple piece of cheap rubbish and yet it had still led to him making a whole series of rash decisions.

The first and most crucial of these decisions was made in Zurich. Johnny had been sent there by Sir George, his superior in the diplomatic service, to deliver official correspondence and deposit funds into his Swiss bank account. It was a regular trip, and he enjoyed the perk and was generally able to overlook the fact that he was being used as a glorified errand boy by a man he detested. The telegram summoning him back forthwith had shattered his revelry. He was normally allowed a week to complete 'his travels' and he'd made arrangements. An urgent recall was unheard of for someone of Johnny's limited responsibility. He could only assume that Sir George had found out about one of his indiscretions, most likely a gambling debt. Johnny was finding them impossible to manage.

There had been little choice but to double up and make a last stand. With the necessary documentation for Sir George's account he had been able to make a sizeable withdrawal, once he'd perfected Sir George's signature – he'd seen it replicated by an expert a thousand times before. Johnny had planned to win enough to pay the money back and head off whatever trouble lay in wait on his return. That money had long since gone and he'd had to resort to further deception.

A woman next to Johnny brushed against his arm, obviously trying to attract his attention, which was par for the course as far as he was concerned. The idea that there was a woman impervious to his brash, physical charm, forged on the playing fields of England, was beyond his comprehension.

Johnny stood up to his full height of six feet. He was immensely proud of his build which combined the elegance and grace of a winger, with the strength of a front row prop. Almost out of instinct, rather than from any sense of desire for the woman, he tilted his head at an angle, showing off the fine line of his cheekbones. It was, he realised, his appeal to women that had got him into this mess.

He glanced across the casino and saw Lady Smyth, looking bored and annoyed, as she distanced herself from the rabble. Her sequined dress gave the impression of shooting stars bursting into showers of light, and Johnny thought that it bestowed a bearing and dignity on her which was way beyond her twenty-one years. It would be bad enough for her to be in a place like this, he thought, but to be in a place like this and be losing must be intolerable.

La Fontaine d'Espoir was a down-at-heel, back-alley gambling den, kept open by a nod and a wink. It was not the sort of establishment that Lady

Smyth was used to, especially in comparison with the splendour and opulence she usually enjoyed in Vittel.

Johnny wondered if it was called 'The Fountain of Hope' in reference to the town's famous spas or the despair of its patrons, who like Johnny, had well and truly fallen through the cracks by the time they'd made it there. The desperation in their eyes was blatant. He caught Lady Smyth's eye and looked away before she saw the same desperation in his own.

The woman next to Johnny was actually pressing against him now to get to the table, all modesty gone in her attempts to place her bets. Her future was also at stake – financial security or the streets. Johnny had seen many such women who'd lost their position in society and, in dire need, would ply their trade in the slightly more up-market brothels he'd patronised before ... before he'd met Lady Smyth.

The last of his rash decisions had been to send her a telegram confirming their arrangement to meet at the spa; he'd needed to see her. She was the most haunting woman Johnny had ever known and if anyone could make him forget the trouble he was in, it was her. Lady Elizabeth Smyth could make him forget everything.

He pushed out his last stack of chips, doubling up his bet on nineteen again, and the croupier sent the ball spinning round with his customary smug sneer, which Johnny found particularly galling. They both knew he was on his last legs.

Captivated, Johnny watched the ball spinning around the wheel. He loved the way it dropped and flitted about the pockets, teasing and caressing his hopes and dreams before finally landing in a pocket.

'Yes! Huzzah!' Johnny was shouting before he'd fully registered what had happened. 'Nineteen! It's actually, bloody-well landed on nineteen!'

That wiped the smug look off the croupier's face and he sullenly pushed a large stack of chips towards Johnny.

'Thank you. I think I'll call it a night,' Johnny said, smirking. He hurriedly started picking up the chips, ignoring the piteous looks from the people around the table.

'Come on, Johnny – play up and play the game!' The crisp, precise voice of Lady Smyth was like cold steel. The jolt caused him to drop his chips. She'd pushed through the crowd and was standing over him. 'You've hardly broken the bank at Monte Carlo.'

'Lady Smyth, we've had our win. The strategy worked,' Johnny said discreetly.

'Aren't you bored with playing the inside, Johnny?' She always looked down on his success as slightly tasteless, believing that it wasn't the winning that counted but how boldly one played. 'Why don't you take a chance on the outside, for once?'

Lady Smyth's elegant, cat-like features formed a smile, her words a not-so-subtle reminder that he was an outsider. He might look the part, in her husband's old evening dress, but he wasn't quite the thing. Johnny gave in to his anger and pushed the chips back out onto the table.

The ball bounced and flicked about the wheel with all the mean-spirited flirting of a bored and frustrated debutante. Johnny had thrown everything on red. It seemed the most fitting. The ball bounced slowly to a stop and the croupier smirked for the last time. 'Noire.'

The crowd stared at Johnny. They knew what it meant and thanked whatever luck they had left that they weren't him.

Johnny pulled together the last shreds of dignity that his education had given him and addressed the crowd. 'I may have lost everything tonight, but as Sir Cecil Rhodes said: "I am an Englishman, so consequently have won first prize in the lottery of life."'

He bowed stiffly and guided Lady Smyth out into the foyer before she could goad him into making any more bets.

'You lose with such style, such vigour,' she purred. 'Oh, to show such superiority, such contempt for money!'

'Where there is disaster to be averted, I will bring catastrophe,' Johnny said glibly and then stepped outside.

The night air cleared Johnny's head and focused his mind. He'd won Lady Smyth's admiration at the expense of every penny he could get. He now owed over two and a half thousand pounds. Not a huge amount, in the grand scheme of things, and certainly not enough to break the bank at Monte Carlo, but it was enough to break him. The sheer scale of it staggered him, when he chose to think about it. Assuming he kept his position in the diplomatic service, he could work for twenty years before coming close to repaying it.

Johnny knew he'd have to return to Paris; there was nowhere else for him to go. He shoved Lady Smyth into a cab, in as gentlemanly a manner as he could manage under the circumstances, and climbed in after her, shouting, 'Station!' at the driver.

'But we've only just got here,' Lady Smyth snapped. She still didn't grasp the full enormity of Johnny's situation. To emphasise the point, he took the telegram out of his pocket.

'Sir George has called me back to Paris, Lady Smyth. Our happy time is over.'

'I do wish you'd call me Libby, when we're in private.'

'I'm required at the embassy, immediately.'

'Nonsense – I'm sure my husband can spare you for a day or two. All he does is gorge himself on the latest scandal in the popular press.'

'You could still take your spa treatment,' Johnny suggested. Sir George tried to moderate his wife's wayward nature with soothing spa cures, even to the extent of allowing her to go out of season. It made an excellent pretext for Johnny to meet her, away from the inquisitive eyes of Paris's diplomatic community.

'That's not the treatment I yearn for.' She ran a suggestive finger down Johnny's face, but nothing could soothe the churning in his stomach.

'You needn't worry about the money,' she said, sensing his anxiety.

'What?'

'I renewed all of the notes before I left Paris. We've got a month to pay it back.'

That gave Johnny some comfort, but he was too stunned by what had just happened in the casino to really care about next month.

'So we might as well spend a few days at the spa and have another little flutter. I'm sure we can find somewhere decent that will still take our notes.'

'My instructions are explicit, Lady Smyth. I really must go back,' Johnny replied, starting to feel temptation well up inside him.

'I see. George did mention something about one of his juniors being for the high jump,' she added casually.

Johnny convulsed. 'He ... *what*?' A thousand possibilities flooded his mind, but he instinctively understood why he'd been recalled. 'Sir George must have found out about us.' Johnny looked at the telegram in his hand, not quite believing it to be true, but if Libby had settled the debts, it was the only possible explanation.

Chapter 2

'It is announced from Sarajevo that the Archduke Heir Apparent and his wife will come to Sarajevo and participate in manoeuvres.' The cafe's gaslight flickered as Gavrilo watched Nedjo grip the newspaper clipping. Franz Ferdinand's arrogant face stared back at them.

Gavrilo shared his friend's restlessness. They both knew that the visit by the 'arch tyrant' would give them the perfect opportunity to take a sweet and bloody revenge for the suffering his empire had inflicted on the South Slav people.

'Rereading the notice won't get us the means to destroy the heir,' Trifko, the third person at their table, remarked curtly.

Nedjo reacted to the edge in Trifko's voice. 'I don't want to stop the visit. Like you, I want to go home and welcome them. It's our moral duty to give the heir a proper reception.'

'Is that a boast or do you actually mean to take action? Trifko replied calmly, ignoring Nedjo's bluster.

All three had resolved to take action a month earlier, after Nedjo had received the clipping from a friend in Sarajevo. They'd made contact with an ex-partisan, a fellow Bosnian Serb, who'd once shared the same lodgings as Gavrilo. He'd agreed to help them obtain the means, but little progress had been made since then and tension was starting to show.

Gavrilo was equally frustrated, but for now he was content to let the other two squabble. Gavrilo Princip tried to have as little to do with people as possible. Wherever he went, people took him for a weakling, seeing only his gaunt features and slight build, the legacy of a childhood under Austrian rule. Gavrilo often played along, pretending to be weak, but he knew that one day he would prove them all wrong.

He gazed at the other two as they argued. Like Gavrilo, they had trimmed moustaches and wore dark suits, rejecting the traditional dress of their parents. Gavrilo had known Nedeljko Cabrinovic for two years. They were both nineteen and committed to their cause, but Nedjo was often too emotional. He had a tendency to speak without thinking and would brag about the heroics he'd perform. It seemed to Gavrilo that he was desperately trying to throw off the stigma of his father, who was generally believed to be a police informant.

Trifko Grabez, Gavrilo's old friend, would be nineteen the following month on Vidovdan, the Serbs' national day. The son of an Orthodox priest, Trifko often appeared reticent, but Gavrilo knew his physical strength ensured he could take action when needed, as he'd proved when he was sentenced to fourteen days in prison and expelled from Bosnia for hitting a teacher who'd insulted him. The experience had left Trifko with the desire to make his country's invaders pay for what had happened to him. It was a desire that Gavrilo had encouraged since Trifko's arrival in Belgrade.

Gavrilo glanced at the gas light above them – it still seemed like a marvel compared to the darkness of the peasant house he grew up in. The light cast a glimmering sheen on the other youthful dissidents from Bosnia and Herzegovina who gathered in the cafes of Belgrade's Green Wreath Square to drink coffee and talk, always to talk. The Acorn Garland was their favourite venue, as this was where the veterans from the Balkan Wars came to tell their stories.

'I will commit a true and noble deed for our people,' Nedjo crowed, drawing Gavrilo out of his thoughts.

'Action, action – enough of words!' Gavrilo protested, unable to listen any more.

'We must have the means, Gavro,' Trifko said. 'We still need weapons, money and a safe route out of Serbia and into Bosnia.'

Gavrilo glared across the cafe at Milan Ciganovic, a decorated partisan officer and their contact. He was at the centre of attention with a group of tough looking ex-partisans.

Ciganovic hadn't been quite so commanding after the last Balkan War, Gavrilo reflected; he'd fallen on hard times like many former soldiers. Legend had it that Ciganovic had been so lice-ridden that he was actually thrown out of the Green Wreath Cafe. Gavrilo found that hard to imagine, looking at him now. A respectable clerk in the Serbian railways, he cut a powerful figure and Gavrilo knew that he wouldn't be moved or hurried.

'Perhaps I should go and ask Cigo for the means, now,' Nedjo said, seeing Gavrilo's apprehension. 'He will not refuse me!'

'Who could refuse the mighty hero?' Trifko said dryly.

Gavrilo cut them short, before they started to argue again. 'I will go.'

The Assassins

He made his way towards the veterans and Ciganovic looked up as he approached, calling across to him, 'Gavrica!'

Gavrilo smiled wearily – he hated the nickname, 'Little Gavrilo'. 'Do you have any news?' he asked.

Ciganovic looked at his companions then back at Gavrilo. 'News? There is no news?' he answered mockingly.

The ex-partisans laughed. Gavrilo shuffled nervously; he felt slightly uneasy in Ciganovic's presence. Ciganovic was six years older than him and had actually done what Gavrilo could only dream of.

'Come Gavrilo – sit and have a drink. I'm just teasing. There's nothing doing.' Ciganovic smiled good naturedly and offered him a glass of plum brandy.

'I don't drink, Cigo.'

'No, of course - your cause is all you need.' Ciganovic drank the brandy and added matter-of-factly, 'Preparations can't be made until it is known whether or not Emperor Franz Joseph will survive the bout of bronchitis he's currently suffering.'

Gavrilo hid his impatience – it was the same story he was always given. The gentleman with whom Ciganovic was working to get the means didn't think that Franz Ferdinand, as heir, would travel, in case the old tyrant died.

'You must be patient, Gavrica. Now leave us in peace,' Ciganovic said, much to the amusement of his comrades. Gavrilo ignored them and turned away. He knew that all he needed was the opportunity, and he would prove himself.

Chapter 3

A commissionaire escorted Johnny into the embassy chancery and left him to wait in the full glare of his colleagues. He was in a state of disgrace and Sir George wanted to make sure everyone knew it. The staff were certainly enjoying the spectacle, and judging from their contemptuous looks they thought that Johnny would finally be getting his comeuppance. He hadn't seen people quite so gleeful since he'd been expelled from school.

The gilded door in front of Johnny eventually opened and he was summoned into a large, elegant office. The Duke of Wellington had purchased the imposing Parisian town house from Napoleon's sister, Pauline Borghese, complete with imperial fixtures and fittings. It was rumoured to have become Pauline and the Iron Duke's love nest, when he was ambassador to France.

A hundred years later and Johnny could feel the puritanical disapproval of the people now occupying the embassy conducted through the self-regarding figure of Sir George Smyth. Johnny was starting to think he should have returned to Paris when he was first summoned, instead of running up even more debt.

'This is exactly the sort of behaviour one should expect from a person of your ilk,' Sir George said with distaste. 'Left to your own devices you revert back to your primitive state, in much the same way that a perfectly good tennis lawn is ruined by a persistent and indestructible weed.'

'Sir George, I ... ' Johnny began.

'Damn your eyes, I'm speaking!' Sir George bellowed and then sat back, enjoying the imperial splendour of his chancery rooms. He was thirty-five, the same age as Napoleon had been when he crowned himself Emperor of France. Sir George liked to style himself as the Napoleon of the diplomatic service.

'How on earth someone with your antecedents got into the diplomatic service is beyond me, Swift. Putting aside your questionable legitimacy, you're the son of a scullery maid.'

'My mother was a governess,' Johnny replied as blandly as possible. He knew it didn't pay to rile these sort of people.

'And your father is a school master? I can only assume you're here through nefarious means,' Sir George jeered. Johnny had found that the primary purpose of the diplomatic service was to provide outdoor relief to the aristocracy, not to be a means of social advancement to 'jumped up louts'.

'I passed the entrance examination and board. My father – my stepfather – is a languages master, which helped.' Johnny had a fleeting image of an angry Welshman shouting at him while he struggled to conjugate verbs.

'Smacks of vulgar professionalism – it will never replace the patronage of breeding and the nobility of the gentleman amateur,' Sir George replied. He'd told Johnny often enough that administration should be practised as a sport – a leisurely sport, Johnny judged, from the copy of 'Le Petit Journal' on his desk. Its banner headline screamed the latest revelation from the Caillaux case, the current talk of Paris.

'I do have a connection through my uncle, whose patronage was, I believe, of some assistance,' Johnny countered.

'Well, your "uncle" can't help you now.' The note of sarcasm in Sir George's voice stung Johnny. He had clearly heard the rumour that Johnny's mother had fallen prey to the grizzled charms of a retired cavalry general. He'd remained something of a shadowy figure in Johnny's life, introducing him to all manner of vice, and to the civil service. Most importantly, he'd taught Johnny that discretion was the better part of valour.

'Sir George, couldn't we settle this amicably, as gentlemen?'

Sir George's refined features darkened. 'Gentlemen don't forge their superior's signature on gambling markers.'

'Gambling markers? Not ... ' '– 'Not having your wife?' Johnny almost added.

'Imagine my surprise when I received a demand for the immediate payment of my outstanding balance – on a debt secured under your snivelling name!' Sir George barked.

Johnny felt himself flush. Betraying emotion was the worst thing one could do, but Libby had told him that the notes had been extended.

'I did win the money back, briefly. Well, some of it.'

Sir George was not amused. He detested flippancy, something Johnny had discovered to his cost. 'How did an ill-bred functionary manage to run up such astronomical debts?'

'It was a redistribution of wealth,' Johnny shrugged. There was no way he could explain himself. He couldn't drop Libby in it, not just like that.

Sir George turned deathly pale. 'If I could, I would have you thrashed and thrown in prison, but to avoid a scandal you will be quietly dismissed. I can't have you reflecting badly on me, as your direct superior.'

Johnny looked again at the newspaper on Sir George's desk. Henriette Caillaux, the wife of France's former Finance Minister had gone to the office of Gaston Calmette and shot him four times with a Browning automatic in response to the smear campaign Calmette had been running against her husband.

By comparison, Johnny's little indiscretion was relatively minor, but the damage it would do to Sir George's reputation in Whitehall multiplied its severity exponentially. Johnny grinned.

'I don't know, Sir George. There's nothing they understand more in France than a cordial agreement between a man and someone else's wife.'

'What the hell do you mean by that?'

'The wife of a senior British diplomat forging her husband's signature to secure gambling debts for an "ill-bred functionary" would, I'm sure, go unnoticed with the minimum of scandal, in France anyway.'

Sir George was dumbfounded for a moment, then he looked coldly at Johnny, 'My wife ... yes, I should have guessed that someone like you, born of scandal, would stoop to something like that.'

Johnny watched patiently as Sir George got up and turned his back on him, slowly regaining his self-control. After a moment he pulled down a large wall map of Europe and every iota of his brilliant and ruthless mind focused on one question.

'What to do with Swift? Can't sack him, can't shame him – can't shoot the blighter.'

'We could call it a pyrrhic victory,' Johnny offered. He knew it was a forlorn hope, but he had to suggest it, nonetheless.

'What we need is some dangerous backwater. Pity the Boer War's finished.'

'I hear the Caribbean can be perilous,' Johnny suggested. People posted there often complained about the heat and yellow fever, but he was willing to take his chances.

Sir George paused for a moment and Johnny thought he might have cracked it. Unfortunately, Sir George chose to stab his finger onto the Balkan Peninsula.

'Bosnia!'

'Bosnia? Surely not, Sir George ... '

'The ambassador in Vienna compares Austria's trouble in the Balkans to our problems with the Transvaal. You speak the language of course?'

'Russian is more my specialty. I lived – '

Sir George cut him short. 'Our embassy in Vienna has requested someone to ferret about. Serb nationalism over there is becoming a nuisance.' He looked up from the map, gleefully. 'Yes, that's the poisoned chalice. At best you'll get your bloody head blown off, at worst you'll end up buried in some nowhere consulate, picking up goat droppings.'

Johnny desperately tried to remember what he could about the place. Bosnia and Herzegovina had been put under Austro-Hungarian administration by the Congress of Berlin in 1878 to 'restore order' after they'd risen up against the Turks, but Bosnia and Herzegovina had remained part of the Ottoman Empire until Austro-Hungary annexed the two provinces in 1908.

'Isn't Bosnia more Austro-Hungary's bag, Sir George?' Johnny asked in a bid to dissuade him. 'It's not really our business.'

'The Balkans are the fault line of Europe, Swift. We don't want the delicate balance of power in the region upset by the Austrians, trampling their filthy great boots over it, especially after all our hard work clearing up the mess from the last Balkan bunfight!'

Johnny had heard Sir George rage about this often enough. He'd been heavily involved with the Treaty of London, which had settled all of the territorial disputes in the area after the first Balkan War. It had been the pinnacle of his career. A month later, the Balkan states had fallen out again and the second Balkan War had broken out, undermining all Sir George's hard work. He'd taken it very personally and as far as Johnny could see, had maintained a morbid fascination with the region ever since. He considered it to be wild, unruly and above all, the backwoods of diplomacy – the converse of everything he held dear. Johnny could feel any hope he had of a career slipping away.

'But surely the Austrians can do what they want to stabilise their southern border?' Johnny persisted.

'No, they bloody well can't. They're fanning the flames of Pan-Slavic nationalism and if Russian influence continues to spread in the region it could drag everyone into a war.'

'Do you seriously think that's likely, Sir George?'

'Probably not, but that's not really the point is it, Johnny?'

No, the point had been made pretty bloody clear to Johnny – he was banished to the wastelands of Europe, never to return. He still had his post, and if he made a fuss now, he'd just look like he was blubbing and couldn't take his medicine.

'Who exactly in Vienna do I need to see about all this?' Johnny asked, accepting his lot.

'I don't know! Am I expected to be on intimate terms with every member of their embassy staff?' Sir George answered, exasperated by Johnny's lack of initiative. 'Try Pinkie, he should know something about the Balkans!'

Johnny walked towards the gilded door of Sir George's office; he doubted he'd see its like for a while. 'Oh, and Swift,' Sir George called after him. 'In the unlikely event that you do find out something useful on your travels, you're to bring it straight to me, is that understood?'

'Yes, Sir George,' Johnny said a little too enthusiastically, clinging to the lifeline he'd just been thrown, however doubtful it might be.

Chapter 4

Gavrilo Princip looked at the people drifting past him in Green Wreath Square, each one of them creating a purpose for themselves, while he sat aimlessly outside the Cafe Moruna with Nedjo and Trifko. Given the means, he would create more of an effect on their lives than these good people could have thought possible.

He underlined a passage in the poem he was reading, 'Our Today' by Sima Pandurovic. It articulated everything he was feeling. Gavrilo may not have been able to express his ideas about love and life, or to extol the glory of his heroes as a poet, but he believed that something new and noble, a truly free anarchist society, would be created from his actions.

Such actions however, were continually being blocked, and while he sat around in cafes, things were in motion in Sarajevo. He'd written to Danilo Ilic, his most trusted friend and confidant, telling him of the plot and instructing him to start organising a second cell in Sarajevo. They had been friends since childhood and Gavrilo was certain that no one else but Danilo would be able to understand the allegorical style of the letter. Word had come back that Ilic was recruiting a second cell; all they needed were the weapons, but Gavrilo still had no news from Ciganovic.

He listened to the melancholy tune of a guslar folk singer drifting across the square, retelling the tale of Milos Obilic, who'd faced the Turkish Sultan on Blackbird's Field. It reminded Gavrilo of his childhood and the smell of a wood fire as his family gathered to hear the mystical tales of their ancient heroes. He longed to continue his mystic journey and face his sultan.

Gavrilo rubbed an old wound he had taken at the start of that journey two years previously, when rioting broke out across Austria's Balkan provinces, in response to the Austro-Hungarian monarchy's oppressive policies in Croatia. The most violent riots were in Sarajevo, where he'd marched at the head of the schoolboy protests and was sabred by the police for his dissent.

The demonstrations had brought Serbs, Croats and Muslims together. Despite all of the in-fighting, they had been one. Gavrilo knew then that a full-scale revolution could have an even bigger effect, uniting the South Slav people and obliterating their Habsburg rulers.

He hoped that such an uprising could be achieved through individual acts of vengeance against the tyrants, destroying the most harmful people in the government and undermining its status, whilst instigating a rebellious heart in his people with the smell of blood.

'Gavrilo – the day has dawned.' Milan Ciganovic slapped him on the shoulder, bringing him out of his thoughts.

'You have news, Cigo?' Nedjo asked as Ciganovic took charge of the group.

Ciganovic grinned affably. 'Your waiting is over. Old Joseph has fully recovered.'

'Thanks be!' Nedjo shouted, drawing unwanted glances from the people around them.

'There hasn't been an official confirmation, but I'm sure you can expect to greet the heir in June and make your mark alongside your Balkan brothers who've taken up arms against the Austrians,' Ciganovic said.

Gavrilo forgot the irritation of the past few weeks and sat up. They'd been inspired by a number of plots across the Balkans to assassinate leading members of the Austro-Hungarian establishment. Now he would be able to emulate them and with the death of Franz Ferdinand and ignite a revolution. 'It's been decided?'

'The gentleman I've been discussing your request with wants to meet one of you for himself.'

'Who is this gentleman?' Gavrilo asked.

'My old commander, Major Tankosic,' Ciganovic replied.

Gavrilo went silent, anger burning in his heart. Enduring poor health, he had been determined to pursue his revolutionary dreams. He'd even been part of a group, with Ilic, which had planned to assassinate the emperor. His studies had eventually suffered and Gavrilo had been expelled from school. He'd gone to Belgrade and tried unsuccessfully to pass his exams there. A year later the second Balkan War had started, giving him the perfect opportunity to fight for the freedom of his people. Gavrilo cringed to suppress the bitter sting of that memory. He'd volunteered to serve in the partisans and had become acquainted with Major Tankosic.

'Nedjo, you should go,' Trifko suggested.

Nedjo laughed, 'It would be an honour to show the major what a true Serb hero looks like ... but I laugh at everything. Gavrilo, you should go. You're always so sombre and grave.'

Gavrilo couldn't suppress his anger any longer. 'I will not see Tankosic. He's a naive man! Trifko will go.'

'What's this?' Ciganovic asked, taken aback by the snub.

'Major Tankosic threw him out of the partisans,' Trifko explained hurriedly, before Ciganovic could react to Gavrilo's insult.

'Because he's so small and sickly,' Nedjo added, making Ciganovic laugh.

Gavrilo bristled, reliving the humiliation. Tankosic had taken one look at him and dismissed him out of hand, but for Gavrilo, the worst part had come when he left. The other recruits had watched as he was led to the gate and a rival of his had shouted. 'So they've thrown out the bad stuff!'

He went back to his studies after leaving the training camp, drifting between Bosnia and Belgrade, devastated, but he'd resolved to prove himself one day and continued to plan attempts against a Habsburg dignitary – plans that were frustrated and never realised.

Ciganovic looked at Gavrilo, clearly deciding whether or not he still wished to vouch for him. Gavrilo met the former partisan's gaze, his eyes blazing – nothing would stand in his way this time. Ciganovic nodded and turned to Trifko. 'Very well, Trifko, you must be the one. Do not be taken in by the major's mild manner; he is a key figure in both the army and the underground movement. Ask any of the veterans here – the major was a ferocious warrior during the war.'

'Is it true that his men obeyed his orders to the point of jumping in rivers, if Tankosic so willed it?' Nedjo asked, chuckling.

'Yes,' Ciganovic replied coldly.

Chapter 5

Major Tankosic waited as Ciganovic led a tall youth into his rooms, saluted and introduced the visitor he'd brought with him. 'Major, this is Trifko Grabez.'

The youth shot Tankosic a defiant look. He and his friends had been pestering Ciganovic for weeks; now it was time to see if there was any iron to their zeal.

'So you are one of the snotty brats who have been making a nuisance of themselves,' the major declared. 'You think yourself capable of taking action?'

The youth did not flinch. 'My friends and I wish to serve our people.'

'And you are resolved to do so, even if it means sacrificing your life?'

'Yes,' Grabez replied plainly.

Tankosic glanced at Ciganovic – he was satisfied. The major had supplied weapons for similar operations before but nothing had ever been done with them and he doubted that they'd even been fired, however, the young dissident struck him as capable of doing what was needed.

'Can you shoot a pistol?'

'No, Major.'

Tankosic took a pistol from his desk drawer and handed it to Ciganovic. 'Take this and teach them to shoot.' He glanced back at Grabez. 'I'll make the necessary arrangements for your return home.'

He dismissed them and headed for Belgrade Fortress, the traditional halfway point between Constantinople and Vienna for warring armies. It bore the scars from centuries of battle; it had almost come to symbolise Serbia's continuous struggle to resist invasion and subjugation.

The major saluted the sentries on the clock gate and passed into the upper town of the old citadel. The man he sought within these walls was the living embodiment of that struggle for freedom – Colonel Dragutin Dimitrijevic, Director of Serbian Military Intelligence.

Tankosic entered the general headquarters of the army and was shown into Dimitrijevic's office. He was sitting at his desk hunched over a report. The colonel had been nicknamed Apis, after the ancient Egyptian bull god, and Tankosic thought him well named. Dimitrijevic's strength and force of personality were immediate.

The Major had been with him in 1903 when a cadre of officers stormed the Royal Palace, assassinating Aleksandar Obrenovic, the king who'd turned Serbia into an Austrian vassal, and his hated wife, Draga. Apis had been seriously wounded and still carried the scars from three bullets he'd taken that night.

Apis looked up from his report briefly. 'Major, what can I do for you?'

'Ciganovic has brought me some Young Bosnians. They want to go back home. Do you have any objections?'

'Of course not,' the colonel answered, still engrossed in his report.

'They want to attempt something against Franz Ferdinand when he visits Sarajevo next month,' Tankosic replied, and then waited as Apis considered his request.

The major knew Apis shared his view that Archduke Franz Ferdinand would not be happy until he had Serbia stuffed and mounted as a trophy to his imperial ambition. He was already working to pacify the South Slavs living within his empire in a bid to frustrate Serbia's expansion. Now the Hapsburg heir would be attending manoeuvres on Serbia's doorstep in a rehearsal for invasion. Such continued provocation could not go unanswered.

The Austro-Hungarian monarchy had adopted an increasingly aggressive policy towards Serbia in the years since the 1903 coup, forcing the Serbian government to make one humiliating concession after another, the worst of which was accepting the annexation of Bosnia and Herzegovina.

Tankosic and many other officers in the Serbian Army were appalled by the way their government, under Prime Minister Pasic, kowtowed to Austria, and in response had formed a new organisation to challenge government policy, stand up to Austrian aggression and ultimately to unite the South Slavs into a Greater Serbia. They called the new organisation, Union or Death. It had subsequently become known as The Black Hand. It was in Apis's capacity as head of Union or Death that Tankosic sought final permission from him to carry out their plan.

Apis frowned. 'Is it possible? The emperor was so well guarded when he visited Sarajevo – they won't stand a chance.'

'They're good patriots; the avengers of Kosovo walk with them.' Tankosic hoped his inference was clear – the colonel would not be risking key men by letting them go. 'What they lack in experience they make up for in enthusiasm,' he added. Apis had ordered him to find willing recruits from the hordes of dissidents that thronged the city's cafes, for operations such as these.

'The necessary preparations will be made?'

'Yes, Apis.'

'I don't imagine anything will come of it, but if they succeed, so much the better. If not, it will show the Austrians just how dangerous it is to interfere in Serb affairs. We must fight our enemies with all means available.'

Chapter 6

Johnny was starting to get annoyed by the steady rocking of the Vienna train. He couldn't sleep – his mind kept churning over the events that had led to this fool's errand, as his bunk swung in time to the rhythm of the pistons.

Libby the Libertine murmured contentedly to herself as she turned over, pressing him against cold steel. He wasn't finding his sleeping compartment really suitable for this sort of thing.

She began to move against him in time to the rhythm of the train and it was suddenly obvious to him how he'd got here; the story of his coming of age could be told by the graceful contours of her body.

He'd read somewhere that Australian Aborigines used stories to find their way through the bewildering landscape of the outback, each tree and mountain becoming a signpost with its own story passed down from generation to generation, telling the way home. Johnny had developed a similar method to find his way through the bewildering landscape of women.

He touched the shapely ankle wrapped around him as he began to retrace his journey, step by hard-won step. The story passed down to him from the captain of the first eleven was that the ankle is the key to a woman's heart, the place where everything begins. This had proved to be a good crib, judging from the giggling of his first fumble with Daisy, a milkmaid from the local village. Johnny had steadily progressed on his journey, gaining more stories and insights at every new signpost. By the time he reached the upper sixth, his skill on and off the field of glory was such that he came to the attention of Simpson, his head of house.

Johnny flinched as Libby dug her claws into his thigh and ran her fingers along a scar he'd taken winning the inter-house cup.

'You can be quite a wonderful little man, can't you Johnny?' Libby sighed, letting slip an uncharacteristic compliment.

'I wasn't the captain of the school rugby team for nothing,' Johnny said, lost in reminiscence. Simpson had generally ignored Johnny's questionable legitimacy and natural intelligence, as they were mitigated by his athletic prowess, but his reputation as someone who gave consequence to the village girls couldn't be tolerated.

Prize day gave Simpson the opportunity he'd needed to humiliate the false hero. When Johnny mounted the podium to receive his usual accolades, Simpson unceremoniously announced that people of breeding didn't engage with the daughters of tradesmen. Johnny, never one to be put off by the bitter sting of laughter, began to engage the charms of Simpson's three lovely daughters, Faith, Hope and Chastity. All three lived up to their names, exulting him to the heights of faith and hope, but ultimately practising the virtue of chastity, until finally, the gates of paradise were slammed shut in his face when he was expelled for instigating a school strike.

Johnny didn't have a great deal of opportunity after that, having attached scandal to an already-jaded name. That was, until his 'uncle' decided to take an interest in his prospects. Even then, the choice was a stark one – the army or the civil service, both institutions his uncle had served with distinction.

The rigour and discipline of army life wasn't for Johnny, so he made a play for the diplomatic service. He quite liked the idea of a career in diplomacy, emulating the heroes of his classical education.

His uncle exerted a certain degree of influence to get Johnny nominated, but as it was he still had to pass an exam, which he did with flying colours. The interview board, however, was slightly trickier and he had to carefully contrive a future for himself as a career diplomat serving the empire to his dying breath and deflect any barbed comments about his background with sporting anecdotes and quotes from his Latin primer.

It was enough to secure him a billet in a lower grade and the doors of establishment paradise opened up to him again. His 'uncle' took Johnny to a sporting club to celebrate, where he taught him to gamble and where the madam introduced him to some classical phraseology he hadn't learnt at school and was now competently performing with Libby.

His dreams of a glittering diplomatic career were soon rudely awoken. The main purpose of his grade of chancery was to carry out mundane tasks within a highly disciplined and authoritarian hierarchy. Even compared to the repressive regime of his school, which was meant to prepare him for a life of clerical work, it was soul-destroying. To top it all, his uncle had insisted that Johnny join the army as a special reserve officer before he'd help him with the nomination system, so he had six months of button-polishing and close-order drill.

Johnny spent his days meticulously copying out Sir George's dispatches and the minutes of his meetings. Sometimes he'd daydream about studying at the Sorbonne, but then all of his money would go as he played at the hedonistic lifestyle of a demi-monde in the city of light.

On his first day in Paris, on 28 June 1913, Johnny saw Mata Hari perform as a Spanish dancer at the Folies-Bergère and that set the tone for his time in the city. Following the tedium of work, he'd have the time of his life, finding solace with the five o'clock ladies of Paris's mid-range maisons de rendezvous. Between five and seven o' clock seemed to be the accepted time for patrons to call, on their way home from the office. Afterwards, Johnny dined at Maxim's before doing the rounds of the fashionable haunts of Montmartre, carousing until it was time to go to work again. It didn't take long for his funds to run out, and he was forced to find some other form of distraction.

Libby stirred in his arms, tightening her grip as his story reached its peak. What they had wasn't so much love, as an escape strategy.

'Libby, are you sure this is a good idea?'

'What? How can it not be a good idea?' she hissed, irritated by the interruption.

Libby had been an untamed and impulsive debutante, so the embassy tittle-tattle went, married off to a promising diplomat in the hope that the ministrations of an older man would calm her. She had reluctantly agreed to the match; as a married woman she'd be away from the cloying influence of her family, which insisted she was constantly chaperoned. Two years on and it was obvious to Johnny that Libby was bored to death. Her only distractions were the spa treatments her husband believed were conducive to her 'nervous condition', and impetuous young men willing to venture with her into the wild.

'You're coming with me? ... I mean, how did you even find me?' Johnny asked.

'I'll always find you.'

It had been a very pleasant surprise to discover her in his sleeping compartment. He wasn't sure if he was more touched that she'd followed him, or shocked that she was prepared to rough it in second class.

'I felt bad about my little fib,' she added.

'So you didn't get the notes extended?' he asked, not that that mattered to him anymore. Johnny's only consolation from this whole fiasco was that Sir George hadn't asked him to pay the money back.

'Well, I didn't get them all extended. I didn't want you to worry.'

Johnny felt an unaccustomed sense of guilt that he'd saved his skin by shopping her. 'Sorry I dropped you in it, Libby. I didn't know how else to save myself.'

Libby giggled dismissively and kissed him. He could taste violets on her lips. 'George was rather annoyed, but you'll pay the money back, won't you. I mean, if you want to return to the embassy, that is.'

Chapter 7

Johnny found it hard to enjoy Vienna's intense attack on his senses after Libby's ultimatum. He'd wasted most of the day searching through the city's cafe society, trying to ignore the overwhelming aroma of coffee, the clamour of argument and the dazzling array of cakes. The only thing more distracting was the famous carefree, muddled atmosphere of the place.

'Pinkie', the man Sir George had said might be able to help him, was not in his office and nobody at the British embassy knew where he was or when he might be expected back. The staff could tell you all about Archduke Franz Ferdinand's latest spat with the high court chamberlain. Anything else could take care of itself, as far as they were concerned.

Finally, after sustained questioning, it was thought that Pinkie might be at the chess school. By all accounts he was a bit of a dandy and Johnny would probably be able to identify him by his flamboyant taste in waistcoats. Johnny really missed being the unhelpful official on the other side of the desk.

After further chasing around, Johnny discovered that 'the chess school' was the nickname for the Central Cafe, an old bank building with a richly decorated, high-arched ceiling. It reminded Johnny of his recent trip to Zurich and the money he owed, further fuelling his anxiety.

To add to his problems, Libby had totally fallen in love with Vienna. Her English reserve was fading, and with it her connection to Johnny; every moment they stayed there increased the danger of her finding an alternative means of diversion. Under the circumstances, he was starting to regret leaving her at a table unsupervised while he searched the cafe in peace.

Trying to find an embassy official who'd play chess amongst the bohemian types who patronised the Central was easier said than done. After accosting every man in the place wearing a vaguely flamboyant waistcoat, Johnny eventually came across a dandy in a garish pink waistcoat and cravat. He was playing chess against an intense looking man in his thirties with steel rimmed glasses and a thick shock of black hair.

'Excuse me. Are you Pinkie?'

The 'dandy' glanced at Johnny, who adopted a suitable air of deference. Satisfied he'd been shown the correct amount of respect, he gave Johnny an amused look. 'Actually, it's the Honourable Pinkston Barton-Forbes ... and who might you be?'

'Jonathan Swift, sir, of the Paris embassy.'

'Are you really? How extraordinary, and here you are in the land of bureaucracy and music. This land doesn't fly though.'

'No, sir,' Johnny said impassively. He was used to his superiors making whimsical reference to his famous namesake's work. By the look of him, Johnny guessed that the Honourable Pinkston Barton-Forbes had been in his post ten years too long, with little opportunity to further his career. All he had to live for now was aggravating his juniors. Not having achieved a suitable rise from Johnny, he pointed at his hand.

'What on earth is that?'

Johnny passed him a postcard he'd brought from a down and out on the way in; it was a painting of the Rathaus, Vienna's town hall. Johnny had thought that the doom evoked by the Gothic spires would appeal to his mother and stepfather.

Barton-Forbes gave a snort of derision and handed the postcard back to Johnny. 'A competent Biedermeier reproduction – mawkish and moral, for middle-class tastes, I think.' It seemed to convey everything Barton-Forbes needed to know about Johnny.

Johnny felt a sharp nudge in his back. Libby had evidently seen that he was talking to one of her sort and had wandered over for an introduction.

'The Honourable Pinkston Barton-Forbes, may I present, Lady Elizabeth Smyth. I've been escorting her to Vienna, on behalf of her husband.'

Barton-Forbes stood up and greeted Libby with dignified disdain. He then established who her 'people' were and offered her a seat at his table. He raised a questioning eyebrow to Johnny.

'Are you the Johnny that my connections tell me diddled George Smyth out of the family silver?'

'I was attempting a redistribution of wealth,' Johnny replied. He didn't know what else to say, but Barton-Forbes had already lost interest in him and begun to exchange pleasantries with Libby.

Johnny wasn't surprised that Barton-Forbes knew about his trouble with Sir George. Someone in his position, desperate to further a stalled career, would have cultivated contacts across the diplomatic service who were willing to do him favours and exchange information. Sir George was ideally placed to return such favours and information, and if Barton-Forbes knew about Johnny's difficulties, Johnny hoped that meant he might actually know what he was supposed to be doing here. He was about to commit a cardinal sin and interrupt a conversation about the coming season, but his flippant comment had aroused the interest of Barton-Forbes's chess opponent.

'Why were you attempting a redistribution of wealth?' he asked Johnny, exhaling cigar smoke and evidently surprised. 'That is quite a subversive term to hear from such an earnest looking office boy dressed up in a frock coat.'

'I beg your pardon?' He had an accent and Johnny suspected he might be some kind of Russian emigre.

Barton-Forbes turned round. 'Oh Swift, this is Leon - Leon Trotsky. Isn't that what you call yourself these days? Leon, the lower ranks of the diplomatic service aren't used to being addressed by dangerous revolutionaries.'

Trotsky blew out more cigar smoke, ignoring Barton-Forbes. 'So tell me, now we've been introduced, why do you want a redistribution of wealth?'

Johnny struggled to reply – he'd once been thrashed by his head of house for reading Trotsky's newspaper, *Pravda* and now he was talking to the man himself. He saw that Barton-Forbes was watching, so he answered Trotsky in Russian; he didn't want to damage his reputation any further. 'I would like a redistribution of wealth – '

'You speak Russian?' Trotsky asked, interrupting Johnny. 'Forgive me – I am so used to your countrymen shouting slowly in English to make themselves understood by foreigners,' Trotsky said, glancing at Barton-Forbes.

'I lived in St Petersburg, when I was a child,' Johnny replied.

'Really? How so?' Trotsky asked.

'My mother was a governess to the children of a rich industrialist,' Johnny said, embarrassed. He hoped that Barton-Forbes didn't understand his shameful admission.

Johnny's 'uncle' had arranged the position for his mother to avoid the scandal of having a child in England out of wedlock. She'd pretended to be a widow in their new home and had encouraged Johnny to become bilingual in Russian, while he ran around the grand nursery with the children of the house. Johnny had had a natural talent for languages ever since; it was a talent he shared with his uncle and he often wondered if it ran in the family.

Trotsky nodded shrewdly, understanding the implications of what Johnny had just said. 'So, you would like a greater distribution of wealth to gain justice for your poor oppressed mother, who occupied one of the worst roles in a bourgeois household, with little status amongst the other servants and no doubt attracted the unwanted attentions of the master of the house?'

The master of the house had, in fact, been very kind and only having daughters, had treated Johnny like one of the family. The only unwanted attentions Johnny remembered his mother receiving were from the man who tutored the children in French. Unfortunately, he eventually wore Johnny's mother down and by the time Johnny was five they'd married and returned to England. It was a shock after the pampered life he'd had in Russia and to add insult to injury his new stepfather had subjected him to a regime of rugby to toughen him up. He was also determined that Johnny receive the start in life he'd never had, so pushed him to study and made him develop his aptitude for languages.

'I would like a redistribution of wealth to pursue my class interests and increase the power of the petty-bourgeois.' Johnny said, trying to steer the conversation away from the more colourful aspects of his family history.

'Bravo – and do you plan to do this as a stepping stone towards a revolution and the greater good, or for your own ends?' His lively, intelligent eyes flashed at Johnny, making him uncomfortable; he wasn't used to people listening to him.

'Well, by throwing off the feudal stranglehold the aristocrats have on society,' Johnny nodded towards Barton-Forbes, 'it will allow the dominance of the bourgeois, who will eventually create conditions bad enough for a full-scale proletarian revolution.' Johnny hoped that was evasive enough, and Trotsky seemed amused by his interpretation of historical materialism. All Johnny wanted to do was clear out the dead wood to make room for his own advancement – maybe then he could regain some of the carefree privilege of his early life.

'Swift, do stop showing off – it's rather vulgar,' Libby said, addressing him in the correct manner that the wife of a senior British diplomat should use when speaking to a member of her husband's staff. 'Tell Mr Barton-Forbes why you're making a nuisance of yourself.' Trotsky, one step ahead of the forces of oppression, responded to Libby's tone by migrating to another table.

'Come on, out with it man. I haven't got all day,' Barton-Forbes ordered, eager to continue his conversation with Libby.

'I believe the Austro-Hungarians have a problem with Pan-Slavic nationalism in their southern provinces,' Johnny said, not really sure where to begin.

'Yes, it's quite exasperating,' Barton-Forbes replied. He had a supercilious manner which Johnny longed to perfect for himself.

'I've been sent here to write a report for you,' Johnny said.

'For me? Reporting what, precisely?'

'Well, that's what I was hoping you could tell me.' Sir George hadn't said 'report' exactly, that was Johnny's interpretation. 'I had something of an open brief from the ambassador in Vienna – to ferret about, in fact.'

Barton-Forbes looked appalled. 'Ferret about? Sir Maurice de Bunsen doesn't request people to ferret about for him!'

'Could you give me details of exactly what you need to know about the Balkan nationalists?' Johnny asked, desperate for this to be over.

'His Britannic Majesty's embassy in Vienna does not trifle with cranks and anarchists. We deal with governments, and even if we did deal with that type, we certainly wouldn't ask our colleagues in the Paris embassy for help.'

It was obvious to Johnny then that Sir George had sent him on a wild goose chase, which must have amused him terribly.

'Where does that leave me? I mean, where does one even start?' Johnny asked. He at least needed to find out something to tell Sir George. 'There was a suggestion that I go to Bosnia.'

'Bosnia!' Barton-Forbes exchanged a wry look with Libby. This didn't seem to him to be a job for a gentleman. 'Well, you could try the consulate in Sarajevo. They might know about the local state of affairs.'

'There's a British consulate in Sarajevo?' Johnny asked, trying to hide his relief.

'I believe so – there's some old sweat down there who's been sending reports regular as clockwork for twenty-five years. If he's not part of the consulate then God alone knows what he's about. Harding-Brown or something, I'd give him a nudge,' Barton-Forbes said, and then dismissed Johnny with a curt wave of his hand. 'Now, clear off. Go send your postcard or something, there's a good chap – the lady and I are talking.'

'Yes, I'll be ready to leave in an hour, Swift. Kindly have a cab ready,' Libby said, playing the part of his superior's wife to the full and then giving him a conspiratorial smile.

*

Johnny watched the imposing Gothic spires of the Rathaus drift past as the cab drove them back to their hotel along the Ringstrasse.

'Pinkie has invited me to stay on for a few days.' Libby's eyes sparkled as she spoke and Johnny didn't think he'd ever seen her so radiant.

It sometimes felt to Johnny that their whole relationship was defined by various car rides. The affair had even begun in a car, when Sir George had instructed Johnny to drive Libby around the boulevards of Paris in his Austin Endcliffe Phaeton 18/24, on her regular shopping excursions.

The idea that the innocuous office boy might pose any kind of a threat to his property or chattel didn't occur to Sir George, until Johnny crashed his car into the wrought iron railings of a metro station.

'You're staying here … with him?' Johnny fought to keep the disappointment out of his voice.

'Alternately, we could take a gamble; you could stay here with me and try to win the money back, Johnny.'

They'd spent most of the journey to Vienna arguing about this, Johnny reflected bitterly. Libby had insisted that they repay Sir George. Apparently, it was the right thing to do and she had a position in society and wouldn't have it threatened for the sake of a few brass farthings. The idea of compromising her marriage any further than she already had was totally unacceptable to her.

'We have to win the money back. I have no intention of ending up like one of your brothel women,' Libby continued.

'How are we going to do that?' Johnny tried to explain patiently for the hundredth time that Sir George wouldn't risk the scandal of a divorce and that they had no money, which Sir George obviously knew, as he hadn't asked for any back and was happy with just ruining Johnny.

'Look, if you're not going to help me, go and do this nasty little job for George, then come and find me at the spa. I'll think of some way of winning the money back.' By all accounts there was a very acceptable spa near Sarajevo, soon to be patronised by the Austrian heir apparent. 'If you do a good job and we pay the money back, George might actually allow you to return to the embassy without destroying too much of your career.'

They drove past the Statue of Athena, outside the parliament building, and she seemed to look down on him – regal and daunting. Johnny turned back to Libby; he knew that in her own way she was trying to be kind and help him. He nodded his agreement – he would do as she asked, somehow.

Chapter 8

Gavrilo thought that the old oak tree had the same shape as a man's body, making it a perfect target for the test. Ciganovic and two of his associates from the partisans, Djuro Sarac and Milan Mojic, had been teaching Gavrilo and Trifko to shoot for the past six days.

Sarac, who'd been Major Tankosic's bodyguard during the war, now wanted to assess them, so he paced out a firing position from two hundred metres and another one from sixty. The deserted forests around Topcider Park made a good training ground, evoking in Gavrilo the memory of Mihailo Obrenovic, a Serbian prince murdered in these woods by Austrian agents as he planned to free Bosnia.

Gavrilo opened fire at distance first and managed to score six out of ten. Closing to sixty metres he hit with all eight shots and watched with satisfaction as chunks of wood and bark flew from the tree.

Sarac then ordered him to run past the target whilst firing. At two hundred metres Gavrilo scored two hits, but from sixty metres he achieved three. Gavrilo felt as if he was following in the traditions of his ancestors as he ran through the trees. They'd laid ambushes for smugglers and brigands in the woodland around their village in the Grahovo Valley, Western Bosnia, where his father and grandfather had risen up against the Turks and beaten them before his homeland was given to the Austrians.

Sarac congratulated Gavrilo. 'You've passed.'

'Well done, Gavro,' Trifko added. 'You're the better shot.'

Gavrilo shrugged off Trifko's praise. 'I trained with a Browning before Tankosic threw me out of the partisans,' he said with a scowl.

'This will even things out, Gavro,' Trifko said, excited to have passed the test. 'We will be the spirits of revenge – avengers for Mihailo Obrenovic.'

'You should get in close to do it, if you can stand to,' Ciganovic told Gavrilo, grinning.

'I will think of Obrenovic and everyone murdered in our cause,' Gavrilo answered flatly. He wasn't sure if Ciganovic was mocking him for his score over distance.

A guslar's song filled Gavrilo with nervous excitement; maybe one day the guslars would sing a song of his exploits to the students and dissidents of The Green Wreath. The idea amused him briefly but he wasn't interested in personal glory – all he wanted was a chance to prove himself.

Princip had his books and a paper to read as they waited for Ciganovic, but he couldn't concentrate. 'The Russian Tsar has been killed,' he announced.

Trifko and Nedjo looked at him doubtfully and neither of them cheered. Gavrilo shook his head in mock shame. 'I'm joking. I wanted to see what kind of revolutionaries you are and how you'd react.'

'How are they supposed to react to such news?' Ciganovic asked as he joined them.

'How any true revolutionary should react to the death of a tyrant,' Princip answered.

'The Tsars have been the saviours of the Slav people since Peter the Great. Tsar Nicholas could be our only chance now against the Austrians,' Ciganovic replied.

'For Serbia maybe, but where were our Russian "big brothers" when we were annexed? Licking their wounds after their humiliation against Japan. Maybe we Bosnians should look out for ourselves,' Gavrilo countered. Now he'd passed the test he did not feel quite so much in the shadow of the mighty partisan. They were both, after all, Bosnians. Ciganovic was from a village not far from where Gavrilo had grown up.

'With a little help from our Serbian cousins, maybe?' Ciganovic said, indicating the sack he was holding.

Princip flinched at the jibe. He didn't know if Ciganovic was playing devil's advocate or if he believed Russia would come to their assistance, but he'd made his point.

Ciganovic smiled before discreetly handing him four Browning automatic pistols. The others looked around, but they were the only people there. Ciganovic carefully passed Princip the sack, which he opened. There were some boxes of bullets and six plain grey, rectangular bombs inside, each the size of a large block of soap and fitted with a safety cap.

'They're not ideal,' Ciganovic explained. 'They're the offensive type of bomb, made at the Kragujevac arsenal and filled with nails and pieces of lead. They're meant for military operations.'

Princip guessed the bombs were surplus from the war. He knew Ciganovic had such bombs, which was why they'd approached him for help.

'To use them, unscrew the safety cap, then hit the loop inside against something hard to prime, and throw. They have a twelve-second fuse, so if you're close to the target you'll need to wait before throwing it.'

Princip looked at Nedjo – the bomb would be his primary weapon. He'd had to work at a typesetter's while they'd learnt to shoot. He was the only one of them with a trade and they were desperately short of money.

'You can't be caught in Serbia with these things,' Ciganovic said. Gavrilo nodded agreement. He knew that the Serbian government was still submitting to Austrian demands, which included the curtailing of subversive activities in Bosnia.

'Wouldn't it be safer to send the weapons on to us separately?' Gavrilo asked. They'd travelled to and from Sarajevo many times; their main concern was how to do it safely with the weapons.

'What do you think we are, a bloody post office? If you want safe, stick to your studies,' Ciganovic replied tersely.

'We will take the weapons. We are not scared of a little risk,' Nedjo said.

'Good – a true hero. You'll be travelling underground to Sarajevo,' Ciganovic informed them.

'There is an actual secret tunnel into Bosnia?' Nedjo asked in awe.

Ciganovic grinned, not quite believing what he'd just heard. Gavrilo was furious with Nedjo for asking such a ridiculous question. He didn't want to give Ciganovic any reason to doubt them, not now when they were so close, but in the end Ciganovic chose to ignore the question.

'You'll take the steamer to Sabac and once there, hand this to a customs official called Popovic.' Ciganovic handed Princip a card with his initials 'M.C.' written on it. 'Popovic will arrange for you to be smuggled into Bosnia. Once you're over the border head for Tuzla – you're familiar with the place?'

Trifko and Princip nodded; they'd both been to school there. 'If you feel it's not safe to take the weapons with you to Sarajevo you can leave them with a local merchant, Misko Jovanovic.'

'We'll need to buy train tickets,' Princip said.

Ciganovic handed him a purse and Princip counted the money inside – one hundred and thirty dinars. 'That's not enough,' he complained.

'This is all I have.' Ciganovic gave him another twenty. Nedjo's wages had been forty dinars and Princip had pawned his coat for eight. That would have to do.

'It won't have to last you long,' Ciganovic grinned. The black humour wasn't wasted on the three. Then Ciganovic gave Princip a glass tube wrapped in cotton wool. 'Remember, dead men tell no secrets,' he said, and with that, he left them.

Princip looked at Trifko and Nedjo as the words sank in. They knew what was in the vial – cyanide of potassium. Each of them understood what had to be done for their cause, and were willing to sacrifice themselves for their people, but this was the first time they'd come face to face with the prospect.

Gavrilo saw that now was the moment to unite their purpose. 'We must swear that we will never betray one another or our sacred mission. We will not talk to anyone on our journey or tell anybody our purpose.'

'I swear,' Trifko agreed.

Nedjo did the same. 'I swear.'

All three listened to the guslar sing. Their mystic journey was about to begin, walking in the footsteps of their greatest heroes.

Chapter 9

Archduke Franz Ferdinand watched as the sunlight started to fade over Vienna, the heart of the empire he would reign over one day. The marble hall of the upper Belvedere Palace gave an excellent view of the skyline, dominated by St Stephen's Cathedral, the great target for the Turkish cannon.

Prince Eugene of Savoy had built the palace after his great victories over the Ottoman Turks, the last major threat to come from the East. Savoy drove them back, sacked Sarajevo and took Belgrade, establishing the Habsburg Empire as the pre-eminent power in Central Europe and the Balkans. Franz Ferdinand wondered whether if his Habsburg ancestors could have retained Belgrade from the Turks, many of the empire's current difficulties could have been averted.

He looked up to God in frustration and found himself staring at a large ceiling fresco depicting the eternal flame of Prince Eugene of Savoy, with history celebrating his achievements.

The heir apparent was fifty-one and still lived in the shadow of other men's achievements, while he waited in the wings to ascend the throne of an empire that was slowly disintegrating. It infuriated him, but there was nothing he could do until he succeeded his uncle as emperor.

He marched out onto the balcony to calm his frustration and smiled as a lone coach pulled up in front of the porte cochère. Some of his anger lifted – Sophie, his wife, had returned. If he'd accomplished one great deed it was to marry the woman he loved, the archduke thought with satisfaction. He'd stood here before leaving to give his oath of renunciation, making that marriage possible.

Franz Ferdinand came back into the marble hall to greet Sophie. She'd been in her early thirties when they married. It was said that her beauty had been starting to fade but the Archduke disagreed and watching her as she entered the hall he knew that marrying her was the most intelligent thing he'd ever done. It was certainly the hardest.

Since coming of age, Franz Ferdinand had been subject to the Habsburg family Law, which decreed that members of the family must marry a person of 'equal birth'. Franz Ferdinand had found the only appropriate princesses to be ugly, underdeveloped ducklings. He'd neither had the time nor the inclination to educate a wife several years too young for him.

It was inevitable that when somebody from his circle found a person they loved there was always some triviality in their family tree to make the marriage impossible, and so invariably with such limited choices, a man and his wife were always related to each other twenty times over, with the result that half their children were cretins.

His cousin, Archduke Friedrich and his calculating wife Isabella, had had the temerity to think he'd be willing to form this type of union with their daughter, Maria Christina. This misconception developed because Franz Ferdinand was a constant visitor to their palace in Pressburg. When the truth was discovered, it caused a terrible uproar.

Franz Ferdinand's blood boiled at the memory. He'd forgotten his pocket watch after a tennis match in the palace gardens. Isabella had been brought the watch and was incensed to find it contained a miniature of Countess Sophie Chotek, her lady in waiting, and not her daughter. Isabella assembled her household and confronted Sophie with the picture. Shrieking, she denounced Sophie as a schemer who'd deceived her and betrayed her kindness, then she promptly dismissed her. Subsequently, Isabella ran to the emperor and informed him that his nephew had trifled with her daughter's affections, whilst forming an attachment with her lady-in-waiting.

Sophie came from a noble Czech family – her father had been a great diplomat for the empire, but in court circles she was a glorified maid. The archduke had established an understanding with Sophie five years previously, and she'd been all that had kept him going through years of bitter illness and convalescence. He'd hoped to keep the matter quiet until the emperor passed away and then, as head of the family, he could at last, marry whom he pleased.

The emperor had demanded that he give his Sopherl up but Franz Ferdinand refused. Franz Joseph had married Empress Elisabeth, his Sissi, for love, and even though she was a lady of equal birth, it had been against his mother's wishes. The archduke considered that to be the only thing his uncle had ever done for love. Franz Joseph had then destroyed his marriage with protocols and unflinching court etiquette.

Considerable pressure was brought to bear on both Franz Ferdinand and Sophie, but in the end, the emperor had little choice but to accept Sophie as

Franz Ferdinand's bride. If he'd expelled Franz Ferdinand from the family his younger brother Otto would have been next in line and his scandalous life made that prospect impossible. Equally, Franz Ferdinand could choose to stick to his original plan and wait until the emperor died, meaning that Sophie would then be crowned when they were married – something that Franz Joseph could not allow. The only solution was a morganatic marriage, with the archduke renouncing his wife's and descendants' claims to the throne, which he did on 28 June, 1900.

They were married three days later. He'd worn full dress uniform for the simple ceremony, which no male member of his family attended, though they had witnessed his oath of renunciation.

The controversy eventually died down, but the malicious gossip continued, inspired by Isabella's vilification of Sophie as an ambitious schemer who'd bagged the most eligible bachelor in the monarchy. At court, protocol dictated that Sophie's birth ranked her lower than the youngest archduchess. She couldn't accompany Franz Ferdinand on any official task within the empire, be that sitting at the top table with him at state banquets, escorting him to official balls or even driving in court carriages together.

These ceremonial rules and protocols of court were zealously enforced by the court underlings, led by the high court chamberlain, Prince Montenuovo, whose own father had been made legitimate by a morganatic union. Nonetheless, Prince Montenuovo did all he could to make things impossible for Sophie. Franz Ferdinand hated him with a vengeance.

It was as a result of these medieval rituals, inherited from the Spanish Habsburg court, that they'd arrived at the palace separately. He was in a 'golden' court carriage and she in an ordinary one, reserved for ladies in waiting. The absurdity was breathtaking, and it infuriated Franz Ferdinand to see her treated in such a way.

Sophie bore it all stoically and in spite of the indignities, they had been very happy for the fourteen years of their marriage and had three healthy children. She was currently more concerned about an item on his summer programme.

'Franzi, are you still expected to observe the manoeuvres in Bosnia?'

'Nothing was discussed today, but now my uncle's health is improving ...' Franz Ferdinand shrugged.

'It's your health I'm concerned about. The summer heat in Bosnia is unbearable.'

The Assassins

'My wife, my doctor, my advisor – my entire happiness. It's my duty to go.' The emperor had recently made Franz Ferdinand inspector general of the army, partly to keep him out of the way and partly to help prepare him to become emperor, but the post offered him very little opportunity to do anything. What chance he had, he felt honour-bound to take.

'Is it safe? The people didn't exactly give you a rousing welcome when you visited Herzegovina and Dubrovnik.'

Franz Ferdinand turned away; he didn't want Sophie to see the anger in his eyes. The memory of all of the faces, staring at him in silence eight years previously still galled him.

'And there have been threats.'

'Threats are an occupational hazard, but it might be as well not to tempt fate.' Franz Ferdinand had already been subject to a number of assassination plots. He'd postponed his last visit to Bosnia in 1910 at the recommendation of his advisors, who feared a Serb ambush. Franz Ferdinand was reminded of the time he'd been in the king of Spain's wedding procession, when an anarchist threw a bomb at the king's carriage, narrowly missing him.

'I'll speak to the emperor,' he said.

'If you're expected to go to Bosnia then I must accompany you.'

'You know as well as I do, Sopherl, that it is dependent on the Emperor's permission. The protocols are quite clear.'

'With a woman at your side it is unlikely that anyone would attempt anything for fear of killing me,' Sophie said firmly.

Chapter 10

Gavrilo Princip put down the postcard he was writing to watch the River Drina meander along the shoreline of Koviljaca. He felt a deep spiritual affinity with this stretch of river. It was a powerful emblem of his people's struggle for freedom. A hundred years ago the whole area had been at the centre of resistance against Turkish rule.

Gavrilo, Trifko and Nedjo had left Belgrade on Ascension Day, 28 May. Following Ciganovic's instructions, they'd taken the steamer to Sabac and from there they'd been directed on to Loznica, where they'd met with Captain Prvanovic, a frontier guard who'd told them to come back the next day when he'd arrange their crossing into Bosnia.

Koviljaca wasn't far, so they'd decided to rest on the border between the free Serbs and the oppressed. Gavrilo was starting to feel the symbolic weight of the journey and the responsibility for what he was trying to accomplish. It wasn't a responsibility Nedjo had chosen to share. Koviljaca was a holiday town and Nedjo was in full holiday mood. Forgetting the oath they had made, he chatted to all and sundry and was even going to show an acquaintance he'd met the bombs tied around his waist.

Gavrilo and Trifko had managed to get Nedjo away before he gave the game away, but there had been an ugly scene. Tension still rippled between the three of them as they sat by the River Drina, writing their postcards. Gavrilo saw this as an excellent opportunity to misdirect anyone who might be tracking them through their mail. He picked up his postcard and continued to write the note he was sending his cousin, telling him that he was on his way to a monastery to study.

'Gavro, would you like to add your greeting?' Nedjo handed him a postcard, waving the peace offering. 'It's for Vukosava.' Gavrilo warmed at the memory of Nedjo's clever sister and took the card, easing the anger he felt towards his friend.

Gavrilo scanned through Nedjo's words and flushed. Evidently Nedjo had felt the same sense of nostalgia that Gavrilo had at being in Koviljaca – but none of the responsibility. Nedjo had written out the lines of a poem commemorating the Serb heroes who'd fought the Turks here. It would be a clear indication to anyone who intercepted the postcard that Nedjo intended to become a Serb hero himself.

Gavrilo had had enough and showed the postcard to Trifko with a stern look. Trifko nodded his agreement; they both knew what had to be done for the good of their mission. Gavrilo tried to calm himself and spoke as quietly as he could. 'Nedjo, we're not meant to draw attention to ourselves, and what do you do?'

Trifko grabbed Nedjo's belt, exposing the two flask shaped bombs he'd tied to it, and said, 'You try to show off your weapons to the first person you meet.' Gavrilo was glad to have the big man with him for the confrontation.

Nedjo tried to shove Trifko back, infuriated. 'He was an ex–partisan and a friend!' he shouted.

'You were going to tell him our purpose,' Gavrilo said. He was angry with himself for trusting someone so unreliable.

'You know the man. He's one of us,' Nedjo retorted. He plainly couldn't understand what he'd done wrong.

'What your enemy should not know, do not tell, even to your friends,' Gavrilo said. It was one of the first things he'd learnt. 'The gendarme you were gossiping with on the ferry was not one of us,' he added. Nedjo had flouted his oath and endangered the mission from the very beginning, striking up a conversation with a policeman he'd met on the steamer from Belgrade. Gavrilo cringed at the memory.

'A true Serbian hero does not skulk from his enemies, like a dog,' Nedjo said.

'A hero does not signal his purpose to his enemies on postcards!' Gavrilo rammed the postcard back into Nedjo's hand.

'A few lines of poetry to my sister,' Nedjo explained, exasperated.

Gavrilo saw that there was no talking reason to him. Nedjo was a liability and they had to get rid of him. 'We think it would be better if you travelled separately – otherwise you'll wreck everything.'

'But you cannot mean it?' Nedjo was stunned.

'Give us your weapons. You can't be trusted with them and they will only implicate you the next time you open your mouth,' Gavrilo said, as forcefully as he could.

Trifko stepped closer and handed Nedjo his student registration card, adding his physical presence to Gavrilo's order. 'Here, you can use this to cross the border legally, without arms, and meet us in Tuzla.' Broken, Nedjo untied the bombs from his belt.

*

Gavrilo fought to keep up with Trifko as they hurried through Tuzla. He was exhausted from the journey; they'd been travelling at night, roughing it across country through appalling weather. He'd hardly eaten or slept in days and fatigue was starting to play on his nerves.

They'd been smuggled across the Drina into Austro-Hungarian territory without official papers, making them vulnerable to police checks, and while being passed from safe house to safe house it had proved impossible to keep their weapons or purpose a secret from the peasants helping them.

Gavrilo had resolved to follow Ciganovic's suggestion and hand their weapons over to Jovanovic, the merchant in Tuzla who Cigo had said would transport the weapons to Sarajevo for them. A local teacher in the underground had arranged a meeting for them and they'd gone to a great deal of trouble and expense to tidy themselves up before entering the city, not wanting to run the risk of being charged as vagrants.

Misko Jovanovic had been extremely distressed by their request and refused to take the weapons into Sarajevo. After some cajoling, Gavrilo had eventually persuaded him to look after the weapons until someone could collect them.

Gavrilo was relieved to have dumped his burden but he still felt edgy as he and Trifko neared the station. He saw a uniformed figure approaching and pulled Trifko into a side street. He'd already been recognised by an old schoolmate and didn't want to be seen by anyone who might know his political views and wonder why he was in the city.

'It's too dangerous to go straight to the station,' Gavrilo said. He knew they could be subject to spot checks while they waited for the train.

Trifko looked around nervously. 'We can go to the tavern near the station,' he suggested. Gavrilo agreed that would be as safe a place as any to try and stay out of sight. They both knew the city well from their school days and proceeded without further discussion.

Things could have been so different, Gavrilo reflected – but for new underwear he would be one of the very people he thought to avoid. Gavrilo's elder brother, Jovo, had been able to exploit the opportunities presented by their new Austrian masters, by setting up his own business hauling lumber. Jovo had hoped to give Gavrilo a similar opportunity when he left primary school at thirteen. He had encouraged their parents to send Gavrilo to military school in Sarajevo, a good prospect for a peasant's son.

On the way, his brother decided to buy Gavrilo new undergarments, so that the poor boy from the villages wouldn't be disgraced as an officer cadet. The shopkeeper, an old family friend, advised Jovo not to send Gavrilo to be a persecutor of his own people. He said that the merchants' school in Sarajevo would be a quicker way to make a profit and bring bread. His brother, ever the entrepreneur, agreed. Changing Gavrilo's fate forever, he found him lodgings in Sarajevo and enrolled him in the merchants' school.

The three years that Gavrilo spent there, supposedly learning to be a capitalist, became his initiation into a new world of ideas and poetry, nationalism and anarchism. His eyes were opened to the suffering of his people and he knew that he must act to change things.

The meaninglessness of studying to be a merchant became too much for Gavrilo, and he implored Jovo to send him to the classical high school in Tuzla. Jovo eventually agreed, seeing it as an opportunity for his intelligent brother to enter a profession.

Trifko jabbed Gavrilo in the ribs sharply, interrupting his introspection. They'd reached the tavern and Trifko had spotted danger through the window. Nedjo was sitting inside making a spectacle of himself with a middle-aged man; from what Gavrilo could tell he was boasting about his success with the local women.

'I think we should continue to travel separately,' Trifko urged.

Gavrilo agreed. It would be too risky to meet Nedjo and they went straight on to the station. Gavrilo was glad to be leaving the city. He'd been a restless spirit during his time at school in Tuzla. He was badly treated by his teachers and missed classes, preferring to read and spend time with the other radical students. He'd eventually transferred to Sarajevo high school to avoid expulsion and joined the front line of nationalist protest.

*

Nedjo finally gave up on Gavrilo and Trifko and took the train from Tuzla on his own. They'd evidently decided to travel on to Sarajevo without him, thinking him unworthy or too dangerous to travel with, but Nedjo knew he would still get the opportunity to show himself to be a hero of his people.

He didn't doubt that he'd find Gavrilo in Sarajevo. Trifko was going to his family in Pale, but Gavrilo was staying at his usual lodgings in the old town. They had much to discuss and organise; the newspaper clipping hadn't told them the date of the tyrant's visit or what he would be doing in Sarajevo.

Nedjo watched the familiar forests rush past his window, as the train carried him home to his family. He felt in good spirits, as he'd had an easy journey into Bosnia using Trifko's documents, and without the encumbrance of the weapons he'd been able to travel freely and enjoy the hospitality of friends and family. Any resentment he felt towards Gavrilo and Trifko had been soothed by Jela, a generous girl he'd met in Tuzla, who had provided his food and lodgings while he waited. Nedjo grinned as he thought of how he would promenade her through Sarajevo.

'Nedeljko Cabrinovic.' Nedjo looked up with a start. Lost in thought, he hadn't noticed the train stop in Doboj and now he was being confronted by two police detectives who'd just got on.

'Detective Vila – hello again,' Nedjo grinned. He had bumped into Vila at the tavern while he'd been waiting for Trifko and Gavrilo.

'Do you mind if we sit with you?'

'Yes, please join me.'

The two men sat down opposite him and began to chat amiably. Nedjo was well acquainted with Ivo Vila, who was a frequent visitor at his father's cafe.

'I thought I'd see you again,' Detective Vila said good-naturedly as the train began to slowly judder forward. They'd had a meal at the tavern before Vila went off to meet his colleague and finish some formalities.

'Did you manage to get your business concluded?' Nedjo asked.

'Oh yes, just student idealists causing trouble about some play or some such nonsense. They're nicely locked up in Tuzla jail now,' Vila said winking. Nedjo flinched, wondering if the detective was familiar with his politics. 'I'm sure we didn't have as much fun as you did. Still daydreaming about that girl?'

'She is a relative, helping me while I look for work,' Nedjo said. He'd had to tell Vila something during the meal as he didn't want to dishonour the girl's reputation.

'I'm sure she was very helpful. I take it you didn't find work in Tuzla. You're a printer aren't you?'

The Assassins

'That's right. Hopefully, I'll have more luck in Sarajevo,' Nedjo said. The detective didn't look impressed by his lack of concern.

'I'm sure your good father will smarten your ideas up,' Vila said.

That was the only black cloud on the horizon, Nedjo thought. His father would demand to know what he'd been doing with himself and start pontificating about the wonders of their Austrian rulers.

'So, you were telling me you've been away.'

'Yes, I've been living in Belgrade,' Nedjo answered, glad not to have to think about the coming reunion with his father.

'Belgrade?' Something caught Vila's eye before he could continue. 'Who's that fellow over there who keeps staring?' the detective asked, pointing across the carriage.

Nedjo looked around with a start. Gavrilo was sitting behind him, in a different compartment, with Trifko. They were both looking at him very intensely.

'That is Gavrilo Princip, a friend from Belgrade.' He was so surprised to see Gavrilo that he blurted out his real name.

'What were you doing in Belgrade, exactly?' Vila glanced over Nedjo for something incriminating. Not seeing anything, he seemed satisfied that Nedjo wasn't a criminal.

'Have you seen my father recently?' Nedjo asked, trying to deflect attention.

'I saw him yesterday, as it happens. He and your family are well,' Vila answered.

'I'm glad.' Much to Nedjo's disgust, his father had got very friendly with the police so that he could get a licence to open his cafe.

'We're all very excited by His Imperial and Royal Highness Archduke Franz Ferdinand's visit to Sarajevo,' Vila said.

'I hear it is to be soon?' Nedjo enquired.

'The 28th of June.'

'Vidovdan? Our most sacred day!' Nedjo was furious. He couldn't believe that the tyrant was coming on the day the Serb people remembered the great defeat by the Turks.

'Yes, he does us great honour,' Vila said solemnly. Nedjo thought that he would bestow his own honour on the heir, now that he knew the exact date on which he would take his revenge.

Chapter 11

A court lackey showed Franz Ferdinand into the billiard room at Schonbrunn, the emperor's summer residence, to await his audience with Franz Joseph. A great chandelier shone above the billiard table, which was placed in the centre of the room, no doubt to help the emperor's petitioners pass the time while they waited. He glanced around at the familiar paintings and white-gold rococo design on the walls.

The archduke was agitated; he disliked having to come here, cap in hand for the sake of protocol. He ignored the billiard table and paced across the blocked wooden floor in military step, to calm himself before his audience with the emperor.

He glanced at a small wall clock in the corner of the room without registering the time. Franz Ferdinand was impatient to get this ordeal over with, but the emperor would not disturb his routine for anyone, least of all for his nephew, the heir apparent.

Emperor Franz Joseph described himself as the first public servant of the state. He lived a solitary and ritualistic life, repressed and self-disciplined, working tirelessly in the service of the monarchy from four in the morning until eight at night. He even took his meals at his desk. Franz Joseph wasn't an intellectual, but he was certainly meticulous and thorough in his duties, with a reverence and devotion to detail. Franz Ferdinand remembered that the emperor's wife, Empress Sissi, had said that Franz Joseph had the soul of a drill sergeant.

In what was a constant battle to maintain order in his empire, routine and protocol were the emperor's guiding lights, taking the place of innovation and change. He'd told Franz Ferdinand that a dynasty without ritual or protocol was a dynasty without meaning or defence.

Franz Joseph had been emperor for over sixty years, holding the empire together through some of its most turbulent times, but he had only slowed the decline. He and his 'cabinet of mummies' had lost territory to Italy, suffered humiliating defeats to Prussia and made concessions to Hungary, resulting in the Habsburg Empire being split in half and recreated as a dual monarchy. To Franz Ferdinand's abhorrence, Hungary now governed the eastern half and Austria the western. Both had separate parliaments, with financial, military, and foreign policy administered by three joint ministries. It was an abnormal and diseased condition, in Franz Ferdinand's opinion, and the confusion and conflict this joint system caused was the single greatest threat to the stability of the realm.

The archduke stopped pacing to study the painting that covered the central wall of the room. It depicted the first investment ceremony of the order of Maria Theresa in 1758. It was one of the empire's highest military honours, and had been founded to celebrate victory over Fredrick the Great. The room had two other paintings commissioned by the emperor to commemorate the centenary of that event and to relive the past glory of Maria Theresa's reign. Franz Ferdinand felt the whole monarchy ran on nostalgia. It was time for a new approach.

He was determined to restore everything that the iron House of Habsburg had lost. He'd been systematic in his preparations for taking the throne, building up a personal intelligence network and a shadow cabinet, which kept him better informed than even the emperor himself. The one overriding message to come from his network was that the situation was getting worse.

The rise of nationalism was seriously threatening the internal and external security of the Austro-Hungarian monarchy. At home, its eleven different nationalities were all clamouring for equal rights, and in some cases, self-determination. Abroad, the Austro-Hungarian monarchy had sought to expand to the east and open new markets to compensate for the loss of territory it had suffered in the west, but they were being resisted by the new Balkan nations rising from the crumbling Ottoman Empire, all of them with competing territorial claims that were destabilising the region.

Serbia had emerged as the monarchy's main rival; it had grown in power and prestige after its success in the two Balkan Wars, and now Serbian nationalists dreamed of recreating a Greater Serbia out of Austro-Hungarian territory in the region, where they spread dissension among the populace.

The Austro-Hungarian monarchy had adopted an increasingly aggressive foreign policy in a bid to bolster its prestige and secure the Balkans from nationalist dogma. The wrongheadedness of this approach frustrated Franz Ferdinand. All it achieved was the further straining of relations with Serbia, driving them into the arms of Mother Russia, who was also trying to increase her influence in the region. A number of hardliners in the government and military believed that war was inevitable, and advocated a pre-emptive strike against Serbia, arguing that any risk of war with Russia would be mitigated by their alliance with Germany.

Franz Ferdinand had reservations about the prudence of such a war and had argued against it. When he gained the throne he planned to stabilise the country by reducing Hungary to a Habsburg crown land and create a centralised state – a United States of Austria, crushed and reshaped back into a feudal society subservient to the will of its emperor once again. Then he'd deal with the South Slavs and re-establish Habsburg hegemony in the Balkans once and for all.

Franz Ferdinand was eventually shown into the Walnut Room, where the emperor conducted his audiences surrounded by dark walnut panelling, lavishly detailed in grand rococo style. The room was both austere and refined, like the emperor himself. Franz Joseph rose from a consort desk, his kind, benevolent features greyed by his recent bad health. Uncle and nephew greeted each other formally; their relationship was always gracious, but never intimate.

'Your Imperial and Royal Majesty – I am glad to see you are recovered.' If the emperor had succumbed to his illness, Franz Ferdinand pondered, he wouldn't have had to go through this ridiculous charade.

The emperor returned to his consort desk and checked his notes. 'I believe you requested this audience to discuss the Bosnian manoeuvres, Franz Ferdinand?' In his youth, the emperor had been noted for his love of such things, riding bolt upright for hours on end and sharing the men's hardships. However, he'd shown a declining interest in the military with the arrival of modern warfare, finding it all rather bewildering. Franz Ferdinand wondered if that was why the emperor had made him inspector general of the army, handing over the responsibility for attending manoeuvres.

'Your Majesty. I have concerns about the intense summer heat of Bosnia. I'm uncertain whether my health could stand up to it.'

'I see.' The emperor gave his nephew a hard look. Franz Ferdinand stood up to the unflinching gaze. Despite his current state of infirmity, the emperor was rarely sick and appeared less than sympathetic to his nephew's concerns.

In his thirties, Franz Ferdinand had contracted tuberculosis and had been exiled to die. The emperor had even cut Franz Ferdinand's allowance and had begun preparing his younger brother to become heir. The archduke felt a flush of anger at the memory. He was determined not to get sick again and the chances were that the extreme heat could bring on an asthma attack.

'You understand the importance of a visit by my successor?' Franz Joseph asked. From his brusque tone it appeared he still viewed Franz Ferdinand as weak and sickly.

Franz Ferdinand knew that if he missed the manoeuvres it would reflect very badly on his commitment to his role as both inspector general of the army and heir to the throne. Franz Joseph often expressed reservations about his heir's character, suggesting that he was blunt and overly aggressive, and he refused to share official documents with him, let alone the reins of power. Franz Ferdinand would not give his uncle any further reason to question his suitability to be emperor.

He looked at a huge wall map that described the monarchy in a great blur of blue, at the centre of Europe. He would not be responsible for losing any more of it. Franz Ferdinand touched his 'life certificate', the letter his doctor had given him to certify that he had fully recovered from tuberculosis. He carried it with him everywhere. 'Yes, Your Majesty. The visit would help check Serbia's growing influence over our Balkan provinces by increasing support amongst those subjects in the province who are loyal to the monarchy. They would therefore act as a defence against Serbian expansionist policies.'

'Precisely,' the emperor agreed. 'I was under the impression that you'd asked for the 15th and 16th Army Corps manoeuvres to take place in Bosnia.'

'Yes, Your Majesty.' Franz Ferdinand suspected that the army was in no condition to launch any kind of military campaign in the Balkans, least of all the pre-emptive strike against Serbia that the hardliners were calling for. 'I would like to know how well the army performs in the region,' he explained.

The emperor almost nodded approval then remembered, 'Yet you do not actually wish to attend the manoeuvres yourself?'

Franz Ferdinand bristled, but managed to control his temper. The emperor looked at his nephew through tired eyes and, sensing the archduke's rage, he took on the pallor of a sick old man, making Franz Ferdinand feel like a bully.

'It's a matter for your own discretion, Franz Ferdinand. If you feel your health will prevent you from doing your duty, then so be it.'

Franz Ferdinand disagreed with many aspects of his uncle's rule, but he'd always been taught to revere the position of emperor, and he held the old man in the deepest respect.

'If Your Majesty so commands, I am more than willing to do my duty.'

'Quite so.' The emperor expected nothing less.

Franz Ferdinand didn't feel it was worth mentioning that the police had received warnings of assassination plots. Such things were common when dealing with the volatile people of the Balkans. The king of Greece had been murdered last year and the Serb royal family had been gunned down and hacked to pieces in their own palace. The Croatian secretary of education had been murdered and the imperial governors of Bosnia and Croatia had been shot at and wounded.

The archduke would not be prevented from doing his duty by thugs. Even the emperor had been attacked by a Hungarian nationalist and had brushed shoulders with an assassin when he visited Bosnia. Yet he still took walks on his own, a tempting target for any radical crackpot. His maxim was, 'If we must go under, we'd better go decently.'

Franz Ferdinand wholeheartedly agreed. He'd been humiliated enough by the mob when he'd visited Herzegovina and Dubrovnik in 1906 and he would not disgrace himself by refusing to go to the Balkans again.

The emperor inclined his head to the side, his usual way of saying an audience was over. 'It's been a pleasure,' he concluded. Franz Ferdinand baulked; he was being dismissed like a common petitioner at one of the emperor's weekly audiences.

'Your Majesty, if I'm to attend the manoeuvres, might it be possible for the Duchess of Hohenberg to accompany me?' Now that the archduke had assented to the emperor's wishes, he felt that it was time to ask for something in return.

The emperor looked world-weary and annoyed. He'd thought the audience was over. 'Yes – yes, what of it? Did she not accompany you at the autumn manoeuvres?'

'As I'll be visiting Sarajevo in a military capacity, I believe protocol permits my wife to accompany me on the official state functions.'

Franz Joseph gave him an astute look and Franz Ferdinand knew what he was thinking; the heir to the throne wanted the commoner he'd married to play at being empress for the day. Franz Ferdinand suppressed his fury at his uncle's perspicacity. Then the emperor smiled. Had being old and lonely made him whimsical, Franz Ferdinand wondered. Perhaps he didn't want any further confrontation, or maybe he remembered how his unflinching belief in protocols had driven away his Sissi, his angel. Whatever it was, the emperor was giving his consent. 'Do as you wish.'

Chapter 12

Johnny Swift fought the urge to fidget with his collar while he waited for Mr Harding-Brown to mull over his request. Johnny had caught him during his mid-morning repast and every new mouthful he took gave him the opportunity to ignore his visitor.

By the look of Harding-Brown, Johnny thought that he must have spent the past twenty-five years completing meaningless forms and memos. All he had was the simple pleasure of a hotly-buttered muffin. For Johnny, it was like seeing his future laid out before him and it almost made him want to give up there and then.

'I'm sorry, I don't understand. You say you're from the Paris embassy?' Harding-Brown asked, his eyes flickering enviously as he said the word 'Paris'.

'That's right, sir.' Johnny replied smugly.

Harding-Brown finished his muffin and Johnny hoped that he was at last going to turn his mind to helping him. 'And you say the Honourable Pinkston Barton-Forbes told you to come and see me?' Harding-Brown was clearly perplexed and irritated by the interruption to his daily routine.

'Yes, Mr Harding-Brown.'

'But what on earth for?'

Johnny felt sweat sting the back of his neck and at last allowed himself to show the weakness of adjusting his collar in front of a superior. He'd had to battle the summer heat as he trudged through the strange sights of Sarajevo trying to find the British Consulate and now it looked as if his efforts had all been for nothing.

'I fail to understand why you're here. I believe the briefings I've been sending to Vienna are perfectly adequate,' Harding-Brown stated grandly.

'There is no implied criticism of yourself,' Johnny said. He hadn't anticipated his arrival putting Harding-Brown on the defensive. Johnny glanced round the drab little office; there were no imperial fixtures and fittings and he realised that there wouldn't be anywhere left for the man to fall if he was cast out of a consulate in the backwoods of nowhere.

'From what I understand, your efforts are very much up to the mark, which is why I was advised to come and see you. I'm here purely to supplement the excellent work you've already produced, with the hope that I will be able to put together a more immediate picture of events,' Johnny said, with all of the false servility he could muster under the circumstances.

'Are you suggesting that my work isn't up to date or relevant?' Harding-Brown asked, steadily building himself up into a rage.

'No, not at all. I'll be happy with background information about the political situation over here, or if you could at least point me in the direction of someone who can provide it.'

'Everything that is salient to the past, present and future political situation in Bosnia is in my reports. I won't have you suggesting otherwise to the people in Vienna, Paris or Timbuktu for that matter!'

'I don't think you understand the purpose of my assignment. Honestly...' Johnny ran out of words; this man was too practised in the subtle civil service arts of obstruction for Johnny to overcome.

'Honestly! – Honestly!' Harding-Brown mimicked in a mock cockney accent, while adopting the relaxed, supercilious expression of Barton-Forbes. It was the same look Johnny had received all his life from his social superiors and now it would seem, also from washed out old hacks. 'Young man, you're right, I don't understand you. I have absolutely no idea what you're about or why you've been sent here, other than that it obviously isn't something that would occupy a gentleman.'

Johnny tried to stifle a smile. He had made a name for himself at school by behaving like a cad on the rugby pitch and introducing dirty play no gentleman would dream of using. He'd proved so effective that he was made one of the school 'bloods'. Despite the rhetoric of playing fair, nothing mattered except having the school colours on a cup. Johnny took his collar off and marched out of the consulate. It was time for him to take a different tack.

Chapter 13

Lazlo Breitner stared blankly at his basement office. It was little more than a storage cupboard, but it had served its purpose. He picked up a copy of his report and made his way through Sarajevo's City Hall to the police station on the top floor of the building.

He was oblivious to his surroundings, as he planned what to say. The meeting he was going to was the culmination of months of work. Breitner knew that it would be an uncomfortable experience, he'd had to beg and plead for it, but he could not allow himself to be distracted by cynicism. If things went well he would be back on the path of the righteous.

Breitner entered the police station, receiving a terse greeting from the gendarme behind the desk, and knocked on the door of Leo Pfeffer.

'Come in,' Pfeffer called from behind the door. Breitner entered.

Leo Pfeffer, an investigating judge of the Sarajevo district court, languished behind his desk. He was in his late thirties, bloated, pasty and already wore a bored expression.

Viktor Ivasjuk, Sarajevo's chief of detectives, paced around the room. Neither of them looked pleased to be wasting their time on Breitner.

Pfeffer picked up the copy of the report that Breitner had sent him when he first asked for the meeting. Breitner would have preferred to see someone more senior, but it was said that Pfeffer was a rising star.

'You seem to think that there is some kind of plot going on in Sarajevo – is that correct, Breitner?' Pfeffer asked, and looked wearily at Viktor.

Breitner took hold of himself and tried to ignore the hostility that surrounded him. In his time he'd dealt with threats to the Austro-Hungarian monarchy far beyond the capacity of these men, but then he reminded himself he'd had the support of the cream of the imperial army.

'Yes, that is correct, Herr Pfeffer. I believe there to be a very serious situation developing in Sarajevo.'

'And how is this any different from the other myriad of idiotic rumours that pour into this office every day?'

'We are facing a wave of nationalism that is sweeping through the Austro-Hungarian monarchy. There have been attacks across the Balkans and I believe that there is a very real threat from local nationalists here, the so-called "Young Bosnians",' Breitner said, prompting Viktor to stop pacing.

'Peasant school children,' Viktor Ivasjuk snarled. He was a tall, lean man with an aquiline nose and a reputation for intimidation.

Breitner had faced worse. 'I believe that these peasant school children are working with Serbian intelligence.'

'But you have no evidence for that,' Pfeffer said.

Breitner opened and closed his fists in frustration. The decaying, medieval institutions of his beloved monarchy were completely incapable of understanding, let alone combating the new threat emerging in the Balkans.

The emperor had decreed that his ministries only concern themselves with their own immediate areas of responsibility. The joint ministry of finance, which Breitner served, only dealt with Bosnia and Herzegovina. This meant there was no circulation or assessment of intelligence, or any coherent study of the South Slav problem. Consequently, Vienna had little or no idea of the increasing anger amongst the South Slav youth towards its rule.

Breitner had been trying to correct this disaster, at least in the provinces for which he was responsible, by attempting to build a coordinated approach to intelligence gathering.

'As you can see from the report, I've cross-referenced information gathered from intercepted mail, rumour and the propaganda pouring across the border from Serbia,' Breitner said.

'You've come to us with, at best, speculation derived from nothing more than the adolescent ramblings of Serb delinquents.' Pfeffer waved Breitner's report at him.

'And wild threats put about by Serbian intelligence to have us running around chasing our tails,' Viktor added.

Breitner shrugged. He was struggling to weld these different strands of half-truths, boasts and hearsay into a comprehensive profile of the threat presented by the Young Bosnians and to filter out the talkers from the doers who might be in league with Serbian intelligence.

He'd been in his post for a year and was only just starting to understand the tidal wave of contradictory information and misinformation which the Serbian intelligence was adept at producing, and the apocryphal statements which the Young Bosnians used. Each one fancied himself a poet, and they wrote cryptic letters to each other, full of metaphor and analogy to disguise their true meaning.

A knock at the door saved Breitner from answering Ivasjuk's or Pfeffer's criticisms. A handsome young clerk entered with the careless air of a matinee idol and handed Pfeffer some papers to be signed.

'Ah Pusara, you're a fair representative of Bosnian youth?' Pfeffer asked.

'Yes sir, I believe that I am,' Pusara answered.

'Would you say that there is a wave of nationalism sweeping through the youth of the monarchy?' Pfeffer asked.

'I don't believe that there is any doubt where the loyalties of the young men of the monarchy stand,' the youth answered, with an amused smile.

'There you are Breitner,' Pfeffer said, as if he'd presented the decisive argument in the cross-examination of a witness. Breitner knew all about Mihajlo Pusara and didn't doubt what the answer would be if questioned precisely what his loyalties to the monarchy were.

'May I go to lunch now?' Pusara asked with a theatrical bow. His name had come up in one or two of Breitner's lines of enquiry; he was a member of various nationalist groups and an associate of the man Breitner wished to investigate. An actor by calling, Pusara had opted to stay in his homeland and work as a clerk, rather than follow the path of fame and fortune elsewhere.

Breitner watched Pfeffer look at the clock and saw that it was 12.30 p.m. The judge appeared annoyed, Breitner suspected, because he was missing his own lunch. 'Yes, of course, my dear fellow. You are a creature of habit aren't you?' Pfeffer waited until he had left before adding, 'Excellent fellow – a good clerk is so hard to come by.'

Breitner thought it best to keep his observations to himself. As far as he knew, Pusara hadn't done anything illegal and he didn't wish to bring down any further derision on his investigation.

'What exactly is it that you want, Mr Breitner?' Pfeffer asked.

'I've identified a member of a Young Bosnia cell. He lives a few streets away from here and is recruiting members to carry out an act of great Serbian patriotism.'

'And you've gleaned all this from the scribbling of these semi-literate rejects? It doesn't seem a very solid premise from which to turn the city upside down,' Pfeffer said.

The Assassins

'I'd like to have him brought in for questioning, or at the very least a few men to help carry out surveillance of his boarding house,' Breitner replied, trying to maintain his dignity.

'Have you taken these mad ideas of yours to your own chief? You are part of the political section for goodness' sake.'

'A very lowly member of the political section,' Viktor added.

'Yes, with very limited power to take action. My chief has passed my warnings on to Governor Potiorek, who chose to discount them,' Breitner said, 'along with those of the chief of police and the speaker of the Bosnian parliament.'

'I see – doesn't that tell you something, Mr Breitner?' Pfeffer asked, harshly.

Breitner finally lost his temper. There was only so much scorn he could take. 'It tells me that our dear, beloved military governor is just as dull and mutton-headed as the dull, mutton-headed bureaucrats he serves in Vienna.'

The two men looked at Breitner, lost for words, although eventually Pfeffer managed to say, 'I understand that you came to Sarajevo with a jaded past, chased out of the army and with something of a reputation.'

Breitner inadvertently touched his chest where his service ribbons had been worn, but they were gone. He no longer wore the uniform of the emperor, and a year on still felt its loss deeply and expected to mourn it for the rest of his life.

'Breitner, you may not have any regard for the consequences your actions have on your career or the careers of those around you or the monarchy in general but I do care, and I have no intention of letting you drag me down with you. Now leave my office and do not trouble me with this nonsense again,' Pfeffer said coldly.

Breitner managed a half bow and hurried back to his basement office – the path of righteousness would have to wait.

Chapter 14

Johnny Swift admired Sarajevo from a terrace cafe on the western edge of Bascarsija, the old town, where Sarajevo merged into the new imperial buildings of the Austro-Hungarian monarchy. The city had been built on the banks of the shallow Miljacka river, at the bottom of a thickly wooded valley. Two storey, whitewashed houses with red-tiled roofs spread out from the city up the surrounding mountains, making Johnny feel as if he was at the bottom of a giant basin.

The centuries-old conflict between east and west had become fused in the city. Minarets, domes and artisan shops, their wares spilling out onto roughly cobbled streets, stood side by side with ornate neo-Renaissance banks, hotels and offices. The call to prayer and the sound of the gentle flow of water fountains mingled with the roar of the trams and the bustle of a modern western city.

He finished his burek, which seemed to be a kind of pasty, and poured himself another thimble of coffee from a long-handled copper jug. He dipped a sugar cube into the rich, dark sediment; it had taken him a while to work out that this was how to drink it, but it was almost second nature to him now. Johnny was at one with his environment; the contrasting character of the city echoed the conflict that was going on in his mind. He was sorely tempted to stay here and revert back to his true self, letting the perfectly cut tennis lawn which the diplomatic service had turned him into, run wild with the persistent weed of his self-destructive side, but he knew that that would prove Sir George right, and that would never do.

Johnny remembered what he was about and glanced at the crowded street below. The mix of cultures was most apparent in the dress of the people. It reminded him of an *'Arabian Nights'* themed party he'd attended in Paris with Libby.

He watched as a blonde man wearing a fez and baggy oriental clothes walked past a group of mountain people in crimson scarves and pointed shoes, then stopped to say hello to a man in a suit and tie. The variety of dress was endless but what really caught Johnny's eye were the women in brightly coloured veils. They had a serene passion about them as they returned his admiring looks with a seductive sway of the hips.

It had taken Johnny a few days to acclimatise to the city as he brushed up on the language and planned what to do next, but now, as he sucked coffee from a sugar cube, he felt like the great British explorer Richard Burton, preparing for his journey to Mecca.

Distant chimes of the Catholic cathedral sounded, followed by those of the Orthodox church and a minute later the sound of the Muslim clock tower. It was then that Johnny saw him among the colour of the swirling crowds, out of sync but regular as clockwork – the lone, frock-coated figure of Harding-Brown, the quintessential Englishman. A bulwark against everything that was not quite right and foreign, he skirted the edge of the old town trying to keep to the safe western parts of the city, while being drawn to the mysteries of the Orient. Johnny finished his coffee and left.

He caught up with Harding-Brown as he passed a rather seedy looking basement cafe. Johnny had been watching him since being dismissed from his office and couldn't help but notice the way he always idled outside the cafe, both fascinated and appalled, desperate to go inside and yet repelled at the same time.

'Good afternoon,' Johnny said. Harding-Brown turned around, startled. Johnny held out his hand and Harding-Brown was forced to shake it.

'Good afternoon,' Harding-Brown replied warily. Johnny had caught him as he'd been looking helplessly at the veiled women going into the cafe. Judging from the way Harding-Brown was staring at the mysterious figures drifting past, he'd never once lifted the veil on his inhibitions.

'My name's Swift – we spoke briefly in your office,' Johnny said, pretending not to have noticed Harding-Brown's embarrassment.

'Yes, yes, I remember,' Harding-Brown replied, his eyes flitting about, trying to find some means of escape.

'I was hoping I might be able to talk to you. I still have a few questions that I need to ask,' Johnny said.

'I think I've said all that I have to say to you, Master Swift,' Harding-Brown answered, desperate to get rid of Johnny. 'I don't know how you conduct yourselves in Paris, but here we don't solicit one another in the street like common hawkers.'

'Quite right, maybe we should go somewhere to talk. This cafe has, I believe, a most amenable atmosphere.' Johnny grinned knowingly.

Harding-Brown baulked at his barefaced cheek. 'Certainly not ...'

'Perhaps I should go to the British Consulate again,' Johnny said, raising his voice.

Harding-Brown glanced around, mortified to hear the place of his employment mentioned in such a scandalous part of town.

'When would be a convenient time for me to see you at the British Consulate?' Johnny asked, even louder.

Harding-Brown started to move away but Johnny caught him as he was off balance and hauled him towards the cafe. He hadn't been the captain of the school rugby club for nothing, he reminded himself.

'Come on, we'll have a drink and enjoy the show. As you say, the street isn't really the place to talk,' Johnny said and Harding-Brown stopped struggling; he wasn't very strong.

*

Gavrilo Princip left the police station and headed back to his boarding house through the crowded streets of the merchant district. He hated Sarajevo, hated the commercialism of the place and the decadence it harboured. Most of all he hated the feeling of being under the control of a foreign power in his own country. The oppressive feel of the invaders screamed out from the very architecture of the city, echoing the corruption they had brought.

He turned into his street and opened the door of his lodgings – the corruption had even found its way into his boarding house. It was the same boarding house where his revolutionary spirit had first grown, under the mentorship of his friend, Danilo Ilic. The house belonged to Ilic's mother, who had furnished it in the eclectic mix of East and West that characterised this city, with worn but brightly coloured rugs contrasting with shiny new dressers and a chest of drawers made in Vienna.

To his annoyance, Gavrilo found Nedjo taking coffee with Ilic in the kitchen. He was showing Ilic a new sports cap he'd brought. Gavrilo ignored Nedjo and greeted Ilic with, 'I've done it.'

'Good. I know it couldn't have been easy for you Gavro,' Ilic answered, with a concerned expression on his pale, raw-boned face.

Gavrilo shrugged in reply and sat at the table. He'd just undergone the indignity of registering his arrival in the city; with his radical background he didn't want to give the police any reason to suspect him.

Ilic silently handed him a small cup of coffee and sat down, nervously brushing a hand over his closely cropped blonde hair. Gavrilo saw that he'd quickly realised his mood and although Ilic was taller and older than Gavrilo, he knew better than to antagonise him further by continuing the subject and risking his fury.

'I have already registered,' Nedjo said. Gavrilo bristled – he had never known Nedjo to exercise Ilic's good sense. 'My father insisted.'

Gavrilo continued to ignore Nedjo. As well as Nedjo's lack of tact, Gavrilo was still angry about his behaviour during the journey from Belgrade and he couldn't bring himself to forgive Nedjo's recklessness.

'We must start to make plans to act, for when the tyrant comes,' Nedjo said, unperturbed by Gavrilo's coldness.

'You will be told if and when you are needed,' Gavrilo said.

'But it was me who was sent the clipping when we were in Belgrade,' Nedjo said in disbelief.

'How am I to trust you, Nedjo, after the way you behaved on the journey from Belgrade?' Gavrilo asked, acidly, and Nedjo sat back looking stunned and hurt.

'We are still making plans, Nedjo. Nothing has been decided,' Ilic said conciliatorily.

'We will act, that is for certain,' Gavrilo said, annoyed at his friend's indecision.

'Are you sure that now is the right time? There is still much to be done, Gavrilo. I am still trying to recruit people.'

'Now is our time,' Princip snapped.

'But there is no plan,' Ilic said.

'We know the tyrant will be staying at the Hotel Bosnia; I've started to observe it,' Nedjo said, twirling his sports cap around his finger.

'You will maintain a low profile, Nedjo. You will not give the game away. The plan will be decided by Ilic and myself in due course when we know what the tyrant's movements will be when he comes to Sarajevo.'

'Are you sure that now is the right time to carry out individual acts of vengeance against the Habsburgs, Gavrilo? There are many ways we can serve our cause. We may be able to accomplish more if we delay...'

Gavrilo held up his hand to stop Ilic. 'Do you forget the harm done to our people by the tyrant, Archduke Franz Ferdinand? Do you lack the resolve to take revenge for what has been done to our people? Or would you rather meet your friends for lunch or talk in kitchens?' Gavrilo pointed towards the bazaar. 'Maybe you have been so long living in this place that you have become addled by the cheap trinkets sold in the market and have forgotten the oppression of our people.'

Ilic became sallow. 'No Gavrilo, I have not lost my resolve.'

'Good. Nothing will be accomplished by delaying. We must act when the tyrant comes to Sarajevo. Only through our sacrifice will our people ever be freed.' Gavrilo had come too far to stop now because of some convoluted idea of Ilic's.

*

A dark-haired goddess in sequined muslin was performing the most original rendition of the Dance of the Seven Veils Johnny had ever seen. Harding-Brown watched transfixed as the secrets behind the veils were finally revealed to him. They were obviously more spectacular than anything he could possibly have imagined.

From a purist's sense it might not have been the most conventional belly dance, but the effect was truly hypnotic. Johnny poured Harding-Brown and himself another glass of wine.

'So you're familiar with the situation in Sarajevo?' Johnny asked.

'Yes – yes,' Harding-Brown replied, unhappy with the distraction.

'Anything you could tell me would be extremely useful.' The two of them had been there half the night and once Harding-Brown had overcome his social embarrassment he ignored Johnny and focused on the floor show.

'I mean, a man in your position must have a tremendous amount of contacts,' Johnny said, persevering. He knew that if his report was to have any credibility he would require something official from the Sarajevo authorities. He assumed they'd have files on local agitators and the dangers they posed to international relations, but to get at them, he would need help.

'I don't want you badgering the authorities about nationalism in Bosnia; this is a sensitive time for them – we've just received word that the heir to the Austro-Hungarian throne will be visiting the province next month to attend manoeuvres and I can't have you creating difficulties. I don't really know you from Adam, do I? You could be any old Johnny off the street,' Harding-Brown said, amused by his word play.

'Maybe I should leave. It's getting a bit stuffy in here.' Panic flickered across Harding-Brown's face. They had a special table at the front, because Johnny was a special customer, and Harding-Brown was under no illusions that if Johnny left he'd have to tip someone to keep it. The lady on stage began to shimmy, rotating her breasts in perfect harmony. Harding-Brown spluttered as he tried to think.

'Nationalism here's a bit of a vexed question. I can't really say I begin to understand it myself.'

'Could you give me some background information? I mean, do you think it's likely that the South Slavs would join together to revolt against Austro-Hungarian rule?' Johnny asked hopefully. That could be just the thing that Sir George would want to know. A revolt of that kind would seriously destabilise the region and have implications for the rest of Europe. Harding-Brown ignored Johnny until the performance was over and the dancer left the stage, then he faced him with a sigh.

'I suppose the best example of what the situation is like here can be expressed through the synchronisation of the clocks that belong to the different denominations.'

'Clocks?' Johnny couldn't believe it. Harding-Brown had spent his entire career in one place and the only thing he'd noticed about it was that the clocks didn't keep time.

'Yes. The clock on the Catholic cathedral is more than a minute ahead of the Orthodox church's clock and the Muslims' Sahat tower clock is even further out of sync. These people won't even agree on the time of day, let alone uniting against the Austro-Hungarian monarchy. A lot of them are very happy under its rule.'

'I see.' That made sense – Johnny had wondered about the different clocks chiming out of sync.

'Of course, the Muslim clock is English-made, by the same chaps who cast Big Ben, so I'm inclined to err on the side of Islam.' Harding-Brown stopped and looked at his empty glass. Johnny poured him another drink – he was starting to earn it.

'Look, go and see Leo ... Leo Pfeffer. He's a jolly nice chap – you can find him in the City Hall.' Harding-Brown handed Johnny his calling card. 'Say I sent you. He's an investigating judge of the Sarajevo district court, so if anyone knows what's going on, he should.' Harding-Brown spun round dismissively as the music began and a different dancer took the stage.

Chapter 15

The City Hall had been built by the Austrians in a grand Moorish style, with yellow and orange stonework, battlements and a large galleried entrance. It reminded Johnny of a modern hotel designed to give a taste of the Orient to tourists, but with all the conveniences of the west.

Leo Pfeffer's office, luckily for Johnny, was directly opposite a medical room, so he was able to beg a handful of aspirin from Pfeffer for his hangover.

'Sorry, Mr Swift, but I think you may have had a wasted trip,' Leo said as he ushered Johnny into his office. 'We don't have a nationalist problem in Sarajevo.' He was certainly friendly, even if he didn't really impress Johnny as someone who'd have his finger on the pulse of local affairs.

'There have been reports of growing nationalism in the Balkans,' Johnny said, trying to be as tactful as he could.

The judge was about to offer Johnny a seat, then thought better of it, waving his hand to dismiss the absurdity of what Johnny had said. 'There is always unrest of one sort or another, whipped up by propaganda, sent across the border by the Serbian government.'

'There is unrest – I mean, tensions, between the authorities and the local population,' Johnny said.

'Mr Swift, there is no significant political activity in Sarajevo. We have only had the usual criminal acts; perhaps if you're interested in that sort of thing you should talk to a detective.'

Pfeffer smiled and took Johnny to see Viktor Ivasjuk, who reminded Johnny of Simpson, his old head of house, who was just as intimidating.

'It's very good of you to see me, Mr Ivasjuk,' Johnny said after Pfeffer had made the introductions and left. Viktor's close-set eyes looked straight through Johnny, directly into his corrupted and tainted heart. Johnny would have confessed anything to the man at that moment.

'I'm not entirely sure how I can help you,' he said.

'No one is.'

'So you thought you'd try Sarajevo's very busy chief of detectives,' Viktor said.

Johnny thought it better to dispense with the social niceties and cut straight to the crux of his problem. 'My instructions are to gather information about the Pan-Slavic nationalist movements in the region.'

'I see.' Viktor immediately lost interest and started to read through the papers on his desk. He dipped a pen in an inkpot and started writing. Johnny almost gagged as he realised that the inkpot was a human skull. He assumed that it must be a stage prop and that the chap was into amateur dramatics. He thought it extremely unlikely, but it could be a way in.

'Alas, poor Yorick!' Johnny said with a grin. Viktor looked up at him, his eyes summoning all the elemental forces of darkness against Johnny.

'This isn't frippery, Mr Swift. It's the skull of Bogdan Zerajic.'

'You mean – it's actually real?'

Viktor turned the skull slightly to show Johnny a bullet hole.

'Yes, it is quite real. It belonged to a lunatic who tried to murder General Varesanin, our previous governor, in 1910.'

'I see.'

'Zerajic shot at the governor five times as he made his way home after opening our parliament, then saved the last bullet for himself.'

'And you didn't think to bury him?' Johnny asked. He couldn't understand why this man kept a real skull on his desk and why he used it as an inkpot. Viktor was in a whole different league to the usual despots Johnny had dealt with in the British civil service. Viktor looked pleased by Johnny's reaction.

Johnny took a deep breath and steadied himself; he'd read about similar assassination attempts in the Austro-Hungarian monarchy.

'You, don't think that this could have been some kind of protest by Bosnian nationalists? It was in 1910, did you say? Maybe it was connected to the annexation of Bosnia and Herzegovina.' That had only happened a year or so previously; Johnny felt pleased he was connecting the dots and made a note of his theory.

'We carried out a full investigation and found no evidence linking Zerajic to any nationalist group or ideology. His assassination attempt, if that was in fact what it was, seems almost accidental – he just blundered into the governor. Zerajic had previously spent time stalking the emperor when he visited Bosnia, but didn't act on his lunatic instinct. General Varesanin was not so fortunate. The investigation concluded that it was the action of a man who, broken by poverty and living a fantasy life, was seized by a fit of paranoia against the governor.'

'So it was the act of a lone gunman? A madman.' Johnny crossed out his notes.

Viktor held the skull up to the light and spoke in much the same way that Johnny's head of house might have. 'Look at the contours of the skull – what do they tell you?'

'That he was a bad shot?' Johnny said dryly, trying to hide his unease. He had no idea what Viktor was talking about; all of this was totally beyond his area of expertise and experience. It looked like a perfectly normal skull to him, not unlike the one that had hung in the science lab at school.

'Zerajic was clearly a lunatic.' Viktor ran his hand along the top of the skull.

'You can tell that just from the shape of the skull?' Johnny asked and Viktor closed his eyes in annoyance. That wasn't the response he wanted.

'Are you familiar with Lombroso's theory of criminology?'

'No, I'm not.'

'Lombroso states that people are "born criminal", which can be identified by an asymmetry of the face and cranium.' Viktor broke off as something occurred to him. 'Perhaps there is someone who could help you. Come back tomorrow.'

Johnny left City Hall and wandered through the jostling streets of the old town. He had no idea where he was or how to get home. He expected that the next bureaucrat the chief of detectives was sending him to would give him the same old flannel and pass him onto someone else. He was going round in circles – he didn't know how he could write a report about the nationalist situation if one didn't exist, but he knew he couldn't go back to Paris empty-handed. Johnny assumed that Sir George had known that all along and now he was trapped here, unable to go forward or back.

The friendly aroma of hookah pipes drew Johnny into a cafe that looked as if it had been converted out of the owner's front room. He ordered a pipe and a bottle of wine. The sweet watermelon-flavoured tobacco gave him a head rush and blew his frustrations away. He wasn't sure how much longer his money would last, but he was determined to make the most of it while he could.

Johnny was halfway through his second bottle and a helping of apple-flavoured tobacco when a conversation behind him drew his attention. He tried to ignore it and concentrate on his binge, however something in what was said drew him out of his stupor.

'The South Slavs must unite and fight the Austro-Hungarian monarchy with force.'

'We should do it soon, while we still can. The Austro-Hungarian heir is coming to our home for manoeuvres that are surely a dress rehearsal for an invasion of Serbia.'

Johnny turned around and found himself face to face with a group of belligerent looking men, not much older than he was. They immediately stopped talking and stared at Johnny, with hard, unflinching eyes. He glanced around the cafe and noticed for the first time, murals depicting bloody medieval battles.

The people in the cafe didn't say anything to him, they just stared, which was unnerving, but Johnny had enough presence of mind to finish his wine before leaving. He wasn't beaten yet. Just because the authorities didn't know that there were nationalist feelings afoot in their city, it didn't mean they weren't there.

The next day he returned to City Hall, as he'd been instructed by the chief of detectives. A short dapper man in his twenties greeted Johnny with a wry, unsymmetrical smile and signalled for him to sit down.

'Lazlo Breitner?' Johnny asked.

'You must be the intrepid Englishman, sent to tame the savage hordes of the East,' the man replied, in clear, if accented English.

Johnny smiled and sat down in front of Breitner. He glanced around the office, which looked like a converted storeroom. He'd had a terrible time trying to find it, until someone directed him down to the basement.

'Do you think you could help?' Johnny asked.

Breitner thought for a moment before answering; he seemed to be taking Johnny's measure. Johnny sat up, adopting a no-nonsense, straight-talking persona, which seemed to amuse Breitner and make up his mind to help him.

'Tell me, Mr Swift, what do you know about the current situation in Bosnia and Herzegovina?' Johnny couldn't place his accent; it wasn't German or Bosnian.

'I don't know much about what's going on in Bosnia apart from a lunatic tried to assassinate the governor.'

'A lunatic? What nonsense!' Breitner raised an eyebrow and Johnny realised that he was Hungarian. He thought about replying in Hungarian, but Breitner was starting to make him feel silly. He didn't want to risk aggravating the situation. He decided to stick to what he was sure of. 'Yes, you can tell he was a lunatic by the shape of his skull.'

'You didn't let our good chief of detectives intimidate you with that skull?'

'But the chap, Zerajic, must have been deranged. He shot himself,' Johnny said, trying to regain some of his dignity. The chief of detectives had made it sound so obvious.

'This lunatic, as you call him, was Bogdan Zerajic – an icon for the Young Bosnia Nationalist Movement.'

Johnny's ears pricked up. 'Sorry – what movement?' He hadn't heard that name before and took out his notebook, wondering if this funny little chap might actually know something.

Breitner put on a pair of pince-nez, as he got down to business. 'I understand you're interested in the nationalist movements within Bosnia and Herzegovina, and obviously the difficulties they present to stability and good order in the Balkans, particularly in any effects their activities may have on the rather strained diplomatic situation between Serbia and the Austro-Hungarian monarchy?'

'Yes, I suppose so.' Johnny hadn't heard it put quite so succinctly before and quickly wrote it down, which entertained Breitner.

'The main nationalist threat to the Austro-Hungarian administration in this province comes from the younger generation, from people of student age, some a bit younger, some a bit older – most are 19. Your age, I'd imagine?'

'Yes, that's right sir,' Johnny answered. 'Is that important?'

'The older generation has pretty much accepted our rule, so they are less eager to adopt violence as a political weapon to force rapid change.' There was a look in Breitner's eyes, as if he was still trying to decide something. It made Johnny uncomfortable.

'The "Mlada Bosna" or "Young Bosnia" is the term increasingly applied to these peasant students who like to form secret societies and plot a revolution that will unite the South Slav people and destroy the Austro-Hungarian monarchy.'

Johnny wrote down the information; it had sparked something in his memory – the people he'd overheard the previous night had said something like that. 'I've heard similar talk in cafes here.'

Breitner raised a questioning eyebrow. 'Have you now? That's surprising – maybe you're not as artless as you pretend to be.'

'The thing I don't understand is that the other local officials I've spoken to told me that there isn't a nationalist problem in Bosnia,' Johnny said, too overcome with excitement to worry about Breitner's backhanded compliment. At last he felt as if he was getting somewhere.

'As I say, they're young and haven't committed any major outrage in Bosnia, so they largely go unnoticed and ignored by the authorities. Zerajic should have been their wake-up call.'

Johnny stopped taking notes – he was still going round in circles. 'The police carried out a full investigation of Zerajic and found nothing to connect him with a conspiracy or a movement.'

'Did the police speak to everyone who knew him? Did they tell them the truth?' Breitner asked.

Johnny shrugged. From his limited experience, he assumed that it wouldn't occur to anyone in Britain to lie to the police, but he realised that this was the continent. 'So why has he become an icon to the nationalists? He botched the assassination and shot himself – doesn't that suggest he wasn't in his right mind?'

'Zerajic showed the Young Bosnians that they can take action, like the anarchists in Russia and the nationalists in Serbia and Croatia. The fact that Zerajic failed and killed himself for the cause makes his actions that much more heroic. They believe that only people of noble character are capable of attempting political assassinations. Martyrdom, tragedy and assassination make up the psyche of the Young Bosnia Nationalists.'

Johnny was getting irritated by the chap's insistent use of jargon. 'Their psyche?'

'Are you familiar with the practice of psychoanalysis? Understanding human behaviour by analysing our rational and irrational drives?'

'You think that's a more valid way of identifying these types of people than studying their skulls?' Johnny asked, getting annoyed – this was becoming too much.

Breitner smiled, 'It's not a question of identifying them, but understanding them. Zerajic has become a hero for the Young Bosnians. They want to emulate him and Milos Obilic.'

'Sorry, who?'

'Milos Obilic is a hero of Serbian folklore. He was accused of treachery the night before the Serbs were due to fight an invading Turkish army at Kosovo in 1389. It was also the eve of Vidovdan or St. Vitus Day, a very sacred Orthodox Christian feast day. Obilic refuted the charge against him and said that on Vidovdan we would see who was, and who was not, a traitor.'

Johnny grew impatient as Breitner continued his litany; he'd actually thought he'd been getting somewhere.

'The following battle was a catastrophe for the Serbs and resulted in them being subjected to four hundred years of Ottoman rule. After the battle, to prove himself true and avenge the Serbs, Milos Obilic pretended to defect to the Turks. When he was presented to the Turkish Sultan, Obilic stabbed him in the stomach and was immediately cut down by the Sultan's bodyguards. The whole thing is commemorated every 28 June, on Vidovdan.'

Irritated, Johnny put down his pen. 'That's all very interesting Mr Breitner, but what's actually happening now?'

Breitner gave Johnny an insolent look. 'You're clearly a fool.'

'I beg your pardon?' Johnny said, jumping up. 'I'm not going to take that from some glorified lackey locked away in a store cupboard.'

'You haven't understood anything I've tried to explain. The personality of the Young Bosnians is largely defined by the outrage they feel over the Battle of Kosovo and the honour they have from Obilic's actions. That is what drives and inspires them, and that is why they present a danger to the stability of the Balkans and Europe.' There was a hardness under Breitner's calm reserve which made Johnny take a step back and regroup.

'Look here, I asked you a perfectly civil question.'

'What a pity there is no one left for you to ask your questions to, after this glorified lackey in the store cupboard.'

Chapter 16

Johnny made his way through the enchanted forest around Ilidza, an ancient spa on the outskirts of Sarajevo. It was a beautiful summer evening and the forest was in full bloom. He wondered if everything seemed so bright and vibrant because his back was well and truly against the wall. His plan may not have come off, but he still had one more ace to play – if he could find her.

Libby had been extremely vague about when she would arrive at the spa and Johnny's only hope now was that a week or so would be ample time for her to bore of Vienna's coffee house fops. He needed her; a woman in her position could exert influence on the local consulate to get something for him to pad out his report.

The distant howl of wolves brought him sharply back to his surroundings. Johnny quickened his pace. He felt that he was in a really strange place, something akin to being trapped in a Grimm's fairy tale where he was desperately trying to find his princess hiding in one of the Hansel and Gretel hotels which the Austrians had built.

Johnny had done a full circle of the spa without so much as a trace of Libby's vibrant, sequined presence. His mood started to brighten as he came to the Hotel Bosnia, the last in the circuit. It was a grand building, with potted palm trees and balconies elaborately decorated with ornate carved woodwork – just the sort of place to amuse Libby.

He entered the foyer, passing a tall, swarthy youth in a sports cap who was lurking at the door. He strolled nonchalantly towards the reception desk where he was greeted by a concierge flexing an elegantly waxed moustache. The concierge recognised Johnny as someone of a comparable class, who had no business on the other side of the desk.

'Yes, how may I be of assistance?' he asked abruptly.

'Good evening,' Johnny replied politely in reproof. The concierge was immediately put on the back foot. False servility was Johnny's stock-in-trade in the diplomatic service and it immediately showed up the concierge as having no manners, which he acknowledged by repeating the greeting more respectfully.

'Good evening, sir.'

'Yes, could you tell me if Lady Elizabeth Smyth is staying at this hotel?' Johnny asked, keeping his tone brisk and businesslike.

'Lady Elizabeth Smyth?' the concierge repeated, suspiciously. Johnny obviously wouldn't be on friendly terms with a lady, not in society, anyway.

'My name's Harding-Brown. I work at the British Consulate in Sarajevo,' Johnny said, showing the concierge Oliver Harding-Brown's calling card. 'I've been instructed to welcome Her Ladyship and invite her to a consulate function.'

The concierge sneered as he realised that Johnny was no more than a glorified messenger boy, certainly lower down the pecking order than himself. Satisfied that he'd regained his superiority, he began to look through the register.

'No, no one of that name is listed at this establishment.'

'Would there be a lady under the name of Swift?' With her coquettish sense of humour, Johnny thought it might be possible that she'd used his name. 'She sometimes likes to travel incognito.'

The concierge flicked through the register once again and shook his head. 'There most certainly is no one of that name staying here either.'

'Is there anyone under the name of Barton-Forbes?' Johnny knew she was capable of anything.

The concierge didn't have to check the register for that name. 'No. Tell me, is it usual for the British aristocracy to travel under such fanciful pseudonyms?' he asked, his moustache twitching with suspicion.

'Don't be impertinent,' Johnny replied, as he flicked a coin onto the desk, significantly under-tipping the concierge and then strolling away.

There was nowhere else to look for Libby so Johnny repaired to the bar, consoling himself with the thought that at least she hadn't brought Pinkie to Sarajevo – that really would have been the limit. Johnny ordered a glass of rakija, the clear plum brandy that was a speciality of the area. It made him want to retch and swallow at the same time, the perfect drink to match how he was feeling. He quickly ordered four more and was contemplating a fifth when the familiar clatter of a rolling ball caught his attention.

He turned and watched a roulette wheel spin, immediately drawn by its power and wondered if it would summon Libby back to him. She always appeared when he was winning.

He cashed the last of his expenses money into chips. He was planning to try spread-betting, in a low risk, low return strategy, but then he saw '19' emblazoned in gold on the green baize and knew exactly what to do.

*

Laszlo Breitner surveyed the storeroom that acted as his office. It was a constant reminder of just how far he'd fallen. While his friends in Vienna and Budapest advanced their careers towards grand offices, he worked in the basement of a provincial city hall. Breitner was usually phlegmatic about his situation, but the young Englishman had hit a nerve and brought home just how impossible his situation was.

He'd hoped for a moment that this Johnny Swift was the answer to his prayers, but inevitably he'd proved to be just as unperceptive and frivolous as everyone else.

Breitner thought he was onto something, a small thread through the labyrinth. He just needed a mythical hero, like Theseus, to follow that thread. He shook his head in disgust – he hated metaphors and had spent far too much time trying to think like the young dissidents he was tracking.

Breitner had learnt his craft in the cold, hard world of the Intelligence Bureau of the General Staff, conducting counter espionage operations within the monarchy under the mentorship of Colonel Alfred Redl, who at the time was considered to be the brightest and ablest officer in the imperial army. He'd completely transformed the Intelligence Bureau, introducing modern methods and equipment, and he had proved to be an inspiration to Breitner.

After years of isolation serving in the Ninth Hussars, Breitner had found that he possessed an aptitude for this line of work and earned a transfer to intelligence.

The Ninth was an elite Hungarian cavalry regiment, famous for its dash and revelry, with promotion dependent on whether or not you were a daredevil rider and gambler. Breitner was only ever going to be a junior adjutant, responsible for mucking out the stables. They were bad days: he wasn't popular with the young bloods who thought nothing of betting a month's pay on the turn of a card. The young Englishman had reminded Breitner of them, which, he realised, was why he'd taken such a dislike to him.

He was starting to feel that he should have stayed in the cavalry – his life would have been simpler. The last time he'd pulled a thread like this, everything had unravelled.

A sharp knock at the door interrupted Breitner's reflections. 'Come in!' he shouted, annoyed with his self-indulgence. An official looking, middle-aged man, who undoubtedly wished to store something in his office, entered. 'Yes, what is it?' Breitner asked impatiently.

'Sorry to disturb you, Mr Breitner. My name is Ivo Vila. I'm a detective here in Sarajevo. I understand you're interested in information about dissidents coming into the area, from Serbia?'

'Yes, that's correct,' Breitner replied, trying to soften his tone. He didn't want to alienate a potential source. Not having either the time or the resources to set up a comprehensive network of informants, Breitner had to rely on the varying cooperation of acquaintances and the local police for first-hand reports.

Vila looked uncomfortable about what he had to say. 'I met the son of an old friend on the train returning to Sarajevo. My friend is a solid, respectable person, a confidant – but his son, well, his son was expelled from Sarajevo for radical behaviour. He went to Belgrade and fell in with students and the such like.'

'I see.' Could be something, probably nothing, Breitner mused.

'There wasn't anything suspicious about him. We just discussed the impending visit by His Imperial Majesty, the heir apparent.'

Breitner's attention pricked. 'His name?'

'Nedeljko Cabrinovic,' Vila replied. Breitner knew that name. He stood up and started to shuffle through his notes, trying to remember where he'd heard it before. 'Was he old or young?'

'Just a boy – nineteen, I think.'

'And he was returning from Serbia. Was he travelling alone?' Breitner was firing off questions more to himself than to the detective. 'When was this?'

'A week ago.'

'You've waited a week to tell me this!'

'I mentioned it to my chief and was told to leave it alone. Cabrinovic hasn't got a prison record, his expulsion has been expunged and his father is a friend.' Vila coughed; he was going behind the boss's back, any more information would cost. Breitner knew he'd have to make his first tug on the thread. He threw down everything that was in his wallet – a month's pay.

*

General Oskar Potiorek, the military governor of Bosnia and Herzegovina, was in no mood to take any chances. He preferred to administer his provinces from the comfort and security of his residence. However, he'd felt compelled to come to Ilidza and oversee the conversion of one of the Hotel Bosnia's rooms into a chapel for the archduke's devotions on the Sunday morning of his visit.

The conversion had cost over forty-thousand golden crowns, not an inconsiderable part of his budget, but General Potiorek felt that it was money well spent. The archduke was an extremely devout man, who'd publicly rebuked Conrad von Hotzendorf, the Chief of Staff, for not attending mass during the autumn manoeuvres.

The governor was determined that that would not happen to him. The heir apparent had already twice blocked his attempts at promotion and he felt he couldn't leave something as important as the conversion to his subordinates, so he had decided to make a spot inspection.

Since inviting the heir apparent to come to Sarajevo after the summer manoeuvres, Potiorek had taken it upon himself to personally supervise every detail of the stay, from the temperature at which the heir liked his wine served, to the correct length of the stirrups he used.

Potiorek had staked a great deal of his reputation on the success of the royal visit in the hope that it would boost the prestige of the monarchy in the provinces. He'd replaced Varesanin as a 'strong' governor three years previously and was expected to top a brilliant career by becoming chief of staff, and he wasn't going to fall now at the last fence.

His inspection had been satisfactory, and now he could retire to the Konak, his splendid residence, for the evening. He was still feeling uneasy, as he knew it would take just one simple event to set the archduke on a rampage and to ruin both the visit and his career.

He saw a tall youth with a short, black moustache and a sports cap in the hotel's lobby – exactly the type he didn't want loitering. General Potiorek, realised he'd left his security detachment outside and he was about to have them called when a coarse shriek echoed across the hotel lobby, striking horror into the governor's heart.

'Here, take your pound of flesh!' a lumbering great oaf in a frock coat was shouting as he was being dragged towards the exit by a croupier and a concierge. He shrugged them off and threw a handful of coins onto the floor.

Potiorek was outraged; things like this simply could not happen. He stormed across the lobby towards the altercation, as the oaf continued his spectacle with the croupier.

'I'm sorry, sir. We only accept official chips at the table,' the croupier was patiently explaining.

'I don't have any official chips left!' the oaf shouted back at the top of his voice.

'Then perhaps you'd like to retire from the game,' the croupier said. He wasn't having much luck pushing the man towards the door.

'No, I wouldn't like to bloody well retire from the game. Don't you understand? I have to win it back!'

'What the hell's going on here?' Potiorek demanded.

The oaf gave him the same look of cold fury that the governor had seen all too often on the faces of Serb students. 'This lackey refuses to take my note.'

The croupier bowed, embarrassed as he recognised the governor. 'I'm sorry, Excellency. The gentleman has lost rather heavily.'

Potiorek addressed his comments to the Serb 'child'. 'Young man, I don't take kindly to Serb ne'er-do-wells entering exclusive establishments and causing a scene.'

'You puffed up buffoon! I'm – ' but before he could finish his sentence, a slight man in his thirties had run through the door, grabbed the oaf and kneed him in the groin, causing him to double up on the floor.

The slight man tipped his hat to the governor. 'Excuse me, Excellency. I'll throw this scum out.' The governor eyed him suspiciously. He knew this man; his name was Breitner and he was a pariah – but he evidently had his uses.

'Come on, you Serb riff raff!' Breitner ordered.

'But I'm not – ' the hapless oaf yelped, cut off as Breitner kicked him in the face, and then, with the aid of the croupier and the concierge, started pulling him up, ripping his frock coat in the process.

Chapter 17

Johnny felt battered and sick as he came round. He remembered being dragged down a corridor which stank of carbolic. He thought he might have won something – he certainly felt as if he'd been in a rugby match. He remembered getting the beating of his life in the final of the inter-house cup, and still managing to smash his way through to score the winning try in the dying seconds of the game.

The metallic screech of a door opening brought him back to the present. He was lying on the floor of a cell, his clothes in rags and his whole body throbbing. A slight figure was grinning at him from the doorway.

'Good, you're awake. I trust you slept well?'

'Breitner ... ' Johnny recognised him and tried to sit up. He didn't understand how this had happened. He'd been winning and then it had all gone bad. Breitner had beaten him up and dragged him into the police station above City Hall.

'What the hell do you think you're playing at, Breitner? I'm a member of His Majesty's Civil Service.'

'Call me Laszlo. This isn't one of your English public schools,' Breitner said, helping Johnny to sit up.

'No? Well you certainly act as if it is.'

'Do they teach you how to lose so ignobly, in those schools?' Breitner handed him a glass of water. Johnny spilt most of it, but enough went down to make him start to feel human again.

'I didn't go to public school. Well, not one you'd have heard of, anyway.' Johnny didn't think there was much point in trying to explain the subtleties of the English class system and the ranking of its schools.

'That explains your rather ungentlemanly behaviour.'

Johnny knew that Breitner was right; he'd made a total arse of himself. 'This assignment's a joke. I thought if I could win the money back – now look where I am.'

Breitner smiled warmly. 'As it happens, you're in exactly the right situation to help me.'

'Help you?' Johnny almost laughed at the barefaced cheek of it.

'Yes, help me,' Breitner repeated impassively.

Johnny pointed at the bruising on his face. 'You've got a very funny way of asking for help over here.'

Breitner led Johnny out of the cell and into the medical aid room. An orderly started to clean Johnny's cuts while Breitner floated about in the background, ever the enigmatic foreigner. He turned abruptly as a young man entered the room.

'Mihajlo Pusara, what do you want?'

'Mr Breitner, I understood that you wanted a clerk to take notes.'

'Who told you that?'

'Forgive me I was told …' The young man turned and looked in horror at the state Johnny was in, Johnny took an instant dislike to him – he was far too good looking. The last thing Johnny wanted was to be reminded that he might have lost his looks, thanks to this dandy little Hungarian.

'This is a special prisoner – no one is to know that we have him. Is that understood?' Breitner shouted and Johnny wondered if he might have had some kind of military training.

'Yes, sir. I won't mention it to anyone.'

Breitner walked up to Johnny and grabbed him around the neck. 'This boy is a troublemaker; he insulted the governor last night.' He slapped Johnny a stinging blow around the face. 'I will show him how we treat troublemakers who insult their superiors. Now get out.'

Pusara looked sickened as he left. Breitner turned his attention back to Johnny. 'I am afraid that such things are necessary.'

Johnny grinned back belligerently; he'd had worse from his stepfather and wasn't going to show any weakness to a man like this.

'Now you say you're here to report on the nationalist problem in the Balkans. Are you interested in how Austro-Hungary plans to combat nationalism?' Breitner asked, matter-of-factly.

Johnny shrugged and fought the urge not to whimper, as pain raced down his back.

'Franz Ferdinand plans to reform the Austro-Hungarian monarchy when he takes the throne, creating a kind of federal state with Austria at the centre. He also plans to increase the franchise to include minorities within the monarchy, thus reducing the power of my beloved Hungary; he thinks this will stem the rise of nationalism and stabilise the monarchy.'

'Will that be enough to stop you going the same way as the Ottoman Empire?' Johnny asked, enjoying the chance to put a dig in.

Breitner grimaced at the comparison. 'In the West, you define a people by the borders of where they live. In the East, such boundaries do not exist; your nationality is what you feel in your heart and the blood that pumps through your veins. As I explained before, the Young Bosnians want to unite the South Slav people in some form of self-rule. The complications are endless, but the only thing you can be sure of is that they want to be free of Austria's corrupting influence.'

The orderly finished dressing Johnny's wounds and left. 'A lot of our population is loyal to the monarchy and will welcome the reforms, but the nationalists are not going to quietly submit to Austrian rule, with a few extra rights given to them as an Imperial gift,' Breitner added.

Johnny tried to straighten himself up, but his shirt was too badly torn. The last vestiges of his identity had been ripped from him with it. 'It sounds as if you sympathise with them,' Johnny said.

'I understand them. I am also subject to Habsburg rule, but ultimately I believe in the stability and security the monarchy provides, which is something the nationalists fear. They don't want the people happy and content, as part of Austro-Hungary.'

'I need something a bit more substantial than that to tell my overlords,' Johnny said, giving up on his shirt. He was nowhere – no shirt, no money and no information worth a damn. Breitner handed him a clean, white shirt with a stiff collar and a pair of black trousers.

'Put these on and we'll have breakfast.'

*

Breitner found his office even more cramped and stuffy than usual, as he prepared coffe for his guest. He wasn't sure if this was the right course of action, but he needed to find out what was going on. It felt incredibly like the debacle that had got him sent to this place. That had started with intercepted mail and a suspicious address.

His career had been progressing nicely and when Redl moved on to continue his meteoric rise, everyone had moved up the ladder. The new chief brought in a system for checking suspicious mail, for which Breitner was responsible. It was dull but important work and it appealed to his meticulous mind.

A routine check of a suspect package found that it contained a large amount of money and two addresses known to be used by Russian agents. He had had the package resealed and returned to the post office for collection. It was thought that a mole in the army staff was passing information to the Russians and the amount of money found suggested to Breitner that the package was the first thread in uncovering the traitor.

Nothing happened for six weeks, then the package was eventually claimed by none other than Colonel Redl himself, the former chief. That was the day Breitner's career ended.

His new office might be hot and stuffy but it was private; Breitner was thankful for that as he passed Johnny his coffee. Dressed in his new clothes, the young Englishman looked suitably belligerent. It sent a shiver down Breitner's spine to think that his plan could actually work.

So far it had all been pretty textbook – beat the suspect up and then be nice to him. He'd even started to build a fairly credible backstory for him. Breitner offered Johnny some bread rolls and cold cuts. It had been simple enough to find him, after Detective Vila had alerted him to the arrival of the Young Bosnia cell. Breitner had telephoned all of the high-end establishments in the vicinity and sure enough, a concierge at the Hotel Bosnia had encountered a young Englishman, purporting to be from the British Consulate. The rest of the plan had been the best Breitner was able to come up with on the spur of the moment.

'Breakfast?' Breitner spoke in Serbo-Croat, wanting to see how good Johnny's grasp of the language was.

'Yes, thank you.' Johnny started chewing the bread with some difficulty. Breitner suspected that his kick to the jaw might have been overzealous.

'My job is to monitor the nationalist problem in Bosnia and report back to the joint ministry of finance, whose administration it falls under.' Breitner knew this was going to be a risk, but there was no one else.

'So tell me what's going on.' Johnny cringed as he bit on a loose tooth but somehow he managed to keep his composure. If it wasn't for the colouring of his cheeks it would have been hard to guess that he was in discomfort.

'I've been receiving anonymous warnings of a plot to assassinate the Archduke Franz Ferdinand when he visits Sarajevo this month.' Breitner watched as Johnny's face registered the news.

'Is there anything definite?' Johnny asked, clearly assessing the information to see how it could be used to benefit him. 'Do you think the threats are connected to the army manoeuvres your heir will be attending?'

'It's reasonable to assume so, but these sort of rumours are not uncommon, Johnny. However, they tie in with information I've gathered from intercepted mail.' Breitner had seen a clipping announcing the

Archduke's visit, sent from Bosnia, to one Nedeljko Cabrinovic, care of a cafe in Belgrade known to be a place where Young Bosnia dissidents congregated. Cabrinovic had also sent a number of postcards in allegorical form from a border town, but the meaning was fairly clear that an act of great Serb patriotism was being planned.

'I've also had a report of a Young Bosnia cell returning to Sarajevo,' Breitner added. He was sure it was a cell – everything he'd seen so far pointed to it. Vila had even told him that he thought Cabrinovic had two travelling companions who'd been trying to distance themselves from him. Vila had said that one of them was called Gavrilo Princip; his name had cropped up in the piles of intercepted mail Breitner spent his day sifting through. Breitner couldn't quite believe that Cabrinovic had given Vila his name, but Gavrilo Princip was a known associate of Cabrinovic's in Belgrade so it was possible that they were travelling together.

'Two members of the cell have registered with the police in Sarajevo. One of the addresses is of a known police sympathiser, so nothing much will be going on there. The other is altogether more interesting.'

Breitner saw that Johnny was fully alert now, taking in every word and analysing it for this report he'd been shouting about all over town. 'Have you passed your concerns on to the archduke? Doing that should clear things up nicely and draw my report to a logical conclusion,' he said.

'There are protocols for such things, Johnny,' Breitner replied.

'Even so, if you went directly to him, it could be a feather in our – your – cap. I mean, do you want to spend the rest of your life in a place like this?' Johnny waved his hand at the drab surroundings.

'I doubt the archduke would listen, even if that were possible. He's not overly fond of Hungarians, especially Hungarians with my heritage. Also, I'm not currently in favour with our illustrious heir. How do you think I ended up in this place?'

Breitner had had to clear up the mess when Colonel Redl was exposed as a spy. Conrad von Hotzendorf, the Chief of Staff, had ordered Breitner to go and see Redl, give him a gun and make it plain that he should do the honourable thing.

That should have been an end to it. A discreet announcement was made, explaining that the colonel had been overworked and had taken his own life; he was to be buried with full military honours. Unfortunately, the full extent of the colonel's treachery was discovered by the press. Redl had been living a secret life of debauchery well beyond his means. To pay for it, or because he was blackmailed as a result of it, the Russians had induced him to give away his nation's secrets. When the story broke, Breitner and the chief of staff had been summoned by Franz Ferdinand.

Breitner had heard stories about the archduke's temper – it was still part of the folklore of the Ninth Hussars years after his tenure as colonel, but nothing could have prepared him for the maelstrom that confronted him. Breitner had thought Franz Ferdinand was going to choke with rage.

He was incensed that Colonel Redl had been allowed to take his own life, firstly because it was a mortal sin, and secondly because he hadn't been properly interrogated to discover the full extent of the damage he'd done.

Breitner and Conrad von Hotzendorf both tendered their resignations. The emperor refused to accept the chief of staff's, but Breitner was not quite so fortunate. Along with a number of other members of the Intelligence Bureau he was forced out of the army. He counted himself lucky to have salvaged enough from the situation to get his current position.

The Bosnian civil service was predominantly Hungarian, and one of his contacts in the joint ministry of finance had been able to get Breitner attached to the political section. After that experience, Breitner wasn't willing to approach the archduke and risk the wrath of those pale eyes again.

'I can report to my superiors that there is a plot to assassinate the heir,' Johnny suggested, looking desperate to be able to tell them something. 'Maybe they can pass it along to your chaps.'

'We need to know what the Young Bosnia cell is planning. Our best hope is to try and persuade the governor, General Potiorek, to call off the visit or at the very least, increase security. The visit is being organised by the army, not the joint ministry of finance, and thus comes under the governor's control.'

'Can't the governor just go and arrest them?' Johnny asked.

'As you have found out for yourself, the authorities here don't believe that there is a nationalist problem and the governor is chief among them. He isolates himself behind the walls of his residence and has no idea about the realities of the province he governs. He's aware that there are student protests in Bosnia, but he thinks they're isolated instances and tries to control them with strong-arm policies, that only further anger the Young Bosnians.'

The Assassins

'Well, it sounds as if you've done all you can. I'll make a full report praising your diligence and, er, hospitality,' Johnny said.

Breitner laughed. He thought Johnny was perfect – impetuous, youthful, malleable and his Serbo-Croat was excellent. 'Tell me, young Johnny, how did you come to speak the local language so well?'

'I had to as a special condition of my entry into the diplomatic service, so I spent a few months seeing a Serbian emigre living in Paddington. I could already speak Russian and, well, I do have a gift for languages,' Johnny said haughtily.

'That is most interesting. You see, I have intelligence that people of your age are being recruited to carry out the assassination,' Breitner said.

Johnny went pale, finally grasping why Breitner had taken such a sudden interest in him. 'Oh, no – no!' He made a leap for the door.

*

A bored policeman pushed Johnny back into Breitner's office and slammed the door shut in his face. He'd got half way down the corridor before he was grabbed by four gendarmes.

Johnny tried to regain his dignity. He hadn't meant to behave in such a cowardly way but he remembered the hard stares he'd received in the cafe and it felt as if all of Sir George Smyth's greatest hopes had come true.

'If the plot to assassinate the archduke succeeds it could have untold implications, for your country as well as mine,' Breitner said. He was nonplussed by Johnny's attempt to escape and carried on the conversation as if nothing had happened.

'You want me to join up with a gang of assassins!' Johnny repeated Sir George's prophetic words. 'You want me to get my bloody head blown-off.'

'Tell me, Johnny, why were you sent here? You aren't stupid, but you clearly understand nothing.'

'It's all part of the cult of the gifted amateur. Whitehall and the diplomatic service thrive on it.'

'Not even the British government would send someone so inexperienced here without a reason.' Breitner didn't appear to understand how a gentleman behaved any more than Johnny did.

'This whole region is considered to be the backwoods of diplomacy – a highly volatile backwoods, where they can send someone expendable on a fool's errand.' And now it looked as if Johnny was going to be stuck in the middle of it for the rest of his life – if this man Breitner didn't get him killed first.

'So you're a fool, disgraced and clearly degenerate, sent here to be killed or forgotten? Unless of course, you help me.' That cut Johnny to the quick. Breitner had read him completely.

'Why can't you use one of your own chaps?' Johnny asked.

'I don't have any "chaps".'

'What about that fellow that just dragged me in here?' Johnny said, pointing back at the door.

'A few well-placed bribes allowed me to keep you under guard in City Hall. No one would be willing to risk any more than that for me, and even if they were they wouldn't be the right "sort".'

'What, a disgraced, degenerate British diplomat? I'm sure I would blend in perfectly with the local fanatics.'

'You'll be able to blend in much better than you think. And of course there's your performance last night at the hotel, insulting the governor.'

Johnny flushed with anger at the memory. 'He insulted me ... ' Johnny trailed off. He'd been so angry with the way his evening had turned out that he hadn't realised he'd been shouting in Serbo-Croat.

'Obviously, I embellished things by giving you a thrashing and dragging you into prison and then that little scene with the clerk just now. He's sure to tell all his Young Bosnia friends what happens to those that disrespect the governor. Such is the current feeling in Sarajevo, that that's likely to be enough to qualify you as an assassin.'

'What wonderful foresight and initiative,' Johnny said acidly. 'But how could I possibly pass myself off as a Bosnian revolutionary?'

'Draw from your own life. I'm sure you've been in plenty of scrapes. The best lies always come from the truth. Besides, Bosnians don't make good conspirators, they're very open and extrovert, which is how I found out that a Young Bosnia cell has returned to Sarajevo.'

'I'm not convinced.' Johnny was starting to feel distinctly uncomfortable about this whole conversation.

'The heir to the Austro–Hungarian throne is bound to reward you for saving his life.' Breitner smiled, he knew that he had struck the mark. 'The British diplomatic service might even forgive whatever crime you've committed. You're a gambler – why not take your chances?'

It was common knowledge at the Vienna embassy that Franz Ferdinand was one of the richest men in Europe. He owned huge estates and had inherited vast sums of money from dying branches of Europe's aristocracy.

'What kind of reward?' Johnny asked.

'The thanks of the Austro-Hungarian monarchy,' Breitner said enigmatically.

'Some type of commendation, from the heir, at least?' Johnny asked. He thought a cash reward might be considered a bit uncouth for saving the life of the heir apparent, but a commendation could be useful when he had to face Sir George again. If he could actually pull this off he might even get a decoration and a title. They'd have to take Baron Swift back into the diplomatic service. He'd also be in a position to find out what the nationalist situation was and 'ferret about' from the inside.

Breitner stood up, offering Johnny a faded, black suit jacket. 'At the very least, I can promise you a letter of commendation, even if I have to write it myself.'

Johnny still felt reluctant, but in his hungover and concussed state he couldn't see any other way out of the mess he was in. Libby wasn't coming any time soon and he didn't even have the money to get back to Paris, let alone pay off his gambling debts. He could stay in Bosnia goat-herding or, as Breitner said, take his chances with a gang of fanatics.

'Why not? Might as well take a chance on the outside, for once,' Johnny declared. 'Play up and play the game.'

Johnny took the jacket from Breitner. With the white shirt and black trousers he'd already been given, he felt like an undertaker.

'You look every bit the young revolutionary,' Breitner smiled, acknowledging his own genius. 'Complete with the bruising from a night in police custody.'

Breitner took down a battered Gladstone bag from one of the storage shelves behind his desk and handed Johnny an identification card. Johnny glanced at the name. 'Jovo?'

'It's the nearest equivalent of Johnny I could come up with, at short notice.' Breitner replied and beckoned for Johnny to follow him out.

'You want me to go now?' Johnny was dazed – he'd thought he'd have a few weeks at least to familiarise himself with the Young Bosnia movement.

'The sooner you start, the sooner it will all be over,' Breitner said, enjoying Johnny's alarm.

'Surely, you're joking?'

'The archduke is coming to Sarajevo at the end of the month, Johnny. That only gives you three weeks to infiltrate the cell and find out what's going on.'

'But I haven't got a clue how to do that,' Johnny said, trying to make Breitner see sense.

'The first thing is to make contact with Danilo Ilic. He's a local journalist with strong nationalist leanings. I've been monitoring post to his address for some time now. He recently received instructions to start recruiting members for a Young Bosnia cell here in Sarajevo.' Breitner patted Johnny on the back. 'That is where you come in. Ilic was sent these instructions by a man called Gavrilo Princip who crossed the border with the other cell I mentioned, and registered at Ilic's address. My guess is that Ilic is acting as an intermediary between the two cells.'

Breitner took Johnny out through the back entrance of City Hall. It still reminded Johnny of an expensive hotel, but it certainly wasn't a safe place for the discerning traveller to experience the pleasures of the East – quite the opposite in fact.

Johnny was still suffering from his beating and struggled to keep up as Breitner pulled him through Sarajevo's old town. The dome and minaret of its mosque rose gracefully from behind the red tiled roofs of the ancient market. The city was still full of the same exotic sights that had charmed Johnny so much before, but they felt different to him now, as if he'd been absorbed by the city.

Breitner used the Gladstone bag to ram his way through the crowds into a roughly cobbled side street, crookedly lined by long, slender houses with whitewashed walls and overhanging roofs. Johnny doubted if it had changed much since the fifteenth century. Something suddenly occurred to him. 'How am I supposed to make contact with this person, Ilic?'

Breitner put his hand on his forehead in an absent minded gesture, which didn't fill Johnny with confidence. He stopped and looked through his Gladstone bag.

'Maybe I should go to my hotel and collect my luggage and ... settle the bill,' Johnny suggested, wondering if it wasn't too late to get out of this. Breitner had been moving so quickly that Johnny hadn't thought about how he was actually going to win the confidence of these assassins.

Breitner gave Johnny a knowing look. 'I'll collect your belongings and settle your bill.' That was something, at least, Johnny thought.

'But I'll need a change of clothes.'

Breitner showed Johnny the contents of the bag – there was nothing in it, just some old books and a shirt.

'A good revolutionary doesn't need baggage. These people have little more than the clothes they stand up in and their books.' Breitner pointed at the books in the bag. 'Commit those to memory,' he said.

'What are they, Serb poetry? Oh, and Kropotkin's "History of the French Revolution",' Johnny said, looking into the bag and taking out a book with a picture of a man carrying a scythe on the cover.

'You're familiar with Russian revolutionary writers?' Breitner asked, handing Johnny the Gladstone bag.

'I heard of him when I was at school,' he replied.

'Bogdan Zerajic was wearing a homemade badge with that picture on it when he died; a contact of mine in the Budapest police identified it.'

'I never really understood the difference between Kropotkin and Lenin.' Johnny said. When he was at school all he'd ever wanted to do was revolt against the oppressive forces that kept him down – the whos and whys of it all were just detail.

Breitner gave Johnny a worried look, 'There's no time to explain everything to you now.'

Breitner carried on, leading Johnny around a blind bend where the houses curved outwards. 'So am I meant to walk up to this Ilic, start quoting a revolutionary tract and he'll let me into his cell?'

'Don't worry, I've got some ideas about that. Just try and make friends for now. His mother runs a boarding house – *that* boarding house.' Breitner pointed at a corner house as they came round the bend. 'Be in the park opposite the embankment at lunchtime tomorrow and make sure you bring the Kropotkin book. If I'm not there don't worry, just send me a note when you find something out. Oh, and good luck.'

Chapter 18

Archduke Franz Ferdinand watched as the 'battue' began, his beaters driving tiny roebuck towards him through a narrow wattle trap. Hunting, for the archduke, as with most of his contemporaries, was not an exercise in tracking but a test of marksmanship. He lifted his double-barrelled Mannlicher rifle and took aim. The rifle had been specially made for him, as Franz Ferdinand believed that repeater rifles didn't enter into the spirit of the hunt.

The first roebuck sped gracefully past the stand, the sun shining on its red-gold fur. When it came to marksmanship, the archduke was in a league of his own. He pulled the trigger, hitting the roebuck cleanly on the shoulder. He fired again and again, bringing down a roebuck with every shot and pausing only to reload.

A dark shadow drifted over the traps. Franz Ferdinand instinctively switched target and fired at an itinerant pheasant, surgically bringing it down, then turned back to the roebuck and without missing a beat, felled the final one of the batch.

'You haven't lost your touch Franzi,' Sophie said, while the next roebuck were brought up. 'You're still King Gun.' She occasionally liked to join him when he hunted; hunting was part of the story of their relationship.

Franz Ferdinand had first met Sophie during a hunting party organised by his cousin Archduke Friedrich and his indomitable wife, Isabella. They'd been good friends at the time and they were Sopherl's employers. It had been the archduke's first hunt since returning from his grand tour of India, the Far East and America, however nothing could replace the sport of his homeland. He'd been 'King Gun' at that hunt – the person with the biggest 'bag'.

'But that was not the prize I sought,' Franz Ferdinand said, taking Sophie's hand. Sophie may have been a lady-in-waiting, forced into the shadows by the rich and highborn, but she had stood out instantly.

She was one of eight children, five of whom were daughters. Her father, a career diplomat, did not have the means to support unmarried daughters. The only choice they had when coming of age, if unmarried, was either to become a lady-in-waiting or a nun, both of which were considered equally untouchable for a man in Franz Ferdinand's position.

'Don't you think you should have left me alone? Surely, I was more trouble than I was worth,' she responded teasingly.

'Not for a moment,' he answered. She'd enthralled him from the first. There was something defiant in her large, brown eyes that betrayed intellect and strength, and had captivated him, like the dark-eyed dancers he'd seen on his grand tour. She was the self-assured swan he'd been seeking in a pool of inbred ducklings. To prove the point, Sophie had been unimpressed by the advances of the heir to the throne, rejecting him with firm politeness.

Unbowed, the archduke continued to pursue her whenever they met at balls or hunting parties. He even arranged for a transfer to an infantry regiment near his cousin Friedrich's palace in Pressburg, where he could visit Sophie twice a week. In the elegant gardens of that majestic chateau they eventually fell in love. It was when Franz Ferdinand came down with tuberculosis that he resolved to marry her, regardless of what society thought.

'I don't regret anything, Sopherl. Your letters were my lifeline when everyone else had given up on me.'

'Are you certain your health can stand up to a Bosnian summer, Franzi?' The memories of that time still ran raw in both of them. Sophie was ever worried that he would relapse.

'I am determined to do my duty, Sopherl,' he answered, but he knew it wasn't his health that really concerned her.

Franz Ferdinand watched Janaczek, his estate manager, personally oversee the beaters as they drove the next roebuck through the traps before he opened fire. This was his passion, his release from the endless wait for the throne. His power may have been limited, but that did not stop him from exerting influence. He'd invited the German kaiser to his country retreat in Konopischt. It was vital that a strong union with Germany be maintained and Franz Ferdinand hoped to build on their friendship by obtaining the kaiser's support for the reforms he planned to implement when he finally took the throne.

He brought down the last of the roebuck and waited for the next lot to be driven up, while the beaters cleared away the dead. It was an impressive total; Franz Ferdinand would at least be 'King Gun' today. The archduke's total bag as a huntsman was close to a quarter of a million heads, all carefully recorded in his game book and mounted on the walls of his country retreats, with the date and place the trophy was taken. Most of Europe's leading sportsmen had similar totals, including Franz Ferdinand's British equivalent, the Prince of Wales.

'What kind of reception can you expect in Bosnia, Franz?' Sophie had taken the pause in shooting as an opportunity to further press her concerns. His beaters were taking their time and these interruptions to the hunt were starting to irk him.

'One is always in God's hands, Sopherl. Worries and precautions cripple life.' Franz Ferdinand had a sense that something could happen in Bosnia, but he had chosen to ignore it. 'Fear is always one of the most damaging things,' he affirmed.

If something did happen, Franz Ferdinand had left instructions with his nephew, Charles, the next in line, on where to find his plans for reforming the empire. Franz Ferdinand had also made arrangements for his burial at his family seat of Artstetten, ordering the construction of a crypt so that he could be interred with his wife and children, who couldn't be buried with him in Capuchin Church, the traditional resting place of the Habsburgs.

Sophie wasn't placated by his stoicism. 'Sopherl, His Majesty the Emperor has assented to your accompanying me, so you can at least look after me,' he reminded her.

Sophie seemed to draw some comfort from that at least, but having to ask the emperor's permission still galled Franz Ferdinand and brought to mind all of the indignities his wife had suffered as a result of the emperor's obsession with court protocols. The fact that they couldn't even ride in the same carriage together, in the empire which he would one day rule, was a never-ending source of outrage to him.

The roebuck still hadn't been brought up, but lost in the fervour of the hunt, it appeared that the archduke had brought down a white roebuck. It was said that to shoot anything white was a portent of death and the bad omen was causing a certain degree of apprehension amongst the beaters. The heir finally lost his temper, 'Janaczek, you useless peasant! Do you mean to keep me waiting all day?'

Sophie pressed his arm and whispered, 'Franzi – Franzi'. The flash of anger left as quickly as it had come. He smiled, feeling that she was as good for his health as she was for his peace of mind.

'I'm sorry, Janaczek – forgive me,' Franz Ferdinand said, regaining his self-control. Janaczek bowed graciously and hurried away to look for the roebuck. Janaczek may have been the son of a peasant, Franz Ferdinand mused, but he trusted him implicitly; he was more like a family member than a servant.

Franz Ferdinand turned his attention back to Sophie. 'We can mark the fourteenth anniversary of my morganatic oath by riding in an open car, side by side, within the borders of the Austro-Hungarian monarchy – and you, my everything, can enjoy the full recognition of your rank.

The idea pleased him. It was one of a series of small victories in a campaign to present Sophie as his consort on the international stage. They'd already visited the Romanian and German royal courts, been entertained by the King and Queen of England at Buckingham Palace and Windsor Castle, and in a few days they'd be playing host to William II of Germany.

The roebuck appeared at last, taking him by surprise, but the Archduke automatically lifted his rifle and fired two shots in quick succession, bringing down two of them.

Chapter 19

The sound of voices carried into Johnny's room; there was a heated discussion about something tedious and political going on in the house. Johnny tried to ignore it, as he'd been doing for most of the previous day, while he prepared to meet his new housemates. He glanced around his bare, whitewashed room. It looked as if it had seen better days, although some effort had been put into making it look presentable. It had cost fourteen crowns, barely leaving him enough money to pay for food. Breitner had said that carrying around any more money would raise suspicion.

Johnny sighed and turned over on the bed. There was nothing to distract him in the room so he went back to the books Breitner had given him, which were all written in Serbo-Croat. Johnny was a bit rusty, but he'd had to learn the language in order to assist Sir George in case he needed to conduct supplementary negotiations for the Treaty of London. However, by the time Johnny had got to grips with the language, the second Balkan war had started and the treaty was in tatters.

Johnny was totally lost with the poetry. It was very rich, with tales of betrayal and noble sacrifice, and he'd have liked to have been able to study it properly but his head still throbbed and he needed something to eat. The out-of-sync chiming from the bells of the various denominations informed him that it would be lunchtime soon. He thought he'd better see if he could find something out before he met Breitner.

He picked up the Kropotkin – it brought back memories. Kropotkin was one of the plethora of revolutionary writers coming out of Russia. Johnny hadn't read any of his work; he'd mainly been interested in Lenin and Marx, who wrote about modern industrial society, and they'd been hard enough to get hold of at his school. He pulled himself off the bed – he'd just have to wing it as best he could.

Still holding the book, he followed the sound of the voices along a narrow corridor to the next bedroom, and seeing that the door was open, he stopped in the doorway of a grimy, book-lined room. Two men were inside, reading Kropotkin. Johnny grinned; Breitner had actually done his homework.

They were still deep in conversation and didn't notice Johnny. The younger, intense one sat on what looked like a pull-down bed and was in full flow. 'Danilo, can't you see? Kropotkin is quite correct. The state crushes the individual. What we need are systems of mutual aid and collaboration.'

Johnny guessed the man who spoke was the same age as him, but Johnny was twice his size. He looked sallow and delicate with a sharp featured face accentuated by a pencil moustache.

'I agree, Gavrilo. I am not saying that we should create a state, but we must lay foundations first,' the older one said conciliatorily. He was sitting on a bed opposite the door. Johnny supposed he was some sort of intellectual.

They were dressed in the same style as Johnny, except the older one was wearing a black tie. Breitner had told him the names to look out for: Danilo Ilic and Gavrilo Princip. They looked as likely a pair of revolutionaries as he was ever going to meet. Johnny knocked and they broke off their conversation.

'Good afternoon,' Johnny said, waving his copy of Kropotkin as they looked up. 'My name is Jon – Jovo. I have the room next door.' He received the same hard, blank stares he'd had in the cafe a few nights previously. 'I see you're also reading Kropotkin. Tell me, are you familiar with the pamphlet, "What is to be Done?" by Lenin?'

Gavrilo scowled and stood up. 'I am sure that whatever is to be done has nothing to do with listening at keyholes,' he said and slammed the door in Johnny's face.

Johnny left the boarding house, retracing the route he'd taken the day before with Breitner, through the meandering streets of the old town and past the City Hall, which now seemed an incredibly desirable place to be after a night in his lodgings.

He turned right onto Appel Quay, a long, straight embankment which the Austrians had cut through the city to control the flow of the Miljacka river, and followed the elegant new Austrian style buildings along the embankment.

It was obvious to Johnny just how pointless this whole venture was; he'd exchanged views on historical materialism with Trotsky but he couldn't strike up a conversation about anarchism with some simple peasants.

Johnny crossed a cobbled bridge and sat in the park opposite the embankment, then reluctantly opened the copy of Kropotkin that Breitner had given him. It was starting to look as if he'd actually have to read it.

'I don't think that I've ever seen such a reluctant anarchist before.' A smooth, liquid voice immediately distracted Johnny and he turned to see that a pretty girl had sat next to him. She had a perfectly oval face, with a cute, upturned nose and long auburn hair neatly plaited and tied back in a bun, but it was the mocking look in her amber eyes that shook him.

'You do not find his work interesting?' she asked.

Johnny shrugged indifferently. 'It's not that I don't find it interesting, it's that I'm more familiar with the works of Lenin.'

'Really? That is unusual amongst the local youths. In fact, I think you're the first person I've met who is.' She eyed Johnny suspiciously.

'I'm sure that Lenin and Kropotkin aren't so different. They both want a revolution and to change society,' Johnny said pompously. He doubted that this simple creature would have read Lenin or Kropotkin – probably too busy plaiting her hair.

'Lenin believes in a strong, centralised state while Kropotkin argues for communities based on mutual aid and cooperation,' she said, taking a bite from a burek and reminding Johnny just how hungry he was. Her eyes mocked him and she broke a piece off for him.

'Here – solidarity amongst the workers,' she smiled.

Johnny nodded his thanks and took a bite from the pasty, savouring the spicy meat and wondered if he could afford to buy one after she'd gone.

'Lenin wants to replace one form of authoritarian state with another. True freedom can only be achieved if we have no state,' she said.

'I see, thank you. I'll bear that in mind the next time I talk to an anarchist,' Johnny replied, wondering if that was where he'd gone wrong with Princip and Ilic. 'But surely, they both believe in revolution?'

She looked at her watch before saying, 'Revolution is more than a slogan; it needs to be a change in the way you behave and feel.' She stood up. 'Come on, you can walk me back – it's the least you can do after I fed you.'

'I say, you're very forward,' Johnny said. He'd been on the back foot ever since he'd met her and he wasn't comfortable with the sensation.

'There is a revolution going on and you stand on social niceties.'

'I'm supposed to be meeting someone.'

'A girl?' she asked coyly.

'No, as it happens,' Johnny said, looking around for Breitner.

'I see. Perhaps you don't like girls.' She smiled teasingly and walked away, swaying in a long billowy skirt. Johnny waited a moment before following. He couldn't help himself and he didn't have anything to tell Breitner anyway.

They walked along the opposite side of the river, from the embankment, past whitewashed Turkish style houses, until they came to the emperor's mosque.

'So do you often do this – dally with strange men in the park?'

'Is that what I'm doing? I thought I was educating an ignorant youth.'

Johnny was used to this type of charade. 'I might be ignorant, but I'm sure that I can satisfy your needs – as a woman.'

'That's very funny, but inaccurate.' She turned her head away, hiding her smile and guided him across the Emperor's Bridge.

Johnny saw a good looking man on the other side of the river stop at the bridge and take his cap off.

'Right on cue, that's good,' she said and pulled Johnny's cap off. 'You know what this place is, of course?'

Johnny shrugged. He looked down at the Miljacka river, its blood-red waters running a few inches deep in the June heat. 'The Emperor's Bridge,' he said tentatively, not sure why she was asking.

'This is where Bogdan Zerajic made his sacrifice,' she said curtly.

'Is it really?' Johnny replied, not sure how to respond to that statement.

'Zerajic showed us that we too could be like the Russians and take action against our oppressors,' she said and handed him his cap back. 'If you want to be a revolutionary, you'll do well to remember these things.'

Johnny looked solemnly at the bridge where Zerajic had made his attempt to assassinate Governor Varesanin before turning his gun on himself.

'Hello there. How are you?' He looked around, but the girl with the mocking eyes had disappeared. 'You took a hell of a beating the other night.'

Johnny saw that the good-looking man who'd removed his cap was advancing towards him. 'You probably don't remember me. You were getting your wounds attended to in the medical room. It's Pusara, Mihajlo Pusara. I'm a clerk at City Hall.' Johnny shook the offered hand. 'I usually meet a friend or two for lunch at this time – would you care to join us?'

'That's good of you,' Johnny said, 'but I have very little money.'

'Nonsense, it's on me. The very least I can do for a hero of our people – the man who dared to insult the governor and lived to tell the story.'

*

Danilo Ilic looked at his kebab, deciding whether or not he could eat it. He had a stomach ulcer and didn't wish to aggravate it any further.

His best friend, Gavrilo Princip, was making him anxious. Ilic had known Gavrilo since he'd been a boy boarding in his mother's house. Ilic was five years his senior and had taken Gavrilo under his wing, introducing him to his friends and his ideas. Now there was no holding him back, as he persisted in the need to assassinate the tyrant.

'Are you sure now is the right moment to act, Gavrilo?' Ilic asked, pushing his plate back. His friend had continued the discussion from his mother's house to the cafe and it was gravely interfering with Ilic's appetite.

'How can it not be? We have the means, you have recruited most of the other cell and the tyrant will be here within the month. All the pieces are in place for us to win a great victory for our people – are they not?' Gavrilo asked, turning his hard, piercing eyes on Ilic.

'Yes, they are.' Ilic looked away. He'd begun to recruit people to form a second cell after he'd received Gavrilo's instructions from Belgrade. 'They are good men; nonetheless they're young and largely unproven.'

'What does that matter, if they believe in what we are trying to achieve?' Gavrilo retorted. Ilic nodded his agreement, but he wondered if his friend was trying to reassure himself about his own lack of experience.

Ilic knew he would have to support the other cell. When the time came he might also need others, but he was reluctant to take the risk of recruiting any further members into the cell. Ilic could feel his friend's eyes boring into him, searching for any sign of weakness.

Gavrilo's eyes at last turned from Ilic as someone approached their table. 'Hello Danilo,' Mihajlo Pusara said. Ilic nodded a hello to his friend as he joined them. 'Gavrilo, good to see you back in Sarajevo. Nedjo received the clipping I sent, then?' Pusara asked.

'You sent it to him?' Gavrilo asked abruptly.

'I saw the announcement for the archduke's visit in the newspaper and sent Nedjo a clipping,' Pusara said, looking surprised by Gavrilo's manner. 'It is well known that Nedjo intends to make an attempt on the life of a Hapsburg dignitary.'

'Naturally,' Gavrilo said bitterly.

'And now look, you are here. Ready to act.' Pusara said, pleased with himself. Pusara signalled to someone lingering in the doorway. 'Come Jovo, don't be shy – join us.'

Gavrilo glared. 'I'd already planned to act against the heir. When Nedjo received the clipping, we decided to work together...' he trailed off as they were joined by a bruised and battered figure.

Pusara smiled, 'This is Jovo. You can talk freely in front of him.'

'Yes, we know him. He is a boarder in my mother's house,' Ilic said. 'You seem to be turning up a lot today.'

The newcomer blushed and shrugged, embarrassed.

'You can trust him. He insulted the governor and took a beating for his trouble,' Pusara said.

'Is that true?' Princip asked Jovo.

'Yes, but it was nothing – I've had far worse,' he said with an air of arrogance that Ilic disliked.

'Your accent – where are you from?' Ilic asked. He felt that there was something odd about how Jovo spoke that he couldn't quite put his finger on.

'I've been studying in France,' Jovo answered. Ilic felt his curiosity rise.

'Where?'

'Paris, but I travelled a lot.'

'We have friends in France. Have you met Vladimir Gacinovic?' Ilic asked. Many Bosnians, including leading figures of the Young Bosnian Movement had studied in France, so it seemed natural that this stranger had also.

'I'm afraid I didn't have the honour of meeting any of our people there, I er, had certain other distractions,' Jovo said, looking at Ilic's half-eaten meal. 'I say, can I have that? I'm sorry, but I'm starving and have no money for food.'

Before Ilic could refuse, Gavrilo pushed his plate towards Jovo. 'Of course. There is no shame in being poor and hungry,' Gavrilo said as Jovo started to eat.

'Oh, I'm sorry, I was going to buy you a meal,' Pusara said and signalled to a waitress.

'I see you're reading *The History of the French Revolution*,' Princip commented approvingly.

'Yes, I'm just getting to grips with it all,' Jovo replied, looking at the book. He'd forgotten he had it with him. 'There is much I need to learn.'

'There is much we could teach you,' Gavrilo said.

'I'm eager to learn. All I could really read when I was away was Lenin and Marx,' Jovo said, picking up the book. 'Now hopefully, I can broaden my knowledge and find the true meaning of freedom. Revolution is more than a slogan; it is a change in the way you behave and feel.'

'It seems you have made a good start on your studies,' Ilic said. He was about to question the youth more on the true nature of revolution, but Gavrilo interrupted him.

'So you got those bruises in a police cell?' Gavrilo asked. He seemed to be testing the stranger to see if he was someone he could mould, as Ilic knew he'd been doing with Trifko Grabez.

'Jovo certainly did. I saw it myself,' Pusara said proudly, turning back from the waitress. 'The flunky who beat Jovo up told me that that is what happens to those who insult the governor!'

'It was worth it to take on the governor; I don't think I've met anyone quite so pompous,' Jovo said, gleefully.

Ilic wondered if this stranger might be someone who could be used as a decoy and water carrier. He seemed essentially a harmless boaster, like Nedjo, but his heart appeared to be in the right place and if it wasn't, Ilic would give him enough rope too hang himself.

*

Johnny followed Gavrilo and Ilic as they walked down Appel Quay. They'd been talking to him all day, taking it upon themselves to explain their world view. Johnny was doing his best to play along, repeating what the attractive woman in the park had told him. Their idea of social progress and his were very different; they wanted everyone to live in mud huts with little in the way of comfort other than the idea that they were living in equality.

'I am a peasant's son and know how life is in the villages. The peasantry must be made aware of their social inequalities,' Gavrilo said. 'There must be sweeping change through revolution.'

'Do you really believe we could achieve such a revolution? Marx said that revolution is not possible with a peasant population.' That was about the only thing Johnny could remember from his time as a schoolboy revolutionary.

'If the Austro-Hungarian Empire was thrown into turmoil, such a revolution would be possible,' Ilic said. 'Their empire is like a broken pot held together by string. One good kick and it will fall apart.'

'Once that is achieved we can create a society held together by a free and natural bond of fraternity, as Kropotkin suggests,' Gavrilo said.

'But could we accomplish something like that?' Johnny asked eagerly. He was actually interested. He'd read about these things, but being with people who believed them was a whole new experience for him.

They entered a cafe garden further down Appel Quay and a tall, suave man wearing a peaked sports cap watched them as they walked through. He was laughing and joking with a group of girls and Johnny thought enviously that he was enjoying the attention.

Gavrilo and Ilic greeted him but there seemed to be some tension between them. Ilic introduced him. 'Jovo, this is Nedjo Cabrinovic.' Johnny nodded, recognising the name from Breitner's briefing.

'He serves our cause by promenading his girlfriends along the embankment,' Gavrilo said, cutting Cabrinovic to the quick.

'Are you too serious for such things, Gavro?' Nedjo asked, in a slightly mocking tone, which made the girls laugh.

Gavrilo didn't look pleased by the comment and pushed his way into the cafe and ordered coffee. They didn't seem to have much else to do apart from hanging around in down-at-heel cafes. Johnny knew this one. It had an intimidating aura. He recognised the murals of the bloody medieval battles between armoured knights and elaborately dressed Turks. He'd been here before but this time no one stared at him and Johnny started to relax. He was being accepted and he hoped that all he had to do now was keep his mouth shut and pick up enough scraps of information to pacify Breitner, and then this whole sorry affair would be over.

Ilic gave Johnny a stern look, almost sensing his thoughts. Johnny tried to look as sullen as he could in response, which seemed to be their way. 'You ask how a revolution would be possible, Jovo? It is possible by following Zerajic's example.'

'Zerajic, the man who shot at the former governor on the Emperor's Bridge?' Johnny asked.

'He is our role model,' Gavrilo replied.

'Now he is mine,' Johnny said. He got the feeling that they wanted to guide him and he knew enough to let them. He was enjoying the sensation of being part of something bigger than himself again.

'When Gavro was a schoolboy he lodged with my mother and me,' Ilic continued. 'We'd sneak out and listen to our great leader, Vladimir Gacinovic speak – he'd been at school with Zerajic in Mostar.'

'Gacinovic instigated a revolution in our souls, with more than just words – he had a plan of action,' Gavrilo said. 'We were to follow Zerajic's act of courage and take revenge ourselves, as individuals, against those who would oppress our people.'

'In this way will a revolution be born, through our sacrifice.' Ilic said. 'As Zerajic's sacrifice inspired us, so will our actions inspire those of our people to rise up. Although that may not be possible until we have laid the foundations for revolution.'

Gavrilo glared at Ilic. 'The governor actually got out of his carriage and kicked Zerajic as he lay bleeding to death in the mud.' Gavrilo said, fighting to control his rage. 'And you talk of "laying foundations". We must act, there is no time for words.'

'I've seen his skull,' Johnny said, to quieten them. The last thing he wanted was for them to start squabbling. 'I've seen Zerajic's skull. The chief of detectives uses it as an ink pot on his desk.'

'He will be revenged.' Gavrilo's eyes flared, but before his outrage could fully consume him, Nedjo sat down at their table. He took off his hat and brushed back his wavy hair excitedly. 'I've been surveying the Hotel Bosnia. I think... '

'I told you to keep a low profile! I don't want you involved,' Gavrilo growled, interrupting him.

Nedjo looked taken aback and glared at Johnny. 'Are you planning to replace me with this angry fellow?'

Johnny squared up, wondering if he would have to fight Nedjo to become part of the group. Then he saw that Nedjo's aggression wasn't directed at him; the revolutionaries weren't completely united.

'What if we are? He shows far more conviction than you do in your endless boasts and bragging,' Gavrilo said.

Nedjo looked at Johnny, 'Have we met? Do I know you from somewhere?'

'I don't think so.' Johnny answered, looking round the cafe, which seemed very inhospitable again.

'We don't know him, Gavrilo. He could be a spy,' Nedjo said, trying to stifle a cough.

'How do we know *you're* not a spy, Nedjo, like your father?' Gavrilo asked scornfully. Nedjo looked crestfallen and began to cough.

Johnny saw his chance to win everyone's trust and look magnanimous at the same time. 'Was not our great hero, Milos Obilic, accused before Vidovdan of being a traitor?'

All three looked at him approvingly, but unfortunately he'd brought himself back to the attention of the group. 'When were you in the chief of detectives' office?' Ilic asked suspiciously. Johnny got the impression that he didn't like him very much.

'As you know, I had a slight altercation in the Hotel Bosnia,' Johnny said, pointing at his bruises.

'Yes, we know you had some trouble with the police,' Ilic said, 'but we only have the word of the flunky who told Pusara that you insulted the governor. The governor rarely leaves his mansion.'

Nedjo managed to control his coughing sufficiently to be able to speak. 'I remember now, I do know him. He called General Potiorek a buffoon and got a kick in the face. I was there, in the hotel, conducting reconnaissance. If he hadn't been pulled away before he could act, I'm sure he would have taught old Potiorek a bloody lesson.'

'Another boast Nedjo?' Ilic said and turned back to Johnny. 'Where exactly are you from? You didn't go to school in Sarajevo.'

'I'm from a small village, across the Drina from Koviljaca. It's a spa town on the Serbian border.' Libby had wondered about staying there and Johnny thought it was sufficiently far from Sarajevo for them to be as unfamiliar with it as he was. 'It's the oldest...'

'I know it,' Gavrilo said, interrupting him. 'Do you not feel the responsibility of history, coming from such a place?'

Johnny shifted uncomfortably – he'd forgotten that they'd only just arrived from Belgrade. It looked as if he was going to be caught out on his first lie. He decided to follow Breitner's advice and switched to the truth. 'I do not consider myself to be from any one place, not since I was expelled from school for organising a student strike,' he answered, although officially the headmaster had called it a mutiny. 'So, as I told you, I went to Paris to continue my education.'

'How could you afford that?' Gavrilo asked.

'I had a scholarship,' Johnny replied. Johnny's stepfather had seen both his potential and his natural self-destructive tendencies, and had fought to ensure that Johnny won a scholarship to attend a minor public school, so that those respective qualities could be best developed and suppressed.

'A scholarship wouldn't cover your expenses to study in Paris,' Gavrilo said. He'd evidently been a scholarship boy himself.

'I knew a patriot who helped me get a job in the civil service. My intention was to work and save to study. Once I'd managed to pass my exams I hoped to go to the Sorbonne.'

Gavrilo looked away, brooding, and Ilic continued the interrogation. 'What brought you to Sarajevo?' Ilic asked.

'I fell for the wrong woman,' Johnny replied. He remembered the way that Libby had stood demurely in the casino, before he lost everything. He wondered briefly where she was now.

Nedjo grinned, 'The expensive kind.' Gavrilo looked at him disapprovingly.

Johnny shrugged. 'She was also the boss's wife. I was forced to gamble to accommodate her. I lost everything. I couldn't go home, so in my shame I came here to escape corruption.'

'And what did you find when you got here? The Austrians undermining the morals of our national spirit, with gambling dens and brothels!' Gavrilo said, identifying with his despair.

Johnny made his eyes blaze with the same indignation he saw in Gavrilo's. 'When I saw General Potiorek, the living embodiment of the people who have corrupted our country, I had to act'.

'We might have need of someone like you.' It had been Ilic who spoke but all three added their agreement.

Chapter 20

Franz Ferdinand admired the gardens of Konopiste, his Bohemian castle, where the roses were at their zenith, a blaze of colour in honour of his royal visitor, Wilhelm II. The kaiser was so impressed by the display that Franz Ferdinand had enthusiastically guided him to the room that gave the best view, a water closet next to his private apartments.

The roses were a source of immense pride to Franz Ferdinand; he'd created the gardens from scratch, commissioning an army of gardeners, who'd worked for twenty years to transform the five hundred acres around his fairy tale castle.

As pristine as the bathroom was, the archduke was starting to appreciate that their current location may impinge on the dignity of his honoured guest and so he suggested that they retire to the castle library. There were a number of pressing matters he wished to discuss.

The kaiser concurred, and Franz Ferdinand led him through whitewashed corridors lined with hundreds of antlers, hunting photographs and stuffed animals. He directed the kaiser into a lift and invited him to sit on one of the chintz-covered sofas. Along with the bathrooms, the lift was one of many modern innovations Franz Ferdinand had installed in the castle. He had turned it into a haven from the pressures of his position, filling it with hunting trophies, paintings and the curios he loved to collect. Far from Vienna, it was somewhere the archduke could relax with his family, without the intrigues or petty rules and slights of court life. He hoped this would make it a conducive environment in which to build on his previous discussions with the kaiser.

The lift stopped and Franz Ferdinand guided the Kaiser into his library of gold-bound books and offered him a cigar. Although the visit was largely social, they'd allowed an hour to review the alliances their respective empires had entered into with Italy and Romania. The key issue for Franz Ferdinand was Hungarian nationalism and the destabilising effect it was having on the Austro-Hungarian monarchy and on these alliances.

'My main hope is that the Hungarians can be made to adopt more lenient policies towards the Romanians living in Transylvania. This would strengthen our position with Romania, keeping them sympathetic to our cause and prevent Russia from luring them into an alliance.'

The kaiser glanced over a memorandum before answering. He'd scrawled notes inside the margins, in the same way that his hero, Fredrick the Great did. 'I understand that we need allies in the Balkans to help buttress your position against a Serbian and Russian league, but does this really need to be done at the expense of the Hungarians?'

Franz Ferdinand was aware that Germany was developing a stronger relationship with the Magyars as a potential ally against the Slavic hordes, but he thought the kaiser really needed to be dispelled of the opinion that the Hungarians were largely blameless.

'There has been very little political or social advancement for non-Hungarians living in the Hungarian half of the monarchy. Nearly all the seats in the Hungarian parliament are held by Magyar aristocrats, even though they are in the minority. This conflicts with the Austrian half of the monarchy, where we have extended the franchise. This deviation in policy is forcing us apart,' explained Franz Ferdinand.

The kaiser scowled, irritated, and flicked his cigar into Franz Ferdinand's favourite ashtray – the foot of an elephant he'd bagged on his grand tour. This evidently wasn't what the kaiser wanted to hear and he attempted to deflect Franz Ferdinand with a joke. 'I will command my ambassador in Budapest to remind the Hungarian prime minister about the Rumanians whenever he sees him!'

Franz Ferdinand was compelled to press the point. 'The really worrying aspect of this business is the idea that Hungarian nationalism can transcend loyalty to the monarchy and the emperor.' The archduke felt his temper rising and glanced at a portrait of Sophie, to calm himself. 'There is a cadre of Magyars that are constantly conspiring against the monarchy, to gain advantage for their country to the detriment of Austria.'

'I'm sure that isn't the case, Franzi. The Hungarian prime minister, Count Tisza, is an excellent fellow. He strikes me as an unusually gifted statesman – you should make more use of him to solve these domestic issues of yours.'

The archduke would have liked to have told the kaiser exactly what he thought of the treacherous Count Tisza, but his guest stretched his legs out onto a tiger skin rug, one of Franz Ferdinand's most prized trophies, and abruptly switched topic.

The Assassins

'Now as to your other little difficulty – don't you think it's about time you resolved the situation with Serbia and stabilised the Balkans? I understand there have been calls for a pre-emptive attack to be made before the situation deteriorates any further. I believe it is a strategy you should consider.'

The archduke was familiar with this view; it was one that Conrad Von Hotzendorf, chief of the Austrian staff, regularly pressed, and one that the archduke was vehemently against.

'Could we count on Germany's support if we were to take such a course of action?' Franz Ferdinand asked. He knew any military intervention against Serbia would provoke the Russians, and as such would be disastrous without German backing.

The kaiser avoided the question with his usual eccentricity. 'The only possible relationship Serbia should have with Austro-Hungary is that of dependency, like a planet to its sun. I believe the best course of action Austro-Hungary could take is to bring Serbia back into the fold, offer them military aid…finance. If she declines, then force should be applied.' Franz Ferdinand fought to remain patient; the kaiser had a reputation for making varying arguments.

'Once I have established good order in the monarchy I will turn my attention to our petulant neighbour, if the need arises,' Franz Ferdinand replied.

He didn't want to tell his ally just how unprepared the Austro-Hungarian Army was for any form of military action, even though it would have furthered his case against the Hungarian parliament, which had blocked every step to modernise the army, seeing it as an opportunity to wrest more control of their country from Vienna.

'The current political sanctions against Serbia haven't stopped their influence from spreading in the Balkans. If you do not take decisive action your position will only get worse and you will appear weak,' the kaiser said.

The archduke clenched his fists and fell back on his usual line of defence against the hawks at court. 'What would we get out of war with Serbia? We'd lose the lives of our young men and we'd spend money better used elsewhere. And what would we gain, for heaven's sake? A few plum trees, some pastures full of goat droppings, and a bunch of rebellious killers.'

Chapter 21

Gavrilo guided Johnny past the shuttered stalls and shops of the old town and onto Appel Quay. Reluctantly, Johnny followed him into the night, unsure why Gavrilo had asked him along.

They walked past the Emperor's Bridge, then a few hundred yards down, they crossed over to the other side of the city, onto the narrow, cobbled Lateiner Bridge and stopped at a wine shop. According to the Cyrillic above the door it was called Semiz's. It was a very grimy looking place of ancient Turkish design, but a wine shop, nonetheless. Johnny was overjoyed. He could hear rowdy singing coming from inside, reminding him of the rugby games his stepfather used to take him to.

Gavrilo opened the door, pushing Johnny in, and he was immediately hit by the overpowering smell of stale wine. The singing stopped as soon as he entered and the door slammed shut behind him. It was pitch-black, and for a terrible moment Johnny thought he'd been lured into a trap and would be found the next morning in the blood-red mud of the Miljacka, with his throat cut.

Gavrilo walked up behind him and Johnny tensed. He was pretty badly bruised, but was determined to make a good account of himself.

'Jevtic, light a candle for goodness' sake. I can't see a thing!' Gavrilo called.

'Gavroche! Come in my friend – forgive me. We did not notice it getting dark,' a cheery greeting came back at the same time as a candle was lit. Johnny exhaled slowly, relieved. He saw that he was in a cramped room with young men dressed much the same as Gavrilo and himself, all sitting at plain wooden tables and drinking red wine. Johnny's heart lifted at the sight of all the casks and barrels around him.

'Gavroche, over here!' the cheery voice called. It belonged to a slightly more flamboyant member of the group who was signalling to Gavrilo. Rather than the den of cutthroats he'd been expecting, he realised that they were in some sort of Bohemian hangout. 'Come join us, and bring your new friend,' Jevtic said. To emphasise the invitation, they resumed their singing.

'Maybe later, Jevtic,' Gavrilo answered and led Johnny to a table near the only window in the place. Johnny took a seat and leant against a wall sticky with red wine.

He looked out at Lateiner Bridge and then turned back to Gavrilo. 'Gavroche?'

'A nickname – it's after the character from *Les Miserables*,' Gavrilo answered as Jevtic came to their table.

'Like Gavroche, poverty and injustice intensifies Gavroli's spirit and purpose,' Jevtic said, putting down a carafe of wine and two cups. 'Here, on me.'

'Thank you,' Johnny said, pouring himself some wine and ignoring Gavrilo's indignant look.

'Jovo, this is Jevtic,' Gavrilo said. Jevtic bowed and went back to his friends.

'Nice chap,' Johnny observed, sipping his wine, which was surprisingly good.

'Jevtic was a housemate of mine in Belgrade. He and his intellectual friends come here to drink wine and sing.'

'Very decent chap,' Johnny reiterated, drinking more wine and feeling it warm and relax him.

'He's a good friend but is unwilling to take action for our people. I find coming here a good way to be inconspicuous to the police and to appear to be acting as every other person our age acts,' he said, giving another disapproving look as Johnny poured a second cup of wine.

'Sorry – would you like some Gavrilo? Very rude of me,' Johnny said. Gavrilo shook his head. 'What do they do?' Johnny asked, glad to be amongst some lively company again.

'Jevtic's a writer. They're all poets and writers,' Gavrilo answered, in a tone which Johnny thought attached a great deal of prestige to their chosen vocations. 'These people, however, are for the most part, incapable of a great idea.'

'Do you have any particular poet or writer you admire?' Johnny asked. He was hoping that if he could get Gavrilo to talk about himself he wouldn't ask him any difficult questions about where he came from.

'I enjoy reading Dumas, Walter Scott and of course Sherlock Holmes.' That was safe ground for Johnny; he could talk about them. 'I also greatly admire poets like Sima Pandurovic and the elegant way he expresses his mistrust of life, and Vladimir Vidric, wary of his own pipe dreams about love. And you?'

'What?' Johnny's mind went blank. This was precisely what he'd been trying to avoid.

'Who do you admire, Jovo? You must have a favourite writer or thinker.' Johnny swore under his breath, wishing he'd read the primer Breitner had given him. 'You must be an admirer of Nietzsche at least,' Gavrilo said.

'Nietzsche, yes. He's very good.' Johnny finished his wine and poured himself another. Gavrilo glared at him, his clear blue eyes burning, but there wasn't anything brutal or threatening in his face.

'Jovo, if we are to restore what our people have lost, to instil a revolution in their hearts, we must be true to our ideals. We must forgo our bodily pleasures – be that women or alcohol. We have to remain pure and unstained.'

'I'm sorry?' Johnny said quietly. He couldn't believe what he'd just heard.

'I thought you understood that, after we talked of how the Austrians corrupt the morality of our people.' Gavrilo's eyes burned with fury again, but still there was nothing threatening in his face, which Johnny found particularly unnerving, as he wondered just how much rage lay beneath the surface of Gavrilo's calm exterior.

'Yes, yes of course,' Johnny said, trying to look shamefaced. 'I am not capable of great ideas.'

'Your political character is not yet fully formed. I will continue to guide you.'

Johnny involuntarily reached for the wine, then stopped as the shop door creaked open and Ilic entered. He greeted the Bohemians and joined Johnny and Gavrilo at their table.

'Is it arranged?' Gavrilo asked.

Ilic nodded. He exchanged a discreet glance with Gavrilo and turned to Johnny. 'Jovo – you wish to take action?'

'I do.' Johnny's bowels tightened.

'Come, I will have need of you in the morning,' Ilic said.

The three of them got up to leave, but Jevtic called over. 'You can't leave good wine undrunk! We must have a song – stay, stay!' The others around him joined the chant. It was clear that they wouldn't be able to leave quietly.

Johnny smiled. 'We'd better do as they ask. The idea is to appear the same as everyone else.'

Chapter 22

Misko Jovanovic lit another cigarette and, unable to remain still, paced along the platform of Doboj station searching for the man he'd arranged to meet.

This had all started one terrible morning two weeks before, when he'd been woken from the sleep of the innocent by two peasants who had come to his home in Tuzla. They'd handed him a note from his friend Veljko Cubrilovic, asking him to 'look after these things'. Jovanovic had asked the peasants what 'these things' were and to his dismay they had untied six bombs and four pistols from around their belts and placed them on his kitchen table.

Jovanovic had not been able to believe what was happening; he was a pillar of the community – a respected businessman. He'd been married less than a year and had a newborn baby. He'd felt sure that 'these things' were to be the ruin of everything.

'They're from the honourable teacher,' one of the peasants had said.

Veljko Cubrilovic was one of his closest friends, his child's godfather and a respected teacher. They were both members of the Sokol, an organisation that celebrated Pan-Slavic culture. Veljko had introduced him to Narodna Odbrana, another patriotic organisation that celebrated Serbian culture, but also carried out covert activities, principally distributing illegal propaganda.

Jovanovic had been reluctant to join, but he had eventually decided that it was his patriotic duty to do all that he could for his people, even though distributing pamphlets was a far cry from handling weapons.

The peasants had started to look anxious and Jovanovic saw that it had become dangerous to be with him. 'The things belong to some students,' one of them had said, as if that settled everything.

'I don't know any students,' Jovanovic had replied, trying not to shout.

'They will be at the Serbian Reading Room at nine o'clock.'

Jovanovic had hidden the weapons and then hurried to meet the students. The Serbian Reading Room was on the floor below his apartment, directly above a cinema he'd just opened.

They'd looked bad, Jovanovic remembered. The two of them had made an effort to clean themselves up, but they'd still looked as though they'd been sleeping rough for days.

Jovanovic had taken them into a side room where they could talk. He'd been relieved they were there, although he hadn't been able to stop shaking. The small one, Gavrilo, had seen this and had stared at him coldly throughout the whole interview. Jovanovic's relief at seeing them had soon started to fade when they asked him to take the weapons on to Sarajevo. Jovanovic had explained as firmly as he dared that there was no way he was prepared to take that kind of a risk.

In the end, he'd agreed to look after the weapons. He couldn't force them to take them back and Gavrilo, the one who'd stared at him, had said that someone would come in a couple of days, and had then asked for a way that he would be able to identify himself to Jovanovic. Jovanovic had suggested a box of his favourite brand of cigarettes, Stefanija. He was going to need them.

He'd had to wait ten days with the weapons hidden in a box under his dining room table before another young man had turned up. This one was slightly older and much better dressed than the previous two and wore a black tie. He'd shown Jovanovic a box of Stefanija cigarettes and had introduced himself as Danilo Ilic.

That had been yesterday morning and to Jovanovic's horror, Ilic had told him to put the weapons in a discreet package and find someone to take them on the following day to Doboj, a town up the line. Ilic had explained that he couldn't carry the weaponry in his pockets and as he was a stranger in town, the gendarmes could well stop him.

There wasn't anyone else to take them and Jovanovic had business in Doboj, so reluctantly he'd said he'd take them himself. They'd agreed to meet in Doboj station's waiting room, early the next morning.

When Jovanovic got to Doboj, with the weapons wrapped in newspaper in the most inconspicuous box he could find, there was no sign of Ilic. He began to panic. The weeks of worry finally caught up with him and his only thought at that moment was to create as much distance between himself and the weapons as possible.

Jovanovic put the package on a table in the second-class waiting room, placed his cape over it and went to look around the station in case the student type had wandered off. The walk calmed him and then the realisation of what he'd done caught up with him. Jovanovic had left a box full of contraband weapons in the middle of a public area – anyone could steal or report them. Rushing back, he found that nothing was amiss. The station cat was sleeping peacefully on the package, digging its claws into his expensive cape.

He decided to take the package into town and leave it with a friend who owned a tailor's shop, after which, he went off to conduct his business, unencumbered.

Jovanovic got back to the station in time to meet the next train from Sarajevo. He could have wept with joy as the gaunt figure of Ilic at last appeared from the smoke and soot of the train.

*

Johnny was in a bad way. They'd spent most of the night at the wine shop and one drink had quickly followed another in his bid to blend in. The Bohemians were very hospitable and didn't mind standing a drink or two, but now he was paying the price. He really wasn't used to drinking wine, not by the jug anyway. Princip had managed to stay out of the drinking though, and had been able to wake Ilic and Johnny when they'd overslept.

The last thing Johnny needed was a train ride to goodness knew where. Ilic was furious with him; somehow the drinking to excess had been his fault, and now all Ilic's plans had fallen through and their whole venture could collapse because of one foolish night of indulgence. Ilic went so far as to suggest that they had acted like common tavern roughs, or worse yet, the Austrians themselves.

Johnny fancied that Ilic had been looking at him rather curiously since they'd got on the train and he had started to test Johnny's knowledge of Kierkegaard, Edgar Allan Poe and Walt Whitman, all of whom Ilic had translated into Serbo-Croat. Johnny hadn't read any of them. He wasn't overly fond of poetry, or philosophy for that matter, which did nothing to ease the tension or to prove Johnny's credentials as a Young Bosnian.

As the train went further and further into the unknown, Johnny started to worry that he was being taken out to be shot in the forests that endlessly rushed past the window. He decided to try and lighten the mood.

'Do you really need to wear a black tie today?' Johnny asked. Ilic never took it off.

'I wear it as a constant reminder of death.'

Johnny smiled. 'Yes, but when we're this hungover we really don't need to be reminded of death.'

Ilic looked at him sourly. It hadn't been a good joke admittedly, but Johnny at least expected him to play the game.

'I have a stomach ulcer and shouldn't drink, ' Ilic replied sullenly. Evidently he felt that was Johnny's fault as well.

It was a relief when the train stopped at Doboj and Ilic pulled him up from his seat. 'Follow me, but don't be seen. If you think I'm being followed by a police agent, distract him.'

Johnny stopped – he thought he might be getting set up to give himself away as an informant.

'How am I meant to distract a policeman?' Johnny asked.

'I don't know – sing him a song. You didn't have any difficulty singing last night.' Ilic smiled enigmatically and jumped off the train. Johnny vaguely remembered singing the 'Eton Boating Song', which had caused great amusement, but he was seriously starting to wonder if this whole thing was just an elaborate plan to get him out of the city so that Ilic could discreetly dispose of him.

Ilic was met at the station by an elegant man in his early forties with a thick handlebar moustache – not the usual sort he'd seen associating with the gang. The chap nearly broke down when he saw Ilic, but he managed to pull himself together and led Ilic out of the station.

Johnny followed from what he thought was a safe distance but he had no idea how to trail a man. He turned around; there didn't seem to be anyone about and having seen the state of the person Ilic had met, Johnny felt confident that he would be able to deal with them both, should they lead him down a blind alley.

He relaxed and gazed up at the medieval castle that overlooked the town, almost missing Ilic and his contact entering a tailor's shop. He glanced around but there was no sign of an ambush or a tail. He stepped into an artisan shop and started examining the wares on display, trying to appear inconspicuous. Something caught his eye amongst the coffee sets and brass plates. It was a curved knife, about six inches long, which looked like something from Beau Geste; Johnny thought it could come in handy if things turned nasty.

He bought the knife and returned to the street in time to see Ilic come out of the tailor's shop with a box under his arm that had been tied up with thick cord. Seeing Johnny, he signalled frantically for him to come with him. Ilic was very nervous and Johnny guessed the reason, as he neared him. There was an ominous metallic clank from the box and Johnny suspected that he was desperately under-armed. Whatever it was that fate was going to throw at him next, he knew that it was neatly tied up in that box.

The train journey back to Sarajevo was even more of an ordeal than the outgoing one. Ilic was extremely tense and so, in consequence, was Johnny.

'Do you believe in our cause, Jovo?' Johnny baulked at such a direct question. 'Do you believe that tyranny against the people justifies the use of violence to overthrow or kill a tyrant?'

'The tyrant must be destroyed,' Johnny answered. He'd heard Gavrilo talk like that and assumed that was what Ilic wanted to hear, but Johnny had misjudged him. Ilic became melancholy and stared out of the window as he spoke.

'My father was a cobbler. He died before I started school and left us in poverty. My mother took in washing to support us and then boarders. I had to share my room with Gavrilo. He had real fire, but knew nothing – a peasant from the mountains. I taught him about poetry, the Russian revolutionaries, political philosophy...' Ilic trailed off, lost in memory.

'You were a worthy teacher,' Johnny said.

'And now he has surpassed me, that small, sensitive boy, five years my junior. Tell me Jovo, what is your background? You don't strike me as a peasant's son.'

Johnny smiled, guessing what Sir George would have said about that statement. He couldn't tell if Ilic was probing further into his background or trying to remember why he was sitting on a train with a box full of illegal arms. The only thing Johnny knew for sure was that if Ilic did suspect him and was going to do him in, he would use whatever was in that box to do it.

'Well, like yours, my mother was forced to do work that was beneath her,' Johnny replied. His mother had been significantly better placed than a common laundry maid, but he was hoping that if he could make some sort of connection with Ilic he would be less likely to shoot him. 'She eventually married a school teacher. They disowned me when I was expelled from school. As you know, the older generation don't share our idealism.'

'You were expelled from school for organising a student strike?' Ilic asked looking back from the window.

Johnny tensed. 'Yes, that's right.'

'What were you striking for?'

Johnny had organised the strike to protest against having to do double prep. He'd roused his brother pupils to rise up – they'd had nothing to lose but their chains. It was meant as a harmless prank to get at Simpson, the housemaster, and everyone had laughed. Unfortunately, the school, caught up in the moral outrage over the Tonypandy riots and working class unrest in general, had unceremoniously kicked Johnny out in disgrace.

Johnny wasn't sure how that would sit with Ilic. The train was coming to a stop at one of the outlying stations, but that didn't distract him. Ilic wanted an answer.

'The school tried to make us sing the national anthem of our oppressors,' Johnny said eventually. He'd heard that some Young Bosnians had organised school strikes for similar reasons. Ilic cringed at the answer and stood up abruptly; he'd plainly been hoping for something a bit more profound.

'I had thought you might be different Jovo, but you're a zealot, like Gavrilo and the rest.' Ilic picked up the box, which made a bloodcurdling clank. 'We're getting off here.'

'What?' Johnny looked at the sign outside – they were at Alipasa Most station, miles from Sarajevo.

'The express is subject to searches by the police,' Ilic said, in answer to Johnny's confusion, and then he jumped out of the train. Johnny felt for the reassurance of the knife in his pocket and followed him.

'Here, take this.' Ilic passed him the box and Johnny took it gratefully, assuming that if he was holding the box, Ilic couldn't use whatever was in it to kill him. Then it dawned on Johnny that his sole purpose for being there was to act as a decoy. If they were stopped, it was Johnny's neck on the block.

They took a branch line train going to Ilidza and Johnny wondered fleetingly if Libby had arrived there yet or if she was still in the arms of the preening dandy. Ilic kicked Johnny out of his gloom as they got into Mariendvor station in the suburbs of Sarajevo. From there they had a hot and sweaty tram ride to the Cathedral of the Sacred Heart and a short walk back to the boarding house.

Ilic finally took the box back when they were in his room.

'You got them?' Gavrilo asked, looking up from a book as they entered.

'Yes,' Ilic answered and started to struggle with the cord tied around the box.

'Here use this.' Without thinking, Johnny handed him the knife he'd brought and Ilic cut the cord and unwrapped the newspaper. To Johnny's surprise, there was a black sugar box inside. Ilic opened the box and looked reassured and worried, almost in the same moment. Then he pulled out a small automatic pistol and pointed it straight at Johnny.

Johnny recoiled, caught unaware. Jumbled thoughts tumbled through his mind: being with Libby, betting every penny he had on the spin of a wheel. Johnny had done all he could to live a full life and still had so much more to do. He couldn't understand why Ilic had waited until he was home to do this.

Ilic lowered the gun, his demonstration over. 'You kept your nerve today, Jovo. Are you willing to swear your allegiance to our cause?'

'I am,' Johnny said, regaining his composure. 'With my dying breath I will fight for what is right.'

'On Vidovdan, we shall honour the memories of Obilic and Zerajic by killing the tyrant, Archduke Franz Ferdinand and sacrificing ourselves for our people. Are you willing to join us?' Gavrilo asked.

'I would be honoured.' Johnny smiled with relief and pride. He looked from the lofty intellectual to the slight, intense adolescent and couldn't believe they'd be capable of such an act. 'Will it just be us?'

'No, there are others,' Ilic replied.

Johnny nodded. 'Nedjo also?'

Ilic and Princip exchanged a look. 'Nedjo may be one of us but we have one other in our group. There is also a second cell known only to Ilic,' Princip replied as he started to take the rest of the guns out of the box. Johnny decided to leave it at that – he'd already gone above and beyond the call of duty. This little escapade was over.

Chapter 23

Johnny was entranced by the nimble figure of a belly dancer. She moved sinuously, as if she was making love – she was wild and beautiful.

They were about the same age, but the dancer was epochs ahead of him in every other respect. He'd tried to catch her eye, but she'd continued to beat out the rhythm with hypnotic hips, giving nothing away under her green veil. Johnny had never seen a woman out of his league before; it was a disquieting and arousing sensation.

He glanced over at Breitner, sitting next to him in judgement, waiting for Johnny to finish his report. He'd been hoping that Breitner might be as distracted by the entertainment as the little chap from the British Consulate had been. Instead, it was Johnny who was caught in the trap, unable to think or talk.

'You did ask for this meeting,' Breitner said piously. Johnny had sent him a note after his little adventure with Ilic. As nerve-racking as that had been, Johnny felt he'd met the challenge manfully and was now enjoying the new experience of a job well done. 'Did you see what was in the package?'

'You say that as if it was nothing,' Johnny replied, gulping down his wine and signalling to the waiter for another. Now that it was all over, he could afford himself a little insolence.

Breitner sighed. Johnny stole another glance at the belly dancer, trying one last time to catch her eye with a rakish smile, but it just made her stop dancing and sashay off the stage in the same heartbreakingly provocative way in which she'd owned it.

Spell broken, Johnny faced Breitner, who was smiling as he enjoyed Johnny's disappointment. It was the first time that Johnny had seen Breitner since he'd been press ganged into this whole sordid affair. He hadn't been in a fit state then to realise just how irritating this jaunty Hungarian could be.

'Yes, I saw what was in the box, Breitner.'

'Good. They must trust you.'

'In a manner of speaking.' Johnny related how Ilic had pointed a pistol at him.

'There couldn't have been a dry pair of trousers in the house,' Breitner said wryly. Johnny shrugged. He should have known he wasn't in any real danger – Ilic hadn't cocked the pistol.

'So, there were pistols in the box?'

'Yes, four Browning semi-automatics – modern and compact, lethal-looking things.'

Breitner nodded, surprised. 'You sound quite knowledgeable.'

'I am a special reserve officer in the British Army.' In truth Johnny had recognised the pistols as the same type used in the Caillaux case. 'There were also six bombs, about the same size and shape as a half-decent hip flask and ammunition for the guns.'

'Where are the weapons now?'

'In the Gladstone bag you gave me, under Gavro's fold-down bed.' They'd needed something damp-proof to keep the weapons in, so they'd naturally taken Johnny's bag.

'He hid them under his bed? Incredible.' Breitner smiled, amused by the calibre of people he was dealing with. 'Did they tell you exactly what they plan to do with this arsenal?'

'On Vidovdan, we shall honour the memories of Obilic and Zerajic, by killing the tyrant, Archduke Franz Ferdinand,' Johnny said, repeating what he'd been told.

Breitner raised an eyebrow. 'You haven't, as you English say, "gone native"?'

'Of course not – you knew that's what they're planning to do,' Johnny snapped. He felt glad that he wouldn't have to suffer Breitner for much longer.

'Did your new friends tell you how they intend to kill the tyrant?' Breitner asked, with a mocking tinge to his voice.

'Why don't you just go and arrest them? Surely you have enough evidence now?' And leave me to get on with my life, or what's left of it, Johnny thought.

Breitner gave him a sceptical look but Johnny ignored it, too distracted by the long elegant fingers that had just tapped him on the back. He gazed up into a pair of amber eyes, shining from the veiled face of the dancer. They were slightly hooded and gave her an irreverent, mocking look that seemed somehow familiar. He had only caught her eye for a split second, but there had been a definite summons.

'Have you met the third person who came from Belgrade with Gavrilo, or any of the members of the local cell which Ilic is recruiting?' Breitner asked, pretending not to have noticed the dancer.

'Not that I know of.' Johnny resented this constant nitpicking. None of that was important now, as he watched the dancer sway through the cafe.

'I've met that girl before – in the park!' She'd stopped to stand in a side door. He still hadn't met a woman who could resist his brash charm, he thought cheerfully, as he got up to follow her.

Breitner put a hand out to stop him. 'You have to find out who else Ilic has recruited.'

Johnny's legs buckled and he sat back down. 'You want me to go back?'

'Surely, you don't think what you've just told me is enough to regain your honour? We don't even know how they're planning to carry out the assassination, or if they're being supported by anyone.'

'Isn't waiting dangerous? They're armed now. Anything could happen ... to me,' Johnny said, his mind reeling. He looked around but the dancer had disappeared, the side door most definitely shut.

'You'll have to spike their weapons, Johnny.'

'How do you expect me to do that?'

'You're a special reserve officer are you not? You must know about such things,' Breitner replied smugly.

'Square bashing is all I know – and how to polish buttons.'

Breitner smiled softly; he knew Johnny was lying. 'It's important that you render the weapons safe, so that your new friends won't pose a danger to you ... or to the heir, while you discover what Gavrilo and Ilic are planning, and who else is involved in the plot.'

'But not even Gavrilo's met the other cell. These are expert revolutionaries we're dealing with, Breitner.'

'I think not, my dear Johnny,' Breitner smiled. 'Nedjo Cabrinovic has registered at an address in Franz Josef Street. No doubt his father made him do that; he owns a cafe nearby and believes in the benefits of our rule, which I'm sure is a bone of contention between them. Go to the cafe and see if you can find out anything else. Nedeljko Cabrinovic is not exactly discreet, so you might pick something up. Other than that, keep trying to ingratiate yourself with Gavrilo and Ilic. We must know everything about their plot before we can ensure the safety of the heir and you can claim your reward.'

Johnny groaned. He had no choice but to carry on. 'They're expecting me to have cash. I told them I was going to visit my maiden aunt to beg for money.' Breitner gave him a few coins – any more would obviously have aroused suspicion.

*

The Cabrinovics' cafe seemed pretty shabby compared to the wonders that Johnny had just witnessed and come so close to experiencing at his previous port of call. The sound of shouting in some far-off backroom did nothing to lift the gloom of the place. He couldn't believe Breitner had cast him out of paradise to come here.

However, Johnny soon forgot his woes when he saw a striking girl sitting in a far corner. She was about seventeen, her face an attractive blend of strength and sensitivity. Everything about her radiated a bright, vibrant nature. To Johnny's surprise, she was talking to Gavrilo. He knew this was too good an opportunity to miss.

'Hello there,' Johnny called as he headed towards them. Gavrilo turned around and scowled at him. 'Please, introduce me to your friend, Gavro.'

'Jovo, this is Miss Vukosava Cabrinovic,' Gavrilo said grudgingly.

'Good evening, Miss Cabrinovic. Pleased to meet you,' Johnny said.

Vukosava looked up at him, her eyes smiling even before she greeted him. 'Good evening. Please join us.'

Johnny ignored Gavrilo's withering looks and pulled up a chair at the end of their table.

'Cabrinovic – are you a relation of Nedjo Cabrinovic?' Johnny asked.

'Nedjo is my elder brother,' Vukosava said. 'How do you know him?'

'Hasn't everyone heard of Nedjo Cabrinovic?' Johnny answered, for want of anything sensible to say.

Gavrilo frowned. 'Jovo has heard Nedjo talk of the great deeds he will perform for our people.'

'Nedjo is your friend and comrade, Gavrilo,' Vukosava cut in, before Gavrilo could say anything further about her brother.

'We have a common cause,' Gavrilo agreed.

'Nedjo used to bring Gavro home. He was a poor, half-starved wretch and we'd feed him.' Vukosava grinned at the memory.

'Even with nine children to feed, they always had a place for me,' Gavrilo said.

'Do you remember, Gavro, when you caught me reading *The Secrets of the Istanbul Palace*? You were so annoyed that you took it away and made me read Uskokovic and Oscar Wilde.' She made a mock sad face. Gavrilo beamed – the poor peasant boy was definitely sweet on this smart, city girl.

'Someone had to take charge of your moral well-being, Vukosava,' Gavrilo said, making her laugh.

'What would my father say if he heard you talk like that?' She chided him gently and ruffled his hair. Gavrilo blushed, embarrassed. Johnny wondered if Gavrilo had decided not to deny himself love in the name of his cause after all; Johnny would certainly have forgotten about everything he believed in for a girl like her.

'Will Nedjo be joining us? Johnny asked. He hadn't completely forgotten his own cause and it was time he got on with it.

Vukosava inclined her head towards the shouting. 'Nedjo is talking with my father.'

'Oh I see, sorry.' Johnny quickly changed the subject. 'Your father owns this cafe?'

'That's right, Jovo,' Vukosava replied.

'A self-made man?' Johnny asked.

'He certainly understands the value of thrift and hard work.'

'You and your brother must have learnt a lot about the practicalities of life from such a man,' Johnny said gently, trying to steer the conversation back to Nedjo.

The shouting in the backroom started to get nearer and Vukosava smiled, embarrassed. 'Vaso Cabrinovic is a very practical man. When I was at school I had to read a poem in a pageant. I longed for a new dress and shoes to wear for the occasion, but I knew my father would never buy me them without good reason, so I told him that if I didn't have a new dress and shoes we would be shamed in front of our neighbours.

He saw my point, but instead of the pretty dress I dreamed of he brought me the most hideous thing you can imagine, made from the strongest material he could find. It was several sizes too big for me so that it would last for years and I had a new pair of boots to go with it.'

'Do you and your brother follow in his footsteps?' Johnny asked.

'No, Nedjo is a dreamer. He doesn't follow my father's lead in anything, as you can hear. I, on the other hand, well, I'm studying to be a dentist.'

'A dentist?' Johnny was genuinely surprised.

'She likes to inflict pain,' Gavrilo said sarcastically. He was tired of being ignored. 'My brother is cut from the same cloth as Vaso Cabrinovic. He thinks more of making money than freeing his people from oppression.'

'Maybe he feels they can free themselves by following his example and exploiting the opportunities the monarchy has given us, rather than pursuing ideas and pipe dreams,' Vukosava replied, teasing him, but Gavrilo looked angry. He might have lost his temper if an argument backstage hadn't burst out into the cafe.

Johnny recognised Nedjo Cabrinovic as he was pushed into the cafe by a giant of a man. 'I do not wish to live like you, father!' Nedjo pointed at the coffee grinder in the serving area. 'A bean counter in every sense!' Nedjo stopped shouting, and with energetic dark eyes and an insolent smile, looked around the cafe.

'You talk to me like that, in my place of business!' The giant was beside himself with rage. For a moment, Johnny was at home again, facing the full fury of his stepfather after he'd been expelled from school.

'Why not? Will you get your friends in the police to lock me up again, or will I be expelled from Bosnia by your masters once more?' Nedjo was enjoying the stir he was causing, as he deliberately tried to provoke his father. 'I wish to live free from the taint of Austro-Hungarian capitalism.'

'Do you get these naive ideas from those peasant boys?' the giant said, pointing at Gavrilo and Johnny. 'Under the monarchy we have security and modernisation.' He addressed the people in the cafe as much as his son.

'And illiteracy and the same feudal system that we had under the Turks, leaving our people no better than serfs.'

'Franz Ferdinand will reform things,' the giant said.

Nedjo shrugged. He was lost in the heat of the argument. 'Franz Ferdinand will not rule here. In a year's time we shall all be under Serbia.' Nedjo broke off, coughing.

Gavrilo slammed the table in rage, but managed a curt goodbye to Vukosava before leaving quietly. Johnny did one better, and kissed her hand. He followed Gavrilo along Franz Joseph Street as they headed towards the embankment.

'The fool will give the game away,' Gavrilo hissed.

Johnny knew that now was the time for him to exploit Gavrilo's anger and find out what was going on. 'Gavro, is it safe to have included someone so ... I'm sure Nedjo is a great patriot, but...' Gavrilo shot him a hard look and Johnny let his sentence drift off. Nedjo was Gavrilo's friend and Johnny didn't want to sound overly critical of him.

'Nedjo included himself in the plot. Well, Pusara included him – he sent Nedjo a clipping announcing the heir's visit while we were still in Belgrade,' Gavrilo said.

'Does Nedjo know how you plan to destroy the heir?' Johnny asked.

'You heard him in the cafe. Nedjo can't keep a secret. I haven't even told him the weapons are in Sarajevo.'

Johnny looked longingly at the Hotel Europe, an elegant Austro-Hungarian building, as they continued down the street. If his own plans had worked out he would have been sleeping there tonight before going to find Libby in the morning.

'Franz Ferdinand will be staying in Ilidza. When he comes, would that not be the best place to act? Is that why Nedjo has been going there?' Johnny asked, hoping to get some idea of what Gavrilo was thinking.

'The tyrant will be too well guarded at his hotel,' Gavrilo said. 'Don't worry Jovo, we have the means. We will act.'

They rounded the corner at the covered bazaar. The domes and ancient stonework reminded Johnny of a picture he'd seen on a Christmas card and he said a silent prayer as he speculated on how he could render the 'means' safe.

They continued to the end of Franz Joseph Street, past Schiller's delicatessen on the corner where the street met the embankment. 'Rum' and 'Lager' were emblazoned on the sign above the arched windows, and further along there was a massive picture of a champagne bottle on the wall. Johnny hoped that they were going to cross over Lateiner Bridge and visit the wine shop again. Gavrilo stopped and looked up and down the embankment.

'The only question is how and where we act, Jovo.'

'The attempt will be made when the heir comes to Sarajevo?' Johnny asked, unsure how he was going to discover a plan that hadn't been made.

Gavrilo nodded confirmation. 'Once we know the programme of the tyrant's visit, we will make our plans and move quickly.'

There was a certainty in his voice that chilled Johnny; it was the voice of someone who intended to die in two weeks.

Chapter 24

'Do you want to abort, Apis?' Major Tankosic asked, as he took a seat in the colonel's office. Apis looked at Tankosic. There was an innate guile in the major that made him invaluable to the head of Serbian intelligence as he walked the political tightrope in front of him.

They'd just returned from a meeting of the executive council of Union or Death, where they'd been ordered to cancel the Sarajevo operation.

'Word of our planned outrage must have filtered through to the government,' Apis said, trying to order his thoughts.

Tankosic nodded agreement, 'It was to be expected. The government has its agents as well.'

Pasic, the Serbian prime minister, had closed the border, but been too late to stop the major's Young Bosnia cell from getting through to Sarajevo.

'And so Pasic has put pressure on the executive council to get the operation stopped,' Apis reasoned.

Although the primary goal of Union or Death was to fight the Austro-Hungarian Empire and undermine Pasic's appeasement of Austro-Hungary, all of which the Sarajevo 'outrage' would accomplish, Apis knew that it didn't always do to pull the tiger by the tail. The organisation couldn't operate if the government decided to crack down on it completely.

'Major, I want you to let Sarajevo know, through the usual channels, that the council has ordered the mission to be cancelled.'

That should satisfy the council and word would filter back to the government that he'd sent an envoy to stop the operation, Apis reflected.

'At the same time, I'd like your envoy to suggest that this is the council's decision, not your own.' Apis looked sharply at Tankosic and paused to make sure that Tankosic understood the inferred implications of the statement. 'Our line will then be that we tried to stop the attempt on the archduke's life, but the outrage was carried out by his own citizens beyond the control of Union or Death.'

Tankosic smiled, 'I will make the necessary arrangements.'

*

Danilo Ilic settled himself at the arranged cafe overlooking the Sava river. This was the third time he'd been made to travel across Bosnia for the sake of the conspiracy. Unlike the other plots he'd been involved in, things were starting to take shape and spiral out of his control, and now he'd been summoned to the Serbian frontier for a meeting with someone so notorious that he couldn't risk a visit to Sarajevo.

Ilic ordered a glass of milk in the hope that it would soothe his troubled stomach. He'd had a very difficult journey; the uncertainty of what awaited him here caused his ulcer to flare up. It hadn't been right since that awful night in Semiz, when the idiot Jovo cornered him into drinking jug after jug of wine, for the sake of the plot. Ilic was starting to doubt the prudence of recruiting Jovo into the cell. He'd picked up all the licentiousness and none of the culture of Northern Europe. The drinking had at least provided Ilic with a temporary escape from the doubts and anguish he felt about the assassination.

He firmly believed that people had a right to take action against an unjust ruler, as was happening all across Europe. These were acts of desperation, of despair against tyranny – unselfish acts, to reclaim the moral order which a tyrant had corrupted. Kropotkin wrote of a moral urge that would destroy authority and create a free society.

Tyrannicide is the principal part of the moral urge to destroy such authority, but that didn't dispel Ilic's philosophical misgivings about assassinating the archduke. He'd tried to express these doubts in a recent review he'd written of *The Seven Who Were Hanged* by Leonid Andreyev. The book examined the meaning of death through the stories of seven people sentenced to die, five for a failed political assassination, and it looked at the spiritual crisis each underwent as they strove to overcome death in the name of a higher goal. It was a crisis that was mirrored in Ilic.

Ilic was also uncertain as to whether now was the right time for such direct action. He shared the same view as his friend and mentor Vladimir Gacinovic, who was considered to be one of the key thinkers in the Young Bosnia movement. Gacinovic believed that there was a need to form a political party to fill the power vacuum that a revolution would cause. Only after this party was established should a political assassination be carried out to instigate a revolt.

Lost in thought, Ilic barely registered the arrival of Major Tankosic's envoy, Djuro Sarac. Ilic understood that this was going to be more than a progress report if the major had sent his former bodyguard and the person who'd been entrusted with Gavrilo's training. They greeted each other and Sarac signalled for coffee. Ilic also realised it could be a golden opportunity to gain an insight into Gavrilo's capacity to commit tyrannicide.

'You taught Gavrilo to shoot?' Ilic asked.

'Yes,' Sarac answered tersely.

'What were your impressions of him?' Ilic asked, as their coffee arrived. He looked at it wearily.

'Gavrilo is a fair shot,' Sarac said noncommittally, placing a sugar cube in his coffee.

'But do you think he will be able to act when the time comes?' Ilic decided to leave his coffee, dreading the corrosive effect it would have on his stomach.

Sarac shrugged. 'Gavro is certainly driven, but you can never tell about a man until he's placed in the moment.' Ilic's heart sank; Sarac's tone suggested that Gavrilo wouldn't falter.

Sarac leaned forward. 'But that is neither here nor there. The central committee has ordered that the attempt on the heir be cancelled.'

Ilic couldn't believe it. This was more than he could have hoped for. 'How – why?' he asked.

'The government has discovered the plot and is concerned about Austro-Hungarian reaction to such an outrage.'

'I understand.' It was a qualm Ilic also harboured.

'However, I've been told to tell you that this message does not come from the major himself.'

'I don't understand – who does it come from then?' Ilic had heard that Sarac had trained to be a priest before joining the partisans. He judged from Sarac's ability to dissemble that he might have done well in that vocation.

'I was told to relay the decision of the central committee, but also to tell you that it wasn't the major's choice.'

Ilic was unsure whether this meant that Tankosic didn't back the decision to cancel and that they should continue, or just that the major didn't agree with the decision. His ulcer began to settle. He decided that, like most things told to him by a priest, he would ignore it.

Chapter 25

Johnny strolled along Appel Quay, enjoying the summer sunshine and trying desperately hard not to scratch his moustache, which was really starting to irritate. He'd grown it in an effort to blend in with Gavrilo and Ilic, but the thing itched remorselessly.

The Young Bosnians didn't seem to go in for the big, bushy Empire moustache that he'd been unable to cultivate, but which his contemporaries in the diplomatic service twirled with effortless charm. They opted instead for pencil-type efforts, and keeping the thing in trim was proving to be extremely tedious. The worst part was that he couldn't stop self-consciously touching and smoothing it, making him feel like a gigolo.

That idea inevitably caused his mind, with a lonely pang, to drift to Libby. The thought of her elegant contours and the journey they'd taken him on focused Johnny's mind and brought him back to the task at hand. He only had a small window of opportunity to act.

Ilic was due back from one of his jaunts and Gavrilo had arranged to meet him on his return, with one of their out of town cronies. Johnny had been expected to go, but he'd told Gavrilo that he needed to see another relative about money. Gavro had understood, as he was also desperately short of cash, although he'd managed to borrow a few crowns from Ilic, a courtesy not extended to Johnny.

He concluded his turn along the embankment and double backed on himself, heading for home, as he thought the coast should be clear by then. He briefly toyed with the idea of following the embankment up to City Hall and dropping in on Breitner; he wanted to see a friendly face, or at least a face that knew him for who he was. Breitner was the first person Johnny had met who he didn't have to pretend with and with whom he could truly be himself.

He would have to find some way of contacting him eventually. If he walked into City Hall he was bound to be seen by someone. The last time he had arranged a meeting he'd gone to the police station above City Hall to register his arrival in Sarajevo and left a note for Breitner.

He reached Lateiner Bridge and crossed the road, following Franz Joseph Street past Schillers' Deli and into the bustling back streets of the old town, rich with the scent of hookah pipes coming from the myriad of cafes. The shutters of the shops were open and their colourful wares spilled out onto the street like the blooms of flowers. He threaded his way around them and through crowds of people dressed in a kaleidoscope of traditional and Western clothes.

Johnny emerged into the central square of the old town, ringed by single-storey shops. He stopped to have a drink at the mushroom-shaped Sebilj Fountain, in the middle of the square and saw Ilic's mother at one of the fruit and vegetable stalls. She went there at roughly the same time every day.

He moved on. He knew there was no point in worrying about how to communicate with Breitner until he actually had something to tell him. He turned into the winding side street where his boarding house was. With Mrs Ilic out of the way, Johnny intended to take advantage of Gavrilo and Ilic's absence from the house as well to render the weapons 'safe'. He prayed that the other boarders would also be about their business, as this was the best chance he was going to get for a while.

The house was quiet, and Johnny made his way to Ilic and Gavrilo's room. The door had been kept shut since they'd brought the weapons here, in order to dissuade Mrs Ilic from going in, but Johnny didn't think it was actually locked, so he turned the handle, cringing as it squeaked.

He stopped dead as the door was pulled open by a burly chap with a trademark pencil moustache. Johnny involuntarily stroked his own moustache and glanced around the room. Gavrilo was sitting on his pull-down bed and Ilic was standing in the centre of the room, trying to make an announcement. He glared at Johnny.

'Sorry, I was hoping ...' Johnny said, looking round at the books lining the walls and wishing he'd prepared an excuse beforehand. 'After my recent journey with Danilo I realised how little I knew and wanted to educate myself about ...'

'Jovo, I thought you were seeing your uncle?' Gavrilo interrupted, before Johnny could get the rest of the tortured explanation out.

'He wouldn't give me any money,' Johnny replied, automatically. 'Sorry to disturb you.' He started to back out of the door.

'Jovo, since you're here, you might as well stay. I have news,' Ilic said, trying to call things to order.

'I would have knocked...' Johnny was too dazed to pay Ilic any attention. 'I thought you were meeting a friend, Gavrilo.'

'And so I have.' Gavrilo pointed at the man who'd ripped the door out of Johnny's hand. 'Jovo, meet Trifko Grabez. Like you, I am helping him to shape his political views. He will be with us on Vidovdan.'

Johnny and Trifko exchanged greetings. All might not be lost, Johnny thought – at least he knew who the other member of the cell was now.

'So why are you here?' Johnny asked. 'You said you were going to a cafe. I was hoping to stay out of the way and hide my poverty.' He didn't have to make that up; he barely had the price of a coffee in his pocket.

Ilic wasn't interested in Johnny's ability to think on his feet. 'What I have to say is of the gravest importance and I couldn't risk meeting Nedjo or his cohorts,' Ilic said, drawing their attention. 'Belgrade wants to cancel the attack.'

Gavrilo's face darkened. 'What are you talking about?'

'The central committee of Union or Death has issued orders that we cancel the assassination,' Ilic answered.

'Why?' Gavrilo was pale with shock. It was now clear to Johnny why they were here. Ilic wouldn't want someone as volatile as Nedjo present for the meeting; he was going to have his hands full with Gavrilo as it was.

'The Serbian government has discovered the plot and is concerned about the Austrian reaction if we succeed, or even attempt to assassinate Franz Ferdinand.'

'There was nothing else?' Trifko asked, surprised. 'No other message, from Major Tankosic? He gave us his support.'

'No,' Ilic said flatly, although Johnny thought he looked shifty.

'I don't care what the Black Hand or that naive idiot Tankosic thinks,' Gavrilo said, starting to seethe. There was clearly no way he would submit to their authority. 'They may have given us help, but that doesn't mean we answer to them.'

Ilic was nonplussed. He couldn't believe that Gavrilo would refuse a direct order from the central committee. 'Gavro, please put your personal feelings aside and think. Are you sure that we're taking the correct course of action?'

Trifko looked as if the ground had crumbled beneath him. This was challenging everything he'd been taught. 'Are you saying we no longer have the right to act, Ilic?'

Ilic saw Trifko's uncertainty. 'How do you reconcile the killing of a man? Your father is a priest – would he not say it is a sin? Have you no faith?'

'My faith is a faith in the nation,' Trifko answered, although it sounded as if his resolve was starting to wane.

'Have you thought what could happen to that nation if we succeed?' Ilic looked to Gavrilo. 'What if Austro-Hungary seeks revenge against our people?'

Gavrilo was in no mood to compromise. 'After me, let the deluge come.'

Ilic managed to remain calm. 'Killing the heir will achieve nothing and will provoke a reaction from the Austrians that will only increase the suffering of our people.'

Trifko nodded. Ilic's words were striking home, but Gavrilo was unmoved. 'We must unite our people, whether by killing leading personages to ignite revolution, or by eliminating those who stand in the way of unification. The archduke is the foremost enemy of the South Slavs. He is ruthlessly opposed to our unification and as the heir to the throne and inspector general of the army, he is responsible for the oppression and suffering of our people. I was one of nine children – six of them died because of the inequalities he perpetuates in his empire.'

Trifko looked reassured by Gavrilo's words. Johnny thought it best to keep his mouth shut during this exchange; he didn't want to destroy his guise as a Young Bosnian and he doubted he could make much of a difference to the outcome of the argument. What Gavrilo was saying might come true if Franz Ferdinand became emperor, but at present even as the Heir Apparent and Inspector General, Franz Ferdinand didn't have a great deal of say in how the monarchy was run. According to the accounts Johnny had heard from the British embassy staff in Vienna, the emperor kept him out of policy making as much as possible.

Ilic stood his ground, although he was uncomfortable arguing like this with his best friend over something he fundamentally agreed with. 'We need to build a political party ... to lay foundations, Gavro, and expound the ideas of our cause, before attempting to incite a revolution.'

Gavrilo was too angry to listen to any more of Ilic's abstract and convoluted arguments. 'Words have made you slack, Danilo. I need action. I have a certain morbid yearning awakening in me.'

A cold feeling fluttered through Johnny. If the plot went ahead without Ilic's involvement, he'd have no way of finding out who the other conspirators were and he'd never get out of here. There was only one chance. 'Ilic, are you going to betray us?'

Gavrilo nodded agreement. He couldn't bring himself to ask his friend outright, but Johnny was playing the hard man, someone who could do the dirty jobs.

'You question my loyalty?' Rather than being angry, Ilic was terrified that he'd be thought a traitor.

'You sound as if you're having second thoughts about what must be done,' Johnny said.

'No, it's as Andreyev said. The death penalty confuses the conscience, even of resolute men. How can they face it? Unless at the cost of their rational consciousness, ravaged to the depths of their souls.'

Ilic was obviously scared and Johnny couldn't blame him. If things went to plan he would die on the same day as the heir's visit to Sarajevo. Johnny had read Andreyev – he also said it would be impossible to live if a man knew exactly and definitely the day and hour of his death.

'I am committed to our cause and will continue to take part, especially now everything is in place. We have the people and the means to carry out a great victory,' Ilic confirmed.

'Are you sure the other cell is ready?' Trifko asked.

Ilic shrugged. 'They're very young, but you can't question their loyalty or commitment to the cause.'

Johnny saw his chance to find out who they were. 'Could I join their cell? Maybe I could bolster them.'

'I don't think so, Jovo. It is better to keep things separate,' Gavrilo said. 'Besides, you need to stay with us. I've got you a job.'

'A job?' That threw Johnny.

'Yes – you are short of money and like myself you have been borrowing. We must clear our debts next week and leave our affairs in order.'

Johnny was taken aback. There was no way he was going to die next week, not when there was still that amazing belly dancer to consider. It would be very bad manners to die before he'd had a chance to charm her a little. That was one account he had no intention of leaving unsettled, even if he had to find some way of stopping the plot.

*

The cafe was crowded with people watching a loud folk band. Apis pushed his way through, searching the faces, hoping to recognise the man he'd come to meet. It was a hard task in the maelstrom of the live performance. Rade Malobabic was an undistinguished man, apart from his large feet. There seemed to be nothing about him that stood out, allowing him to blend in as he unobtrusively went about his business, gathering information. It was an ability that had enabled him to become Apis's chief intelligence man in the Austro-Hungarian monarchy.

Apis found Malobabic as he sat lightly tapping his big feet in time to the music. Apis had felt it was more discreet to meet him in a cafe rather than his office, where government spies could monitor his visitors. To an observer, he would be passing pleasantries with a grey, middle-aged man as they enjoyed the show. Malobabic had come a long way to make his report. It was too important to be trusted to the usual means of communication and Apis didn't want to run the risk of anything getting back to Prime Minister Pasic.

Malobabic carried on watching the band as Apis sat at the table next to him. 'The Serbian minister in Vienna has paid a visit to Count Bilinski and expressed fears about the archduke's visit to Sarajevo,' Malobabic said.

'Has he warned him of the plot?' Apis asked, wondering if perhaps the government hadn't been entirely bluffed by the cancellation order, or if he had a spy in his ranks.

'No, not outright. The good minister said that the heir should be careful when he goes to Bosnia. Some nonsense about a young Serb putting a live bullet in his gun rather than a blank and then firing it.'

Apis nodded. He could imagine the minister, bogging himself down in doubletalk, trying to warn of a plot, but not wanting to make it too obvious in case it looked as if the Serbian government was involved. 'What did the Austro-Hungarian joint minister of finance make of that?'

'Not a lot. It was a very vague comment and could even have been interpreted as a veiled threat, but from what my sources tell me, Bilinski's feathers have been ruffled by the visit. It was organised by the military governor who completely bypassed his ministry, so Bilinski has washed his hands of the whole affair.'

Apis smiled. If that was the best Pasic could do there was nothing that could stop the operation now. 'Good work, Rade.'

'There was one more thing. I have a regular chess opponent at the British embassy in Vienna – the usual arrogant, self-assured type of diplomat. He's been a great source of information.' Apis nodded impatiently; the longer their conversation lasted, the greater the risk of discovery by the prime minister's spies.

'The last time we played, he was extremely unhappy. A woman he'd been mooning around after for weeks had decided to go off to Sarajevo. She is the wife of a senior English diplomat.'

'Why would such a woman go to Sarajevo?'

'Apparently, she was pursuing some Englishman, a 'bad sort', who's been sent to Sarajevo by the British embassy in Paris on something unofficial.'

'What sort of unofficial – an operation?' Apis asked, concerned.

'That's just it. Pinkie couldn't find out. He has an extensive network of contacts throughout the British diplomatic service, but his enquiries couldn't locate the woman or the man she was pursuing. She may not even have gone to Sarajevo yet. No one knows anything. He's been erased, almost as if he's been sent to do something clandestine ... something deniable and off the books.'

'You think it might be connected with the archduke's visit to Sarajevo?' Apis asked.

'Why else would anyone be interested in the Balkans, just when we have an important operation in progress?'

Apis turned and spoke directly to Malobabic. He was too concerned by what he'd heard to stick to security procedures. If his government had tried to warn the Austrians, he thought it possible that they'd told the British and hadn't been quite so circumspect about it. Perhaps the British feared any further diplomatic tension, which might bring the Russians into the Balkans, thereby threatening British interests in the Mediterranean.

'Rade, I want you to go to Sarajevo and stop this Englishman from interfering with the operation.' Apis wouldn't have the so-called 'great powers' making sport of him or his organisation. 'Be careful – we have no idea what kind of man we're dealing with.'

Chapter 26

Archduke Franz Ferdinand finished his breakfast with little enthusiasm; his usual two boiled eggs were barely touched. He drank his tea and surveyed the grounds of Chlumetz through the bars of the nursery's window. It might not be as impressive as Konopischt, he reflected, but the attractive baroque chateau had a homely feel to it.

He loved to take breakfast with his family in the nursery and afterwards he'd often stay to read over the newspapers and enjoy the chaos his children created, while Sophie maintained a relaxed order to it all.

Today Franz Ferdinand abandoned any attempt to read the news and remained a little longer than normal. He had a thousand and one matters to attend to, but he was reluctant to leave his family.

He looked at his children in their white sailor suits as they ate their breakfast, oblivious to the turmoil he was feeling over leaving them. Little Sophie was thirteen, Maxi twelve and Ernie, ten. They were fine looking, intelligent children and a source of unending joy and pride to the archduke.

The bliss he felt at that moment overwhelmed him. Franz Ferdinand never ceased to be amazed by how much he loved them. He yearned to stay and spend the long summer days taking them hunting or on long walks, and then in the evenings, to watch Sophie do her embroidery while the children played, trying their best not to knock things over.

Janaczek brought in his mail and stood watching, until Franz Ferdinand glanced at him. 'Excuse me, Your Highness, the preparations for your departure are nearly complete.'

'Thank you, Janaczek,' Franz Ferdinand said in a flat tone. He knew there was no point in worrying what disaster fate might bring, but he couldn't shake off a feeling of apprehension about the trip to Bosnia.

'Papi, why are you going? Maxi, his eldest son asked. 'When the emperor said you don't have to, he said you can do as you see fit!'

Ernie and Sophie looked round at their father with worried expressions and Franz Ferdinand saw that he hadn't hidden his feelings from his children as well as he'd hoped.

He took a deep breath. He had infinite patience when it came to his children, but they were old enough to understand duty. 'I am inspector general of the Austro-Hungarian armed forces. I must go to Sarajevo. Do you think the soldiers would understand my absence if I wasn't there?'

Franz Ferdinand had tried to sound cheery, but Maxi would not be put off. 'But when the emperor went to Bosnia, he was stalked by that madman, Zerajic, who tried to shoot the governor.'

'They say he got close enough to touch the emperor,' Ernest added, with scared eyes.

'It was a miracle that he didn't shoot,' little Sophie said, making her father wince. As secluded as the lives of his children were, they still managed to find such things out. 'We cannot allow our feelings to govern us. If we did we would never be able to do anything, and become a prisoner to our slightest doubt and hesitation. And then how could I make a good emperor?'

Maxi tried to continue but his mother cut him off. 'Enough of this, children. Maxi, your only concern should be whether or not you have passed your exam. Now, all of you leave your poor father in peace.'

Franz Ferdinand watched from his study window as their luggage for the visit to Bosnia was loaded. All of the arrangements had been attended to, except one.

He turned from the window and faced Janaczek, who was standing formally, sensing the gravity of the moment. He'd been a good and faithful servant for twenty five years.

'Janaczek, there is no one I'd trust more to run things in my absence,' Franz Ferdinand said, and he presented him with a gold watch.

'Thank you, Your Highness.' The archduke's estate manager knew that the watch was more than a recognition of service.

'I'd like to ask that you never leave my household, Janaczek. Even if something should happen to me, you must never leave the children or the duchess.'

'Never, Your Highness.' Janaczek bowed formally. No further declaration was needed – Janaczek would do his duty.

Franz Ferdinand shook his hand and headed to the hall to make his farewells. He drew himself up, as he saw his children huddled around their mother, but instead of more protests they threw their arms around him.

'We'll be back in a week,' he whispered, drawing them close.

Chapter 27

Johnny finished his baklava and looked up contentedly. Something nice before a day in the office always cheered him up. The same couldn't be said for Gavrilo, who was sitting next to him, calm and impassive, his eyes burning with their usual ferocity, as he studied the *Bosnische Post*.

Johnny signalled for the bill to Vlajnic, the owner of the pastry shop, and turned back to Gavrilo. The official programme for the royal visit had been published in all of Sarajevo's major newspapers, heralding the arrival of the heir.

He was to attend two days of manoeuvres and a large formal dinner on Saturday, followed by a visit to Sarajevo on Sunday. The full details of the visit to Sarajevo had been released to the press, as the lord mayor wanted to ensure that the people of Sarajevo knew where to stand so that they could give the archduke a resounding welcome and show their, 'gratitude, devotion and loyalty' to the monarchy. From the way he was studying the paper, Johnny assumed Gavrilo was deciding just how he would do that.

Johnny winked at the waitress as she brought over the bill. Gavrilo glowered at him and apologised to the waitress for Johnny's ill-mannered behaviour. 'Jovo – how dare you be so disrespectful to a woman?'

'I'm sorry, Gavrilo – she's very pretty,' Johnny replied, trying to sound submissive. Gavrilo and Ilic had continued to argue about the rights and wrongs of the assassination and Johnny didn't want to aggravate Gavrilo any more than was necessary. He still had a job to do.

'Relations between a man and a woman should be of the purest kind,' Gavrilo said curtly.

'As is yours with Vukosava?' Johnny asked.

Gavrilo's cold blue eyes stared at Johnny with controlled fury. 'My relationship with Miss Cabrinovic is strictly platonic, based on a mutual respect and appreciation of poetry and literature. Anything else would trifle with her dignity.'

'I meant no offence.'

'We have sworn off such things, Jovo. We cannot allow ourselves to be distracted, not now that we are so close to the end.'

Johnny assumed that Gavrilo wanted the strength and purity of a cause, not the uncertainties and vulnerability which the love of a woman offered. It seemed that to Gavrilo, everything was superfluous to the journey he was on.

'I know it's not really my place, Gavrilo, as I'm still new to the group, but can we afford distractions that are closer to home?'

Gavrilo glared as Johnny continued. 'I must tell you that I support your decision to act against the archduke and that Ilic is totally wrong to question the course we must take.'

'That is not your concern, Jovo.' Gavrilo said, annoyed by Johnny's comment.

'Surely, the fate of our people is everyone's concern.'

'Ilic is my best friend. He has given me his word that he'll work with us.'

'I'm worried about the other cell,' Johnny said. 'What do you know about them?'

'Ilic has assured me that they are good patriots.'

Johnny thought he could sense an element of uncertainty in Gavrilo's voice. He'd been waiting for an opportunity to exploit the growing rift between Ilic and Gavrilo, and he decided to press on.

'I do not doubt their sincerity to our cause. It's just that if the only contact they have with us is through Ilic, can they be relied upon? Who knows what Ilic is saying to them.'

Johnny waited as Gavrilo thought that over. Ilic was nothing if not an idealist and once he'd had an idea about something, it was almost impossible to change his mind.

'Perhaps I could be of more help to you,' Johnny suggested, 'if I were to keep an eye on him and the other cell as we prepare for Sunday.'

Gavrilo shrugged noncommittally. 'Trifko is coming to Sarajevo tomorrow. We'll discuss the matter then.'

Johnny knew that was the best he could hope for. Gavrilo paid the bill and they left, walking out onto Cumurija Street and up towards Appel Quay. A triangular shaped baroque building had been constructed at the end of the street next to some old Turkish houses and a cafe. They followed a narrow stretch of road on the left hand side of the building and came out into the bright light of Appel Quay, opposite the steel Cumurija Bridge and carried on around the corner past a bank of Austro-Hungary.

Gavrilo stopped under the shade of a tree and surveyed the long line of new, neo-Romantic Austrian buildings that ran along the embankment.

'Sarajevo isn't an honourable place to make our sacrifice. It's just one, big Austrian market.'

Johnny gazed wistfully at a tobacconist's, its yellow paintwork making it look nicotine stained next to the whitewashed bank, which was gleaming in the early morning sunshine. He wondered if he had enough money to buy something that would help him get through the day. It was going to be a long one, by the sound of it. He checked his pockets but there was barely enough to buy a box of matches.

'Would you like some matches, Gavro?' Johnny asked, trying to lighten the mood.

Gavrilo gave him a disgusted look. 'If I could afford a box of matches I would set Sarajevo on fire.'

'That's one way of getting out of going to work, I suppose.'

Gavrilo ignored Johnny and they continued on to a large, elegant building next to the tobacconist's. It had a statue on the roof, of what Johnny took to be Athena, the goddess of wisdom, sitting on a chair dispensing wisdom to Serb children. It was very different to the imperial depiction he'd seen of the goddess outside the Austrian parliament building. He was briefly reminded of the cab ride with Libby down the Ringstrasse and the promise he'd made her.

'How is it that you have never heard of *Prosvjeta* before?' Gavrilo asked, studying Johnny curiously, as they entered the building. 'You said you received a scholarship to study.'

'The church was of some assistance,' Johnny replied, then shrugged, embarrassed, and started to climb the stairs to their office. He had no idea which organisations provided Serbian students with scholarships. The scholarship he'd won had come from the school and the church council. *Prosvjeta* or 'enlightenment', as he'd recently learnt, was a cultural society for the development of Serbs through education and gave support to poor but gifted students. They'd helped, among others, Gavrilo and Bogdan Zerajic.

Gavrilo and Johnny reached their desks and settled down for a day at work. Gavrilo had managed to find himself and Johnny jobs at *Prosvjeta* through its secretary general, who paid them fifteen crowns each to copy out minutes of meetings, which Johnny told Gavrilo would be enough to pay off his debts.

Johnny had done very little else to further his cause in the last week before the archduke's visit to Sarajevo. It was Thursday and he had been well and truly seduced back into the monotony of meaningless work. He was starting to wonder if he should stop gambling and womanising, and accept that he'd be perfectly happy spending the rest of his life engaged in simple clerical tasks.

The stark reality was that he couldn't have hacked it, even if he'd wanted to. He kept making mistakes. The chief administrator had already questioned his work several times. If one thing was for sure, Johnny would have to find some way of making this agreement with Breitner work, as he couldn't go back to the way his life was before.

'This work is of the highest importance, Jovo. Prosvjeta gave me a chance – we must do the same for the next generation,' Gavrilo said, seeing how bored Johnny was.

'You value education more than the great work we are doing for our people?' Johnny asked.

'Education has always been important to me. I was a very earnest child – I hardly played with the other children in my village. Even before I went to school I'd follow our cows and make-believe I was going to school with a bag full of books. My father wanted me to be a shepherd, but my mother took my part and I went to school eventually, when I was nine.'

Johnny looked at Gavrilo's small hands and slight frame, and wondered if he would have survived the harsh conditions of a peasant farmer. 'You were lucky that your father supported you as far as high school.'

Gavrilo shrugged. 'It wasn't easy. The peasants are crippled with taxes and rents, but my brother saw the potential of my education as a means of social advancement, rather than its true purpose of enlightening the people. When he was no longer willing to support me I managed to get a small stipend from *Prosvjeta*.'

Johnny smiled sympathetically. He was starting to feel comfortable in his role as an informant. He'd gradually begun to win Gavrilo's confidence and he was opening up to him. Out of the corner of his eye, Johnny suddenly caught sight of a blurred vision of loveliness and he got up instantly.

He'd have recognised that nimble figure anywhere, even restricted by layers of whalebone. It was the belly dancer he'd seen with Breitner, gliding effortlessly through his office on the arm of a rich old industrialist. If Johnny had believed in such things, he'd have said he was in love.

The man she was with went into the chief administrator's office without knocking, leaving her outside and unguarded. Johnny didn't miss a beat.

'Good afternoon, Miss ...?' Johnny left the last part of the sentence hanging, hoping that she'd fill in the gap, but she just arched her eyebrow questioningly.

'Good afternoon, Mr ...?' she replied, leaving the last part of her sentence to hang too. Johnny choked – even if he could have remembered what his name was, he'd never have been able to say it. She was truly beguiling.

'Didn't we meet the other night?' he managed to ask.

Her amber eyes flashed the same mocking look that she'd given him in the park and the cafe. She recognised him, there was no doubt about it. Johnny couldn't believe he hadn't followed her through the side door in the cafe.

'I'm sorry I wasn't able to join you, but I had a rather pressing matter to attend to.' Whatever it was, Johnny couldn't remember now.

'We have met.' Her eyes were willing him to say where.

'In a cafe – you were performing. Although that wasn't the first time we'd met ...'

'Sir, you seem to have mistaken me. I've never seen you before.' She smiled, making Johnny feel dizzy.

'Just what the hell's going on here?' A harsh voice brought him sharply back to the present.

The industrialist and the chief administrator were standing behind him. 'I asked you a question, boy,' the industrialist said. For the first time in his life, Johnny was caught without a flippant reply. She'd well and truly scuppered him.

'This "gentleman" was insinuating that I'd performed in some sleazy hovel. Like ... like a common trollop! He even had the impertinence to suggest that we were acquainted.' She turned her head away from them and winked, so that only Johnny could see it.

The chief administrator had a face like death. 'Get out! How dare you insult the daughter of one of our leading benefactors?'

The industrialist blew cigar smoke in Johnny's face. Johnny looked around in disbelief; he couldn't understand how this had happened. The whole office was looking at him, but it was Gavrilo's cold eyes that stood out.

Johnny turned on his heels and fled. He'd often fantasized about being dismissed from his job, but he'd always hoped it would be for something big, like having relations with the boss's wife, not by being made to look a total fool by the love of his life.

He wandered along the embankment, taking stock, and realised that he could probably have played that slightly better. If she had been the dancer from the cafe, she would hardly want him spreading it around a place where her father was a respected figure. Even so, he thought getting him sacked was uncalled for.

He should have kept his powder dry, no doubt about it, but he hadn't been able to help himself. Johnny stopped and looked down at the bloody red mud of the Miljacka river. Too late for recriminations now, he reflected. Of all the mistakes he'd made with women recently, this one was relatively minor.

It had been worth getting sacked, just to talk to her. Johnny walked on towards the old town – he still had the more immediate problem of disabling the weapons. He considered just throwing them into the river and blaming Ilic, but the river was only a few inches deep and Ilic was too much in Gavrilo's pocket for anyone to believe he would do it.

Johnny was almost home, and realised that if he was going to do something, now was as good a time as any. Gavrilo would be at work all day and Ilic would probably be at *The Bell*, the newspaper he edited. He made up his mind to act as he got to his street: the archduke's visit was only a few days away.

Mrs Ilic was pottering about in the kitchen when he got to the boarding house. Johnny shouted hello to her and went up to Gavrilo and Ilic's room. The door was shut, but not locked.

He went in and tried to walk silently across creaking floorboards and then pulled out the Gladstone bag from under Gavrilo's fold-down bed. He carefully opened the catch and took out one of the small Browning pistols. The plate on the side stated that it had been made under patent by Fabrique Nationale in Belgium. Johnny had never held an automatic before; it was very different from the service revolvers he'd trained with in the reserves.

He examined the beige cardboard boxes that held the twenty-two calibre bullets and could just make out, 'Browning Colt USA' smudged on the front, under a picture of a Browning automatic. It felt strange to be reading English again, in this environment.

Printed boldly next to the picture of the pistol was the number '25', and he wondered if these were all the bullets they had. Johnny considered just taking the bullets, but Gavrilo and Ilic would be sure to notice they were missing before he completed his assignment.

He put the gun down and ruffled his shirt; his sweat was making it prickly. Johnny picked up one of the oblong bombs, wishing it was a hip flask full of brandy. It felt rough and uneven. Russian revolutionaries had used bombs to great effect, throwing them at leading personages as they drove down the street, the most notable being at Alexander II, the current tsar's grandfather. Johnny wasn't about to let that happen here, but he didn't have a clue how to stop it.

He unscrewed the cap on the top of the bomb – it made a click and he almost dropped the thing in fright. There was a small loop under the cap that Johnny thought must be the priming mechanism. When the loop was struck it would push down, lighting the fuse that set the whole thing off. He thought that if he could knobble the loop, then it wouldn't light the fuse. He was only guessing, as, not having undergone ordnance training, he really had no bloody idea.

He looked around for something to use, but a hacksaw wasn't something Young Bosnians would keep in their bedrooms. Johnny remembered the curved knife he'd bought in Doboj. He still carried it around, just in case things turned nasty.

He started slicing away at the loop and eventually managed to make two small dents, which didn't look too obvious, on either side of it. He hoped that anyone striking the loop would just snap it off without igniting the fuse.

He then placed the bomb back in the bag and took out another one. He had started to unscrew the lid when a knock door to the street made him jump. The bomb slipped, he fumbled it and it hit the floor with a loud clang. For a moment, Johnny thought he must surely be dead.

'Jovo, Jovo – what are you doing up there?' Mrs Ilic shouted up at him.

'Nothing, nothing at all Mrs Ilic,' he managed to squeak.

'Didn't you hear the front door? There is a girl here to see you.'

Confused, Johnny shoved the bag back under the bed and fled downstairs. He had no idea what Mrs Ilic was talking about – he didn't know any girls. Then he saw her standing at the bottom of the stairs in a bright green veil. There was no mistaking the amber eyes mocking him.

Chapter 28

Johnny pressed himself into a corner outside the eastern end of the Catholic cathedral and shivered. Its gothic design didn't offer much cover from the rain. He looked longingly across the street at the green domes of the Turkish baths and thought of the shimmering green silk of the belly dancer.

It had taken him a moment to recover from the shock of seeing her at the boarding house. By the time he'd regained his senses she'd ushered him out into the alley next to the house and slapped his hands away, as he simultaneously tried to lift her veil and robe. It was an instinctive reflex he'd perfected under his uncle's tutelage, but it was completely wasted on her.

'Lazlo sent me,' she said, removing the veil herself.

'Lazlo? Oh, you mean Breitner,' Johnny said, dejected. The name was like a bucket of cold water thrown in his face. 'You work for Breitner?'

'Why else would I share my lunch with you and take the trouble of explaining Kropotkin, so that you could make friends with the other boys.' Her eyes mocked his naivety.

Johnny's anger flared up. 'He told me he didn't have any chaps.'

'I thought you'd noticed. I'm not a "chap".' She rolled her eyes coyly.

'Well, yes, I have obviously .... what I meant was ...'

'I believe what Lazlo actually said was that he didn't have anyone *suitable*. I'm not suitable,' she explained.

Johnny smiled in spite of his rage and frustration. The thought of her trying to make friends with a puritan like Gavrilo was vaguely amusing. Then he remembered.

'You got me sacked.'

'Something had to be done to winkle you out. Lazlo thought you were getting far too comfortable. He needs your information, urgently.'

'So that was a trap? You knew I'd recognise you at the charity?'

'You are a man of certain crude predictabilities. It makes you very easy to manage.'

'Breitner planted you at the cafe!' Johnny couldn't believe he'd gone to that much trouble. Breitner must have known that if he stopped Johnny from following her through the side door at the cafe, he'd completely lose control the next time he saw her. The eye for detail staggered him. 'How did Breitner magic up your father?'

'My father?'

'The chap you were with, puffing cigar smoke all over the place.'

'My father, yes.' She seemed amused by the comment, as if he'd believe anything and everything. 'Oh, Krumpli – that particular "father" is a well known philanthropist, who I met at a Chamber of Commerce function. I pretended to be interested in such matters and he invited me to join him when he visited the *Prosvjeta* office.'

'How does he feel about you cavorting about as a showgirl?'

Her amber eyes flashed angrily. 'You are to wait by the tram stop behind the Cathedral of the Sacred Heart tonight, after last mass. Lazlo will be on one of the trams going past.'

'But I'd rather meet him at the cafe again.'

'Yes, I'm sure you would, but it will create less suspicion if you are on a tram rather than sitting together in a cafe – I shouldn't have to tell you this. Now, you've detained me long enough.' *He'd* detained *her*! Johnny was so taken aback at her gall that he forgot to ask her name.

He had been waiting for hours, watching the trams rattle past, trailing sparks in the rain. Breitner hadn't been on any of them and Johnny wouldn't have put it past that spiteful little minx to have made the whole thing up. The thought gave him a warm feeling. She was magnificent. Scheming women were new to Johnny. Libby, for all her guile, was pretty no-nonsense. You always knew where you were with her, and exactly what was expected. Johnny would have to raise his game if he was going to get anywhere with this sophisticated continental.

He nearly missed the tram when it finally came battling its way through the heavy rain. He saw Breitner sitting at the window; there was no mistaking his ridiculous pince-nez. Johnny did a hundred-yard dash through the rain and jumped on just as the doors slammed shut. Breitner nodded approvingly, obviously thinking it had all been part of an elaborate ruse to make sure he wasn't being followed.

He fell into the seat next to Breitner and said a little too begrudgingly, 'I got your message.'

The Assassins

Breitner smiled. 'You're cutting things a bit fine, Johnny. The archduke arrived in Bosnia today and we have no idea how your friends plan to welcome him.'

'They're not going to do anything before Vidovdan, on Sunday. I've still got Friday and Saturday.'

'Vidovdan,' Breitner repeated the word, ponderously. 'I'd have thought that it would be a lot easier to shoot him during the manoeuvres, when he's standing around in a forest. There must be hundreds of ex-partisans who could do it.'

'They want to slay the sultan on their national day,' Johnny said curtly. He'd already told Breitner all of this. 'They'd hardly ignite a revolution skulking about in a forest.'

Breitner gave him a cold look. 'So, it's definitely a nationalist plot by the Young Bosnians – there's no one else involved?'

Johnny shrugged his sodden shoulders, inadvertently pressing cold water down his back. 'The whole thing seems to be their own idea.'

'You're sure?'

'The weapons were supplied by a group called 'The Black Hand' – whatever that is.'

'It's a Pan-Slav extremist group, connected with Serbian intelligence. Exactly the sort of people to mastermind something like this,' Breitner explained.

'They don't appear to have direct control over Gavrilo. In fact, he's very hostile to a Major Tankosic in their leadership.'

The tram went round a corner and Johnny fell onto Breitner. 'Have you managed to spike their weapons?' Breitner whispered into Johnny's ear before he could sit back.

'One bomb.'

'*One bomb*, Johnny!' Breitner tried to keep his voice down.

That annoyed Johnny – it wasn't his fault. 'I was in the middle of doing it when your dancer turned up. Who is she anyway?'

Breitner shifted uncomfortably. Involving her was obviously distasteful to him. 'She's a compatriot of mine from Budapest. I have reason to find her useful from time to time.'

'I just bet you do.'

'There are more important things to worry about than the life story of one dancer.'

'Not to me there aren't.'

'Johnny, do you want your commendation or not?' Breitner grinned, and it was Johnny's turn to shift uncomfortably.

'I'm meeting the group tomorrow, so hopefully I can find out more. Now the itinerary's been announced they can start planning in detail. Oh, and I've met the other person in my cell, his name is Trifko Grabez.'

Breitner nodded, making a mental note of the name. 'And the other cell?'

'I've been angling to try and join it, but your little stunt at my work may have lost me some stock with Gavro.'

Breitner gave an indifferent flick of the wrist. 'These things can't be helped.'

'Why don't you just round everyone up – you must have enough evidence by now. and then just beat the rest of it out of them?' Johnny asked. 'Ilic is on a knife-edge, I'm sure he'd talk.'

Breitner looked irritated by the question, 'I'm a civil servant, not a policeman. I tried to have the conspiracy dealt with before I ever involved you, Johnny. It doesn't matter how much evidence I have, the authorities won't listen to me. I explained to you that I have something of a past and anyone who involves themselves with me is likely to find their career ended – especially where the archduke's visit is concerned'

'There must be something you can do, Breitner.'

'I have to see Governor Potiorek. No one else will dare interfere with the archduke's visit.'

'Well, go and see the governor then.'

'He's at the manoeuvres with the archduke. I can't get to him until Saturday afternoon. Before that though, I want to know every detail there is to know about this plot, so you'd better complete your mission by then and come and meet me at the governor's residence, around 4.30 p.m. I'll try and arrange an audience,' Breitner said, although he didn't look comfortable with the idea.

'And what happens if I can't?'

'Just come to his residence on Saturday. Hopefully we can talk the governor into cancelling the visit.' The tram stopped and Breitner charged out into the rain.

*

It was still raining the following evening when Johnny met with Gavrilo, Trifko and Ilic at the boarding house. A dull light from an oil lamp cast a menacing glow over the assembled conspirators, hiding their faces in shadow.

The Assassins

Johnny hadn't spoken with Gavrilo since he'd been dismissed from the charity and he couldn't tell if he was still angry with him. All of Gavrilo's focus was on Ilic, who was continuing to bang on about postponing the assassination.

'Now is not a good time to act – we will not profit from it. We must wait until there is a proper political structure in place.'

'Whatever happens after the assassination will only be good for our cause,' Gavrilo replied abruptly, his mind made up.

Ilic held his hands up in surrender. He'd tried to stop it; he was no longer responsible for what happened, or the consequences.

Gavrilo passed Ilic the copy of the *Bosnische Post* that he'd been reading in the pastry shop. If Princip had any concerns about Ilic, he'd brushed them aside; they'd been friends far too long for him to harbour any serious doubts about Ilic's commitment.

Ilic opened the newspaper and started to study the itinerary of the archduke's visit, with what little light he could get from the lamp. 'The royal train will arrive at Sarajevo station, at 9.50 a.m. and from there the tyrant and his wife will inspect the army barracks and meet senior military commanders. Then they drive to City Hall, via Appel Quay, for a reception and municipal welcome from 10.10 a.m. to 10.30 a.m., with drawing room dress required. After this they will tour the new museum between 10.40 a.m. and 11.40 a.m., followed by a nice long luncheon with Potiorek at the Konak. Then a sightseeing tour and back to their hotel in Ilidze by special train.'

'We intend to ambush the heir's motorcade, in the true spirit of our forefathers,' Gavrilo said quietly, his calm scarcely concealing the tension in his eyes.

'Surely it would be easier to act while he is walking around sightseeing, rather than when he is sitting in a moving car,' Johnny suggested. 'If we split up and position ourselves at different points on the tour we'll increase our chances of success.' Johnny hoped this tactic would also make it a lot easier for him to slip away and warn Breitner.

'The station, barracks, City Hall, museum and governor's residence will be too well guarded,' Gavrilo said, studying the route.

'One person may have a better chance of slipping through the cordon and destroying the heir. We should draw lots to decide who,' Trifko said, exchanging a look with Ilic. Johnny thought that Ilic must have got to

Trifko before the meeting, with another idea to divide the group and stop the assassination.

Gavrilo gave no quarter. 'It will be all of us. This can't be an act of a single person, but a collective action of a people taking revenge.' Gavrilo's word's steadied Trifko. 'We will make one concentrated effort while the tyrant is driven through Sarajevo and the gendarmes are most stretched.'

'All of us? Even the other cell?' Johnny said to remind Gavrilo of the concerns they'd discussed previously. 'What do we know of them, other than that they are young and enthusiastic?'

'You cannot use schoolchildren for a job of this kind; it is not right and it will end in a fiasco,' Trifko agreed.

'I have sent for an experienced person to bolster the other cell,' Ilic said.

'Who?' Johnny spoke louder than he'd intended – he'd been angling to fill that role.

'Jovo, you will also join the other cell,' Gavrilo said.

'Gavro, I will ...' Gavrilo cut Johnny off before he could talk of the heroic acts he'd perform.

'That way we will have all the schoolboys together.'

'I don't follow ...' Johnny said.

'I think perhaps they will bolster you.' Gavrilo glared at Johnny. 'I am not convinced that your heart is pure Jovo, not after the way you were dismissed for trifling with the dignity of that poor girl, but there is a role for you in the other cell.' Gavrilo looked away from Johnny in disgust. 'Ilic will let you know when you are needed.'

Chapter 29

Franz Ferdinand watched the mock battle with growing admiration. The army was demonstrating a high degree of morale and efficiency. He nodded to General Potiorek – the governor had done a first-rate job. The simulated battle between the blue and red armies, made up of elements of the 14th and 16th Army Corps was quite a sight, some twenty thousand men fighting across the rugged, wooded terrain of Western Bosnia.

It had been reported to him that the Serbian government viewed these manoeuvres as a dress rehearsal for an invasion of their country, even though they were being conducted well away from their border. The archduke smiled. A fortune teller had once told him that he would unleash a world war. Although these army corps were excellent, whether or not the rest of the army would be in any position to unleash anything other than a superbly executed waltz was another question.

The field exercises that he was currently observing were a simulated attack on Sarajevo from the Adriatic, which the defenders had successfully repulsed. He kicked his horse to follow the stand-in Italians as they were driven back and, thankfully, found that someone had thought to check the correct length for his stirrups. The archduke viewed the Italians as a very real threat; it was well known that they harboured designs on the monarchy's territories of South Tyrol and Trieste.

The archduke stopped to allow the rest of his suite, and the gendarmes assigned to protect him, to catch up. He turned to General Potiorek. 'Truly exceptional, Governor – beyond all commendation.' The governor looked relieved, as well he might. If he'd failed, he would have been lucky to get a command in the swamps of the Eastern frontier, Franz Ferdinand would have seen to that.

'Thank you, Your Highness,' Potiorek beamed, fighting to maintain his hard-bitten professional persona. He'd been under considerable pressure to perform and he'd clearly stood the strain.

'I'll make a full report to the emperor of your excellent preparations,' Franz Ferdinand added. The manoeuvres had indeed been a great achievement; the soldiers were well drilled and the excessive heat that had so worried his Sopherl hadn't transpired. It had mainly rained and there had even been snow. 'In fact, this whole visit has been a success, Governor.'

'Thank you, Your Highness. I trust your accommodation is satisfactory?'

'Very pleasant.' His rooms at the Hotel Bosnia had been extensively decorated with rich carpets and oriental objets d'art. He'd been so impressed that he and Sophie had paid a trip to Sarajevo's bazaar to add to his collection at Konopiste. They'd had a wonderful afternoon exploring the maze of back alleys, full of artisans working at their various crafts, and all the way they'd been followed by an enthusiastic crowd of cheering, loyal subjects.

'I trust Her Highness was pleased with her itinerary, while you've been observing the war games?'

'Yes, very pleased.' Sophie had been engaged to make a number of humanitarian visits, mainly to orphanages – good work which would increase her profile within the monarchy. 'I'm very pleased.'

'I'm gratified, Your Highness. I was afraid that the difficulties you experienced on your journey might have been a bad omen.'

'Yes, we didn't get off to a promising start,' Franz Ferdinand said. The royal couple had been forced to abandon their private railway carriage because an axle had overheated, filling the carriage with steam. 'I thought, now the carriage has broken down, what next – a murder attempt in Sarajevo? And finally, if all of that doesn't get anywhere, an explosion on board my ship on the way home,' the archduke joked. The governor laughed politely. Sophie hadn't found the jest quite so amusing.

'As I boarded the new train the electricity cut out, plunging us into darkness. They had to light candles – I thought I was sitting in a tomb!' he continued.

The archduke heard a sudden cry of alarm and saw a man in an ill-fitting black suit, jump out of a copse and hurry towards him. He stopped just short of Franz Ferdinand, the sun glinting on a black barrel. Franz Ferdinand sat up straight on his horse and faced the man, as a gendarme seized him. The archduke laughed. 'What are you doing? That's the court photographer. Let him go.'

Franz Ferdinand caught the governor openly sighing with relief. The heir apparent was safe.

Chapter 30

Johnny paced around his room, frustrated after the meeting with Gavrilo and the others. He'd spent the rest of Friday and now the best part of Saturday waiting for Ilic to summon him. He wasn't sure what else he could do. It was the eve of the archduke's visit to Sarajevo and he'd been banished from any further discussions with the group. Gavrilo was still insisting that the two cells be kept separate. Johnny got the distinct impression they didn't trust him and he couldn't say he blamed them.

Ilic was certainly playing his cards close to his chest and Johnny had started to feel pretty edgy. He only had a few hours left before he was due to meet Breitner at the governor's residence. A loud knock at the street door had raised Johnny's hopes for an instant; he'd thought that Breitner might have turned up with a posse of gendarmes to arrest the conspirators.

The sound of Mrs Ilic's voice calling for her son soon dashed that idea. It was just a visitor for Danilo, and whoever it was had made a heck of a noise banging around with great clod-hopping feet. Johnny watched from his window as the visitor left and then he glanced impatiently around the room for the thousandth time. He picked up the book of Serbian poetry that Breitner had given him and began to thumb through it.

'It's good to see you using your time wisely, Jovo.' Johnny looked up with a start – Ilic had come in unannounced.

'Do you need me for something, Danilo?' Johnny asked hopefully.

Ilic looked at the book of poetry and nodded. 'Yes, come with me.'

Johnny followed Ilic into his room. Ilic looked decidedly ashen as he pulled the Gladstone bag from under Gavrilo's bed. He took out two bombs and tied them around his waist with a piece of cord.

'What's going on?' Johnny asked.

'I've arranged to meet the second cell,' Ilic answered, putting two guns into the pockets of his jacket and padding them out with newspaper. Johnny assumed that he needed the paper to show the other cell the archduke's route through Sarajevo.

They left the boarding house just after two and strolled through the busy streets of the old town. The rain had started to ease up and Johnny felt a tremendous sense of relief as he enjoyed the first sunshine he'd seen in days. Things were finally starting to happen.

They came out of the old town and passed City Hall. Ilic looked around wearily before steering them towards Bembasa, a quiet district on the edge of the city where the Miljacka river meandered into Sarajevo.

'Are you okay, Danilo?' Johnny asked.

'It is possible the police might have heard about our plans, Jovo.'

'How do you know that?' Johnny asked, trying to keep his voice steady. He was pretty sure that Ilic was just nervous and didn't suspect him of being an interloper who was counting down the minutes before he could betray him – not that Johnny felt much guilt about that. The simple fact was he had a job to do and that job was furthering his career. No matter what, he would not crawl back to Sir George empty-handed.

'Are you going to give me my weapons today?' Johnny asked, but Ilic ignored him. 'Am I to be finally told what the plan is? The tyrant is coming tomorrow, so it might be helpful if I knew what is expected of me.'

Ilic stopped and gave Johnny a stern look. 'We are about to meet the other cell, Jovo. They hold very strong views about the destruction of the Habsburgs and the political unity of the South Slav people and will not be so tolerant of your flippant manner.'

'I'm sorry, Danilo. I did not mean to sound flippant. I'm merely anxious to take action against our oppressors.' Ilic nodded acceptance of Johnny's apology and carried on in silence, brooding no doubt about the rightness of what they were doing.

Ilic led Johnny to a small cafe across the road from a large, tree-filled park on the banks of the river. Two members of the other cell were waiting for them at a table. Johnny recognised them straight away by their black suits and trim moustaches.

Trifko had said that the other cell was made up of schoolboys, but they didn't look that much younger than the others. They were both about sixteen or seventeen and burnt with the passion that only an absolute faith in a cause can give.

'There are only two – where is the third, older one?' Johnny asked Ilic, looking round for a likely suspect.

'He is on his way. I'm meeting him later tonight,' Ilic replied and went to greet the two schoolboys. Johnny swore long and silently to himself; he was going to have to mess about to find out who the last member of the cell was.

The Assassins

'Jovo, this is Cvjetko Popovic and Vaso Cubrilovic. Jovo will be with us tomorrow,' Ilic said as he sat at their table. Johnny greeted them. Popovic seemed the friendlier, with sad, melancholy eyes that had trouble focusing on him. The other one, Cubrilovic, reminded Johnny of Gavrilo in both his physique and intensity of spirit, but he had a slightly more refined manner.

The formalities completed, Ilic turned to the youngest member of the group first. 'Popovic, are you ready to act for our people?'

Popovic didn't blink. 'Through Franz Ferdinand I will revenge myself on those who oppress the Slavs. Let our vengeance serve as a warning to the ruling circles.'

Cubrilovic took up the statement of belief, speaking as earnestly and unflinchingly as Popovic had. 'I consider the heir to be an enemy of the Slavs. He represents the regime which harasses and oppresses my home.'

'Very good.' Ilic couldn't fault their zeal. Unexpectedly Ilic turned to Johnny. 'And you, Jovo. Are you with us?'

Johnny shrugged. 'Yes, I'm as ready as I'll ever be.' That wasn't quite the commitment they were looking for, so he tried to put more guts into his declaration. 'The heir must not be allowed to stand in the way of my dream of freedom.' Ilic couldn't question his depth of feeling – he just didn't know that Johnny had a slightly different dream to the rest of them.

Johnny smiled smugly as Ilic unfolded the newspaper he'd put into his pocket. He had passed all of the tests and the full plan was at last going to be revealed to him. Then, to his horror, Ilic started tearing the newspaper up into strips, and sitting there in the cafe, he poured out grains of what Johnny could only assume must be poison onto the table and wrapped portions of it up in the strips of newspaper.

'This is potassium cyanide. You know what to do with it when the time comes. Dead men tell no secrets.' Ilic passed a sachet to each of them. He was remarkably calm and matter of fact, considering the uncertainty he'd expressed about the assassination.

They left the cafe and headed for the park across the road. Ilic handed Cubrilovic a bomb and a pistol as they ambled through the trees. He produced another Browning automatic as they reached a tunnel.

'Have either of you fired a gun before?'

Cubrilovic and Popovic shook their heads, impressed by the sleek modern design of the weapon. Johnny also indicated that he hadn't fired a gun, so as not to raise any suspicion.

Ilic cocked the pistol. 'Where this hits, no medicine can help.' Ilic fired the gun and the shot echoed loudly down the tunnel. Johnny started to think that maybe he should have taken the bullets after all.

Ilic handed the pistol to Popovic who accepted it with due reverence. Ilic then untied a second bomb from around his waist, told them how to use it and passed it to Popovic.

'Don't I get a weapon?' Johnny asked, feeling slightly bereft. How could he be a conspirator in an assassination plot without either a bomb or a gun?

Ilic waved Johnny's concern aside. 'Do not worry. We all serve the cause in our own way.' Cubrilovic and Popovic grinned at him – they had guns.

*

Breitner decided to take a risk on the weather and left City Hall, walking slowly along Appel Quay, over the cobbles of the Emperor's Bridge to the other side of the city. With a reluctant sigh he trudged past the mosque and started up the hill to the Konak, the traditional residence of Sarajevo's governors since Ottoman times.

Breitner wondered if any of the previous governors had been as obtuse as the present incumbent – he doubted it. He skirted the thick, brick wall that surrounded the Konak. It had proved to be an effective barrier in keeping the governor cut off from what was going on around him, but as he went through the gate, Breitner hoped it wouldn't prove to be so today.

It began to rain again and Breitner swore and quickened his pace towards the residence. It looked like a great, big, baroque layer cake, decorated with orange-brown icing. For luck, he patted one of the stone lions that protected the front of the building, and then he leapt gracefully out of the rain into the pillared porte cochère.

At least if the rain continued, the crowds for the archduke's visit would be reduced, making it easier to spot any would-be assassins, Breitner reflected. Then he braced himself and went inside. He wasn't anticipating an easy interview with Governor Potiorek.

An orderly showed Breitner into a waiting room and not surprisingly there was no sign of the shiftless Englishman. Breitner tried to control his anxiety. He'd called in every favour he could to get on the appointment list – he was going to look a total fool if Johnny didn't turn up.

Breitner opened his pocket watch; it was four o'clock. They had three hours before the governor was due to attend an official dinner in honour of the heir apparent. Breitner had no doubt that the governor would wish to be early, to ensure that all of his meticulous arrangements were precisely executed.

He'd have to stall Potiorek until Johnny arrived. Not a pleasant task, but one he'd rather have than face the full fury of Archduke Franz Ferdinand in person.

*

Preparations were in full swing for the royal visit on the streets of Sarajevo. Roads were being repaired and in response to the lord mayor's proclamation to welcome the royal couple, the citizens of Sarajevo had decorated their houses with the yellow and black of the Austro-Hungarian monarchy.

Ilic led his merry band through the commotion, back past City Hall and down Appel Quay towards the bridges, making the most of the cover the trees on the city side of the embankment gave from the rain. Ilic explained that the embankment had been selected as the place of ambush because the heir had to drive along it twice: once from the station to City Hall for the civic reception, and back again after his tour of the museum, on his way to have lunch at the Konak with Governor Potiorek. At least Johnny had managed to find that much out.

Cubrilovic and Popovic definitely had a certain swagger about them as they promenaded along Appel Quay. They'd passed the Emperor and Lateiner bridges, when a friend of Popovic called to him from the river side of the quay. It took a couple of shouts and Cubrilovic pointing him out before Popovic recognised him. When he did, he very nearly showed his pistol off to his friend, but Ilic just managed to stop him.

Five minutes further up the quay they passed the charity where Johnny had worked. Ilic stopped on the corner of Cumurija Street, where Johnny had stood with Gavrilo, opposite the steel Cumurija Bridge. Johnny looked at the tobacconist's but he still couldn't afford to buy anything.

Ilic addressed them. 'You and the other cell will be placed along a three-hundred-yard killing ground from here to the Emperor's Bridge. Popovic, this is where I want you to stand. Jovo will be with you to act as your eyes, which is why he doesn't need a weapon. If the comrades before you fail, then you will attack. Throw your bomb and then in the confusion finish the tyrant off with your pistol. There will also be someone opposite you on the river side of the embankment, who will attack at the same time. If you can't act when the heir comes past the first time, change positions and try again when he comes back from the museum.'

Popovic was not happy with this arrangement, 'Can we not choose our own positions?'

'This is where I need you, for one concentrated effort. If there are too many policemen here on the day, then you can go to where you choose,' Ilic added conciliatorily.

'Can I not stand with Vaso? I do not know this person,' Popovic asked, eyeing Johnny guardedly.

'You could always wear glasses,' Johnny suggested.

'How could he afford glasses?' Cubrilovic asked.

'I have never worn glasses. If I started on Vidovdan, it would only raise suspicion,' Cubrilovic said.

'Very well, but you need someone. You can't see fourteen yards across the street, Popovic,' Ilic said, then led them past the Austro-Hungarian Bank on the corner and across the narrow stretch of Cumurija Street, where it led onto the embankment. They stopped in front of the adjacent triangular baroque building at the end of Cumurija Street, which appeared to house a doctor's surgery. Johnny had never looked at the front of it before. The bottom half of the building was made up of striped stonework, with a plain brown facade above it, topped by an ornamental gable and an onion spire.

'Cubrilovic, this is where you will be, next to the first in line, who will be just over there.' Ilic indicated a cafe and the old Turkish houses at the end of Cumurija, in the gap between the triangular building and the other new neo-Romantic Austrian buildings on the embankment.

'Where exactly?' Johnny asked. He needed to know the precise positions.

'In front of the Mostar.' Ilic pointed to a wooden picket fence around the cafe's garden. Johnny saw Ilic glance quickly into the garden before turning back to the group.

'Cubrilovic, you are to act as soon as you see the first in line throw his bomb.'

'Who is this first in line?' Cubrilovic asked.

'The most experienced man,' Ilic said. 'He will know when to act.'

Johnny wondered how they were going to coordinate their actions if they didn't know each other. He didn't like to ask, as he hadn't been on the friendliest terms with Ilic since he had accused him of being a traitor.

From what Ilic had said, Johnny supposed Gavrilo and his cell would be further up Appel Quay near the other bridges, but there was no way for him to know for sure. Breitner had said that the priority was to find out who all of the members of this cell were, so Johnny decided to put all his effort into finding this other man. If he was as experienced as Ilic said, he would likely be the most dangerous.

*

Breitner snapped open his pocket watch for the umpteenth time. It was nearly five o'clock and Johnny still hadn't arrived. He stood up and began to move impatiently about the waiting room, prompting the officer of the guard, who was busy writing lists of lists, to make a huffing noise. Breitner ignored him – it was because of bureaucratic fools like him that he was in this situation.

Breitner had expected the archduke's visit to be cancelled. There had been numerous warnings about the threat posed by nationalist organisations to the archduke, should he come to Bosnia, which had been issued to both Governor Potiorek and Vienna. Consequently, Breitner hadn't been overly concerned about Johnny's apparent lack of progress infiltrating the Young Bosnia cell over the past few weeks. It took time to establish oneself with people like that and he wasn't convinced that Johnny was up to the task. He'd been pleasantly surprised not to have read about the murder of some nameless youth in his morning reports. However, when it became blatantly clear that the visit wasn't going to be cancelled, what had started out as an experiment to try and flush out a group of possible assassins had become the last line of defence, and all that stood between his world and catastrophe.

The Hofburg elite didn't seem to care whether or not Franz Ferdinand was killed in Sarajevo; he was universally disliked and considered to be something of an ogre. They probably believed that cancelling the heir's visit would only have provoked his anger – a view Breitner could sympathise with.

Breitner had heard through his old colleagues in the Intelligence Bureau that the warnings from the police, consular officials in Serbia and military intelligence which had been pouring into the Interior, Foreign and Military ministries in Vienna had been ignored or lost in the massive bureaucratic muddle of the Austro-Hungarian monarchy.

There was a general distaste for information gathered through intelligence sources, not least because Austrian agents had inadvertently provided forged documents that had become the basis for two recent high-profile trials. Breitner believed that the forgeries had been produced by

Serbian intelligence and passed on through a double agent, as part of an operation to stir up trouble and embarrass the Austro-Hungarian government. The ensuing scandal undoubtedly caused Vienna to cripple intelligence gathering activities in the Balkans.

The considered view of the foreign ministry was that the Serbian government and its army were more concerned with fighting each other than staging an operation against the heir, regardless of what any extremist splinter groups might attempt. The foreign ministry had even asked for the colour-coded ribbons that were put around the warnings to be changed from red to the standard yellow and black. The ministry of the interior argued that Bosnia was not within its area of responsibility. His own superior at the joint ministry of finance, Count Bilinski, whose responsibility it certainly fell under, had washed his hands of the visit as a purely military matter.

At the local level, Count Carlo Gallas, the chief of the Bosnian government's political department, had told General Potiorek of the growing militancy of the Young Bosnians' societies.

Count Gallas had even drafted a report on the subject in the previous year, which Breitner had contributed to. Dr Gerde, the chief of the Sarajevo police, had tried to advise both Potiorek and the military committee about the incendiary nature of the heir visiting on Serbia's patron saint's day. All of these warnings were ignored.

The person who created the biggest stir was Dr Sunaric, the Croat vice president of the Bosnian parliament, who'd urged Potiorek to cancel the archduke's visit because of possible Young Bosnia activity. He'd even attempted to go over the governor's head and telegraphed Count Bilinski directly, which caused a certain degree of indignation, but ultimately, like all of the other warnings, this had been dismissed as being the pessimism of doom and gloom merchants. Unlike other areas of the empire, there had been no violence specifically attributed to nationalism in Bosnia.

Some concessions had been made to security: all of Sarajevo's schools had been closed since the middle of June, and any student who wasn't a resident of Sarajevo had been expelled. The border controls were also more strictly enforced and strangers coming into Sarajevo were to be monitored. However, Breitner knew that that hadn't stopped Gavrilo and his cell from crossing the border or organising their plot.

The police were also allowed to face the crowd, rather than the heir, during the visit, to scan for any potential assassins lurking in the shadows.

That didn't change the fact that there were only 120 gendarmes to provide security for a city of over 50,000 people. Bringing in additional policeman from Budapest was deemed to be too expensive, as all of the budget had gone on building a chapel for the royal couple in their hotel.

There was talk of bringing additional police from the surrounding areas, but even so there was still a lot of ground to cover, unless of course Breitner could tell them exactly who the assassins were and where they were likely to be – which he couldn't do if Johnny didn't turn up. Breitner flipped open his pocket watch again.

Chapter 31

Johnny rhythmically turned his last crown over. He was loath to spend it, but he had to show that he wasn't a vagrant. A waiter was coming to his table for the third time, expecting to take his order. Johnny made a performance of looking embarrassed and eventually shrugging, he told the man that he was waiting for a girl, who was late, and that he didn't want to order until she arrived.

The waiter wasn't particularly sympathetic, but went away. Johnny glanced through a gap in the café's picket fence. Ilic was still sitting in the garden, reading *The Seven to be Hanged*.

He'd finished his briefing next to the Mostar Cafe, which Johnny thought was curious. It would have made more sense to start at the cafe, where the first in line would be standing and then to work his way up along the route the archduke would take. Ilic would then have finished his instructions nearer to the boarding house.

When Ilic dismissed the cell, Johnny stayed back and discreetly followed him into the cafe and found a table, partly hidden by the cafe's picket fence. He was banking on the fact that Ilic would be meeting the third member of the cell, so that he could tell him where to stand for the attack on the archduke.

Although Johnny couldn't account for Ilic's eccentricities (he might just have been enjoying the sunshine), he had no choice other than to wait and watch him make notes in his book. Johnny put the coin back in his pocket and hoped the waiter would think he looked suitably desperate to be waiting for a girl – who would never turn up.

*

Breitner was eventually summoned by Lieutenant Colonel Erich von Merizzi, Governor Potiorek's aide-de-camp. 'I understand you wish to see His Excellency, the Governor.' Von Merizzi spoke without looking up from his work.

'Yes, sir.' Breitner stood to attention and adopted a brisk, military tone.

'You may not be aware of this, Breitner, but we are currently hosting the heir to the throne. The governor is extremely busy attending to his needs.'

'It is a matter of the utmost urgency, sir.'

The colonel slowly looked up from his desk, trying to understand how a junior bureaucrat could possibly have anything of interest to say to the governor.

'Oh come now – aren't you being a little over dramatic, Herr Breitner?'

'It concerns His Imperial and Royal Highness, sir.'

'You're the fellow who was friends with Redl?' Von Merizzi made it sound as if Breitner was guilty of all manner of corruption and treachery.

'Colonel Redl was my superior in the Intelligence Bureau,' Breitner said flatly. Along with his fall from grace he'd come to accept that people would be suspicious of him. Breitner had worked closely with Redl for years, and like everyone else in the Intelligence Bureau, had had no idea that he spied for the Russians, or that he entertained young officers in a lavish boudoir.

Breitner had resigned his commission in the army at the first hint of scandal, but the disgrace to the Kaisersrock, the imperial uniform, would always be there. Nothing Breitner could do would wash the stain from that most revered symbol of imperial honour and duty.

'Don't you just fetch and carry for the joint ministry of finance?' Von Merizzi was stunned that Breitner, of all people, had the gall to seek an interview with the governor.

'I believe the governor is personally supervising every detail of the archduke's visit, sir, including tonight's official dinner for the heir apparent at the Hotel Bosnia.'

'That is correct.'

'I've been approached by an intermediary from one of the dignitaries attending tonight's evening meal. He raised some concerns about the menu, which I urgently need to discuss with His Excellency.'

'Good God man, what are you saying?' The colonel was beside himself. Franz Ferdinand's visit was a make or break issue for any serious, career-minded officer.

'It has been suggested that perhaps there should be a local delicacy on the menu, aside from the fish of course. It could be interpreted as an insult to the loyal subjects of Bosnia if something produced locally wasn't offered to His Imperial and Royal Highness.'

'I see.' Von Merizzi looked ruffled. 'This is appalling. Consolidating local support for the monarchy is key to maintaining a stable government in the province.'

'Yes sir, after some not inconsiderable wrangling and negotiation I managed to reach a compromise on a local wine being served – a Zilavka.' Breitner paused. 'If I could have the governor's approval for its addition to the wine list, and perhaps a letter of authorisation to ensure delivery, then the loyalty of our subject people can be assured. At dinner at least.'

'Yes, quite,' von Merizzi said, ringing the bell for his orderly.

*

The waiter had given up trying to take Johnny's order and had started to smirk at him, which rankled Johnny more than the attempts to move him on. Princip had turned up, which had appeared promising for a while, until he and Ilic started to argue, no doubt about the assassination. They gave no indication that they would be doing anything other than arguing for the rest of the day.

Johnny was on the verge of giving up and going to meet Breitner when a tall man sailed into the cafe garden and greeted Ilic. The man looked a few years older than the other members of the group Johnny had met, which fitted in with what Ilic had told him about the third man.

When Ilic finally left with the stranger, Johnny decided to chance it. He shrugged a goodbye to the waiter, before hurrying after Ilic and the tall man. He followed them up Cumurija Street, towards the centre of the city. He saw Ilic hand the man a metal object, the size of a half-decent hip flask and mime how to use it. Johnny smiled; he'd found the last man.

He continued to trail after them as they walked through the square in front of the Catholic cathedral and watched as they proceeded to the Hotel Sarajevo. He waited a minute then followed them into the hotel, taking out his last carefully hoarded crown.

*

Breitner focused on the gold, floral decoration on the ceiling of General Potiorek's study. Even though he was standing, Breitner felt a little like Sigmund Freud giving a consultation. He looked down at General Potiorek, staring impatiently at him as he reclined on a green and red chaise longue. The governor's close-cropped hair and neatly trimmed moustache added to the severity and dignity of his manner. General Potiorek was the very embodiment of the Austrian military, even in his shirt sleeves. Breitner had evidently disturbed him while he was resting.

'It was very good of you to see me, Your Excellency.'

'Yes, yes – what do you want?' The governor regarded him coldly. He reminded Breitner of the commandant of his military academy. They both

The Assassins

made him feel like an outsider, a Hungarian and a Jew, although he was never sure if either title fitted him. Breitner's parents had converted to Catholicism and fully assimilated into the Magyar way of life, going so far as to send their youngest son off to do his duty as an officer cadet.

The only true identity Breitner had ever felt was that of a soldier. He loved the discipline and ritual of the army. When he joined the Intelligence Bureau of the general staff, Breitner thought he'd found a place where he could actually belong. Under the guidance of Colonel Redl, a fellow outsider from the east of the monarchy, Breitner learnt counter-intelligence, the work he was born to do.

After Redl was exposed as a spy and Breitner had been banished, the only thing he had left was his sense of duty. Duty was his life raft in an ever volatile and unpredictable world, even if that meant further sacrificing what was left of his career for 'the ogre'. He wondered if maybe that was why he had an affinity with the strange Englishman. They were both looking for approval from men who would never give it.

'Your Excellency, I must urge you to cancel tomorrow's royal visit. I believe His Imperial and Royal Highness Archduke Franz Ferdinand will be in mortal danger if he comes to Sarajevo.'

The governor was speechless for a moment; the absurdity of Breitner's statement was beyond his comprehension. Breitner really did feel as if he was psychoanalysing Potiorek. The governor had cut himself off so completely from what was happening outside the walls of his residence that he had no way of understanding the danger he faced, irrational or otherwise.

'Herr Breitner, you are aware that the manoeuvres were shortened from four days to two? Not to mention that the scale of the archducal visit was significantly reduced.'

'Yes, Excellency.' Breitner knew the governor had planned a much longer visit for the archduke, complete with excursions and shooting parties.

'There was even uncertainty about whether or not the archduke would make the visit, right up until the last minute. In spite of that, the manoeuvres were a tremendous success. The archduke is extremely pleased and you want me to cancel the crowning glory of his visit?'

'There's a clear threat to the archduke, from ...'

Potiorek cut him off. 'You people see phantoms everywhere.' Governor Potiorek had given the same response to the local police when they'd tried to warn him of the possible dangers to the heir. 'There has never been any significant political unrest here, Breitner.'

'Your Excellency, an agent of mine has infiltrated a Young Bosnia cell, here in Sarajevo. If I could have a detachment of gendarmes I can arrest them now without any effect on the royal visit.' Not an ideal solution, he reflected – he wouldn't get all of the conspirators, but it might be the best he could manage.

'Breitner, you have no power to act in a military matter. Your involvement is neither desired nor needed.'

This was precisely the situation Breitner had been trying to avoid. Without Johnny, all he had was hearsay and supposition. 'Excellency, these fanatics mean to commit a terrible outrage on the streets of your city.'

'And do you have any evidence of that? Preferably something that isn't one of the forgeries you cloak-and-dagger people like to produce.'

'My agent can provide details of the plan and the names of the conspirators – when he gets here.' Breitner snapped open his watch, trying to suppress his impotent rage.

*

Johnny slowed his pace as he approached the Europa Hotel. Its pavement cafe was teeming with people and he realised that it must be about teatime by now. He didn't have much time to order his thoughts. He looked through the mixed group of patrons in traditional and modern dress, enjoying Viennese cakes and coffee. Framed against the old covered market on the corner, it was like a view of two worlds merging into one. He was coming to the end of Franz Joseph Street and it was just a matter of rounding the corner, crossing Lateiner Bridge and then a short stroll to the governor's residence. He still wasn't sure how he was going to get the maximum amount of credit for all this when he reported to the governor.

Johnny had successfully managed to get the name of the last man, Mehmed Mehmedbasic; with the right inducement a maid at the Hotel Sarajevo had been more than happy to help Johnny. He was now penniless on the streets of a foreign land, with one last chance to redeem himself.

An elegant woman stepped out of the hotel in front of him without any thought of where she was going and started to raise a parasol. The graceful, fluid movement felt somehow familiar. Johnny glanced around as he passed her and found himself face to face with the girl he'd thought would never turn up.

'Ah, there you are Johnny,' she said casually, as if he was just late for tea.

Johnny was dumbfounded for a moment, as his two worlds collided. 'Libby, where have you been?'

Libby stepped closer, covering Johnny with her parasol and bringing him into her realm. 'Where have I been? I've been scouring the streets of this frightful place for a week trying to find you.'

'A week? I've been here for nearly a month!' She'd been fluttering about Vienna with her coffee house fops, while he'd been subjecting himself to all manner of danger and degradation, he thought irritably.

'Well you know how it is, Johnny.' Her green eyes smiled whimsically and his antagonism faded.

Johnny had to get away before she totally overwhelmed him. 'I'm sorry but I'm in a hurry. I'll come and find you at the spa tonight.'

'I can't go back there. The hotel's been commandeered for that blasted royal visit. I'm staying here now.' Libby waved vaguely at the Hotel Europa.

'Well then, I'll come back here.' Johnny stepped out from under her parasol.

'Where do you think you're going? I can't believe you'd just abandon me now I've finally found you,' Libby said mockingly. She never needed anyone, least of all him.

'I'm sorry Libby, it's vital I go now.' If he missed his chance with the governor Breitner would take all the glory and he'd never get out of here.

'I trust you haven't forgotten that you owe my husband a considerable sum of money?' Her well-bred features became hard.

'What can I do about that now? We're not exactly in Monte Carlo.'

Libby gave him a patient look. 'Now that the manoeuvres have finished the local gambling dens are going to be awash with money as eager young officers throw away their pay, desperate for a few hours' amusement.'

'Manoeuvres – what manoeuvres? I really have to go.'

'The manoeuvres – the reason for the archduke's visit.'

Johnny wondered how Sir George would react if he knew that Johnny had put the heir to the Austro-Hungarian throne's life in danger to go off gambling with his wife. It wouldn't surprise him, in fact he would probably expect it. Johnny was determined to prove him wrong for once. He wouldn't let Libby distract him this time. 'I can't do all that now. I'll come and find you later.'

'You promised to win the money back, Johnny and win it back you shall.'

'Libby, I've got nothing.'

'When has that ever stopped us?' Johnny felt the call of the wild. He could hear the ball spinning, feel the nausea as it dropped and the anguish of it landing in the wrong pocket.

'I haven't had much luck recently, Libby.'

'Don't worry about that. I'm sure we can turn things around.' Libby's green eyes sparkled. The first time he'd seen her at an embassy garden party, she'd been a force of nature, a maelstrom at the centre of everything, effortlessly bending servants and guests alike to her will.

Johnny wondered if he'd told Breitner enough about the assassination plot to get the royal visit cancelled. Breitner knew that there were people running around the city with guns and bombs; there wasn't much Johnny could add to that.

If he were to pay the money back, that could well be enough to placate Sir George. However, for the sake of his future career, it would be better to have a letter of commendation from the heir to the Austro-Hungarian throne to complete his report.

'Can't we do it tomorrow? I need to get a few more documents to complete my report.'

'Your report! You're refusing to help me for the sake of your beastly report?'

'You told me to do a good job. Besides it isn't just a report, it's ...'

'Johnny, all of the troops will be gone tomorrow; they've been ordered out of the city for the royal visit,' she said, interrupting him.

Johnny saw her dilemma. He knew Breitner was a capable man – he could get the visit cancelled and Johnny thought he could call round to see him on Monday, tell him who all of the conspirators were and pick up his letter of commendation and whatever other rewards the Austro-Hungarian monarchy chose to bestow on him.

Libby sealed it with a suggestive look. 'I have some new tricks I want to share with you.' It wasn't meant to be seductive, but a command from the head girl. Johnny, grinned. He really did find Libby's direct approach so much easier to negotiate than the coy, will-o'-the-wisp performance of the belly dancer.

*

Breitner watched from the study window as it brightened into a pleasant summer's evening. The rain had long since died away and no amount of praying could bring it back. Providence wasn't on his side today.

'Where is your spy, Herr Breitner?' The governor was becoming progressively more frustrated with every passing minute. It was plain that he hadn't believed a word of what Breitner had told him and was anxious to get to his dinner with the archduke.

'I can only apologise, Excellency. He may have been killed. His work is extremely dangerous.'

'I think we've had quite enough of your flights of fancy for one evening, Herr Breitner.'

Breitner sighed – a first-hand account of someone who'd been living for weeks with the Young Bosnians, seen the weapons and been part of their plans may have made all the difference, or perhaps the governor would simply have dismissed Johnny as casually as he had all the other evidence Breitner had presented.

He'd considered trying to arrest Princip and Ilic on his own. He'd managed it with Johnny, but these people had bombs and guns and without any support Breitner could well cause an incident that would warn all the conspirators that the authorities were on to them. Breitner felt the best thing to do was to get Sunday's visit cancelled and then deal with the assassins. 'Could we at least move the royal visit? The 28 June is the Serbs' patriotic day. As Sarajevo's chief of police has been at great pains to point out, it can only be provocative for the heir to visit on that day.'

The governor reddened. 'I've been through this umpteen times already. There may well be safety issues, and because of that the more people who see the archduke, the greater our victory. It might well alienate some of the Serbs, but it will also inspire and encourage the Muslims and Croats who support the monarchy.'

'I understand that, Excellency and commend your far-sightedness.'

'Oh you do, do you?' the governor replied, dryly.

'If I may just point out that this year's Vidovdan celebrations are of special significance because the Serbian Army has recaptured Kosovo from the Turks after hundreds of years of occupation. As I'm sure you're aware, Vidovdan commemorates their great defeat by the Turks, at the battle of Kosovo.'

'Enough – the date is just one aspect of the myriad of details we've had to contend with for the archducal visit. It must be tomorrow; the spa season starts next week and making any further arrangements is quite impossible.'

Breitner couldn't believe what he was hearing. The weapons were under Princip's bed, barely a mile away and the governor was worrying about the spa season. 'The Young Bosnians are not concerned about scheduling problems; they will only see this as an insult by an imperialist power.'

'I will not ask the heir to the Austro-Hungarian throne to cancel his visit because a gang of half-starved juvenile delinquents might be upset by it!' A polite knock at the door stopped the governor before he could continue, and his valet entered through an adjoining door from the master bedroom, carrying a dress uniform jacket. Breitner decided to change track.

'Your Excellency, could we at least use some of the troops from the manoeuvres as extra security?' Breitner suspected a lot of them would probably have been granted leave by now, or be in camp at the manoeuvre site, but it was worth a try.

'Out of the question. I've ordered all troops not involved in the heir's visit out of the city. A strong military presence would offend the citizens of Sarajevo. Besides, the soldiers don't have their dress uniforms.' The valet started to brush down General Potiorek's jacket.

'Could they not wear their normal service uniforms?' Breitner was pushing his luck to the verge of destruction, but this was the best chance he had of averting a disaster. 'There is also a battalion of soldiers in barracks, here in Sarajevo.'

'Herr Breitner, I understand you were once well thought of, in Budapest at least, but I do not put much stock in your wild theories and marketplace gossip.'

The governor stood up. There were more important matters to consider. 'Now what is this I hear about the wine list?'

Breitner sighed. It was time for the last resort. 'It might be diplomatic to have Zilavka, a local wine, served at the meal tonight – keep the natives happy.'

The governor at last showed some concern. ''You will organise it personally?'

'Yes, Excellency.'

'Good. That may well redress the balance sufficiently for me to overlook this little outburst of yours.' The governor allowed his valet to help him into the dress jacket, ready for the evening's events. 'My ADC will see to your letter of authorisation.'

As he bowed his thanks to the governor, Breitner hid the unease he was feeling. He would do his duty and go to Ilidze spa and approach 'the ogre' directly.

Chapter 32

Johnny waited patiently for Libby to finish locking the door of her hotel room and went in for his *coup de grâce*, picking her up and swinging her round towards the bed. He hadn't realised just how much he'd missed her until he tasted the violets on her lips again.

'What are these new tricks you promised?' Johnny asked.

'No, no – bath time,' Libby said sharply, and gracefully disentangled herself from his grasp. 'What on earth are you wearing, Johnny?' Libby grabbed the lapels of the battered jacket Breitner had given him and pulled it off his shoulders. 'Oh never mind, I'll ring down for something. The moustache can stay – I rather like it.'

Johnny didn't argue and got undressed while she ran the bath. From past experience he assumed that this whole performance was some type of head girl foreplay, and after the past few weeks with barely more than the clothes he stood up in, a nice long soak with Libby sounded just the thing.

However, much to Johnny's disappointment, she fended him off as he fumbled with the fastenings of her dress. 'Johnny, we haven't got time for this nonsense. I've got so much to tell you. I've had an incredible week touring Sarajevo's brothels and gambling dens.'

'So you haven't actually been "scouring the streets" looking for me?' he asked sarcastically. It didn't surprise him.

'Don't be a bore. Where else was I going to look for you?' Libby asked, pushing him into the bath.

'You could have gone to the Ilidze spa as we arranged,' Johnny said, but he couldn't really fault her reasoning.

'As it happens, I did go there ... for a while. I met a splendid old gentleman who knew the lie of the land.' Libby made a few tentative strokes with a scrubbing brush. 'A retired general from the British Army, no less.'

'Oh, really? How nice for you,' Johnny said brusquely – that didn't really surprise him either.

'Yes, it was actually,' she replied. 'He's touring Europe's spas, desperate to find a cure for his gout, biliousness and all of the other blights that affect those fortunate enough to have lived a life of hedonism and vice.'

'Honestly, Libby, for a sensible woman your head is very easily turned.' Her gushing tone annoyed Johnny. All he'd managed to accomplish was a minor, rather irritating flirtation with a belly dancer.

'Don't be ridiculous, Johnny. My general's far too old and infirm to inconvenience me with anything like that. Besides, we had far more important things to worry about.'

Johnny wasn't sure he believed Libby. This general sounded a kindred spirit to his uncle, who was far from infirm: fortified with brandy he was capable of anything. For all Johnny knew, this general may even have been his uncle, blundering through the backwoods of Europe, one eye on a popsy and the other looking out for 'the boy'.

The thought gave Johnny hope as Libby scoured the skin off his back. 'You wouldn't believe how much the soldiers are paid out here. They're considered to be on active service and are paid as such. Not to mention all their admin chaps and support staff.'

'How interesting.' The last thing Johnny needed was a lecture on the pay and conditions of the Austro-Hungarian military.

'But don't you see what that means?' she said, increasing the brutality of her brushing.

'I'm not getting a job in the ...' Libby cut him off with a sharp backhand smash with the scrubbing brush.

'Don't interrupt. Apparently, there were no brothels in Bosnia until the Austrians and Hungarians came. Can you believe it? Now there are thousands of camp followers of every description, come from all corners of the monarchy to provide the type of diversions soldiers need. The Austro-Hungarian authorities have even colour-coded the brothels according to rank.'

Johnny understood then why Princip had been so worried about the corrupting influence of Austro-Hungarian rule.

'Sarajevo's a boom town at the best of times Johnny, but with the manoeuvres it's a bloody gold rush. The city's swarming with nearly two army corps' worth of officers, bursting at the seams with money and ripe for the picking.' Libby stopped scrubbing and, lost in excitement, began to wave her arms about dramatically as she spoke. 'I had a little flutter at roulette while my general was showing me around some of the more choice establishments.'

'Don't tell me you broke your general and now you need me to ... what? I've got no money, Libby. I'm no use to you,' Johnny said, trying to rub his stinging back.

'No, you see, that's where you're wrong, Johnny. You're just the hapless fool I need. I've managed to put together a reasonable stake, but I need a player. I did have an Austrian officer lined up, but you're much better. Just the sort of lumbering great oaf who wins a fortune and nobody suspects anything other than blind luck.' Johnny flinched as she resumed her scrubbing.

'But I never win, Libby, not at roulette anyway. The game defies strategy and reason.' Johnny grabbed the brush and pulled her towards him – he'd had enough. 'Now, about these new tricks of yours?'

'What if I told you that roulette wasn't altogether a game of chance, and that you can in fact predict the numbers that are going to come up, without using one of your brilliant strategies?'

Johnny let the brush slip through his fingers. Libby had tapped his other overwhelming base desire.

*

Breitner was relieved to see that Franz Ferdinand was in good humour and enjoying the fine dinner which Governor Potiorek had organised at the Hotel Bosnia in the company of more than forty local dignitaries, all of whom were showing due deference to the heir and his consort.

The dining room windows had been thrown open so that 'The Blue Danube' could flow around the diners, carried in on the evening breeze from the Sarajevo garrison band out on the lawn below.

Breitner marvelled at General Potiorek's meticulous attention to detail, which ensured the comfort and entertainment of the heir apparent, if not his personal safety.

Breitner had used the letter of authority from the governor's office to deliver the wine, which caused some consternation for the wine waiter. He felt badly for the man as he had to rush about making last-minute changes to the menu, but Breitner had needed a reason to be at the hotel, and using the local wine may even have helped to cement the loyalty of the local population.

The meal had begun with cream soup, a soufflé and local trout, followed by a main course of chicken, lamb, and beef with asparagus and salad, and

The Assassins

was finishing with pineapple cream and burning brandy, a cheese selection and ice creams and sweets, all of which were complemented by a dry Madeira, several clarets, a Rhine wine, champagne and Breitner's favourite, Hungarian Tokay. He could almost taste its rich, honeyed nectar.

He had observed from the wings as each new course was served, trying to gauge Franz Ferdinand's reaction. He was there ostensibly to answer any questions the guests might have about the Zilavka. Not that he could tell them much, except that it was a white wine which you could buy by the case, at short notice. He watched with some trepidation as the Zilavka was served. Fortunately, the archduke seemed to enjoy it without question, as did everyone else.

If the archduke stayed in such good spirits, Breitner thought that he might be able to approach him without too much fear. He began to turn his thoughts to the problem of what he'd actually say to him. He still had very little proof that there was going to be an assassination attempt; the heir presumptive had already ignored the previous warnings, and without the governor's endorsement it would be difficult to persuade him to cancel his visit to Sarajevo.

The room suddenly went quiet. One of the diners, happy in his cups, had made an inappropriate comment. Not quite realising what he'd said, the unfortunate guest looked around in shock and then seeing that all eyes were on the heir apparent, he addressed his comments directly to the archduke. 'I know Your Highness takes an active interest in such matters ... I was merely commenting on whether or not Count Tisza would fall into line with policy in the Austrian half of the dual monarchy?'

Breitner took a step back; he knew exactly how the archduke would respond. 'All the difficulties which we have in the monarchy arise exclusively from the so-called noble and gentlemanly Magyar – that most infamous, anti-dynastic, lying, unreliable fellow!' The archduke shouted in rage across the table at the local dignitaries, including several Hungarian civil servants.

'None is worse than that scoundrel prime minster of theirs, Tisza, who is a dictator in Budapest and would like to be the same in Vienna. All of the current problems in the monarchy are down to the Magyar.'

Breitner choked back his indignation. The archduke's attack had deeply offended him, but he remained determined to do his duty. Franz Ferdinand would after all, one day be the king of those infamous, anti-dynastic, lying, unreliable fellows.

'The ogre' had been woken and Breitner knew that he would never be able to approach Franz Ferdinand directly now, as the archduke wouldn't listen to anything anyone had to say. Not that Breitner was a Magyar aristocrat, far from it. He was perhaps something worse in the archduke's eyes – a fake or 'pinchbeck' Magyar.

Breitner looked around the stunned guests for a possible intermediary. He considered General Conrad von Hötzendorf, the Chief of Staff, as he'd known him in the old days, but the combination of the both of them approaching the archduke might bring back memories better left forgotten. Breitner's eyes finally came to rest on the only woman present, Her Highness the Duchess Sophie of Hohenberg. She'd been seated away from her husband, between the Orthodox and Catholic bishops, and was attempting to politely continue her conversation with them after her husband's eruption. Breitner knew from his contacts in Vienna that Sophie held reservations about the visit to Bosnia, reservations he might well be able to exploit.

*

Johnny began to dress for an evening at the casino while Libby explained her new trick. 'You must have heard of the man who broke the bank at Monte Carlo?'

'I know the song. It's your favourite,' Johnny answered, putting on his new shirt. The arms were a bit long but it was the best the hotel could manage at short notice.

Libby grabbed his shirt sleeve and started to put in his cufflinks. 'You haven't heard of Joseph Jaggers – and you call yourself a gambler?'

'I don't call myself a gambler, Libby. If anything I'm a sportsman.' That made Libby laugh.

'Oh, really, Johnny. You'll be calling yourself a gentleman next.' She finished putting on the cufflinks and began to struggle with his collar.

Johnny grinned and attempted a West Country burr. He liked to play at being the humble servant to her corrupting mistress of the house. 'I ain't no gentleman, right and proper. Just a humble civil servant true enough, but I'm the best you'll ever get.'

'That blatantly isn't true, is it, Johnny?' Libby smiled patiently. It was a tired old joke. 'Anyway, the point is that Joseph Jaggers was a mill engineer. He recorded and studied the results of roulette wheel spins in Monte Carlo.'

'Why would someone do something so pointlessly dull?' Johnny asked, putting on his trousers. The waist was too big, making him feel like a clown.

'Mr Jaggers wanted to identify if the roulette wheels had a "bias".'

'I think we both know roulette wheels have a bias, towards me anyway.' He was starting to think this whole thing might be some elaborate ploy to make a fool of him.

'A bias is a mechanical error in a roulette wheel that prevents it from depositing the ball in a random pocket when it's spun. So if there are thirty-seven pockets on a roulette wheel, you have a one-in-thirty-seven chance of the ball landing in the pocket you have bet on. But if the wheel has a bias or fault, it lands on certain pockets with more frequency than the others, shortening the odds. You of course have to know *which* pockets.'

'Which of course, *you* do.' Johnny didn't believe any of it.

'Yes, with a little help from my general. How do you think I got our stake?'

'I'm sure your general was most obliging,' Johnny said struggling with his bow tie.

'Johnny, really!' Libby snatched the tie away from him and fastened it roughly around his neck.

'Libby, this is absolute tosh. I'm not going to get carried away on your gambling mania again.'

'Mr Jagger won fourteen-thousand pounds in one night, which, of course, was considered to be a lot of money forty years ago, but it's still not to be sniffed at.' Libby smiled. 'You are adorable when you're confused, dearest.'

'That can't possibly be true.' A win that big could set them up for life, Johnny realised.

'You've heard, "The Man Who Broke the Bank in Monte Carlo" – it's performed in music halls, so it has to be true," Libby said mockingly, while forcing him into badly fitting tails. 'My general and I have spent the past three nights in the officers' club with the faulty wheel and I'm absolutely positive.'

'How can you be sure after three nights?'

'I was confirming what my general had already discovered. He's spent weeks observing the roulette wheels.'

'But this is fantastic. Why isn't everyone doing it?'

Libby smiled, reminding Johnny of a Venus flytrap. 'Because most casinos use new wheels which are less prone to the fault, and they rebalance and realign them regularly. Or they move the wheels around so you don't know which one has the fault, or they change the numbering on the pockets. The staff who run the officers' club might not even know the wheel's faulty, or they might think that the people in this backwater, most of whom have never set foot in a casino before, are either too honourable or too stupid to exploit the fault.' Libby smiled acidly, 'Which of course, is where someone like you comes in.'

'Because your general won't use the bias? He's a real sportsman who believes in fair play.' Johnny had heard of such people, when he was a schoolboy.

'Yes, that, and I asked him not to. You'd be surprised what men do when I ask them.'

'No I wouldn't,' he said wryly.

*

Nedjo Cabrinovic saw Princip as he turned onto the embankment. Coughing, Nedjo quickened his pace. He was late and knew Gavro would be annoyed, but it couldn't be helped. There had been a terrible row at home. His house lay on the route the tyrant would take along Franz Joseph Street and his father had been so desperate to show his loyalty to the Hapsburgs, that he was going to fly the imperial flag from their home.

Nedjo had resorted to hiding the flagpoles, but after much frantic searching it became clear that his father blamed his mother for their disappearance. Nedjo had been forced to tell him where they were before matters became violent.

'Where have you been?' Princip asked, as Nedjo caught up with him. His sharp tone annoyed Nedjo and he shrugged indifferently.

'We're meeting at eight o'clock tomorrow morning, in the pastry shop on Cumurija Street. Don't be late,' Princip told him, with a hint of scorn.

'So we are to act on Vidovdan?' Nedjo asked. His exclusion from the preparations had left him feeling slighted, but at least now he would be able to prove himself a hero on such an important day.

'We are,' Princip replied. As they walked along by the river, he told him the plan, leaving out one vital detail.

'What about my weapons?' Nedjo hadn't seen them since Gavro and Trifko disarmed him, during the trip from Belgrade.

'What of them? Did you risk bringing them across the border?' Princip asked.

'No, but I would have, had you not ...'

'You will receive your weapon tomorrow, if you turn up,' Princip growled, interrupting Nedjo. 'Here take this.' Gavro passed him a twist of newspaper.

'What is it?'

'Dead men tell no secrets,' Gavro said and hurried away.

Nedjo returned home in a dark mood and watched in disgust as his father decorated their house with the hated yellow and black flag. Was it any wonder Princip and his friends didn't trust him and thought he was incapable of action, he reflected angrily.

'How can you bend your knee to these people, Father?'

Vaso Cabrinovic shook his head in annoyance. In his view he was merely being practical. He brushed his son's idealism aside. 'You live under the emperor and you're enjoying all the benefits he provides, Nedeljko. If you don't like living under my roof you can always go somewhere else.'

'Don't you see how you betray our people?'

'You're betraying our people Nedeljko, keeping them in the dark ages, with idiotic dreams.'

His father's words provoked a coughing fit in Nedjo. This man, who everyone called a police informant, who put his livelihood before his freedom and that of his people, thought *him* a traitor.

Nedjo managed to control his coughing and looked at the blood on his hands, 'Tomorrow, on Vidovdan, we shall see who is and who is not a traitor,' he said quietly. He had nothing left to lose.

*

After dinner, Archduke Franz Ferdinand and his consort repaired to the hotel foyer to hold court and engage their guests in small talk.

Breitner stood as near as he dared and surveyed the scene. This was the place where the whole thing had started for him, when he had press-ganged Johnny into this ridiculous situation.

The duchess was proudly telling the guests that Max, her eldest son, had passed an examination. Breitner knew she wasn't liked at court and was seen as something of a scheming outsider, which from his perspective made her a perfect ally.

Unfortunately, Breitner wasn't an invited guest and had no business addressing a member of the imperial family. He'd never get through the invisible cordon of aides and hangers on. What he needed was the support of one of the local dignitaries.

Governor Potiorek shoved past Breitner as he fluttered about the more important guests, asking them to disregard the controversial comments concerning Magyars which the archduke had made at dinner. The governor approached Doctor Sunaric, the leader of the Bosnian parliament.

Doctor Sunaric had made himself notorious as a doom and gloom merchant in the warnings he'd given about the royal visit, going so far as to telegraph his feelings to Vienna. Potiorek took the opportunity to remind the good doctor that the royal visit had been a tremendous success, despite his warnings and the archduke's colourful outburst.

When Governor Potiorek moved on to the next dignitary, Breitner took a chance and sidled up to Sunaric.

'Yes, what is it?' The doctor asked, trying to keep his temper. Potiorek had clearly embarrassed him.

'My name is Lazlo Breitner. I work for the joint ministry of finance.'

'Another one of Bilinski's toothless minions.'

Breitner shrugged, 'Yes, precisely. I believe your concerns about the Archducal visit were correct.'

'You seem to be the only person who does,' Doctor Sunaric replied.

'I have information that there are currently two Young Bosnian cells in Sarajevo, plotting to murder the heir apparent,' Breitner said, finally getting the doctor's attention.

'Why haven't you arrested them, then?'

'As you say, I'm toothless in this matter. The visit is in the hands of the military and without conclusive proof the governor refuses to act.'

Doctor Sunaric sighed. 'He doesn't want to spoil his moment of glory.'

'If you might present me to Her Highness ... if we presented our concerns on a joint front, perhaps we could explain the danger her husband is in,' Breitner suggested.

Sunaric thought for a moment, watching the governor make his rounds of the guests. 'Very well. I'll try one more time.'

Breitner followed tactfully as Doctor Sunaric presented himself to the duchess. Her dark eyes lit up immediately.

'My dear Doctor Sunaric, you were wrong, after all. Things did not turn out the way you said they would. Wherever we have been, everyone, down to the last Serb, has greeted us with such great friendliness, politeness and true warmth. We are very happy with our visit.'

Doctor Sunaric was slightly taken aback by the gentle rebuke but maintained his bearing. 'Your Highness, I pray to God that when I have the honour of meeting you again tomorrow night, you can repeat those words to me. A great burden will then have been lifted from me.'

The duchess smiled courteously and Doctor Sunaric looked at Breitner before moving away. He'd made his point and nothing would be gained from further discussion; the duchess had made up her mind. Breitner bowed his thanks to the good doctor and glanced around the foyer for another possible intermediary.

*

Johnny paused at the porte cochère of the officers' club to look up at the large, romantic building. The sunset had cast a pink sheen on the grey stonework. He adjusted his evening dress for the hundredth time and entered, making his way through a series of thick velvet curtains into a salon where an eight-piece band was playing bawdy songs.

It took him a moment to acclimatise after weeks of clean living with the puritan-like Princip. He looked around wide-eyed at the splendid gold-and-red decor, the giant mirrors and the nude paintings hanging from every wall. It wasn't surprising that the locals flocked to these places to revel in Western European decadence.

Libby had made a point of giving Johnny a stack of casino chips to make it difficult for him to spend the stake on any of the other amusements on offer. Even so, he needed all of his strength to resist the daintily clad nymphs who clustered around him as he made his way through something that resembled a combination of Ascot on Ladies' Day and a Roman orgy.

Johnny found an arcade of roulette wheels, swarming with officers of the imperial army. He instantly identified with these bored and lonely young men from the provincial middle class of the Habsburg Empire. They'd had hard, institutionalised childhoods and even worse teens in military academies, before being packed off to serve on the edges of the empire for years on end, waiting for a war that might advance their careers.

Like Johnny, this great palace of vice offered the unfortunate officers some escape from the routine of duty. They were fascinated by the little white ball spinning round and around the glittering roulette wheel, promising all manner of delights and riches. He recognised the look in their eyes – if they won they'd be able to afford one of the women in the next room, or maybe a new horse or even a castle, if the ball would only land on their number.

However, tonight belonged to Johnny. Libby had been right – half of these bumpkins had obviously never seen a roulette wheel before, let alone had any concept of how to play the game; they just kept pouring more and more of their hard-earned money into the all-consuming wheel. They were just the sort of people to provide Johnny with the cover he needed. He didn't expect that the management would particularly mind him winning when everyone else was losing.

He went to the wheel with the bias and placed his first bet, spreading it across the numbers which Libby had said occurred most frequently: seven, eight, nine, seventeen, eighteen, nineteen (inevitably), twenty-two, twenty-eight and twenty-nine. He placed one chip on each.

Johnny gripped the edge of the table in his usual manner, trying to control his excitement. He felt terribly conceited as the wheel span. He would at last be a winner – the odds were on his side for once. He readied himself not to explode in his moment of victory; he didn't want to draw attention to himself.

The ball landed on zero. Johnny couldn't believe it, but managed to stifle his disappointment. He knew his numbers wouldn't come up every time. He placed the next lot of chips on the same numbers and this time the ball impudently landed on thirty-six. Johnny looked about at the cheering officers enjoying their blind luck. He was furious, but knew he couldn't very well cry foul because his cheat hadn't worked.

Suddenly, he felt a sharp yank at his back that nearly took down his trousers.

Chapter 33

Ilic finished briefing Mehmed Mehmedbasic in the room which the veteran had taken at the Hotel Sarajevo. Mehmedbasic had just arrived from Stolac in Herzegovina, where he worked as a carpenter, although Ilic had assumed that he would have been used to a more refined occupation, being the son of a ruined Muslim noble.

'I trust that you didn't have any difficulty on your journey?' Ilic asked respectfully. He was conscious that, unlike the majority of his fellow Muslims, Mehmedbasic opposed Austrian rule, passionately believing in the establishment of a Yugoslav State. This made him extremely valuable to the movement, as he could travel freely without raising suspicion.

'I told the police that I needed to see a dentist, and they gave me a travel pass,' Mehmedbasic answered.

Ilic studied him. Mehmedbasic had come to the fore at the beginning of the year, when he'd attended a meeting with some of the Young Bosnian Movement's leadership, in Toulouse. It was decided at the Toulouse gathering that Mehmedbasic would assassinate General Potiorek and he was dispatched to Bosnia armed with a dagger and a bottle of poison.

'So it wasn't as eventful as your previous journey?' Ilic asked, trying to gauge Mehmedbasic's mood. He had become anxious on the journey back from Toulouse when several gendarmes had boarded his train at the Austrian border, so he'd disposed of his weaponry, only to discover that the police were after a petty criminal.

Mehmedbasic smiled dryly in response to Ilic's question, revealing little of what he was thinking. Ilic wondered for a moment if Mehmedbasic might be losing his resolve. If so, he sympathised, as he still had misgivings about the assassination; however, he'd determined to do what was required of him, not least because Gavrilo was so resolute, but also because he'd received word from Belgrade.

Ilic's mother had called him to the parlour that afternoon, where a man with large feet had been waiting for him. 'I have come from Apis,' the man said.

'Apis?' Ilic asked, taken aback by the sudden appearance of his visitor.

'Don't be coy, Danilo. I've had a very difficult journey and I don't have the time or the patience for play-acting.'

Ilic knew enough of the man's reputation to sit down and be quiet. The visitor looked up at the ceiling as the floor above creaked – Jovo was walking around. He was always moving around up there, Ilic reflected.

'Jovo, our lodger,' Ilic explained, in response to the man's questioning look.

'Can he be trusted?'

'He likes his drink a little too much and he's a show-off, but he is a patriot.'

'Have you noticed anyone suspicious loitering?'

'There are always suspicious people. We live under occupation, but I'm careful,' Ilic replied.

'Our Russian cousins are careful. That doesn't prevent half of them from working for the police. I have reason to believe that an Englishman has been sent to stop your attempt tomorrow.'

'An Englishman? Why would the English concern themselves with this?'

The man dismissed the question as unimportant. 'Has anyone tried to hinder your plans?'

Ilic fought to remain calm; he presumed that Apis had heard he'd been trying to stop the assassination. 'I had received instructions that the attempt was to be abandoned,' Ilic blurted out in mitigation.

'So you haven't made the necessary arrangements?'

'Things are in place, but …' – there was really no right or wrong answer to the man's question. He had been officially told to cancel the assassination by the last envoy from Belgrade, but the specific instructions had all been so cryptic.

'Whatever orders you've received, I countermand them. The assassination is to go ahead.' Ilic had little choice but to dispel whatever doubts he felt and send word for the second cell to meet him. He knew they would have to act tomorrow, regardless of personal feelings. Nonetheless, he didn't plan to physically take part in the assassination; his role would be purely to advise and support his comrades.

'Are you ready to follow in the footsteps of our Russian brethren?' he asked, turning to face Mehmedbasic. The man with the large feet had put Ilic in mind of the great Russian revolutionaries.

'I am,' Mehmedbasic answered sternly, sounding as if he was trying to convince himself more than anything.

'When you stand on Appel Quay tomorrow, with the tyrant's car coming towards you, remember Yegor Sazonov, who threw a bomb into the carriage of von Plehve, the Russian minister of the interior. Or Ivan Kalyayev, who dropped a bomb onto the lap of the Tsar's uncle as he travelled to the theatre, and the comrades who bombed Tsar Alexander II's carriage.'

Mehmedbasic seemed reassured that he would be following the path of a true revolutionary. Ilic didn't mention that many of the assassins had been arrested and hanged. He wondered if they'd faced their fate in the same way as the revolutionaries in *The Seven Who Were Hanged* – they had pitted everything against the horror of inevitable death.

*

Breitner watched as the guests began to leave the Hotel Bosnia. He hadn't been able to find another intermediary – General Conrad von Hotzendorf had dismissed Breitner's concerns as he left, making it clear that he had no wish to incur the archduke's wrath. The dinner was the last of the key events around the archducal visit, and with its conclusion a number of dignitaries from Vienna were taking their leave and returning home. Breitner was hoping that this example might present an opportunity to suggest Franz Ferdinand do the same.

The man to arrange such a change of programme would undoubtedly be Baron Rumerskirch, the archduke's chamberlain. Franz Ferdinand and the remaining guests had retired to the hotel's smoking room, where Breitner found the chamberlain in attendance.

Breitner approached him with due deference. 'Sir, if I may say, His Imperial and Royal Highness's visit has been an absolute triumph.'

The chamberlain regarded him dismissively, evidently thinking that Breitner was another unwanted guest trying to ingratiate himself into the archduke's suite. Breitner didn't think there was much point in trying to dispel the idea.

'You must be pleased with how well your staff have performed,' Breitner said.

'Everyone has behaved as I would have expected,' the chamberlain replied, glancing around the smoking room and checking that the brandy and cigars were being dispensed correctly. As with everyone else associated with the organisation of the archducal visit, the chamberlain was worried that something might happen to blight an otherwise flawless event, and unleash Franz Ferdinand's anger. It was a fear Breitner hoped to intensify.

'It will be a shame for it all to end in ignominy.'

The chamberlain turned on Breitner sharply. 'What do you mean by that?' Breitner had hit his mark at the first attempt.

'Sorry, Baron, I meant no disrespect.' Breitner tried to be as subtle as he could, allowing the chamberlain to regain his composure. He was visibly annoyed that he'd allowed himself to be bated by a nobody. 'I was merely observing that the chief of staff and the other notables from Vienna have left. Perhaps the royal couple could do the same. The most important part of the visit has, after all, been completed, rather splendidly.'

'That's not what you meant. Who the devil are you anyway?'

'Forgive me, my name is Breitner. I work for the joint ministry of finance.'

'And your point is what, exactly?'

'I believe there is a real danger that the archduke will receive a poor reception when he goes to Sarajevo, tomorrow.'

'You think that's possible?' the Chamberlain asked.

'There are a number of malcontents amongst the Serbian youth in Sarajevo, who are unwilling to accept the benevolence of our rule.' Breitner didn't want to mention the plot to assassinate the archduke – that would have only overplayed his hand. The chamberlain's primary concern was to prevent an unseemly spectacle: anything else was too far beyond his purview to be of any consequence to him.

'We wouldn't like a repeat of the cool reception the archduke received on his last trip to the Balkans,' Breitner said mildly.

'No, quite. You work for the joint ministry of finance, you say?'

'Yes, sir.'

'Well the last thing we want is anything to blemish His Highness's visit when it has been such a triumph.'

'I agree. As you say, sir, the last thing we want is to spoil His Highness's visit and cause him to lose his temper,' Breitner said dryly. The chamberlain glanced at Breitner for a moment.

'This might well be an opportune moment to conclude His Highness's visit,' The chamberlain said, then nodded his thanks to Breitner and made his way over to Franz Ferdinand, who was enjoying a brandy and cigar in the company of a number of local officers keen to curry favour from the future emperor.

The Assassins

Breitner noticed that Colonel von Merizzi was staring at him. General Potiorek's aide-de-camp was clearly wondering what he was doing in the smoking room; as far as he was concerned, the letter of authority from the governor's office hadn't been issued to Breitner so that he could hang about amongst his betters.

Franz Ferdinand listened in silence as his chamberlain explained the situation, then gradually looked as if he was agreeing. The chamberlain finished and the archduke addressed the assembled officers and flunkies.

'Gentlemen, I'm cutting short my visit and returning to Vienna, directly.' The archduke smiled – his words had created a stir, changing the atmosphere from genial to tense. He liked to appear unpredictable; it kept the lackeys on their guard. Von Merizzi glared at Breitner, realising that he'd had something to do with the archduke's abrupt change of heart.

'I believe this is the most prudent course of action,' the archduke continued. 'The weather is changing, the rain has stopped and the summer heat is likely to bring on my asthma. Appearing in public is trying enough as it is.'

The chamberlain bowed in agreement, but felt it polite to give further explanation. 'I also explained to His Majesty that a visit to a provincial capital to view some barracks, attend a civic reception and all the rest, might be something of a disappointment after the triumph of the past few days. We can also expect something of a hostile welcome from the local youth.'

'Her Highness has made a number of worthy visits in Sarajevo. The people can't say we have forgotten them,' the archduke added decisively, and that looked to be the end of the matter. He would not visit Sarajevo – in his own mind, Franz Ferdinand was already on holiday with his children. Breitner started to congratulate himself on a job well done.

Then Lieutenant Colonel von Merizzi came to the fore. 'If I may interject, Your Highness?' the colonel said, rising to his feet. 'If you do not complete the programme of events, it would be seen as a public reprimand to General Potiorek, weakening him significantly in front of his political enemies, and it would show that we are willing to back down in the face of a few scrawny schoolboys, giving the nationalists a major victory.'

The colonel glanced briefly in Breitner's direction, evidently remembering their earlier conversation. 'Perhaps most importantly, an early return to Vienna by Your Highness would cause deep offence to the loyal Croat and Muslim members of the population, whose support is needed so badly to maintain the balance of power in the region.'

'Very well, Colonel, you make a fair point. We will proceed as originally planned,' the archduke said cheerfully and then returned to his brandy and cigars. Breitner knew there would be no disturbing him now and made a hasty retreat. He would have to face, 'the ogre' single-handedly in the morning. Then his duty would finally be done.

*

Gavrilo Princip was in a pensive mood, distancing himself from his bohemian friends in the wine shop. He had no wish to join their revelry. He needed to order his thoughts and prepare himself; he could not repeat the uncertainty he had suffered a few days previously.

Gavrilo had been making his way home past the artisan shops of the old town, through the streets he'd been walking since studying at the Merchants' school. It had been unusually crowded, and Gavrilo had found himself caught up in a swirling mass of people. Fighting to make his way through, Gavrilo had seen the solid figure of Franz Ferdinand. 'The tyrant' had been cheerfully shopping for carpets with his wife, enjoying the spectacle he was creating at the centre of the fawning mass.

Princip's blood ran cold at the memory. Caught off guard, he'd been gripped by indecision, allowing the crowd to push and pull him after the heir. If he'd had his pistol he could have finished the tyrant there and then, he'd realised. Gavrilo had known that he might not get a chance as good as this one during the heir's official visit. He'd deliberated running home, as his lodgings were only a few streets away, but he had seen a policeman behind him. If he'd started running he was sure to have attracted unwanted attention. Even if he'd had his gun it had been so crowded that he could have easily shot the tyrant's wife by accident.

In the end, he had done nothing and was disgusted with himself. He hadn't acted when he had had the chance and he was starting to question whether he'd be able to do so when the heir came to Sarajevo.

Jevtic put his arm around Princip and tried to encourage him to sing, but Princip shrugged him off. 'Come Gavro, you have been in a foul mood ever since the heir arrived in Bosnia. With your past, people will make the connection and become suspicious.'

Princip looked at his friend, wondering if he'd understood that he was using him to hide from police spies. 'The day they arrived, I saw them –

the heir and his wife. I could have freed our people in an instant, had I not been so concerned about hitting his wife.'

'Don't worry about that preening tyrant, Gavro – he's too busy tightening his corset and stuffing his face to be of any concern to us. Drink and sing!' Jevtic handed him a cup of wine. Gavrilo took the cup, and unable to resist his friend's good humour, drank alcohol for the first time in his life.

Gavrilo's apprehension faded with the wine and he began to sing of Blackbird's Field and the heroes of Kosovo who'd fought so valiantly for their people. Princip looked through the window. He could just make out Lateiner Bridge in the twilight – tomorrow he would join their fight.

*

Johnny felt the tug on his trousers again and spun round, then almost choked. Libby was dressed in the most extraordinary get-up, with feathers, tassels and garters. He only had a second to take in the apparition before she hissed in his ear.

'Stop gawping. You're at the wrong wheel – idiot!'

'What?' Johnny managed to splutter, before she disappeared into a sea of admirers. Libby had said to go to the second wheel in the middle row, which he had. He examined the wheel, which was spinning gracefully, its smooth unblemished wood gleaming in the reflected light. Johnny swore – the one with the 'bias' had a scratch on the side where it must have been dropped and he'd forgotten to check. Libby had said that the club's management might move the wheels around to stop people taking advantage of the biased wheel.

Johnny gathered up his remaining chips and readjusted himself. Libby had looked quite stunning – apparently her general had organised a hostess position for her in the club. What that entailed hadn't been made entirely clear to Johnny. He'd naturally assumed that it would be something akin to a society hostess, offering guests scones and cucumber sandwiches from a tiered cake stand. It hadn't occurred to him that it would be 'that' sort of hostess. Not that Johnny really cared – one night of playing dress-up wouldn't hurt her. He was the one taking all of the risks, while she sashayed about in feathers.

He found the scratched roulette wheel in the next row along and placed his bets as before, spreading the chips across the enchanted numbers. This time, nineteen came up straight away.

*

Princip left the wine shop suitably fortified, and began a final pilgrimage to the grave of Bogdan Zerajic. He knew the others from his cell would be going there too, but he preferred to pay his respects in private.

Staggering along Appel Quay he could picture General Varesanin's coach driving back to his residence after the opening of parliament – the coach slowing as it turned onto Emperor's Bridge. He imagined Bogdan Zerajic, as he pointed his pistol at the governor's coach. Zerajic had missed his opportunity against Franz Joseph a few weeks before, when he could not bring himself to shoot, but he would not falter at his second chance.

Princip turned off the embankment and began to make his way to the cemetery, envisaging Zerajic as he opened fire on the governor. The first shot had hit the step of the driver's seat, the second had narrowly missed Varesanin's face. The governor had thrown himself forward as Zerajic fired the third shot, which missed, but left a hole in the back of the coach where his chest would have been. Zerajic had desperately fired two more shots at the back of the coach as it drove away and then put the gun to his head. He had saved the last bullet for himself.

Princip entered St Mark's cemetery, raging inside as he recalled the story of how General Varesanin had stopped the coach when it crossed the river, and seeing that his assailant was down, had coolly approached Zerajic as he lay dying in the mud, coughing up blood. Varesanin had kicked him, screaming, 'You filthy cur – you scum!'

Princip found Zerajic's grave in an unmarked corner of the cemetery saved for criminals and suicides. The Young Bosnians had discovered it and made it fit for a hero. Princip stood before the grave and repeated Zerajic's dying words, 'I will be revenged.'

He swore to follow Zerajic's example – to fight their oppressors and avenge his death. He remembered that Zerajic had been wearing a red and black badge depicting a man with a scythe, which he'd copied from the cover of Kropotkin's book on the French Revolution.

Princip turned to make his way home to read Kropotkin and dream of the free society that would be created as a result of his actions on Vidovdan.

*

The officers around Johnny were losing heavily, their hopes and dreams vanishing as they consoled themselves with brandy and champagne. Not Johnny though – he was winning. He knew it wasn't luck, or skill or heart, but knowledge, and not even his knowledge but some randy old goat's. Even so, he was having the time of his life.

The Assassins

At that moment, Johnny didn't care if the whole bloody world fell down around him. For the first time since he'd been expelled from school he thought he might have a chance of controlling his fate. He could clear his debts and turn things around, or he could make a new start, pretend to be someone else – he seemed to have a talent for it. He just had to keep winning.

He hadn't lost his head completely and varied his bets, moving from black and red to odd and even numbers.

He went to place a split bet and knocked the hand of an Austrian lieutenant wearing a monocle and sporting duelling scars. They apologised to one another and continued to play. Johnny swept in another pile of chips and went to place his next bet, putting down an even spread of the numbers, and this time the officer with the duelling scars matched him square for square.

They both won again. Johnny looked around and saw that he was getting a few curious glances from the people surrounding him. He adjusted his bet again and this time a couple of the other officers copied him. When their numbers came up they all cheered, loudly.

It was a bit galling, but there wasn't a lot Johnny could do without creating a scene. The officers were suspicious enough; he could hear them muttering about how a civilian was having all the luck, while the cream of the empire lost.

He continued to adjust his bets – he'd made a note of complicated betting patterns which Libby had recommended. Nevertheless more officers began to copy Johnny, sensing victory over the house for the first time. They were quite blatant; a couple of them even slapped Johnny on the back and stood him schnapps, to show their thanks, calling him 'the goose that laid the golden egg'.

The commotion they were creating inevitably began to attract the attention of the floor manager who, much to Johnny's annoyance, came and stood behind him. It looked as if the manager was trying to work out if they were all cheating or whether Johnny was acting alone.

Johnny tried to think. If the manager thought he was cheating he'd take the money back, have him beaten up and probably taken to the police. Breitner would be sure to find out why he'd missed his appointment at the governor's mansion then and he could kiss his commendation goodbye.

He knew that there would be safety in numbers and so started feigning friendship with the officers, shaking hands every time they won and trying to suggest to the manager that he would have to take them all on if there was any unpleasantness.

More and more people were coming to the table now as the money continued to flow. The next wave of bets nearly broke the bank and the manager decided to suspend play. The officers were furious, but the manager calmly placed a green sheet over the top of the wheel and instructed the croupier to re-fret the wheel.

After his recent experiences, Johnny knew when to cut and run. He started to gather up his chips; the numbers would be in a different order now and he'd never be able to exploit the wheel's bias.

A swarm of beauties from the next room descended on the officers at the table, making them forget their complaints and coaxing them away from the wheel. He pushed one of the more persistent beauties off, hugged his chips to his chest and made an exit. He thought he saw the portly physique and fine whiskers of his uncle, but the figure was lost in a blur and the persistent beauty was on him again, desperately tugging on his trousers. He tried to fight her off, but she clung on for dear life.

'Keep still, imbecile! I'm trying to get us out of here!' Johnny hadn't recognised Libby. She'd put on a black negligee, which regrettably, covered her charms. She led him to the cashier where he exchanged his armful of chips and then they were out through a red and gold door into a seedy area where Johnny assumed the poor girls who worked there lived. He heard a shout and saw that the monocled lieutenant was following them.

'Damn – Matthias has seen us,' Libby said, quickening her pace, her boots clattering on the stone floor.

'Who?'

'The idiot I was going to use, before you turned up.'

'Does he know about the biased wheel? Is he expecting a cut?' Johnny asked.

'Don't be stupid!'

'What does he want then?' Johnny smiled. 'Do I have another rival for your fickle affections?'

'Johnny, please!' Libby said urgently.

Matthias had started to run, but Libby knew what she was about. They were down another corridor and at the service entrance before he could catch them. Libby gave a stack of notes to a thick-set doorman and they were out and into a waiting taxi.

Johnny watched the river fly by as they were driven up the embankment. Tonight he was the victor and all the spoils would be his. Elated, he reached out and took Libby's hand. 'It worked. I can't believe we actually bloody-well pulled it off!'

Libby smiled. 'They knew something was going on, that's why the manager sent the girls in to get the money back. It saves having a riot and having to rough up the gentlemen, but they didn't think you could possibly have been involved. They decided that you must have been copying the others, so they left you to the new girl.'

She started to straddle him. 'I must say, you do play the hapless gambler extremely well, Mr Swift. Reading your bets off a piece of scrap paper – genius!'

This time the tugging at his trousers finally brought them down. Johnny pulled open Libby's negligee, running his hands down the feathers of her bustier to the warm silk of her thighs and then feeling the satisfying snap of a garter. It was like breaking the seal of quality on a whole new world.

Chapter 34

Nedjo followed Princip's instructions, getting to Vlajnic's pastry shop just after eight o'clock in the evening. He found Danilo Ilic and Trifko Grabez in the back. It was Trifko's birthday and he was in high spirits, trying to impress the waitress by telling her that he was a true Serb, born on Vidovdan.

Nedjo greeted them and ordered three of his favourite cakes. He also regarded himself as a true Serb, but was in no mood to join their conversation. He opened a copy of *Narod* which he'd bought on the way to the cafe and began to read. The paper was a special Vidovdan edition, filled with poetry that celebrated the Serb spirit. Nedjo read it avidly, preparing himself for what he planned to be his last day on earth.

He was still troubled by the arguments of the previous night; his mother held him responsible for his father's fury over the fiasco with the flagpoles. It had made leaving home all the more difficult, but he'd put his affairs in order, dividing his money and possessions amongst his closest relations. He'd then sent flowers to Jela, the sweet girl who'd helped him on the journey from Belgrade, to let her know he'd have to take this last promenade alone.

'Are you sure you wish to continue?' Nedjo looked up; Ilic was trying to draw him into the discussion he was having with Trifko. Nedjo ignored them and continued to read his paper. Trifko answered for him.

'What are you saying, Danilo? I thought you'd received word that we are to carry on.'

'Are you ready for the spiritual crisis you'll have to face as you strive to conquer death?' Ilic asked. Nedjo sneered. In his view this was typical Ilic claptrap, theoretical and highbrow.

'We must strike now – the time for talking is over,' Trifko replied.

'Are those your words or Gavrilo's?' Ilic countered.

'The heir must be destroyed,' Trifko said speaking quickly to hide his uncertainty, or so it seemed to Nedjo. 'He cannot be permitted to invade Serbia and stop the unification of the South Slav people.'

'Very well.' Ilic saw that there was no point in continuing. 'We should go over the plan. He unfolded a copy of the *Bosnian Post*, which detailed the route the royal motorcade would be taking through Sarajevo. 'We'll be positioned between the bridges on Appel Quay.' Ilic pointed on the map, to where Cumurija Street led onto Appel Quay. 'The other cell will strike here, with Jovo and myself, as the tyrant travels to the town hall. Nedeljko, you will be opposite them, on the riverside.'

'I know where to stand,' Nedjo said curtly. He wouldn't be told what to do by the likes of Ilic.

'Gavro will be two hundred yards further up, near Lateiner Bridge. Trifko, you will be last, on the Emperor's Bridge.'

'What greater gift could I be given on my birthday?' Trifko smiled – he'd been given the place of honour, where Zerajic had stood when he died for the cause.

'Trifko, you and Gavrilo will be ready in case the motorcade takes a different route. Otherwise you'll be the last in line if the tyrant gets past the others.' Nedjo knew they expected him to fail, placed out in the open by the river with schoolboys.

Nedjo was on his third cake by the time Princip arrived. 'You have the weapons, Gavro?' Nedjo asked as he joined them.

'I do.' Princip handed Nedjo one of the flask-shaped bombs. 'Today we follow Obilic's path and kill the sultan on Vidovdan.' Nedjo was glad to hear that Gavro's resolve hadn't been undermined by Ilic's constant talking. 'Remember, it has a twelve-second fuse, so count to ten before you throw it.'

'And my gun?' Nedjo asked, tying the bomb to his belt.

'That's not the arrangement. You haven't had the training and there aren't enough for everyone.'

Nedjo bristled at Princip's words. It had been bad enough that he'd been excluded from the planning of the outrage, but now it was apparent that Gavro thought him unworthy of a pistol. Nedjo had been the one who'd received the newspaper clipping informing them of the tyrant's visit; he'd asked Princip to join him in the assassination and now Princip would rather give a gun to someone he hadn't even met.

*

Breitner returned to the Hotel Bosnia and made his way to the archduke's suite. He was planning to see Franz Ferdinand before the heir attended low mass. According to his meticulously arranged schedule, mass would start at 9 a.m., in the room which General Potiorek had had specially converted into a chapel for the purpose.

Breitner's letter of authorisation still held sway with the local police, who let him pass without any difficulty. The archduke's regular security detail was slightly more resistant, but eventually referred him to the archduke's staff. Breitner found himself ushered into the atrium of the archduke's suite and face to face with the archduke's chamberlain once again.

'This is most irregular, Herr Breitner,' the chamberlain said, moving to block the doorway into the main apartments of the suite.

'I have to see His Imperial and Royal Highness. It's a matter of the utmost urgency.'

'His Highness is not available,' the chamberlain replied.

'I must insist.'

'You don't insist ...' The chamberlain was indignant, but fell silent as the double doors behind him swung open and Franz Ferdinand came out, followed by Colonel von Merizzi and a small entourage. The heir apparent was dressed in a light blue jacket and black trousers with red side striping, which Breitner recognised as the ceremonial uniform of a cavalry general. The oriental decor of the suite shone behind the archduke like a sultan's harem. Breitner wondered if the nationalists planning to kill the archduke would have enjoyed the juxtaposition of the present imperial ruler taking on the trappings of the last.

'I'm sorry to disturb Your Imperial and Royal Highness,' Breitner managed to get out, caught off guard by the archduke's sudden appearance. The Order of the Golden Fleece hung around the heir's neck – his country's highest award. The design of the medal always reminded Breitner of a sheep caught in an eagle's talons, which seemed particularly appropriate for his present circumstances.

The archduke's hussar's moustache twitched with irritation, as he appeared to remember Breitner. When Breitner had tried to engage General von Hotzendorf as an intermediary the previous evening, von Hotzendorf had cited the audience which he and Breitner had had with Franz Ferdinand after the Redl debacle. The general claimed it was the most unpleasant thing he'd endured as chief of the general staff. It was without doubt the worst thing Breitner had been through; he could still remember the shock he felt when the heir apparent roared that they should have

The Assassins

hanged Redl in front of the whole army, rather than let him take his own life.

'Breitner the Hungarian. So this is the rathole you ended up in,' the archduke said, as he studied him. Franz Ferdinand's eyes were light blue with an inner bright blue iris, giving the appearance of two sets of eyes looking out. Breitner had found this disconcerting the last time they'd met; it made him feel as if 'the ogre' was waiting to jump out at him from behind the shadows of the archduke's affable persona.

'Well, what is it?' The archduke asked.

Breitner couldn't speak, hypnotized by those eyes, which amused the entourage. The archduke's valet handed his master a gold chain – Breitner had evidently caught the archduke as he was in the act of finishing dressing. He watched as the archduke put the chain on. It had seven gold and platinum amulets attached to it, each containing religious icons and charms to protect Franz Ferdinand from evil. Breitner gathered himself and prepared to do his duty; the heir would need something slightly more tangible to ward off the bad luck that faced him in Sarajevo.

'I regret I must ask Your Highness to cancel today's visit to Sarajevo. I believe there will be an attempt on your life.'

'Do you indeed?' The archduke looked around at his aides, none of whom gave Breitner's statement any credence. 'Do you have any proof of this, Herr Magyar?'

'No, Your Highness,' Breitner replied. He was still hoping that Johnny might turn up and tell him what the Young Bosnians were planning. He'd checked his office before leaving Sarajevo, but there hadn't been any messages from Johnny or reports of a body matching his description being found. Breitner had left word for Johnny to be dispatched to Ilidza if he made an appearance at City Hall.

That was about all Breitner could hope for. The idiocy he was currently engaged in would only serve to cause him further discomfort and damage, but he knew he must try everything. 'Your Highness, there are Bosnian extremists in Sarajevo, planning an attempt on your life.'

'Your Highness, if I may? This … person is nothing more than a scaremonger,' Colonel von Merizzi said, trying to prevent all of his hard work from being undone. 'He's hell-bent on ruining Your Highness's visit with these tales of woe.'

'I see.' The archduke smiled at Breitner. 'We are all constantly in danger of death. One must simply trust in God, Herr Magyar.'

'Your Highness, you must understand that this is the Serbs' national day and your presence is a tremendous provocation ...'

Before Breitner could finish, the archduke's face contorted with rage as 'the ogre' jumped out of the shadows. 'Enough! I have made my decision. You say yourself, you can't prove a thing. I won't be dictated to by a "pinchbeck" Magyar! This constant questioning is everything I detest in your people! If you dare to contradict me one more time then so help me, there won't be a rathole deep enough for you to crawl into! You and your sort would do anything to keep me away from my subjects so that you can turn them against me.'

Breitner took a step back, propelled by the sheer force of Franz Ferdinand's anger. The archduke stormed back into his suite, quickly followed by his entourage.

Breitner felt a hand on his shoulder and found that Colonel von Merizzi was next to him. 'You're staying with me, Breitner. I can't have you causing any more mischief today.'

*

Nedjo Cabrinovic left the pastry shop and walked up to Appel Quay, ready to face his destiny. He pondered whether he should record the moment in some way for posterity. He was wearing his best suit, and after the trouble he'd caused at home Nedjo felt he should leave something of himself for his family.

'Why so glum, Nedjo – have you been stood up? All dressed up and no girl to impress?'

Nedjo grinned – his friend Tomo was walking towards him. They'd spent many a happy hour taking girls out along Appel Quay. Nedjo decided for sure then what he would do.

'This will be a momentous Vidovdan, Tomo – a day of great deeds. We must record it with a photograph.'

'Why not?' Tomo readily agreed and they found an open photographer's on Circus Square where Nedjo posed with the copy of *Narod* tightly rolled up in his hand and his arm discreetly covering the bomb under his jacket.

*

Gavrilo Princip crossed Lateiner Bridge and entered the park on the opposite bank. He needed to be as inconspicuous as possible, and loitering at his position next to the bridge was a sure-fire way of attracting unwanted attention from the police.

'Stop, Princip! Wait there!' The sudden shout sent a jolt of fear through Gavrilo and he spun round, trying to identify who was calling him.

Maxim Svara, the son of Sarajevo's public prosecutor, was coming towards him. Princip started to hurry away but a hand grabbed his arm.

'Gavro, where are you going? You remember Maxim?'

'What?' Princip said with a start. It took him a moment to understand what was happening. 'Spiric?'

Rather than the burly gendarme Princip had been expecting, he was being accosted by an old school friend.

'We just wondered if you managed to pass your exams in Belgrade,' Spiric said, as Maxim caught up with them.

'No, I failed,' Princip replied tersely, but then quickly realising his good fortune, he invited Maxim and Spiric to walk with him. There couldn't have been a better ruse than taking a Sunday morning stroll through the park with the son of the public prosecutor, while at the same time blending in with the loyal subjects who'd gathered at the Ottoman-style bandstand to listen to jaunty, marching music.

It all felt seductive and false, something his elder brother would have enjoyed. Gavro glanced up at the ramparts of the imposing police station that overlooked the park and wondered how many more Sunday mornings like this there would be after today.

*

Cvjetko Popovic was frustrated by the change in weather. He'd been hoping for the rain to continue, so that he could wear a woollen cape that would hide the bulges the bomb and pistol made in his jacket. He was afraid that the cape would now make him look conspicuous in the summer heat.

Eventually, Popovic decided to risk the cape as the better option and made his way to Appel Quay, with the bomb concealed in his right-hand pocket and the gun in his left.

Since he'd had the honour of being asked to take part in the assassination Popovic had existed completely for this moment. He'd stopped studying, ignored the news and barely noticed the jokes of his friends; it all seemed pointless and childish. The only thing he cared about was this day – the day he would take revenge on the tyrant for all his oppressive policies and the day he planned to die.

Popovic had lived the assassination a thousand times in his imagination. His friend in the second cell, Vaso Cubrilovic, would be at his side. Vaso would throw his bomb, stopping the archduke's car and in the chaos, Popovic would throw his bomb and open fire. He'd save the last bullet for himself, to use after he'd taken the cyanide which Ilic had given him.

Unfortunately, it would not happen that way now, Popovic reflected sadly; he would be with Jovo, a stranger. He found his place in front of the tobacconist's, on the corner of Cumurija Street, across from the bridge, and he looked at the crowd gathering around him under the shade of the linden trees that lined the city side of the embankment. Ilic's face came into focus through the blurred sea of shapes.

'Where is Jovo?' Ilic asked.

'I don't know. I've just got here,' Popovic shrugged.

'Damn – I knew he was all talk. I'm going to check that the other two are in position, then I'll come back.'

'I can do my duty without a wet nurse!' Popovic was indignant.

Ilic patted Popovic reassuringly on the shoulder and moved out into the blurred mass around him.

*

Archduke Franz Ferdinand and his wife Sophie, Duchess of Hohenberg, glowed in the bright sunshine as they emerged from Sarajevo Station. Franz Ferdinand's uniform was now complete, with a gold-braided ribbon around his waist, white gloves and a peacock-feathered hat. The duchess was elegant in a white silk dress, an ermine fur over her shoulders and a wide-brimmed hat. Breitner thought they presented a splendid target.

If Franz Ferdinand had taken Breitner's warnings seriously he certainly didn't show it, radiating calmness when General Potiorek invited him to inspect the honour guard, which was parading in full dress and service medals. These troops, in Breitner's opinion, would have been much better employed lining the streets, actually guarding the heir. Franz Ferdinand smiled approvingly as the guard snapped to attention and presented arms.

Breitner stayed out of the archduke's way, surveying the crowd. Most of them were hard to see, packed under the shade. He wondered whether if it had kept raining it would have thinned the crowd.

'Look lively, Breitner. You're with me,' Colonel von Merizzi said, hurrying towards him.

'Days of rain and then sunshine today. How is anyone going to see gunmen with all of these people, Colonel?'

'Breitner, stop playing the fool,' von Merizzi said impatiently. 'You're not going to hold us up any more.' The royal couple were running twenty minutes late and von Merizzi seemed to feel that this was Breitner's fault. 'His Highness has also requested that the motorcade drive slowly, so that he and his wife might enjoy the sights.'

'Of course he has,' Breitner said with a sigh and allowed the colonel to march him towards the fleet of seven cars that were neatly lined up outside the station.

The royal couple were courteously guided to the third car in line. A sleek Gräf & Stift Double Phaeton, its convertible roof had been neatly folded down and rolled behind the back of the car.

The archduke helped the duchess into the right-hand side of the back seat and sat next to her on the left. Potiorek perched opposite them on a pull-down chair. Count von Harrach, an officer from the Transport Corps, sat in the front seat next to the chauffeur. Breitner knew that the large touring car belonged to the count and that he'd put it at the archduke's disposal. Seeing the royal couple seated, Breitner climbed into the front of the car behind them, next to Colonel von Merizzi.

Breitner was slightly relieved to observe a detachment of the archduke's special security police climb into the first car. Then, with imperial black & yellow flags flying, the motorcade moved off towards the first item on the programme, the inspection of Philippovich Barracks.

Chapter 35

The bright sunshine gradually woke Johnny from the first proper sleep he'd had for weeks. He listened briefly to the bustle outside, finding it strangely restful and comforting, but it was part of a world that no longer concerned or interested him.

He pulled Libby closer, immersing himself in the silky warmth of her honey-blonde hair. Some of the chips he'd forgotten to change the previous night fell off the bed with a gentle, reassuring clatter. It was exactly a year since he'd watched Mata Hari dance on his first day in Paris and had begun his decline into debt.

That was all over now. He was in the clear and had concluded the sordid journey which Sir George had sent him on in a most satisfactory way.

'You are fantastic, Libby,' Johnny whispered.

'I know,' she murmured back, contentedly.

'Where did you learn to do that?'

'I told you – a very obliging general.'

'I didn't mean the gambling,' Johnny said. Libby turned over and slapped his face playfully. 'So, when shall we make our return to Paris? We must have won enough money to placate your husband and get my post back.'

'It'll take more than money to do that,' Libby said turning to face him. 'You'll still have to complete the report he asked for.'

'You didn't think that was very important last night, when you were persuading me to help you.'

'Don't be a bore, Johnny. The report's important.'

'But what good is it going to do? Yes, the nationalists are very dangerous. Yes, they have the means and the will to do great harm.' The idea of having to write it all up didn't appeal to him.

'You're missing the point, Johnny. It's not about dotting the i's and crossing the t's; it's about helping George further his career and providing him with something to dazzle his superiors. It was obvious that something was stirring between Austro-Hungary and Serbia, and he knew that you're an opportunist street urchin. If anyone could find out what was going on over here it was you. Either that or you'd have died in the process.'

'I'm sure if I had died it wouldn't have made much difference to you,' Johnny said. Libby smiled and coiled herself firmly around him. As warm as she felt, he appreciated that Libby was as cold-blooded as they came. 'So if I could say that there was a plot to assassinate the heir to the Habsburg throne, but that I'd foiled it and the Austro-Hungarian government are deeply indebted to me, and that it is all thanks to Sir George – that would help, do you think?' he asked.

'I should think it would be useful.'

'Well, that's just what we'll tell Sir George, then. I'll pop along to see my chap in City Hall tomorrow, get my letter of commendation and we can be on our way.'

The noise outside started to change pitch with the low murmur of crowded streets becoming cheering, accompanied by what Johnny thought was a military band playing the 'Radetzky March'.

'I wonder what's going on out there,' Johnny said, half interested.

'It must be that tiresome royal visit,' Libby replied, stifling a yawn.

'What?' Johnny's world tilted. The archduke's visit hadn't been cancelled and it was his fault. He pushed Libby off and charged to the window. Franz Joseph Street was lined with people, clearly waiting to see the heir. Johnny started to get dressed.

'Johnny, what are you doing? Get back into bed at once!'

'Breitner was supposed to have cancelled it. I should have gone to meet him,' Johnny tried to explain as he struggled into his trousers, which still didn't fit.

'I take it this means you won't be getting your commendation now?' Libby asked, mildly amused by the spectacle he was making.

'To say the least!' Johnny replied, as he finished dressing and charged out.

*

Ilic met Mehmed Mehmedbasic at his position, outside the Mostar Cafe's garden. The motorcade was late and the veteran seemed tense. Ilic wondered again if Mehmedbasic might have lost his nerve that day on the train back from Toulouse, panicking when he saw the policeman searching the train.

He pushed the idea to the back of his mind – Mehmedbasic was the linchpin, the trigger. When he threw his bomb, the others would join the attack. Cheering could be heard from the direction of the station; it wouldn't be long now and he needed to get back to his short-sighted comrade. If Jovo wasn't going to act as Popovic's eyes then Ilic would do it.

"Be strong, be brave,' Ilic told Mehmedbasic and started to work his way back through the crowd. He passed Vaso Cubrilovic just before the corner of Cumurija Street, but before he could cross the road, the man Apis had sent came out of the shadows and blocked his path.

'Have you seen the English spy?' he asked.

*

Johnny was frantic as he pushed his way through the crowd. He didn't know where to start. There wasn't time to go to City Hall and find Breitner – the royal couple were here.

He thought about going to the place Ilic had assigned for the assassination and stopping Popovic from acting, but Popovic was only one of the conspirators. There were five others, plus Ilic himself, for all the good he was, Johnny reasoned. He considered approaching a gendarme, but it would have taken too long to explain himself and even if he was believed he'd probably end up getting arrested.

Johnny was furious with himself for having been so easily led by Libby. He knew that it was all too late and it was all his fault. Then Johnny saw the onion spire of the triangular doctor's surgery on the corner of Cumurija Street, and he started to pull himself together. He wasn't being fair – any right-thinking man would have behaved in exactly the same way as he had. 'Play up and play the bloody game!' he reminded himself, and decided that this wasn't much different to the time he had won the inter-house cup by leading the comeback to overturn a twenty-eight-nothing lead.

He could take two of them out of the game. He knew where Cubrilovic would be, and Popovic was too short-sighted to be of any danger to anyone apart from the people immediately around him.

*

Breitner watched as Franz Ferdinand and the senior regional commanders finished the tour of Philippovich Barracks without any incident.

An unseemly scramble ensued as the archduke's security detachment and the local police argued over seats in the first car. The motorcade eventually began to leave and Breitner saw, to his horror, that the archduke's special security detectives had been pushed out.

The Assassins

The motorcade turned onto Appel Quay and at the archduke's request, proceeded at a steady ten miles an hour along the embankment. Breitner scanned the crowds that had gathered under the shade on the city side of the embankment, which he thought would be the most likely place the assassins would strike from. Not that there was much that he could do to help, squashed next to the colonel in the front of the car. To all intents and purposes he was merely a passenger.

*

Franz Ferdinand was gratified that black and yellow bunting had been hung across Appel Quay and that the imperial flag was flying from every building – some even had photographs of the archduke himself in their windows.

The governor, sitting opposite Franz Ferdinand, pointed out the Herren Club and the new post office, magnificent examples of Austrian culture and architecture. The archduke waved at the crowd, enjoying the prestige he and Sophie were receiving. It wasn't a huge crowd, but they were cheering enthusiastically enough, actively demonstrating their appreciation of what the monarchy had done for them. Franz Ferdinand wondered whether, given time, the people in this wild and remote place could be tamed and fully absorbed into the empire.

He turned to his wife and whispered, 'At last you're receiving the respect you deserve, my Sopherl.' It had been fourteen years to the day since he'd taken the morganatic oath that had allowed their marriage. Sophie smiled and brushed his jacket; he had also worn the uniform of a cavalry general for their wedding ceremony.

She suddenly jumped at the sound of an echoing explosion and Franz Ferdinand put a reassuring arm around her.

'A twenty-four cannon salute,' Governor Potiorek said, pointing ahead of them to a small, round tower overlooking the city, surrounded by telltale gun smoke. 'The Yellow Bastion, Your Highness,' he explained and indicated a fort behind it. 'That is the newly enlarged Prince Eugene Barracks, headquarters of the Fifteenth Corps.'

The archduke inclined his head to show that he understood the information. The Fifteenth Corps had taken part in the manoeuvres he had been attending.

*

Johnny found Vaso Cubrilovic at his position under the onion spire of the doctor's surgery, on the corner of Cumurija Street.

'You're late, Jovo,' Cubrilovic snapped.

'So is the archduke, by the look of it,' Johnny said, trying not to sound relieved.

'What are you wearing?' Cubrilovic eyed him suspiciously. Johnny looked down and realised he'd put on the evening dress from the previous night.

Johnny shrugged, 'I don't want the tyrant to think we're peasants.'

Cubrilovic nodded, accepting Johnny's explanation. He was also smartly dressed, with a clean collar on his shirt. 'Why aren't you with Cvjetko? My eyesight is fine.'

Johnny sensed that the schoolboy was trying to hide his nerves with bravado. He had seen it a hundred times before big games and he drew strength from it.

'Ilic said we could stand where we wished if ...' Cubrilovic motioned for Johnny to be quiet; they could hear cars approaching and the cheering of the crowd was intensifying.

*

Mehmedbasic prepared himself as he saw the royal motorcade. He took the bomb from his belt, turned to look for something to strike the primer against and stopped still.

A grey-uniformed gendarme had appeared from nowhere and was standing behind him. If he attempted to use the bomb the gendarme would stop him and it would give the game away before the others had a chance to act.

He'd counted seven cars approaching. He had no idea which one the tyrant was in. Ilic had told him only to act if he was sure he recognised the archduke, otherwise he should wait until the tyrant made his return trip. Mehmedbasic turned back and watched the motorcade cruise past.

*

Nedjo was feeling hot and exposed on the river side of Appel Quay, away from the crowd and the shade. He'd taken the cap off the bomb, ready to prime it, and was holding it under his jacket.

He had a clear view of the royal motorcade as it rounded a slight bend in the road, past a mock Moorish building that housed the State Girls' High School and a grey neoclassical building.

His father's accusation that he was betraying his people still burnt, along with the lack of faith his friends had shown in him. He started to move

The Assassins

away from Cumurija Bridge, knowing that he must be the first to throw his bomb on Vidovdan.

The lead car in the motorcade was only a few yards away, but he didn't know which car the tyrant was in. He saw a policeman watching the approaching procession and asked him.

'The third car,' the policeman answered, as excited by the scene as everyone else. Nedjo could see lime green feathers above the third car and knew it was the tyrant. He took the bomb from under his jacket and aimed for the feathers. Today he would prove that he was no traitor.

*

Johnny stood with Cubrilovic, watching the motorcade as it appeared around the bend in the road and went past the picket fence of the Mostar Cafe without being attacked. Johnny guessed that the most experienced man wasn't all he was cracked up to be.

Cubrilovic seemed captivated by the spectacle as the great ocean liner of a car came nearer, the imperial eagles on its flags clearly visible. On the river side of the car, the duchess held a parasol, reminding Johnny of Libby, and a black fan. The archduke was closest to them; he'd rested his arm on the car's folded-back roof. The sun was reflecting on his medals and the gold braid of the red insignia on his collar. It was the perfect picture of royal pomp.

'Is that them?' Cubrilovic asked, coming out of his daze.

'Yes,' Johnny answered.

Cubrilovic unscrewed the cap of his bomb and moved to strike the primer against the striped wall of the surgery.

'Vaso, have pity. You'll kill his wife,' Johnny said, trying one last attempt at reason.

*

The motorcade came onto a long straight section of Appel Quay and for a fleeting moment, Franz Ferdinand had the sensation of being a roebuck driven through the traps towards a waiting hunter.

Governor Potiorek pointed across a steel bridge to a grand imperial building on the other side of the river. 'If Your Highness would care to observe – the Franz Josef Barracks, headquarters of the Gendarmerie Corps.'

Franz Ferdinand turned to wave at the couple of people on the river side of the quay and looked straight into the eyes of a tall, skinny youth in a grey suit. The car suddenly lurched forward as the chauffer accelerated.

*

Cubrilovic hesitated and pulled up short, unsure how to act now that Johnny had planted the seeds of doubt in his mind. 'This is hopeless. We are too badly positioned,' he said.

Johnny smiled agreement and breathed a deep sigh of relief, but just then a loud crack like a pistol shot cut through the noise of the crowd. A tall man across the street was banging his pipe against a tramway mast. Johnny wondered for a brief moment why someone would do something so strange as the heir to the throne drove past. Then he realised it was Nedjo Cabrinovic. He'd just struck his bomb against the mast, to prime it.

*

Ilic heard the crack and, unsure what it was, searched the crowd for some sign of action. Something was going very badly wrong – neither Vaso nor Mehmedbasic had attacked. Apis's man couldn't blame him for their failure; Ilic had stayed next to him on the corner of Cumurija Street so he could see that he hadn't tried to interfere.

Ilic saw Jovo standing a few yards in front of him with Vaso. It wasn't his assigned position and it looked as if Jovo was talking Vaso down. The doubts that he'd had about Jovo began to crowd back into Ilic's mind and he tapped Apis's man on the shoulder.

'That's him – Jovo – he's the English interloper!' Ilic shouted. At that moment Jovo started to tear through the crowd trying to get onto the road. Apis's man set off after him.

There had always been something about Jovo that had never sat right with Ilic. Despite supposedly studying in Paris he showed little interest in anything intellectual and he was always sneaking about asking questions, ready to point the finger to throw suspicion off himself. Ilic had been so focused on trying to talk Gavro out of the plot that he hadn't given much thought to his instinctive distrust. Jovo had always done what he was told and Ilic had made sure that Jovo wasn't armed today or privy to the full plan.

*

Johnny pushed his way onto the road and started to sprint towards the archduke's car, madly waving his arms, before tripping on a huge foot which some idiot had stuck out in front of him. As he fell, he locked eyes with the archduke's chauffeur, a tough-looking, stocky man, who instinctively accelerated to avoid him.

The Assassins

Johnny hit the ground with a thud and tasted blood in his mouth. A shooting pain ran up his leg and for a brief moment he thought he was back on the playing fields of his school.

The archduke turned his piercing blue eyes on Johnny, looking directly at him, then turned back as Cabrinovic hurled his bomb at the car and dropped to the ground.

Franz Ferdinand put his arm up to protect his wife, but the chauffeur's increase in speed caused the bomb to curve over them by inches and hit the folded-back roof of the car. Everything slowed down, as Johnny prayed, 'Please be the spiked one. Please be the spiked one!'

The bomb bounced off the canvas roof and landed on the road without going off. Johnny began to breathe again and felt the same sort of elation he had experienced when scoring the winning try in his inter-house cup.

The bomb continued to bounce along the road, smoking. Johnny thought it was odd; the bomb shouldn't have been smoking if it had been spiked and he watched as it disappeared under the next car along in the motorcade.

*

Cvjetko Popovic waited with growing apprehension; he could hear the motorcade getting closer. The people around him started to cheer and push to the front. Popovic put the cyanide in his mouth and waited with the bomb ready in his right hand and the pistol in his left.

He was in a trance, rhythmically repeating the words of the people around him under his breath. 'Now they're coming, now they're coming, now ...' The first car in the motorcade went past.

As the crowd crushed in, the enormity of the situation started to weigh on Popovic's sixteen-year-old shoulders. The people around him began to shout, 'Long may he live! Long may he live!' Popovic heard a dull crack and a second car drove past – then an ear-splitting explosion, followed by pandemonium.

His nerve left him and he bolted. His only thought was to get rid of his weapons and he turned and ran down to the cellar of Prosvjeta Palace to hide them.

*

Nedjo Cabrinovic swallowed his potassium cyanide and jumped over the embankment wall into the Miljacka river. It was a fifteen foot drop and he landed heavily in the inch-deep water. Ignoring the pain, he tried to submerge himself in the effluent red mud of the river in a bid to drown himself if the cyanide didn't take effect.

There was no time – several policemen and a number of spectators were on him and started to beat and kick him as they dragged him under Cumurija Bridge.

Nedjo coughed and retched; the cyanide had just made him sick and he couldn't get away. The group got to the low riverbank on the other side of the bridge and someone demanded to know who he was. Nedjo replied as proudly as he could, 'I am a Serb hero.'

*

Franz Ferdinand ordered his car to stop and instructed von Harrach, the transport officer, to investigate the scene of the explosion.

'Sophie, are you hurt? the archduke asked.

'Something hit the back of my neck,' she replied.

'You've been grazed,' Franz Ferdinand said with concern, examining her.

'We'll get you attended to, Your Highness.' Potiorek was mortified and clearly wary of how the heir would react.

Franz Ferdinand was too stunned to be angry. He wished that he'd listened to his last intuition about the trip to Bosnia, when he was at Konopischt. 'I always thought that something like this would happen,' he growled.

*

Princip was running with the crowd along Appel Quay towards the site of the explosion. He'd heard the bomb blast and could see that a car had stopped. He couldn't tell who was inside it, because of the mob, but he knew that the plan must have worked and his heart filled with triumph. He saw no need now to throw his bomb and shoot at the car, as had originally been planned when it was forced to stop.

A commotion across the river drew Princip's attention. Nedjo was being pulled out of the river, alive, into the park where Princip had been walking earlier with the prosecutor's son.

*

Von Harrach hurried back to the royal car and reported to the archduke. 'Your Highness, no one was killed. Two people from the car, one of them the governor's ADC, has been wounded and some spectators were injured.'

Breitner the Magyar staggered up to the car, cradling a wounded arm. 'Your Imperial and Royal Highness, might I suggest you continue to City

Hall, immediately. You're extremely vulnerable stopped in the middle of the road like this.'

Franz Ferdinand turned to von Harrach, 'Very well – the fellow must have been a lunatic. Let us proceed.' He'd been subject to an ambush of this kind at the king of Spain's wedding. All that could be done was to carry on.

Breitner climbed onto the running board next to the archduke as the car set off. Franz Ferdinand wasn't overly pleased with his presence, but Breitner had been correct about the threat to his life. If the archduke was ever wrong about people, he tried to make things right. He regarded everyone he met as being a scoundrel at first, and then let them gradually change his opinion, if they could. Breitner had changed his mind and Franz Ferdinand decided he would reinstate Breitner's commission in the army.

*

Princip watched as the police dragged Nedjo through the park, then he looked at his gun, deciding what to do. For a brief moment, Princip thought that he would kill Nedjo and then shoot himself. They had agreed that even if they were successful they should take their own lives.

The car that had been stopped in the middle of the road suddenly came to life and sped past Princip and to his dismay, he realised that the attempt had failed. He returned to his position on Lateiner Bridge, where he heard conformation that the bomb hadn't killed the tyrant.

*

Trifko Grabez stood by the Emperor's Bridge in some turmoil. After the pastry shop he'd gone with Ilic to the boarding house to get his weapons and poison, but Ilic had still tried to persuade him not to take part in the assassination. Trifko had been so desperate to get away from Ilic that he'd forgotten to ask him for his potassium cyanide. It was probably still in Ilic's pocket, he reflected. He would have to use his pistol now to take his life.

However, Trifko wasn't so sure he could bring himself to do anything, Ilic's arguments had thrown him into confusion. Trifko had walked around in the park trying to find Princip and gather his thoughts. In the end, he felt he must take part in the attack. When Trifko heard the explosion, he relaxed, assuming that the others had been successful.

Then, when the first two cars of the motorcade zoomed past, Trifko knew he would have to act and he readied his weapons. He looked at the crowd – there were a lot of old people and children who'd be hurt in the blast. He saw an acquaintance and as they greeted each other, Trifko froze as it dawned on him that if he attacked the tyrant, his friend would be implicated.

He watched, unable to act, as the royal car went past.

*

Johnny mingled in with the crowd, trying to avoid the photographers and police who were out in force at the scene of the explosion. There was no sign of Cubrilovic or the others, nor the man who'd tripped him up with his bloody great feet. Johnny had half expected an apology.

He was slightly dazed and couldn't understand why the bomb hadn't gone off when it hit the archduke's car, if it hadn't been the spiked one. Johnny supposed that Nedjo had been too carried away to count to ten before throwing his bomb.

The bomb had exploded by the left back wheel of the car it had rolled under, badly damaging its underside and blowing a hole about a foot wide and six inches deep in the granite road. The passengers from the car were being treated at the doctor's surgery and it looked as if around twenty people had been injured altogether, but Johnny was relieved to see the royal car drive off up the quay, the feathers of the archduke's hat flapping in the wind.

Johnny thought he saw Libby enter the Bank of Austro-Hungary, on the corner of Cumurija Street, and he debated whether or not to go and see her. In the end, he decided to follow the archduke – there would be time to make things up with Libby later but he had to get to City Hall right now. He'd done it somehow; he'd saved the archduke's life and now he had to claim his reward.

Chapter 36

Breitner held on to the side of the archduke's car for dear life. He hadn't been so scared since he'd left the Seventh Hussars. The sense of balance he'd developed riding horses in those turbulent years stood him in good stead now, as the car rushed towards Appel Quay.

His hand had been scratched by a bomb fragment; it wasn't a serious wound but it was bleeding a lot. One of the duchess's ladies-in-waiting had given him her handkerchief, so he was able to cling to the royal car without leaving a bloody handprint.

The bomb attack had taken Breitner by surprise, coming from the wrong side of the embankment, and he felt that the least he could do now was to protect the archduke until he reached safety.

Colonel von Merizzi, the governor's aide-de-camp, who'd been keeping a watchful eye on Breitner up until then, wasn't so lucky and had received a nasty gash on the side of his head.

Breitner grinned sombrely – he should have known that Johnny couldn't be trusted to spike the bombs. At least the plot was out in the open Breitner mused, and there couldn't be any more blatant evidence of a plan to assassinate the archduke. All that remained was to ensure that Franz Ferdinand stayed locked away while the army was called in to clear the streets and then to get him safely out of Sarajevo.

The car arrived at City Hall without further incident, and with some relief Breitner leapt off the running board to allow the royal couple to alight from the car. The Lord Mayor of Sarajevo, Fehim Effendi Curcic, was standing at the head of Sarajevo's leading religious and civic representatives, who were lined up on either side of the red-carpeted steps in ascending order of importance.

For a moment, Breitner thought that the mayor had gone mad. He was continuing with the archduke's visit, as if nothing had happened. Breitner observed the scene with growing dismay, as the Royal couple reached the top of the steps and the mayor proceeded to give his prepared speech of welcome.

'Your Imperial and Royal Highnesses – our hearts are full of happiness on the occasion of the most gracious visit with which Your Highnesses have deigned to honour the capital of our land ...'

'Herr Burgermeister!' the archduke interrupted him. The numbing shock of the explosion had gone and the archduke was in full fury. 'I came to Sarajevo on a friendly visit and I get bombs thrown at me. It's outrageous!'

The mayor looked stunned. He'd been in the second car of the motorcade, which had carried on along Appel Quay after the bomb had gone off. Breitner presumed the mayor must have thought the explosion was part of the twenty-four gun salute.

Sophie pressed her husband's arm and whispered something to him as he continued to berate the hapless mayor. To Breitner, at the bottom of the steps, it sounded like, 'Franzi – Franzi.' Whatever it was, it soothed the archduke. Breitner wouldn't have believed it if he hadn't seen it for himself. The archduke's infamous rage had been tamed by a firm hand and a reassuring word.

Franz Ferdinand nodded to the mayor, 'Oh, well – you can get on with your speech.'

The lord mayor stumbled through the rest of his welcome and looked expectantly at the archduke, causing an awkward silence while he and the archduke stared at one another.

With a cold shiver, Breitner realised that they were waiting for him. The archduke needed his speech to return the lord mayor's greeting. Von Merizzi had thrust the paper into Breitner's hand as he waited to be taken to hospital. It still had the colonel's blood on it.

Breitner did his best to wipe off the blood and rushed up the steps to pass the speech to the archduke. There was another awkward silence as the archduke looked at the blood, then proceeded as protocol dictated.

'I thank you, Herr Burgermeister, very heartily, for the enthusiastic ovations offered to me and to my wife by the population.'

Breitner looked on with some trepidation as the archduke continued to read out the prepared text, but the heir had managed to regain his composure sufficiently to ad-lib. 'I thank you all the more as I see in the people an expression of their joy at the failure of the attempt at assassination.' The cheering of the crowd followed the archduke as he made his way into City Hall.

Its reception rooms had been made in the same neo-Oriental style as the exterior, complete with pillars and a large domed ceiling. Seeing the

The Assassins

archduke in this artificial setting, Breitner wondered if all the residents of Sarajevo saw Franz Ferdinand in the same way as the nationalists did, as a new sultan trying to mimic their last conqueror.

If that was indeed what they felt, they were masking it well behind worried expressions and hushed conversations. The local representatives plainly thought Franz Ferdinand would be killed. They knew, even if their imperial masters didn't, that if there had been one assassin, there more than likely would be more. They couldn't take their eyes off Franz Ferdinand as he marched around like a soldier on parade, in a type of goosestep.

Breitner suspected that the heir had no other way of calming down without the soothing influence of his wife. The Duchess of Hohenberg had gone to a separate reception on the first floor for a special viewing of the clothes worn by local Muslim women.

Breitner drifted along behind the archduke, who was trying to downplay the attempt on his life. 'You mark my words, the assassin will probably, in good Austrian style, be decorated with the Order of Merit or end up as a privy councillor instead of being made harmless.'

Breitner laughed dryly – no one else did. Most of the assembled crowd were unaware of the gross incompetence that Breitner had witnessed over the past few days. It wouldn't have surprised Breitner if some idiot did reward the would-be assassin exactly as the archduke suggested.

'It looks to me that we might still get a few more pot shots today,' the archduke continued. 'What do you say Potiorek? You said yourself there would be no danger!'

Breitner felt little satisfaction as the archduke taunted the governor for his inability to maintain law and order on the streets of his province.

Potiorek flushed and struggled to regain his composure. 'Your Highness, please accept my regrets for this outrage. I take full responsibility, but be assured that all danger has passed.'

The suggestion that there would be no further attempt made on the archduke's life was so mistaken that Breitner felt compelled to enter the discussion. 'Excuse me, Your Highness. Gentlemen, perhaps we should put out more troops and clear the streets. There must be at least five more armed ...'

'We do not need to clear the streets. Do you think Sarajevo is full of assassins?' the governor barked, interrupting Breitner. Despite his shocked condition, Potiorek knew that any further discussion around the archduke's security arrangements would only highlight his negligence.

'With respect, Governor, what more proof do you need that there are assassins at large in Sarajevo?' Breitner held up his injured hand.

'We have only seen one,' the governor replied, looking at Breitner with distaste.

'I will not lock myself away and cower while the streets are cleared of my sovereign people,' the archduke said. To Breitner's surprise, the archduke had accepted what he had to say and disregarded it without chastising him. Breitner was now at something of a loss, as without knowing the plans of the Young Bosnians, clearing the streets was the only thing he could think of to ensure the heir's safety.

Governor Potiorek seized the initiative. 'Perhaps Your Highness would consider cutting his programme short and proceeding straight to the Konak for lunch? That would also punish the city for this outrage, as the crowd will not have the privilege of welcoming Your Highness.'

'Governor, I'm sorry but changing the programme of events is not enough. We must get His Imperial Highness out of Sarajevo immediately. There are two Young Bosnia cells at large in the city determined to kill His Highness,' Breitner argued.

'So you keep saying, yet you still haven't conjured up anyone to support your wild accusations,' Potiorek said, finally regaining his poise. 'I've told you Breitner, your help is neither wanted nor desired.'

A gendarme tapped Breitner on the shoulder and for a split second he thought that Potiorek had signalled for him to be arrested. 'Herr Breitner, there is someone from the British Consulate asking to see you.'

*

Johnny stayed close to the wall of the marble atrium, the City Hall's oriental design providing him with plenty of alcoves in which to hide. He'd already seen three officers from the club and it would have been terribly embarrassing if one of them had recognised him. The last thing he wanted to do was to have to explain to Breitner that he'd met the officers in a gambling den when he was supposed to have been reporting to the governor.

More worryingly, Johnny had seen Matthias, Libby's monocled lieutenant from the club. He was cutting a dash with his duelling scars and dress uniform, clearly believing that the Austro-Hungarian Army deserved its reputation for having the best-dressed soldiers in Europe.

If Libby had Matthias as an admirer and a pawn, it would explain why she'd been content to spend so much time with an infirm old general in

Sarajevo. Johnny was slowly becoming accustomed to Libby's weakness for dandies; he'd known that he was playing with fire from the moment he'd got involved with her.

If Matthias did have designs on Libby, the last thing Johnny wanted to deal with now was a jealous rival who sported duelling scars, or worse still, a jilted accomplice who thought he was entitled to a share of the winnings.

He was relieved to see Breitner hurrying out of the reception room towards him. Johnny stood up straight, trying his best to look like a representative of His Britannic Majesty's government. He had managed to put his bow tie on as he had made his way through the police and outraged crowds, which with his battered tails, seemed to be enough to comply with the 'drawing room' dress code which the programme demanded, but he still hadn't been able to get into the reception without an invitation.

Breitner regarded him wearily. 'So you've reverted back to being an Englishman?'

'I didn't know how else to get in,' Johnny shrugged, 'so I pretended to be a chap I know from the consulate.'

Johnny took a drink from a passing waiter, before adding, 'I need you to introduce me to the archduke.' Breitner snatched the drink from Johnny and signalled for the waiter to go away. 'I say, that's a bit rum, Breitner. I think the least I deserve is a drink after what I've done today.'

'I take it that by turning up here, in that ridiculous outfit, you think you've successfully completed the task I gave you?'

'Well, don't you? They've shot their bolt. Some of them might still be lurking about, but all you need to do is flood the city with troops.'

Breitner glowered. 'Where have you been, Johnny? I needed you.'

Johnny shrugged again, distracted by a pretty girl in a pink and white silk dress who'd swished past him.

'You were supposed to meet me at the governor's residence, yesterday,' Breitner said pointedly.

'I say, is your hand okay?' Johnny asked, feigning interest. The last thing he wanted to do was to try and explain the last twenty-four hours.

'A bomb exploded under the car I was in. A bomb you were supposed to have disarmed.'

'You were in that car?' Johnny stifled a laugh. He should have guessed. 'Sorry about that, but we did stop it – the assassination.'

'Is that what you think happened?'

'What?' Johnny was half listening, half looking for the girl in the pink and white dress – she'd looked familiar somehow. 'But didn't you see me? I ran out into the road when Nedjo threw his bomb.'

'I didn't see anything, Johnny, no one did.' Breitner waved his wounded hand, 'Even if I had, the archduke doesn't exactly see what happened as a success. I take it you saw the explosion?'

'But the bomb missed the archduke. I warned the chauffeur – he saw me, I'm sure he did. He can tell the archduke I warned him.'

'You're missing the point, Johnny. A *bomb* was thrown at the archduke. He was subject to an act of terrorism within the borders of his empire. Everything else is just detail.'

Johnny could feel all of his hard work slipping away; he might as well have stayed in bed with Libby. 'I'll talk to the chauffeur, he can tell them that I helped. You could tell them how I've worked with you. At least then I could get some sort of commendation. I can go and find him.' Johnny had seen the chauffeurs standing outside, on his way into the reception.

Breitner looked annoyed. 'My main priority is to get the archduke out of Sarajevo alive. If you had actually done what you were supposed to ...' Breitner stopped himself mid-sentence. 'Maybe it's not too late to talk to the governor though. Wait here. Your turning up might actually have been quite prescient.'

'Yes, I think you're right, Breitner old chap,' Johnny agreed wholeheartedly. There was a lot to attend to and he had no intention of standing in the corner while Breitner took all the glory.

*

Franz Ferdinand listened with growing frustration as his staff and the local officials discussed whether or not to amend his programme of events or cancel it altogether and return to Ilidza. Potiorek was of the opinion that the engagement at the museum must go ahead, since members of the government were waiting to greet the heir.

The archduke felt his duty was perfectly clear. 'I wish to go to the hospital and visit Lieutenant Colonel von Merizzi, who I believe was wounded in the attack. From there we can go to the museum.' Franz Ferdinand was the inspector general of the imperial army and he felt he must go to a wounded soldier, aside from the fact that Merizzi was injured while attending the archduke. 'Please inform my wife that I shall be leaving presently.'

His aides and the local officials snapped to attention.

The Assassins

*

Gavrilo Princip crossed the road from Lateiner Bridge and went to his fallback position in front of Schiller's general store and delicatessen, at the corner of Franz Joseph Street and Appel Quay.

He doubted that the archduke would stick to his planned programme now, and deliberated about going back to his boarding house, which was only a couple of streets away. Ilic was probably already there, he thought, as he looked at a large picture of a wine bottle that ran up the full length of the wall, advertising Hungarian champagne. It reminded him of the wine he'd drunk the previous night to wash away the bitter taste of failure and now he'd missed his chance again. Princip controlled his anger and decided that he would not leave while there was still a chance of taking revenge on the tyrant.

Mihajlo Pusara, Princip's actor friend, tapped him on the shoulder, his handsome face glowing. 'Gavrilo, I knew Nedjo would do it if he saw the newspaper clipping announcing the heir's visit.'

'He hasn't done anything, Mihajlo, apart from fail,' Princip replied, irritated that Pusara seemed to be as quick to believe Nedjo's boasts as Nedjo was prone to make them.

'Do you think they are dumb enough to come back this way?' Pusara asked.

'Who can tell?' Princip answered. 'The *Bosnian Post* reported that the motorcade would pass this way on its return from the reception at City Hall.'

Pusara read the street sign with the theatrical flourish of an actor. 'Franz Joseph Street – how ironic. A great act of Yugoslav nationalism could be carried out in a street named after the emperor.'

Princip looked at the narrow, innocuous looking side street. It was the perfect place to set an ambush and prepare to wait for his enemy, just as his ancestors had in the Grahovo Valley.

*

Johnny saw a commotion as he stepped out of City Hall; one of the conspirators was being dragged around the back to the police station, followed by a baying crowd.

He ducked out of the way, realising that things were getting pretty hysterical. The last thing he needed was for one of his former confederates to see him and involve him in a riot. There were more than enough gendarmes and army officers hanging around to make things difficult.

He needed to find the archduke's chauffeur before Breitner took him in to see the governor. He'd only got a fleeting look at the chap as the archduke's car drove past, but he was confident that the chauffeur would be with the line of neatly parked cars outside City Hall.

Johnny recognised the smooth lines of the archduke's car first and then saw the powerful frame of the chauffeur. He'd taken his jacket off and was crouched down at the back of the car, under the petrol tank. A grey-haired officer hovered behind him, waiting to hear his report.

'The damage looks fairly superficial, Colonel von Harrach, just some small scratches and dents from bomb fragments,' the chauffeur said, standing up and putting his cap back on.

'Very well Loyka, we'll see to it later,' the grey-haired officer said and then hurried up the steps of City Hall.

'Hello there – Loyka, isn't it?' Johnny said, taking the opportunity to approach the chauffeur.

The chauffeur looked at Johnny, trying to identify the unfamiliar gentleman. 'That's right, sir. How may I be of service?'

'You might remember me from the incident this morning?'

'I can't say that I do.' The chauffeur's eyes suddenly changed, as he recognised Johnny. 'You're one of them!'

'What? No, I'm not!' Johnny protested, but it was too late – Loyka had grabbed him around the neck. 'I just need to talk to you. I need you to tell them what I did!'

'I'll tell them all right!' the chauffeur snarled before shouting to the gendarmes outside City Hall. 'I've got one of them. I saw him throw the bomb!'

Johnny tried to grapple with the chauffeur, but he was too strong. He could see the angry mob, which had been following the person taken into the police station, coming towards him. He wondered for a moment who it was that had been caught. Then he headbutted the chauffeur and as the man stepped back to hold his nose, Johnny got in a short, sharp jab that knocked him out cold.

He hadn't been the captain of his school's rugby team for nothing, he mused, picking up the chauffeur's cap. He had a vague plan, but before he could do anything, two gendarmes had him.

Johnny struggled to get away, but the mob surrounded them and started to kick and punch. He heard muffled shouts of command and a burly officer pushed his way through the mass of bodies.

'What the hell is going on here?' he demanded.

Johnny's relief turned to apprehension as the sun glinted on the officer's monocle and he recognised Matthias, Libby's lieutenant. He smiled at Johnny, emphasising a livid, duelling scar on his left cheek. Johnny could smell the schnapps on his breath.

Matthias turned to the gendarmes. 'How dare you accost a gentleman in the street like this!' he shouted, but the gendarmes maintained their grip.

'This man is a terrorist – he made an attempt on the heir's life,' one of the gendarmes replied.

Matthias looked at Johnny, enjoying his predicament. 'Who says so?'

'He does,' the gendarme said, pointing at the chauffeur, who was lying on the floor, still out cold and unable to corroborate the story. In his shirtsleeves and without his cap there was no way to identify who he was, which was as Johnny had planned.

'Lieutenant, I demand that you order these men to release me immediately. I work for the joint ministry of finance. You can check with a Herr Breitner at City Hall that I am bona fide,' Johnny's German master at school had been a Pomeranian grenadier in the Franco-Prussian war and the German he'd learnt from him allowed Johnny to muster some authority. Matthias dismissed Johnny's sham with an indifferent shrug of his shoulders.

'Actually, I was hoping for a chance to meet you again. You left with the young lady rather abruptly last night. No need to explain. I know how these things work,' Matthias said knowingly.

Johnny wasn't sure if Matthias was implying something about Libby or if he felt he'd been slighted in some way, but under the circumstances Johnny thought it best not to challenge him.

Matthias turned back to the gendarmes. 'Let him go. Didn't you hear the gentleman?'

'But he's a terrorist, sir,' one of the gendarmes said.

'How can he be a terrorist? He took the house for all he could last night!' Matthias barked, not used to having his orders questioned.

The gendarmes let go. Johnny couldn't work out if Matthias actually believed his story or if Libby had secured his patronage some other way.

'The main reason I was hoping to see you again, was to apologise for my conduct last night. Copying another player's betting strategy is inexcusable.'

'Think nothing of it, Lieutenant, my pleasure.' Johnny smiled – Matthias was just a fellow cheat acknowledging a fellow cheat, he wasn't implying anything about Libby.

'But I must thank you and the young lady.'

'The young lady? What about the young lady?' Johnny asked.

'Without her knowledge of the service entrance we'd never have got out of that place with our shirts,' Matthias grinned. It was impossible for Johnny to tell if he was grinning because of the money he'd won thanks to Johnny, or as a result of Libby's services.

'As it stands, I won enough money to buy a new mount, so I'm very much in your debt.' The lieutenant seemed blissfully unaware of the crowd, who were anxiously watching the exchange. Their blood was up – they needed a sacrifice and Johnny was determined that it wouldn't be him.

'In that case, I'd be grateful if you'd allow me to be about my business and take this man into custody. I believe he's a terrorist. I saw him tampering with the archduke's car,' Johnny said, pointing at the chauffeur.

The lieutenant bowed and signalled to the gendarmes, who took charge of the chauffeur and dragged him through the crowd. Johnny knew he'd come back round presently and start screaming bloody murder. He wanted to be with Breitner before that happened, so he shook hands with the lieutenant and hurried back to the reception.

Chapter 37

Breitner returned to the reception and made his way through a phalanx of officials who had gathered around General Potiorek. The decision to change the programme of events had caused some confusion, and without the local liaison provided by the governor's aide-de-camp, Colonel von Merizzi, the archduke's retinue was struggling to make the necessary arrangements. To Breitner's surprise, they were still discussing possible routes that the motorcade should take when it left the reception.

'Might it not be better if we advanced directly to the hospital along Appel Quay and cut out the planned route through Franz Joseph Street?' one of the archduke's aides asked, as Breitner took up position next to the governor.

'Yes, those backstreets are far too narrow for a speedy exit. Appel Quay provides a much better option,' Potiorek agreed.

Very well, we shall adopt that route,' a staff colonel from the archduke's chancellery said, before turning to catch Dr. Gerde, Sarajevo's chief of police, who was hurrying to leave. 'Dr. Gerde, would you be so good as to repeat the governor's exact words to the drivers?'

'Yes – yes, of course,' Dr. Gerde said impatiently, barely acknowledging the staff colonel and rushing to take his place at the head of the motorcade. Breitner realised he didn't have much time, as the archduke evidently wanted to leave immediately. It was now or never.

'General Potiorek, forgive the intrusion – may I have a moment of your time, please?' Breitner asked, as obsequiously as he could.

The governor barely glanced at him. 'Breitner, I thought I'd made it perfectly clear that the archduke's visit is not your concern.'

'Forgive me, Your Excellency. My undercover operative has returned. If you would care to hear what he has to say, you'd agree that it's imperative we cancel the remainder of the archduke's programme.'

Potiorek glared at Breitner, fighting to hide his irritation. 'Cancel the programme? Quite impossible! Didn't you hear? His Highness has asked to see Colonel von Merizzi in hospital. What kind of intelligence officer are you?'

The governor pushed past Breitner before he could respond, and went to join the Duchess of Hohenberg, who had swept in holding a small bouquet of flowers. Breitner followed in the forlorn hope that he could make his case directly to the royal couple and he watched as the duchess addressed her husband.

'Franzi, are you visiting the wounded without me?'

'Yes, before the official engagement at the museum. My duty is clear, Sophie, but I can't have you exposed to any further danger,' the archduke replied.

'And what of my duty? I will go with you to the hospital,' the Duchess said and Breitner was once again touched by the affection they had for each other.

'But Your Highness, you are not scheduled to attend the reception at the museum,' Potiorek interjected.

'As long as the archduke appears in public today, I will be at his side,' the Duchess said firmly, putting an end to the discussion.

No matter how many undercover operatives he 'conjured up' for General Potiorek, Breitner knew that in the charged atmosphere it would be futile to suggest abandoning the hospital visit, let alone the rest of the official programme.

He wondered whether von Merizzi, wounded and lying in hospital, regretted persuading the archduke to come to Sarajevo the previous night. Now it was also on his account that the archduke was being put in harm's way, yet again.

*

Johnny entered the foyer and began to search for Breitner. This would be his last chance. If the little Hungarian couldn't arrange some sort of commendation, everything Johnny had gone through in Sarajevo would have been for nothing.

'You always remind me of a little boy with his nose pressed up against a sweet shop window.' A smooth liquid voice brought Johnny out of his stupor. The girl in the pink and white dress was standing next to him. She reached across and picked a small grey, metal fragment from the lapel of his jacket. It took Johnny a moment to realise that it was a piece of the bomb casing which Nedjo had thrown. 'A few inches higher and it would have been in your neck,' she said, handing it to him.

'Thank you. Sorry, do I err …?' Johnny bumbled. There was something about her that turned him into a tongue-tied idiot. It was an uncomfortable feeling for him. He usually put the ladies aflutter.

She smiled and arched an eyebrow. 'Don't you know me, Krumpli? This might remind you.' And there in the foyer, surrounded by the leading citizens of Sarajevo, she gave a nimble roll of her hips. Johnny choked, suppressing a laugh as he remembered.

'Sorry, the bomb blast must have knocked the sense out of me.' It was all coming back: the auburn hair now tightly tied back and those amber eyes. 'You're the dancer.'

'At last, Krumpli!' she laughed.

'Why do you keep calling me "potato" in Hungarian?'

'Well, what else am I to call you? You are as stupid as a potato and you never took the trouble to introduce yourself. Too busy trying to lift my robes.'

'That's not exactly true – it was more your veil, actually. I mean, is it any wonder I didn't recognise you, when the last time we met, you were dressed like that!' Johnny flushed. 'Anyway, I apologise. My name is Jonathan Swift, but you can call me Johnny.'

'Johnny,' she repeated with a smile. He liked the way she said his name, full with the richness of European culture and sophistication. It was as if she was trying something new and foreign, and she liked it.

'I am Katalin Zhofia Weisz. You may call me Kati.' They shook hands formally. 'At last we meet properly, just as I am about to leave for Belgium.'

'Belgium – you're going to Belgium?' Johnny bit back his disappointment.

'Yes, in the morning. What's wrong with Belgium? My mother was Belgian,' she said defiantly.

'Nothing. I can see that a lot of good things come from Belgium ….' he replied appreciatively. 'And lace, chocolate, beer. Why are you going to Belgium? Is that where you're from?'

'It's for my father's work – he's a civil engineer.' She pointed out a distinguished man milling around with some austere local dignitaries. He was very different from the showy carpetbagger who'd had Johnny sacked.

'He looks like a very important chap,' Johnny said.

'Yes, he's been specially brought here to advise on the construction of a new railway line. And before you ask, he doesn't know I dance in cafes. That is just for me.'

'Is that your actual father?' Johnny asked, not sure if he could believe anything she said.

Kati rounded on him, self-assured and precise. 'I never said that the gentleman at Prosvjeta was my father. You jumped to that conclusion all by yourself, Krumpli.'

'I didn't actually jump to any conclusion. The chief administrator described you as the chap's daughter,' Johnny said, starting to remember why he didn't trust her. 'Do you work for Breitner?'

'Is this really the conversation you want to have, now that we have found each other and we can be ourselves?' Kati put on a mock pout, which sent Johnny reeling.

'Are you being yourself? Your real self? I mean, you've fooled me a number of times.' Not that that seemed important to Johnny any more.

'I was just doing my patriotic duty,' she said with a bored sigh. 'Can we not talk of how you're going to entertain me, on my last night in Sarajevo?' Kati's voice implied every type of promise known to man. Johnny looked into her mischievous eyes and couldn't believe his luck.

She started to make another teasing motion with her hips but Johnny put up a shaking hand to stop her. 'You'll cause a sensation behaving like that at an official reception for the heir apparent.'

They'd had a few strange looks already and Johnny could hear a commotion from the reception room; for a moment, he thought he was going to be asked to leave without getting a chance to speak to the governor.

'Don't look so worried, Krumpli. It's just the archduke and his wife preparing to leave,' Kati said in her usual, mocking manner.

Johnny wondered for a moment who was going to drive the royal couple if their chauffeur was in custody. He instinctively felt for the chauffeur's cap he'd stuffed into his pocket and knew how he could put things right.

He started to move away. 'Where are you going, Johnny?' Kati's silky voice stopped him for a moment. He looked up, noticing the domed ceiling for the first time, and then at her, but he couldn't let himself be distracted again, not after the terrible mess he'd made of things the last time a pretty girl called his name.

*

Breitner made a quick search of the foyer for Johnny and wasn't surprised to find him missing. He left City Hall and found a position at the bottom of the steps, to add what little protection he could to the heir; as a civil servant Breitner never carried a weapon.

He considered running to his office to try to find his old service pistol, but before he could, the archduke and his wife rapidly descended the red carpet, hardly acknowledging Sarajevo's municipal officers who were standing along the steps.

The royal couple looked nervous when they took their seats in the Gräf & Stift. As in the previous journey, the archduke sat on the left-hand side of the back seat, with the duchess to his right and Potiorek directly in front of him, on a pull-down chair.

Breitner was thankful to see that von Harrach, the owner of the car, had taken Breitner's own previous place on the left-hand running board of the car next to the archduke, to shield him from any further attempt on his life. The last attack had come from the river side of Appel Quay; it stood to reason that they could expect another from that direction on the return journey.

Breitner glanced along the motorcade and saw that the lord mayor and the chief of police were sitting in the first car, so he made his way towards them to offer his services.

The car pulled out just as Breitner got to it, much to the amusement of the municipal officers on the steps behind him. The second car drove past quickly and then the archduke's car lurched in front of him, and to his dismay, Breitner saw that Johnny had dressed himself up as a chauffeur and was driving. He tried to signal to von Harrach, but he was too busy looking along the embankment to pay him any notice.

Breitner jumped onto the running board of the next car in the procession, ignoring the shooting pain in his hand and clung on for dear life. He had a fairly good idea of what Johnny was up to and was determined to prevent the errant young Englishman from causing him any further embarrassment.

*

Johnny pulled at the chauffeur's jacket, which he was finding a bit loose. He'd been relieved to find it on the front seat where Loyka must have left it to examine the back of the car, but he was starting to wonder if he'd ever wear clothes that fitted again.

All he needed was a chance to talk to the archduke in person and make him see sense. Although Johnny was starting to question the soundness of his plan, the archduke hadn't appeared to be in a mood to be trifled with when he climbed into the car. Johnny wondered if driving away from Kati might not have been a bit rash. It may even have been the biggest mistake he'd made so far.

The last time Johnny had driven a car he'd been in Montmartre with Libby and had ended up wrapping Sir George's shiny new Austin Phaeton around the art nouveau railings of Abbesses Station. Johnny was glad that they were going in a straight line along Appel Quay. He was finding the high wooden steering wheel of the Gräf & Stift quite awkward and the gear mounting was unfamiliar, which had caused him a bit of a problem as they set off, but he seemed to have got away with it, apart from a few angry curses from the governor.

Johnny looked out across the river at the grand dome of the Emperor's Mosque and almost swerved. Trifko Grabez was standing by the Emperor's Bridge, but he made no attempt to attack the car from Bogdan Zerajic's historic position. If they'd turned onto the bridge, as General Varesanin had, it might have been a different story.

Johnny steadied himself – so far so good; all he had to do was follow the cars in front. Von Harrach was hanging onto the other side of the Gräf & Stift, behind the passengers, and was more concerned about assassins than who was driving.

The two cars in front began to slow down and turn right into Franz Joseph Street, following the course that Johnny had seen in the newspaper. He slowed to do the same. He saw the familiar advert for Törley champagne on the corner of Schiller's Delicatessen, and struggling with the steering wheel, managed to execute a half-decent turn into the narrow street. He started to straighten up to follow the two cars as they approached the tight, left-hand turn, where the road turned into the main part of Franz Joseph Street.

Johnny heard a snort of consternation from the back seat. 'What is this – Franz Joseph Street? Stop, this is the wrong way.' General Potiorek tapped Johnny on the shoulder, sharply. 'We are supposed to be going to the hospital via Appel Quay!'

Johnny stopped instantly in front of the delicatessen and was not sure what to do next – he had thought they were going to the museum. He stared at the people lined up along the street. They all seemed to think that this was the route the archduke would be travelling, as had the drivers of the first two cars. Johnny wondered if this might be the moment he was

The Assassins

waiting for to talk to the archduke while the people in charge established what was going on.

'Come on! Get us back onto Appel Quay – what's the delay?' Potiorek demanded. Johnny abandoned his plan and reached across for the gear stick mounted next to him on the running board. Out of the corner of his eye he could see the duchess, sitting directly behind him and waving at the people beside them on the pavement.

Johnny crunched the gears as he struggled to find reverse, attracting von Harrach's attention. 'Who the devil are you?' von Harrach said, as he leant in over the front passenger seat, keeping his voice down so as not to be overheard by his esteemed passengers. 'You're not my driver! Where's Loyka?'

'Your driver was taken ill, Herr Colonel.' Johnny involuntarily rubbed his bruised knuckles. None of this was helping him find reverse.

'Nonsense!' Von Harrach looked around at the crowd in front of him and realised that this wasn't the best time to have the discussion. 'Just get us out of here.'

*

Breitner's car stopped suddenly on the corner of Franz Joseph Street. His wounded hand gave out under the sudden jolt and he fell off the running board, flat on his back. Fumbling on the side of the car he managed to stagger back onto his feet. An unfamiliar feeling of panic swept through him as he wondered why they'd stopped. He knew that something must have gone terribly wrong.

He looked around to see if he could borrow a side arm from someone, but none of the officers in the motorcade looked to be armed with anything more dangerous than a ceremonial sword.

He started to push his way through the crowd onto the corner of Franz Joseph Street and was relieved to see the archduke's car slowly starting to reverse towards him. Nothing had happened. The motorcade had just taken a wrong turn. Von Harrach was still on the left-hand running board of the car, shielding the heir.

Breitner was considering whether or not to confront Johnny when he saw a gaunt youth pointing a gun, to the right of the royal car. Panic overwhelmed him as he realised that von Harrach was on the wrong side. He started to run.

*

The royal car stopped abruptly, a few paces from Gavrilo Princip. He recognised the tyrant, fully plumed, and Potiorek, but the presence of the duchess made him pause. She was directly in front of him and so close he could see flowers pushed into a red sash around her waist.

He dismissed his uncertainty and determined that he would not fail this time. A peculiar feeling began to take over him, focusing him on what needed to be done. He knew this was his destiny. He would prove himself.

Gavrilo's first instinct was to throw the bomb, but it was tied to the left-hand side of his belt. The crowd were pushing and shouting, 'Viva, long may he live!' and as his strength started to fade with the nervous excitement sweeping over him, he decided that it would be too difficult to untie the bomb from his belt, unscrew the top, prime it and throw.

He took the automatic from his pocket. Oblivious to the immediate danger, the driver of the tyrant's car was reversing very slowly. Gavrilo lifted his pistol and aimed at the archduke.

*

Johnny was feeling very pleased with himself. He'd managed to overcome all manner of technical difficulties to get the car to reverse and he was even managing to use the high steering wheel fairly competently.

He had the car backing up nicely towards the embankment when he saw Breitner come charging around the corner, causing him to almost stall, which released an outburst of complaint from his passengers.

*

The gaunt youth was only a few feet away. Breitner was confident he would get him when he was hit by a blinding flash of pain that knocked the wind out of him.

*

Johnny gazed in amazement as Breitner crumpled and fell to the ground. Mihajlo Pusara, the actor, had burst out of the crowd and punched Breitner in the stomach. Then Johnny heard the metallic click of a gun being cocked and understood immediately why Breitner had been running. Gavrilo was standing a few feet away from the car, pointing a pistol at him.

*

Excitement was welling up inside Gavrilo as he pointed his gun at the tyrant, turned his head and fired. The people around him immediately started to beat him. He thought he'd fired twice, maybe more, but he couldn't see if he'd hit anyone. He put the gun to his head and prepared to join Bogdan Zerajic. Somebody pulled the gun away before he could squeeze the trigger.

The gun was ripped out of his hand and he dropped his bomb in the struggle, but he managed to unwrap his cyanide and swallow it, amid a swirling torrent of punches and kicks. Gavrilo started to retch violently and was thrown to the ground.

*

Johnny watched the crowd beating Gavrilo, trying to understand what had just happened. Army officers from the motorcade joined the struggle around Gavrilo and one of them hit him with the hilt of his sword. Johnny felt a sudden urge to go and help Gavro, as some of the other members of the crowd were doing.

'Take us to the hospital man, at once, do you hear?' Potiorek snapped, bringing Johnny back to attention.

Johnny thought that Potiorek meant to carry on with his improvised tour. Franz Ferdinand and Sophie were both sitting bolt upright and Johnny assumed that both of the shots had missed, as he'd seen Gavrilo look away when he fired. Everything seemed to be alright; he'd saved the royal couple while under fire. Then, as he continued to reverse onto Appel Quay, Johnny saw a bright crimson sheen of blood in the archduke's mouth.

The duchess saw the blood at the same time and called out, 'In God's name what has happened to you?' She slumped forward onto the archduke's lap and he called to her.

'Sopherl, Sopherl! Don't die! Live for our children!'

Johnny fought to block out the nausea and shame he felt and concentrate on driving the car. He couldn't see a wound on the duchess and hoped that she'd just fainted. Von Harrach, who was still on the running board next to the archduke, held the heir up and stopped him from falling forward as Johnny reversed the car back on to Appel Quay.

Crowds of people had gathered at the end of Franz Joseph Street, blocking the embankment. Johnny glanced around again at the archduke. Von Harrach was wiping blood from his mouth, and asked if he was in pain. Franz Ferdinand repeated over and over, 'It is nothing', but the distress on his face told a different story.

'We'll never get through that mob!' the governor shouted at Johnny. 'Take us to my residence – go over Lateiner Bridge.'

Johnny turned the car onto the narrow, cobbled bridge and drove as fast as he could while the governor barked directions.

They reached the mansion and he stopped the car next to four, resting, stone lions. The archduke had started to make a rattling sound; the jolts from the drive appeared to have aggravated his condition.

Johnny joined the doctors who'd rushed to treat the royal couple and helped carry the archduke as he and his wife were brought up to the first floor of the residence. The archduke was put on an ugly green and red chaise longue in the governor's study, while his wife was taken into the adjoining bedroom. Downstairs he could hear the clatter of cutlery as preparations for the governor's lunch continued.

In his shocked state, Johnny had a vague notion of trying to talk to the archduke to explain what excellent service he'd been to him, up until he was shot.

He immediately regretted the idea. The archduke's bleeding had worsened; there was blood on the gold stars of his collar insignia and down the front of his tunic. His breathing had become barely audible as he started to lose consciousness.

The four doctors in attendance started to cut off Franz Ferdinand's uniform, desperately searching for his wound. Johnny knew it was hopeless; he remembered Ilic's words, "Where this hits, no medicine can help". Dejected, he turned to leave and saw von Harrach with a group of outraged soldiers, blocking the door.

'There you are, skulking in the corner like the rat you are. Waiting to finish your handiwork, no doubt.'

'I beg your pardon?' Johnny replied in disbelief.

'You deliberately drove the archduke into a trap!' von Harrach shouted, drawing some angry glances from the doctors.

'What are you talking about? I most certainly did not,' Johnny said indignantly. He knew he should have done more to prevent this from happening, but he thought von Harrach's accusation was a bit strong.

'Save it for the hangman!' von Harrach bellowed and signalled for the soldiers to seize Johnny.

Chapter 38

Johnny came to on a rough, stone floor with a hazy memory of being hit over the head with a rifle. He could hear muffled voices and a door open and close behind him. He realised that he was in an office and thought he recognised it, but he just couldn't remember where it was, or when he'd been in it before.

The door swung open again. Johnny looked around and saw Gavrilo and Nedjo sitting in a medical room directly opposite him. His stomach turned over – they were in a terrible state.

A bloated, pasty-faced man made sure that Johnny saw the scene, then closed the door. Johnny realised then that he was in the City Hall police station; he'd sat in that same medical room when Breitner recruited him.

'I'd say, under the circumstances, you've got off lightly,' the man said. Johnny tried to get up but his legs gave way. The man signalled to a guard and Johnny was hauled into a chair.

Johnny now recognised the man as Leo Pfeffer. The chap from the consulate had sent Johnny to see him when he had first arrived in Sarajevo. 'Mr Pfeffer, you know me. I came to see you a few weeks ago,' Johnny said.

'Did you really?'

'Yes, I asked you about the nationalist movement in Bosnia.'

'It appears you found them, by all accounts.' The last time they'd spoken Pfeffer had told Johnny that there was no nationalist movement in Sarajevo and it seemed that he wanted to cover up his lack of knowledge by pretending not to know him.

'Look, Mr Pfeffer, there have been some pretty wild accusations flying about, but it's nothing that can't be explained. If you contact Lazlo Breitner he can straighten everything out.' Johnny felt that this was his only real chance to escape this mess. He couldn't expect any help from Sir George, since this was exactly the sort of thing that Sir George had been hoping would happen to him.

Pfeffer put his glasses on, the preliminary side of their discussion over. 'I've been appointed as the investigating judge of this case, and as such it is my duty to inform you that Her Highness the Duchess Sophie of Hohenberg, died on arrival at the governor's residence.'

Johnny was shocked. 'But surely, she just fainted.'

'One of the shots that Princip fired penetrated the right side of the car and hit her in the lower abdomen. His Imperial and Royal Highness the Archduke Franz Ferdinand of Austria-Este died ten minutes later, from a wound to his neck.'

'Princip couldn't have done that … he wasn't even looking at them when he fired.' Johnny felt numb.

'The bullet hit the heir apparent just under the collar of his jacket, nicked the jugular artery and embedded in his spine,' Pfeffer said blandly and then began to charge Johnny as an accomplice in the murder of the archduke and his wife. All that Johnny could think of was the blood in the archduke's mouth. It had been the first time that he had seen anyone shot and he hoped to God it would be the last.

Viktor Ivasjuk, the hawk-faced chief of detectives, whom Johnny had also met when he first arrived, wasn't quite so formal when Johnny was dragged into his office later that night. He examined the contours of Johnny's skull and deduced that he was a degenerate criminal, of the worst order.

'Maybe there is something to Lombroso's theory of criminology, after all,' Johnny said with a smile, trying to hide his unease at the examination.

Viktor struck Johnny in the face – his methodology didn't appear to be a laughing matter.

'Who were you working with to assassinate the heir apparent?' If Viktor recognised Johnny from their previous meeting, he saw no need to mention it.

'Look, as I told the investigating judge, you need to speak to Breitner. I've been working with him – you sent me to see him for goodness' sake!' Johnny was deeply shocked by the deaths of Franz Ferdinand and Sophie and wanted to help in any way he could, but he saw that Viktor wasn't in a mood to listen to reason. Johnny knew that anything he said to him, without Breitner to verify his story, would only implicate him further in the conspiracy.

Viktor picked up Bogdan Zerajic's skull from his desk. If the gesture was meant to be an intimidation tactic, Johnny felt it was a good one.

He levelled his close-set eyes on Johnny. 'You were acting under instructions from Belgrade and Narodna Odbrana. I can smell it on you. They told you to stop the heir's car in front of Princip.'

'No, some old duffer tapped me on the shoulder and told me to stop the car – Potiorek I think his name was – the governor. He's the chap you need to speak to.'

Viktor put down Bogdan Zerajic's skull and punched Johnny in the face. 'How dare you talk of the governor in that way?'

'The only person I took instructions from was Lazlo Breitner, of the joint ministry of finance,' Johnny said, through a cut lip. He'd taken quite a beating since he'd come to Sarajevo and was becoming increasingly concerned that it would spoil his good looks.

However, Viktor seemed satisfied that Johnny wasn't a Serbian agent and began to change tack. 'Give me the names of all of the revolutionary scum you've been associating with. We need to clear them from our streets!' he shouted and punched Johnny again.

'I'd be happy to cooperate fully, but I need to speak to Breitner first.' The names were Johnny's last bargaining chip and he was starting to worry that if he gave them to Viktor, Breitner would have no reason to help him get out of this disaster.

'Maybe you'd be more talkative after a little bath?' Viktor almost smiled.

'A bath?' Johnny didn't like the sound of that.

'Yes, I find submerging my subjects under water to be an effective method of extracting information.'

'You don't really need to go to all that trouble. I've told you all I can,' Johnny said in disbelief.

Two guards picked Johnny up and dragged him to a large tin bath in the corner of the room. They held him over it and blood started to drip off his face into the water. He could just make out his reflection and was glad to see that it didn't look too bad.

'Are you sure you don't want to tell me anything?' Viktor asked.

'Yes, damn it!'

'Very well.'

The guards dropped Johnny. He landed on the floor with a crash.

'What are you playing at, man?' Johnny groaned.

'I know who you are. I recognise the symmetry of your face from the last time we met,' Viktor said.

'Why did you go through this pantomime, then?' Johnny asked in dismay.

'I wanted to make sure you weren't one of them. The indentations on your head suggest you are prone to deceit.'

Johnny was dragged into another interview room and after several hours Breitner entered with a face like thunder. 'What have you done this time, my English friend?'

Johnny pointed at his face. 'Look what they've done to me.'

'Never mind that, just tell me everything you know.'

'You've got to help me get out of here ...'

'I've vouched for you – that's all I can do for the time being. I need to know what else you've found out,' Breitner said patiently.

'Well, I rather think you've missed the boat on that. They've done it.'

Breitner finally lost his temper, 'I am willing to overlook your missing our meeting to go gambling – don't try to deny it. I have found out everything. There is nothing I can do about that now, but if you stand in the way of justice and refuse to tell me the names of everyone who took part in the murders of the heir apparent and his consort I'll leave you to Viktor.'

Johnny told him what he wanted to know and for his trouble found himself back in the same whitewashed cell that Breitner had left him in before. After everything he'd been through, he was in an even worse situation than when he'd started.

This time he had to share the cell with a number of leading Serb citizens who'd been rounded up and beaten after the assassination. If Gavrilo Princip's aim had been to unite the South Slav people through the outrage, he had dramatically failed. Johnny's cellmates told him that the assassinations had caused widespread revulsion in all of Sarajevo's communities. Nonetheless, full-scale reprisals against the Serb population had broken out all across Bosnia and Herzagovina.

Johnny's new cellmates were eventually transferred to the military prison and the bells of Sarajevo, which had been tolling for the royal couple, finally stopped. Johnny was left alone and in silence, to rot.

All he could do was hold fast and wait for Breitner to return. He was worried about Libby; he'd heard that a mob had thrown stones at the Serb-owned Hotel Europe and he had no idea if she'd been hurt. However, his real concern was that she might leave Sarajevo without him. He'd abandoned her with all their money and rushed off. He tried to fight off his nagging doubts about her loyalty. She had, after all, come to Sarajevo to find him eventually, so that she could win back the money for her husband, but only once she'd bored of Barton-Forbes.

Johnny couldn't decide if he'd really seen her go into the bank of Austro-Hungary or not after the bomb went off. Even if she had been there he was sure that there was a harmless explanation, but the thought that she'd banked the money beyond his reach, in her own name, was an unsettling one.

He had to get out of the cell before she did something stupid, like give the money to Sir George. There wasn't much point in Johnny going back to Paris; he'd totally failed to stop the archduke's assassination, and all of the information he'd gathered for Sir George had been superseded by events.

Johnny spent most of the time thinking about what he'd do next. Once he got his half of the money from Libby he could do as he pleased. He hadn't given it much credit before, when he was winning at the club, but the world was on the cusp of untold creativity and innovation. He could be part of that, and, starting with Belgium, he could go anywhere.

After six days, Breitner finally turned up with a supercilious grin on his face and his ridiculous pince-nez gleaming. For a moment, Johnny was overjoyed.

'Breitner, thank God!' he blurted out, before managing some semblance of self-control. 'Where the hell have you been? I've been in this stinking hole for nearly a week!'

'I needed to keep you somewhere safe, Johnny. You have a tendency to wander off,' Breitner grinned. 'Also, I was quite angry with you. If you'd done what you were told we might have prevented the assassination.'

'You deliberately left me in here?' Johnny almost punched him. 'I told you what was going to happen!'

'Yes, that's true, but you drove the archduke right in front of his assassin and stopped. That took some explaining.'

'The governor told me to stop.' There was a whiny tinge to Johnny's voice that made Breitner smile.

'Apparently, you drove the wrong way, as well.'

'I was following the cars in front!' Johnny shouted. He didn't know how many more times he was going to have to say it. 'Which were following the official programme.'

Breitner gave Johnny a hard look. 'Evidently no one thought to tell the drivers that the route had changed. There's an unholy row and I doubt that we'll ever get to the bottom of it all. I can only imagine what you thought you were hoping to achieve by getting into the archduke's car at all. Did you honestly think he'd stop and chat with his driver?'

Johnny shrugged – none of that seemed important now. 'Look, have you been able to clear this mess up? The chap who owned the car was bloody angry.'

'I've spoken to Colonel von Harrach and explained that, as one of my operatives you were doing your duty by stepping in and driving the car when his chauffeur became involved in an altercation with the crowd. Von Harrach is mortified that his driver was taken into custody minutes before he was due to drive the heir apparent, and as I pointed out, he didn't notice you were driving the car until it was too late. He's willing to let the matter drop. Your part in the whole sorry affair will be quietly forgotten and expunged from the records – so you won't receive a commendation.'

'Oh well, that's what I expected. I might as well be on my way.' Johnny made to leave the cell; he needed to get back to Libby and the money. Breitner didn't move out of the way and Johnny thought that he must want a proper farewell, so he went to shake his hand. 'Thanks a lot, old man. It's been fun, but I have urgent matters to attend to.'

'I still have need of you, Johnny.'

'But I've done everything you asked. We tried and failed. It's time to cut our losses and make a run for it.'

'I need you to come with me to Vienna.'

That was the last place Johnny wanted to go. As far as he could see, there was nothing for him in Vienna. 'Why on earth do you want me to go there?'

'For the good of the monarchy and of course, the gratitude of a thankful nation.'

'How long are you going to keep dangling that carrot?' Johnny asked. He waved at the walls of his cell. 'I've had about as much as I can stand of your nation's gratitude. 'You need to offer something new to get my attention.'

'I understand that a lady of your acquaintance went to Vienna a few days ago. She might even still be there.' Breitner handed Johnny a folded piece of paper. 'This was left for you at the Hotel Europe.'

*

Breitner was satisfied to see that Johnny was as upset by the note as he'd planned he would be and so didn't have any difficulty hurrying him out of his cell. Breitner had paid Johnny's hotel bill and collected together the belongings he'd brought to Sarajevo after he'd placed him in Mrs Illic's boarding house. He gave them to Johnny as they left the City Hall police station and then guided him into an official car.

There wasn't much time before their train was due to leave and it had already taken most of the morning to obtain Johnny's release from the local police. Breitner had downplayed Johnny's significance as a source to the investigating judge, in an effort to reduce the embarrassment of having an operative of the joint ministry of finance involved in the shooting of the heir apparent and his consort and then consequently being interrogated by Viktor Ivasjuk.

As a result, Breitner had been kept on the periphery of the investigation by Leo Pfeffer, who ignored the information Breitner gave him with the same disdain which General Potiorek had shown. Breitner's reputation from Vienna had again preceded him.

He was, however, as a representative of the joint ministry of finance, allowed to observe Princip and Cabrinovic's interrogations. The conspirators initially denied that they'd been working together, and Princip had expressed regrets at Sophie's death, stating that his target had been General Potiorek.

Not expecting to survive the assassination, neither of them had given any thought to what they'd say if they were caught, and because of this lack of preparation, they let slip a few important details.

Princip mentioned that he'd been living in Ilic's house and so the house was quickly searched and Ilic arrested. Breitner had tried to tell Pfeffer that Princip was registered at that address and that Ilic had been heavily involved in organising the plot, but he'd been ignored.

Nedjo Cabrinovic also told the investigators that he'd come from Belgrade with two other youths, which led them to deduce that he'd been working with Princip, and that there was a third person on the loose. At first they suspected that it might have been Ilic, but when Trifko Grabez was discovered trying to leave Bosnia without a permit, he was quickly identified as the third man.

When Breitner's car pulled up at Sarajevo Station he was immediately hit by a feeling of sorrow; the last time he'd been there it had been with the royal couple on the day of the outrage. He fought off his regrets, knowing that he still had work to do. He pulled Johnny to the ticket office and purchased two first-class train tickets; it was going to be a long journey to

Vienna and he needed to rest. The past week had been a very difficult time for Breitner. He hadn't approved of many of the methods used by his fellow investigators, but had been totally powerless to stop them, he reflected.

Over two hundred Serbs had been arrested in Sarajevo and many of them were placed under the cell windows of the conspirators, so that Princip and the rest could hear as the guards beat them. All of the known associates of the four were rounded up, including the staff at the Cabrinovics' cafe. Eventually, the conspirators agreed to cooperate with the investigation to prevent any further innocents from being hurt.

As the conspirators gave up more information they corroborated what Breitner had been telling Pfeffer and he was eventually allowed to participate in the investigation fully, helping with the capture of Cvjetko Popovic and Vaso Cubrilovic. Mehmed Mehmedbasic managed to cross the border into Montenegro and remained the only conspirator to evade capture.

Breitner was less successful in preventing inflated reports of Belgrade's involvement in the plot from being sent to Vienna. The police had been keen to make a connection between the assassins and Belgrade from the start. Viktor Ivasjuk had even said that Nedjo had admitted to him that he and Princip had received their weapons from the general secretary of Narodna Odbrana, a Pan-Slavic organisation which had largely abandoned paramilitary activity. This was something which Cabrinovic violently refuted when he was questioned by Breitner and the investigating judge.

More importantly, Princip and Cabrinovic revealed that they had planned the assassination in Belgrade, and mentioned the involvement of a man named Milan Ciganovic, a government employee on the Serbian state railway.

All of this was interpreted in Vienna as evidence of the Serbian government's participation in the assassination. The Serbian government strenuously denied these claims and pointed out that the assassination had been carried out by citizens of the Austro-Hungarian monarchy.

The noise of the trains brought Breitner out of his thoughts. Instinctively he looked round for Johnny and saw him watching the train being shunted. He turned to Breitner. 'Is it true that Kati Weisz's father is an engineer and that he was working on the railway in Sarajevo?'

'Is that what she told you?' Breitner frowned at the lapse in security, but he didn't suppose that it mattered now. 'Yes, her father has worked on every railway from Transylvania to Cairo. She was brought up as wild as a gypsy – how do you think she learned to dance?'

Johnny smiled, apparently pleased that he'd managed to substantiate that much of her story, at least. Breitner moved forward, shepherding Johnny onto their platform.

'So how do you know her?' Johnny asked.

'I knew Miss Weisz while I was stationed in Vienna. We recently became reacquainted at a local Chamber of Commerce function which her father was giving. He needed a Hungarian translator, so I attended and had the privilege of seeing her perform an extraordinary interpretation of a classic Hungarian folk dance.'

Breitner remembered the intriguing, spiralling movements of her dance. 'We have a similar interest in mathematical conundrums. Kati's quite an accomplished mathematician. Her father would be lost without her and her sister, Esther. They've been checking his work for years.'

'Kati's a mathematician?' Johnny asked with surprise. It was clearly the last thing he had expected to hear.

'Yes, although it is Esther who is truly brilliant.' Breitner gave him his most condescending smile. 'When she dances you see the provocative movements of a sensual and accomplished woman. For Kati, she's solving complex mathematical problems, mapping out patterns, searching the rhythms of the universe, the symmetry of a seashell, the spiral of the human ear.'

Johnny walked on in silence towards their train, taking in the information, then asked, 'Does she work for you, Breitner?'

'I'm not a spymaster, Johnny, I'm just a humble civil servant. I have to improvise and make use of whatever I can, as I did with you. I have a few informants who do me the odd favour, picking up coffee house gossip and such things. Kati wasn't a great deal of help until you came along.'

'You planted her at the cafe?' Johnny stopped and looked at Breitner.

'I asked her to perform – it was easy enough to arrange. She is quite fearless and I thought I might need something to tempt you back into the fold.' Breitner had been shocked by how well his plan had worked. 'It hadn't been my intention to get you sacked from your job, Johnny. She was only supposed to pass you a message. I hadn't anticipated the strength of your attraction.'

'No, that surprised me too,' Johnny smiled.

'Haven't you got enough trouble with the ladies, without adding any further to it?' Breitner asked as they clambered aboard the train.

Johnny looked downcast. He had a very mercurial temperament, Breitner noted. A porter showed them to their compartment on the train and Breitner tipped him and asked for a newspaper; he needed to keep abreast of the latest opinion in Vienna.

Ilic had been interrogated earlier that day. Breitner hadn't been present but he had been told that his interrogators had made Ilic false promises, playing on his fear of the noose. Ilic had given them a more detailed account of Ciganovic's involvement in the plot. He told them how Ciganovic had helped Princip and the others to get in contact with Major Tankosic, a Serbian Army officer who not only approved the assassination, but provided weapons and support for the assassins.

This revelation was now being loudly flaunted as proof of the complicity of the Serbian government in the assassination, adding weight to calls by generals Conrad von Hotzendorf and Potiorek for a pre-emptive strike against Serbia.

Johnny had told Breitner of Tankosic's involvement when they had met on the tram prior to the assassination and Breitner had duly passed the information on to his superiors at the joint ministry of finance and his contacts in Budapest and Vienna. He'd assumed the report had been lost in the biggest bureaucracy in Europe. Then today, he had received immediate instructions to bring his informant to Vienna.

*

Johnny looked blankly at the picturesque mountain ranges that streamed past as the train chugged its way towards the Austro-Hungarian homeland.

Libby's note had been written in her usual curt style. She couldn't wait around anymore and had gone to Vienna. She was sure he could make his own way there and that he would appreciate that the spa season was starting and that she didn't have time to play 'silly buggers'. The money wasn't mentioned – Libby would have thought that too vulgar.

Johnny looked over at Breitner sitting opposite him in the compartment, reading his newspaper. He would have liked to have told Breitner where he could stick his precious monarchy, but he didn't even have the money for the train fare home.

They'd barely said a word since they'd got on the train. Johnny had been too busy reflecting on what to do about Libby and what Breitner had told him about Kati. He felt some consolation that she hadn't been lying to him;

the sooner he got this over with the sooner he could go and find her in Belgium, he decided.

'What's all this about, then? Why are you dragging me to Vienna?' Johnny asked.

Breitner looked up from his paper with a sigh. 'The hardliners in my government are blaming Serbia for the outrage and are demanding punitive action be taken.'

'The assassins received help from Serbian nationalists, but Princip was acting independently.'

'Well, that's why we're going to Vienna. I need you to tell your story.'

'Surely, General Potiorek is to blame. There were hardly any police on the streets and he told me to stop the car in front of Princip.'

Breitner waved his newspaper. 'There is amazement that the general hasn't been reprimanded. Potiorek's brazening it out, deflecting attention away from himself by blaming the Serbians.'

'You mean he's kept his post?'

'The emperor has forbidden any internal investigation into the organisation of the visit and hasn't pressed for the punishment of the local officials whose negligence led to the assassination.' Breitner shrugged. 'I imagine that this is all very embarrassing for him. There is a lot of blame to go round. It is a mess from start to finish. Also, there is a lot of support for General Potiorek within the government. Potiorek might have been able to do more but he was in the line of fire. The shot that killed the duchess could have hit him and, God help us, he's one of our top generals. We'll need him if there is a war.'

'The deaths of the archduke and his wife could have been so easily prevented,' Johnny said, wondering if the assassination was going to be put down to the Viennese love of a muddle.

'Potiorek claims that you can't legislate against an assassin who isn't scared of dying, unless you evacuate the whole city,' Breitner said.

'Why didn't he do that then, after Nedjo threw his bomb? Johnny asked.

'Cabrinovic was given that bomb by members of the Serbian military. Don't you think they should be called to account?'

'Yes, but Nedjo shouldn't have been allowed to get anywhere near the city, let alone the archduke,' Johnny said and Breitner gave him a reproachful look. Johnny felt momentarily guilty; he had his share of blame for the debacle.

'The point is, Johnny, they attacked and killed the heir apparent and his consort – that can't go unanswered and whether or not it could have been easily prevented is irrelevant. To even suggest that an Austrian might have been negligent lessens the guilt of Serbia.'

'But you've caught the people who carried out the assassination.'

'Don't be so naive, Johnny. Do you think the hardliners will be content with executing a few Serb peasants?'

'So what's the alternative? Declare war on Serbia, because a few rogue members of the Serbian Army gave their support to Gavro and his friends?'

'The assassination is a godsend for the hawks. It's given them all the moral reason they need to bring the Serbians to heel and make them fear Vienna again. They think the monarchy can then at last reassert itself in the Balkans, at the same time halting the flood of nationalism that is ripping it apart.'

'So the hardliners are in control?'

'Paradoxically, it was Franz Ferdinand who was the main bulwark against them,' Breitner sighed.

'So is there nothing that can be done to force a diplomatic solution?' Johnny asked.

'That brings us back to the purpose of our mission,' Breitner answered wryly, before reopening his newspaper.

Chapter 39

The Honourable Pinkston Barton-Forbes watched patiently as the black flags flew over the Hofburg Palace, the sprawling assortment of buildings that had been the centre of Habsburg power for centuries. The dynasty had survived the Turks, Napoleon and revolution and he had no doubt that it would survive this crisis.

Pinkie had positioned himself at the outer gateway of the palace, alongside representatives from the monarchy's oldest families and Vienna's diplomatic corps. It didn't, however, seem like a good moment to try and add to his list of contacts. His chief had sent him on behalf of the embassy to pay last respects when Archduke Franz Ferdinand and the Duchess of Hohenberg were taken to their final resting place. The cortege was due to leave shortly at 10.00 p.m., and Prince Montenuovo, the preening martinet of a court chamberlain, was ensuring that everything ran like clockwork.

Pinkie looked at the crowd gathering opposite him along the Burgring. There wasn't a great feeling of mourning in the city, but during the prescribed four hours, thousands of people had filed past the royal couple as they lay in state. Then the doors had been slammed shut, regardless of the mourners still waiting outside.

The archduke hadn't been liked at court, and it seemed the court would do no more than protocol dictated for the heir apparent. Many, including the court chamberlain, were safe in their positions now that Franz Ferdinand had gone.

The overriding feeling at the embassy, and, Pinkie assumed, with the rest of the diplomatic corps standing around him, was one of relief. Europe would be more stable without a wildcard reformer like Franz Ferdinand waiting in the wings to ascend the throne of one of the great powers. The Austro-Hungarian monarchy was useful only if it kept peace in the Danube Basin and the Balkans.

Pinkie suspected that the Austrians would go off half-cocked over the assassination, making inflated demands for recompense, but he had no doubt that the whole thing would blow over. He was more concerned about the Russians; they had started playing up in Persia again, encroaching on the neutral territory next to Britain's principal oil supply. In the midst of that emergency, Pinkie had been obliged to attend the official memorial service held that afternoon at the Hofburg Chapel, with his chief, Sir Maurice de Bunsen, the British ambassador. Pinkie had been livid – he was supposed to be preparing for his summer vacation.

The whole thing couldn't have come at a worse time as far as he was concerned; he'd already had to postpone his departure by a week. To add insult to injury, there weren't any heads of state at the service, so Pinkie didn't get an opportunity to advance his career. The Austrian government hadn't been able to guarantee their security after the fiasco in the Balkans and poor old Franz Joseph wasn't up to entertaining an international event. Pinkie presumed that there must have been a number of problems with etiquette behind the scenes. It would have been bad taste to have invited the Tsar, considering Russia's connection with Serbia. However, it would have caused great offence not to have asked him, as a head of state of one of the great powers.

Consequently, only diplomats were allowed to represent their respective countries at the service. All in all, Pinkie felt that Prince Montenuovo was surpassing himself in making a shockingly third rate affair of the whole thing.

The royal couple had been returned to Vienna the previous night with little ceremony. The small cortege made an eerie procession through the capital. Once at the Hofburg Chapel, the duchess's coffin had been placed eighteen inches lower than the archduke's, reflecting the duchess's inferior lineage to that of her husband. A black fan and white gloves were also placed on the lid of her coffin, the traditional symbols of a lady-in-waiting, and a reminder of Sophie's past. Pinkie usually approved of such distinctions being made, but in these circumstances they seemed a bit churlish.

The memorial service itself had been thankfully quick and efficient. The emperor had looked suitably impassive, reflecting the austere, medieval atmosphere of the chapel. Pinkie had heard a rumour that when Franz Joseph was told of the assassination he'd said, 'The Almighty cannot be defied with impunity. A divine will has re-established that order of things which I, alas, was not able to preserve.' This was believed by most to be a reference to the archduke having married beneath himself. To Pinkie's mind, the statement didn't sound like the old man's style.

Some questioned whether or not the emperor felt any grief over the death of his nephew. However, Pinkie's contact at the Hofburg told him that when the emperor had met Archduke Charles, his great nephew and the new heir, he'd burst into tears, saying, 'Nothing at all is to be spared me.' These were the same words he'd used when his wife, Empress Elisabeth, was stabbed to death by a lunatic anarchist.

Very few royal families could have had so much grief to bear, Pinkie reflected. The emperor and his wife had lost a baby girl, Sophie, to illness. Their son, Crown Prince Rudolf, had killed himself in what was thought to have been a murder suicide pact with his lover. The emperor's brother Maximilian, the Emperor of Mexico, was executed in the country's revolution. Franz Joseph's youngest brother, Karl Ludwig, had died of typhoid after drinking water from the River Jordan and now the emperor's nephew Franz Ferdinand and his wife had been assassinated, leaving three orphaned children.

The only wreath in the chapel, aside from those sent by the diplomatic corps, was one made up of white roses and was from Sophie, Max and Ernst. The children were not present at the service; they were in a state of total anguish and paid their respects privately.

On the way out of the chapel, de Bunsen had let slip that he wanted to send Pinkie to Persia to deal with the Russian business. Apparently most of the diplomatic service were already on holiday and they needed a safe pair of hands. Pinkie had said that he didn't speak Russian and that it might be better to send someone who actually spoke the language. The chief had replied curtly, 'Yes, that's a pity, but there's no one else.'

The sound of hooves on flagstones announced the funeral cortege as it began the procession to the Westbahnhof; from there the royal couple would be taken to Pochlarn Station and on to Artstetten Castle, where the archduke had arranged for them to be buried together in a crypt built under the family church.

Pinkie bowed his head as the first hearse came through the central arch of the outer gateway. The cortege was fairly small considering it carried the heir to the throne and inspector general of the army. Pinkie thought again that this was obviously the work of the court chamberlain, intent to the last to do no more than protocol demanded. There was no military parade, aside from a small army detachment, and the only uniformed people were court officials and officers from the archduke's suite. Pinkie was shocked;

he felt that there should have been representatives from all branches of the armed forces and every regiment that the archduke had served in.

The members of the monarchy's oldest families, standing around Pinkie, saw this short measure and over a hundred of them began to walk behind the procession. They'd served the Habsburgs for centuries and wouldn't stand to see its heir slighted. A number of army officers also began to follow the cortege and Pinkie couldn't help but be moved and felt compelled to join them. If there was one thing he hated more than nasty little social climbers it was jumped-up officials, drunk on their own power.

It was a resentment that was becoming all too evident in Pinkie's relationship with his chief; he couldn't believe that de Bunsen had had the temerity to suggest sending him to Persia during the spa season. Pinkie had arranged to go to Marienbad where he'd take his place with the elite of Europe – it would have been perfect. The sensuous Lady Smyth had breezed back into his life on the ill wind from the east, and he felt that she wouldn't be able to resist the draw of Europe's most exclusive spa. Having the beautiful wife of a senior diplomat in tow would ensure he'd be invited to the more choice parties. Pinkie had even managed to secure adjoining rooms in a very discreet hotel.

He couldn't believe that the Russians were threatening to spoil everything, but he had no idea how to get out of the secondment to Persia and he continued to ponder the problem as the cortege arrived at the station. He followed the procession onto the platform to find the usual Viennese muddle. He watched as Prince Montenuovo handed the caskets over to Janaczek, Franz Ferdinand's estate manager, and then how with little grace, he withdrew any further official help for the transportation of the royal couple, stating that the rest of the journey was a matter for the 'private' arrangements the archduke had made for his burial.

After that, Pinkie was warmed to see an impromptu line of the monarchy's archdukes, headed by the new heir apparent, form along the platform to send Franz Ferdinand off on his last journey and no doubt demonstrate their outrage at the court chamberlain's behaviour. Then, through the smoke of the departing train, Pinkie saw the answer to all of his problems – Johnny Swift, strolling through the assembled dignitaries as if he owned the place.

Chapter 40

Breitner gazed around at the plush interior of the Hotel Klomser's restaurant with a melancholy he seldom expressed or felt. Someone certainly had a sense of humour, he decided.

'What's up? You've hardly touched your pud,' Johnny said, stuffing his face with strudel. Despite Johnny's reluctance to come to Vienna, he'd been quick to enjoy the delicacies the city had to offer. He'd made his way through a schnitzel, baked chicken and the emperor's favourite, asparagus and boiled beef. He was now trying every type of cake, tart and pastry he could fit into his mouth.

'This isn't feeding time at the zoo,' Breitner answered.

'I've just spent a week in one of your filthy cells,' Johnny said. He finished his strudel and moved onto a slice of rich chocolate cake, then looked Breitner up and down. 'If I cared, I'd say you were a bit windy, ol' man.'

The phrase didn't translate well in the clear, precise German which Johnny had started speaking since their arrival in Vienna, but Breitner understood the subtext.

'It's being back here – where it all began,' Breitner said.

'In Vienna?'

'The Hotel Klomser.'

'How so?' Johnny asked.

Breitner had never spoken of it before, but as crass as he found Johnny, he'd become the closest thing to a friend he'd had for a year. So Breitner told him how he'd come to this hotel with four other officers to tell his comrade and mentor, Colonel Redl, that he'd been exposed as a spy and to ensure that he did the honourable thing. Redl had been sitting at his desk putting his affairs in order when they'd arrived. He'd gazed up at Breitner, saying that he knew why they were there and then he'd asked Breitner to help him end his life.

Breitner had given Redl a Browning pistol and then left with the other officers. When they'd returned at 5.00 a.m. they'd found that Redl had shot himself. He'd left a note to the effect that frivolity and his passions had been his downfall and he was taking his life to atone for his sins.

The full extent of his sins would probably never be known, Breitner explained to Johnny, but it was rumoured that he gave the Russians 'Plan Three', Austro-Hungary's strategy for invading Serbia. 'When Franz Ferdinand found out that we'd allowed Redl to take his own life, it ended my career,' he recalled. Despite the betrayal and the ensuing catastrophe, Breitner still couldn't shake the remorse he felt about his part in Redl's death.

'Excuse me, gentlemen.' Breitner looked up to see that an aide was standing at their table. 'The count will see you now.'

The aide showed Breitner and Johnny into a stylish suite, where they were greeted by the tall, dignified figure of Count Istvan Tisza, Hungary's prime minster. Breitner immediately stood to attention; he hadn't been expecting to report directly to such an esteemed person. As a true conservative, Breitner greatly admired the count.

'Thank you for coming so promptly, gentlemen. Please take a seat. My aide tells me that you found the restaurant to your liking,' Tisza said, bemused.

Breitner glared at Johnny – they'd evidently taken advantage of the count's hospitality. 'Yes, thank you, Your Excellency,' Breitner stammered, embarrassed.

He considered Tisza the only Hungarian statesman to have the gravitas and strength to walk the difficult tightrope between keeping Hungary's Austrian partners in the dual monarchy context whilst simultaneously dealing with the uncompromising nationalists at home. He was reviled by both sides, and particularly by Franz Ferdinand, who'd been convinced that the Hungarian prime minister was plotting against him and the monarchy as a whole. Breitner remembered with distaste Franz Ferdinand's rant at the Hotel Bosnia the night before he was murdered.

'Please, sit down. I apologise for the subterfuge,' Tisza said in German for Johnny's benefit. 'It's imperative that we keep this meeting strictly between ourselves and I'm told that this is the last place that anyone suspicious of your reasons for coming to Vienna would look for you.'

Breitner couldn't detect any irony in Tisza's statement; he wasn't sure if the count was referring to the exclusivity of the hotel or the unhappy memories it held. He supposed there were people in Vienna who might want to know why he'd returned.

Breitner managed to keep stony-faced and Tisza appeared satisfied with his reaction and so he continued. 'I am in urgent need of accurate information. The reports that we've received from Sarajevo are confusing and contradictory.'

'Hopefully we can clarify matters, Your Excellency,' Johnny said, in surprisingly good Hungarian. Tisza shot him a withering look, making it clear that he should only speak when spoken to, but the count continued in Hungarian.

'However questionable these reports may be, they are fuelling demands for war from many of the most powerful people in the monarchy. I believe that in our current condition such a war would be disastrous for the Austro-Hungarian monarchy. The army hasn't seen action since we took charge of Bosnia and Herzegovina in 1878, and it struggled to overcome the opposition it encountered even then. It is unlikely to fare any better now as it is woefully ill-equipped and undertrained. The nationalist situation within the monarchy is also very delicate: any further drop in its prestige could tip the balance and renew calls for greater freedoms for minorities or worse.' Tisza paused for a moment to ensure that they understood what he was saying, which Breitner assumed was that if Austro-Hungary lost a war with Serbia it would fall apart.

'Diplomatically, the monarchy is also in a weak position. Romania, Bulgaria and Russia will be aligned against us should we attack Serbia. What I need, gentlemen, is solid information, something that can delay the pro-war party, so that I can find a diplomatic solution or create a situation that will give us a more favourable position, should we go to war.'

The great man finished and gestured that they could now speak. Breitner ran through what he knew for sure – that the Young Bosnians had planned the outrage in Belgrade and were trained and supplied by members of the 'Black Hand', a Serbian nationalist organisation connected to Serbian intelligence.

Tisza nodded. 'Are you able to elaborate further?'

'Johnny should be able to – he infiltrated the terrorists' cell, Your Excellency,' Breitner answered.

Tisza turned and looked at Johnny. 'Yes, the spy. Come, speak – that is why you are here, after all.'

Johnny shifted uncomfortably; he didn't like Tisza's tone. 'I have been promised certain recompenses for the services I've performed for the Austro-Hungarian monarchy.'

'Payment! You want *payment* to help prevent a war?'

Breitner thought it opportune to intercede. 'If I may explain, Your Excellency. Johnny doesn't require money, merely a letter of commendation to show his superiors to demonstrate that he has been of service.'

Tisza nodded curtly, 'Let us hear what you have to say, then we shall discuss your "recompense".'

Johnny told Count Tisza that from what he'd observed of Princip and the rest of the cell in the weeks preceding the outrage, the influence anyone in Belgrade had over them was minimal. The Black Hand had even tried to cancel the plot at one point, provoking a full-scale confrontation between the ringleaders. Johnny described how Princip had completely ignored the cancellation order. He had even got the impression that there was a great deal of antagonism between Princip and Belgrade, or one of the members of the Black Hand, to be precise.

'Interesting – certainly grounds for further investigation to verify what you have alleged,' Tisza said, deep in thought. 'There is a meeting of the council of joint ministers of the monarchy tomorrow, to discuss the matter. Breitner, I'm sure you will join me, and this gentleman should be on hand in case there is need for further clarification.'

'I would be honoured,' Breitner replied. 'But I thought you wanted to keep our meeting a secret.'

Tisza smiled apologetically. 'My dear chap, no one there will have the faintest idea who you are. This was the hotel where Redl shot himself, was it not?' Tisza asked shrewdly.

Breitner tensed. 'It was.'

'And in the ensuing scandal, you were exiled to Bosnia?'

'That is correct, Excellency.' Breitner suspected that the real reason for their meeting in the Hotel Klomser was so that Count Tisza could see how well he dealt with difficult situations.

'It is almost as if you've come full circle. I will have need of you as long as the present crisis lasts, and if we prevent a war I will need someone with your expertise to advise on the South Slav nationalist movements and to monitor their activities with a view to preventing this situation from arising again. I may even have you reinstated in the Intelligence Bureau.'

Breitner couldn't believe it. 'Is that possible, Your Excellency?'

'I don't see why not. Franz Ferdinand's gone so there is nothing stopping it.'

Breitner bowed stoically. It was more than he could have possibly hoped for. Johnny coughed, attracting the prime minister's attention. 'Although I have serious reservations about your reliability, young man, what you have told me could be of some small service. If it proves such you shall have your letter.'

'The Austro-Hungarian monarchy could also reward me for my services, financially, if that is more convenient,' Johnny smiled.

Tisza glared at the impertinent youth and then left. He obviously found the whole transaction with Johnny repugnant, but Breitner assumed that he'd needed to gather every piece of information he could before confronting the council of joint ministers, and if he could hear it directly from its source then so much the better.

Chapter 41

Breitner struggled to concentrate as the council of joint ministers discussed the Balkan crisis. Officially, he was there to take Hungarian minutes for Count Tisza, so following convention he had begun by recording the principal participants at the meeting, starting with Tisza himself, then Count von Berchtold, the Imperial Foreign Minister, Count Sturgkh the Austrian Prime Minister, General von Krobatin, the Minister of War, and lastly the minister in charge of Breitner's department, Count Leon von Bilinski, the Joint Finance Minister. Breitner had met generals and the heir to the throne, but these men were the real power in the monarchy he loved so dearly.

After spending a year in the furthest corner of the empire this current situation was a bewildering turn of events for a rational and methodical man like Breitner. When he had started to investigate the Young Bosnians he hadn't dreamt it would lead to him sitting in a state room at the Ballhausplatz, the administrative centre of the Austro-Hungarian monarchy, with the men who would ultimately inform the emperor's decision on whether or not to take his country to war.

Breitner gathered himself and tried not to think about the possibilities the future held; everything still depended on the outcome of this meeting. He began to record the report of Count Alexander Hoyos, a senior official from the Foreign Office. Hoyos had just returned from Berlin, where he'd been dispatched at the beginning of the assassination crisis to determine German support for any punitive action the monarchy chose to take against Serbia.

Hoyos was currently explaining that the kaiser had been at the Kiel Regatta when the news from Sarajevo was delivered; he was reported to have said that the assassination had shaken him to the depths of his soul and that Franz Ferdinand had been one of his closest friends.

Hoyos had met with the German Chancellor, Bethmann Hollweg, and the Deputy Minister of Foreign Affairs, Alfred Zimmerman. They'd given him firm assurances of German support for any action the monarchy chose to take against Serbia. 'They left it to the monarchy's discretion as to what form that action should take,' Hoyos concluded, adding that Germany felt that they should act immediately, while there was still worldwide sympathy for the assassination of the archduke.

'But what of the Russians, my dear Hoyos?' Berchtold, the elegant Imperial Foreign Minister, asked with effortless charm. Breitner could see why he was sometimes compared to a poodle by his political opponents.

'The view in Berlin is that the Russians will not interfere in what is largely a matter of honour,' Hoyos replied.

'I'm not so sure,' Berchtold said, addressing his comments to the assembled ministers. 'I believe it is very likely that Russia will intervene if we invade Serbia. Nonetheless, if we don't act now we are only delaying the inevitable. Russia is continuing to spread its influence amongst the South Slavs and building a Balkan alliance against us. Added to that, we have the growing problem of nationalism within our borders, undermining the cohesion of the monarchy.

'The situation will only deteriorate if we don't make a timely settlement of accounts with Serbia. The South Slavs within the monarchy will align themselves with the new revived Balkan states in the face of the monarchy's perceived decline.'

Breitner quickly wrote down what Berchtold had said, as his view was echoed and supported by the other council members. 'In short,' Berchtold summed up, 'now is the time to take decisive action against Serbia, while unconditional support from Germany is guaranteed. The only way we can stabilise the empire and secure our southern border is to make a decisive show of force and dismember Serbia, absorbing her into the monarchy and dividing what we don't need amongst her enemies. Thus, we will eliminate Serbia as a political factor, once and for all.'

'That is totally unacceptable,' Tisza said, outraged by the suggestion. His objection, Breitner presumed, was that if any more angry South Slavs were brought into the Austro-Hungarian monarchy they would cause more trouble and dilute the Magyar power base, undermining its control of the Hungarian half of the monarchy.

'Is it your personal view that Serbia should be added into the monarchy, Foreign Minister, and not necessarily a view supported by our German allies?'

Berchtold made no reply and Tisza continued. 'As I see it, there is no necessity for overwhelming or immediate action. War would not solve any of our problems. If we were to attack Serbia without any warning it would only undermine our standing and position in the world and start a war with Russia. The rational course of action is to present a list of demands to Serbia. If they agree to them we would win a major diplomatic victory, humiliating Serbia and greatly increasing our standing in the Balkans.'

'What if our demands are rejected?' Berchtold asked.

'Then we'd have the moral justification for taking military action – something along the lines of a short-term occupation of Belgrade, not a full-scale destruction of Serbia, which Russia would never stand for.'

Berchtold pointed out that previous diplomatic victories against Serbia may have increased the monarchy's standing in Europe, but they'd only stirred up further trouble among the nationalists in the Balkans, which had led directly to the assassination of the heir to the throne. It was time for a radical solution and to do away with the Pan-Slav movements once and for all.

Berchtold's statement was strongly applauded. Sturgkh added his endorsement. 'If we employ a policy of indecision and weakness, Germany could lose confidence in the monarchy and withdraw its support.' Bilinski and Krobatin also agreed, arguing that a diplomatic victory would be pointless unless it led to war.

'I am not convinced that the Serbian government was complicit in the assassination,' Tisza said. His statement was met with dismay by the council members. Constitutionally, they needed his assent before any resolution could be passed.

Tisza was nonplussed by the reaction of his council colleagues. 'There is some evidence to suggest that Serbia trained and equipped the terrorists who carried out this terrible outrage, but it is not conclusive,' he said, before looking at Breitner. 'There is even some evidence to suggest that the terrorists were acting on their own initiative. We need proof before an ultimatum can be delivered. I therefore suggest further investigation to find out the extent of Serbia's involvement – then we can put informed demands to the Serbian government. If they fail to meet these demands, military action will be inevitable. We will then legitimately be able to argue that we are acting in self-defence and would not run the risk of alienating the Balkan states and starting a war we cannot win.'

Tisza put in a final caveat. 'While our demands should humiliate Serbia, they should not be so excessive that they couldn't possibly accept them – otherwise the whole exercise would be wasted.'

The Assassins

The joint council had little choice other than to accept Count Tisza's proposal. Breitner was delighted; he may not have saved his country from war, but he might at least have helped to save it from annihilation. He hoped that it would be enough.

*

Johnny waited in a long, draughty corridor, surrounded by the imperial grandeur of an empire in decline. He wasn't sure what possible use he could be now; he'd done his bit and wanted to find Libby, so he could press on to Brussels.

The self-important Hungarian aristocrat had insisted that he be at hand – Johnny thought that his impudence was astounding. It was almost enough to make him want to take up Princip's banner of violent action. Johnny smiled to himself; he couldn't imagine a single rabid revolutionary who liked his creature comforts as much as he did.

He wondered briefly what had happened to Gavro and the rest. Then he decided that it was probably best not to ask; he didn't really care anyway. They'd known it was a one-way ticket from the start and Johnny still had a lot more living to do – something he planned to start immediately with the lovely Lady Elizabeth Smyth, before she went back to her husband and he moved on to his beguiling dancer.

He considered himself to have been dashed lucky to have met Pinkie at the station. Johnny and Breitner had arrived in Vienna some time earlier, but it seemed fitting to make a final farewell to the royal couple, whose lives had become so inextricably entwined with their own.

Pinkie had approached them, introduced himself to Breitner and invited them both to a gathering at the embassy in honour of Franz Ferdinand. Such things were apparently essential to measure the mood of the diplomatic community. Pinkie even hinted that Libby would be there and Johnny decided that he'd been wrong about Pinkie and that he was in fact, a bloody decent chap.

Breitner had declined the invitation, but made no objection to Johnny attending. Breitner hadn't been at the top of his game since their arrival in Vienna and Johnny assumed it was something to do with what had happened to this Redl chap.

Breitner and his new master, Count Tisza, finally came out of their conference and ushered Johnny into a room that had been decorated in a squiggly, white-gold, Rococo style. Tisza handed Johnny a letter with the Imperial Seal on it.

'Lovely job. That should do the trick. Much obliged, governor,' Johnny said. He wasn't sure how much use the letter would be now, but he thought he'd play the game. Unfortunately, his attempt at cheeky cockney didn't cut any more ice with the Hungarian prime minster than his schoolboy Hungarian had. Johnny grinned – it had still been worth the effort of learning it. There had been a very forceful Hungarian maid at his boarding house in Paris. She'd taught him the basics and quickly helped him get over his disappointment at being in Paris and not actually having a French maid. It was a truly unique language.

'I need you to accompany Breitner back to Sarajevo to assist him in his investigations.' Tisza's voice cut through Johnny's memories.

'I beg your pardon. I think I missed something,' Johnny said.

Breitner gave Johnny a fierce look as the count repeated himself. 'It's very likely that there will be a war. If so, as I've explained, we need to enter it in conditions favourable to the Austro-Hungarian monarchy.'

Johnny understood. 'You don't want to look like the bad guys and bring in Russia and half the Balkan states against you. So you want Breitner and myself to go all the way back to Sarajevo and rake up some dirt to prove that the Serbians planned and executed the whole thing. Very wise.'

Tisza looked a little piqued by Johnny's glib analysis, but decided to rise above it. 'The Germans have given us their unconditional support to act as we see fit, but they don't think the Russians will interfere in our bid to get justice for our dead heir. However, if Russia does object to any military action we take against Serbia, I would like to be able to demonstrate that we were acting purely in self-defence against the aggressive actions of a foreign state.'

'And what if we can't find anything?' Johnny asked, 'I've told you that Gavro and the rest were acting on their own.'

Tisza continued to look annoyed by Johnny's informal style of address, much to Johnny's amusement. Breitner spoke, to save Tisza's fury. 'What we need, Johnny, is clear, definite evidence of the role Serbia played in the assassinations of the heir and his consort.'

'If you can find evidence to confirm your claims that the Serbian government wasn't directly involved in the assassination, so much the better. We might be able to prevent a war, but I don't think it's very likely that you will find anything. What we are concerned with here is demonstrating the rightness of our cause,' Tisza stated.

The Assassins

'I see,' Johnny said. He definitely didn't like the sound of that, but the easiest thing was to play along. If he refused to go, Johnny didn't doubt for a moment that Breitner would drag him back to Sarajevo in chains.

'Count Berchtold, the imperial foreign minister, is sending a special emissary, Friedrich von Wiesner, to investigate the assassination in Sarajevo and to ascertain what role the Serbian government played in it,' Tisza continued.

'And you want me to help him somehow?' Johnny asked.

'Dr Wiesner is a diligent and conscientious official, but he is a lawyer, not a specialist on the South Slav people. I think your insight into the assassins might be useful in gaining further information from them,' Tisza answered.

'I'm sure there will be a use for you. We could even send you to Belgrade. As an English citizen you could go there and speak to the leaders of the Black Hand as an unofficial intermediary,' Breitner said indifferently. Johnny looked around at him in horror, realising that Breitner really didn't care what happened to him.

'You will, of course, receive the thanks of a grateful nation for your services,' Tisza said, in the same way he'd thank a servant for polishing his boots, and then pointed at the door.

'When do we leave?' Johnny asked Breitner as they left the Ballhausplatz and made their way past the romantic splendour of the Hofburg Palace into Michealerplatz.

'There is a special train laid on for us in the morning.' Breitner said, distracted as they turned onto Herrengasse.

'So I can still attend that function at the British embassy?'

'I'll send your apologies. We have an early start and we should prepare for the investigation in Sarajevo,' Breitner said.

'We can do that on the train. Really, there is no need for me not to go. I mean, it is in the honour of the archduke and it will be shockingly bad form if I don't go. I might even be able to find out what the thinking is in London about your little Balkan predicament.'

Breitner gave him a preoccupied look as they returned to the Hotel Klomser. 'Go if you must, Johnny. You'll only get in my way if you stay.'

Chapter 42

Johnny relaxed in the warm embrace of the diplomatic service, free to enjoy the restrained elegance of the British embassy in Vienna, surrounded by the sparkle of a well organised function. There was no way he would go back to Sarajevo, not for anything. He'd received his letter of commendation and something special was formulating in the back of his mind. Even if Libby wouldn't play along, Johnny had an idea innovative enough to dazzle his superiors.

Most significantly, Johnny didn't have Breitner with him to stop him drinking. It was a welcome change after the hardships he'd endured and no more than he felt he deserved.

Pinkie was helping Johnny along nicely with the champagne, making sure that the waiters didn't miss him as they circulated the room. Pinkie had even provided Johnny with a frock coat for the occasion; Johnny was amazed by how much of a decent chap he was turning out to be.

'Look, Johnny, I'm sorry about this,' Pinkie said, as he passed him another glass of champagne. 'Awfully sordid to talk shop I know, but we're rather in need of a translator and I seem to remember you talking Russian to that Trotsky chap ... would you mind? It's for the chief.'

'I'd love to.' Johnny flushed – he'd been drinking and hadn't intended to sound quite so keen.

'Yes, quite.' Pinkie tried not to grimace at Johnny's exuberance and led him to Sir Maurice de Bunsen, the British ambassador in Vienna, who was happily conversing in French with his Russian counterpart, Nikolai Shebeko and their respective staff members about some business in Persia. They didn't appear to need Johnny, and so he began to search the crowd for Libby.

'You! Yes, you. Kindly pay attention and translate what His Excellency is saying.' Johnny looked back and saw that de Bunsen and the cream of Vienna's diplomatic corps were staring at him in silent rage. The Russian ambassador had started to speak in Russian.

Johnny apologised to de Bunsen and broke into the fluent Russian of his early, happy childhood. 'I'm sincerely sorry, Your Excellency. Please forgive my eccentricity.'

The Russian ambassador frowned. 'In answer to Sir Maurice's question, we intend to consolidate our position in the Middle East in order to defend against German encroachment on our interests in that region. Germany's association with the Ottoman Empire is a direct threat to Russia's aim of acquiring the Bosporus Straits and Constantinople. We will not allow them to have the door to where we live.' This was obviously a subject which the Russian ambassador felt very strongly about, and he could clearly only express his strength of feeling in his mother tongue.

Johnny translated for de Bunsen, who asked if Russia would use the current crisis developing in the Balkans as a pretext to drive off the German threat and realise their aspirations for Constantinople.

The Russian ambassador glowered at Johnny. 'The Imperial Russian Government has no intention of going to war on behalf of Serbia,' Johnny translated as the ambassador continued to speak. 'However, if the Austro-Hungarian monarchy were to crush Serbia, the predominance of both Austro-Hungary and her allies in the near-East would become a serious threat to Russia's security. Our interests in the region would also be seriously impeded by a drop in prestige if Russia were not to fulfil its historic role as defender of the Slavs. We would be considered no more than a second rate power.'

De Bunsen exchanged a look with Pinkie and his staff. Johnny didn't think Russia would stand for any further drop in status after the humiliation they'd suffered in their war with Japan and Austria's subsequent annexation of Bosnia and Herzegovina.

'Any threat to the sovereignty of our Balkan little brothers caused by the crime in Sarajevo would not go unnoticed in Russia. We would have no choice but to defend the interests of both ourselves and our allies,' the Russian ambassador declared, reminding Johnny of something that Count Tisza had told him.

'But the Germans don't believe that Russia will intervene in what is essentially a matter of honour for Austro-Hungary to gain justice for their dead heir,' Johnny blurted out in Russian before he'd thought about what he was saying. Both the Russian ambassador and his staff eyed Johnny dubiously.

'What on earth are you saying to the Russian ambassador?' de Bunsen asked, sensing a possible diplomatic incident. Johnny repeated what he'd said in English.

'You can't possibly know that is the German government's thinking,' de Bunsen said sharply, putting Johnny in his place and making it clear that he had no business interpreting the policy of a great power.

'I have a contact in the Austro-Hungarian government,' Johnny said proudly, and sensing an opportunity to shine in front of the British ambassador, he relayed what Count Tisza had said to him during their last meeting.

'Who is this contact?' Pinkie asked. Johnny thought he sounded as if his professional pride had been hurt. 'You've been in Vienna five minutes – you couldn't have had time to make such a high-level connection.'

Johnny doubted that they'd believe him if he said that it was the Hungarian prime minister, and he didn't want to show Pinkie up any more, so he told them about Breitner, exaggerating his importance in the joint ministry of finance. Johnny explained that he'd liaised with Breitner during a recent fact-finding trip that he'd undertaken in Bosnia.

'Is that the chap you were with at the station?' Pinkie asked, turning to de Bunsen. 'Swift was in the company of an official from the joint ministry of finance when I met him at the station, sir. They'd both returned from Sarajevo.'

'Yes, that's right. He's been recalled to Vienna to brief the council of joint ministers on the assassination crisis. Very talkative after a couple of drinks,' Johnny said wryly, reaching for a glass of champagne as a waiter floated past.

De Bunsen and his staff were incredulous. 'This contact told you that Germany has given Austria a free hand to deal with Serbia as they see fit, because they feel Russia won't intervene if Austria attacks Serbia?' De Bunsen had switched back to French so that the Russians could follow what they were saying.

'Well, yes. After all, if any nation is touchy about members of their royal family being assassinated, then surely it's Russia,' Johnny replied, also in French, before finishing his champagne.

The Russian ambassador's face darkened and for a moment Johnny saw why the Russians were known as 'the steamroller of Europe'. 'The thing I dislike about the frock coat is that it makes it difficult to separate the gentlemen from the lackey.'

He spoke in French directly to de Bunsen, who flinched, then turned to Johnny and said, 'I think you'd better go before you do any more damage to our alliance with Russia.'

Johnny managed to find solace for his bruised self-esteem in more champagne. It didn't seem to matter what he did, he would never be seen as 'one of us' by his social superiors, but he knew the day of the lackey was coming. The decaying old aristocrats would be cast out soon enough to make room for the middle classes, if what he'd seen in Sarajevo was anything to go by.

Lady Elizabeth Smyth finally turned up an hour later, gliding through the assembled elite in the same sparkly dress she'd worn in Vittel, indifferent to the envious and admiring stares she received. Johnny approached her and she gave him a cool, sideways glance. 'Oh, there you are. Well, you certainly took your time about it,' she said, moving away. Johnny followed.

'I couldn't get here any sooner. I was detained in police custody,' Johnny said, talking to the side of her head because she refused to turn around.

'Well, that was your own silly fault. I can't believe you ran off like that.'

'So you left Sarajevo without me, Libby.' Johnny didn't really blame her for that, not with all the rioting that had been going on.

'Did you really expect me to wait around for you?' Libby said airily.

'No, I'm sure that would have been too much to hope for,' Johnny replied dully. He knew there wasn't any point in discussing it further – as far as she was concerned she'd left him a note and that was that.

'Do stop being tiresome, Johnny.' Libby turned around at last to show off her refined beauty. They were away from the crowd now, on the periphery of the reception and Johnny felt as if he was about to drop off the edge of the world into turmoil once more. She opened and closed her left hand three times, then exited the function room. Johnny waited for a few moments, then followed. It was an old routine they'd perfected at numerous embassy parties in Paris.

She was waiting behind the third door on the left, in an empty office. 'You look wonderful, Libby,' Johnny said when he'd found her.

'No, I don't. I'm an absolute mess. Do you know how many times I've worn this old rag?' Johnny tried to embrace her, but she pushed him away. 'Don't try and butter me up, Johnny. The money is safely deposited in the Bank of Austro-Hungary and that's where it's staying.'

'But we can go anywhere, do anything! You can buy all the new dresses you want – well, within reason,' Johnny said with a laugh.

'You're worse than that insipid fool, Pinkston. He actually wants me to go to Marienbad with him, for goodness' sake.' She moved away from Johnny to look out of the window, but he saw excitement flash briefly across her face.

'Don't do that. Come with me,' Johnny said, although it hadn't occurred to him where they'd go if she did accept.

'It's all right for you to go running off into the unknown – you're a nobody. One has certain standards, expectations of life. How would I show my face in society if I created a scandal? George has made it perfectly clear that if I pay the money back he'll overlook my lack of judgement. People in our position do, after all, expect these things to happen; they're just not generally done with the staff.'

'If that's how you see it, we don't have to stay together, if you'd rather not. Just give me my half of the money and I'll be on my way,' Johnny said.

'Johnny, it doesn't work like that. We won the money together to pay off the gambling debts we ran up ... together.' She almost spoke kindly.

'I see. What about us? Are we going to stay together?' Johnny asked.

'That is up to you. I'm more than happy to carry on our little arrangement in Paris for the time being. Staff or not, you can be most diverting.' Libby smiled and Johnny was glad to see that all of the beatings he'd received over the past few weeks hadn't blunted her attraction to him.

'But we must settle our accounts,' Libby continued. 'I'm leaving tonight before I allow myself to get any more distracted. You can come with me or stay here, as you choose.' With that, she left the room before he could create any more of a scene.

Johnny looked out of the window, across at the Belvedere Palace. The domes of Franz Ferdinand's official residence rose above the buildings in front of him like a giant wedding cake. He could see a flag was flying at half mast; he knew exactly how that felt, he mused.

He stayed in the room for a while, brooding about his options. He'd never had any illusions about his relationship with Libby, but it seemed maybe he was just as susceptible to women's charms as they were to his. The thought worried him. Perhaps he'd overestimated his effect on women and maybe they had used him, rather than the other way round.

Johnny quickly dismissed the idea as ridiculous. If he went poking about in the depths of his soul he knew he'd be sure to end up inventing any number of terrifying things.

What was really bothering him was whether or not to stay in Vienna. Pinkie had implied that he needed someone with his skills and Johnny wondered if, by making a full report of everything he'd discovered, Pinkie would be impressed enough to overlook the Russian ambassador's remarks and offer him a position, or arrange for a posting to Belgium. All he really had back in Paris was uncertainty.

Johnny found Pinkie holding court with a group of embassy officials; they were laughing about something as Johnny arrived.

'There he is – the man of the moment, Johnny Swift. You certainly know how to put on a show.' The others laughed again and Pinkie signalled for them to go away.

'Sorry, Johnny. I don't mean to tease. You've made quite an impression on the chief.'

'Really?' Johnny asked doubtfully.

'Oh, absolutely. He said you were a bit of a loose cannon but that your Russian's spot on and that you have initiative.'

Johnny grinned, unused to praise, while Pinkie went on. 'As a matter of fact, we may have a job for you if you're interested in being transferred to our firm.'

'Yes, definitely.' Johnny fought to control his excitement. He hadn't even had to attempt to sell himself. This was what it was all about, he thought – dazzle people with a bit of insider knowledge and you're off to a flying start. Although he wondered if he could really call what he'd said to the Russian ambassador 'dazzling'.

'Splendid, splendid. We need you to go to Persia to help sort out some difficulties we're having with the Russians in the neutral zone. I'd do it myself but I simply don't have the language skills and well, to be honest, I was hoping to get away for a few weeks,' Pinkie confided.

'Persia. You want me to go to Persia?' Johnny let what Pinkie had said sink in; all he could think of were arid deserts and bandits. He realised that Pinkie had been priming him to join his network of contacts all along.

'I gather hopeless missions are rather your line,' Pinkie said dryly. Johnny knew then what he had to do and he bowed to the inevitable.

He got to Libby as she was about to board the Paris train. Panting, he pulled her aside and fought to get his breath back. It had been a hell of a run.

'Johnny! How dare you manhandle me?' He didn't let go, despite her indignation.

'We can't go to Paris, Libby,' Johnny eventually managed to say.

She scowled. 'Johnny, we've been through this. I've got commitments. I'm not running away with you.'

'No, you don't understand. We have to go to Switzerland first.' If he was going to do this, he thought, he might as well get it right.

'Switzerland?' Libby lit up. 'You want to take me to Switzerland? You're trying to trick me! You know I simply adore it there.'

'The last of the money I lost in Vittel came from Sir George's bank account in Zurich.'

'The secret naughty fund – so that's why you were so funny when we lost. You sneaky little fibber! Yes, we'd certainly better go to Zurich and pay the money back into his account. You can keep your fortune safe from the tax collectors, but not from Johnny Swift. I can see that George is going to have to take a firmer hand with you in future.' Libby frowned, remembering Sir George's other condition for letting Johnny back into the fold. 'I hope your report's going to be up to scratch.'

Johnny smiled weakly. He'd accepted that he'd have to pay the money back, but he didn't really care if Sir George found his Balkans report up to scratch or not. It was the information that he'd discovered since leaving the Balkans that really mattered. Johnny now planned to take that straight to the British ambassador in Paris, with the letter of commendation from Tisza to prove its authenticity. He had no doubt that what he knew could change the course of events in Europe forever.

'We can't stay in Zurich for long, Libby – things are happening. I need to get back to Paris and impress people.'

'Well, we needn't go straight back, surely. It's the start of the season. Nothing can happen – all of the diplomats are on holiday. I mean, even the kaiser's gone off on a cruise around Norway. I don't see why we can't have a holiday as well.'

Johnny shrugged. He had helped stop a war, or at least helped stop the Austrians from going off half-cocked. He deserved some sort of holiday, after everything.

Chapter 43

Breitner put down his copy of von Wiesner's report and sat back to contemplate the special emissary's findings on the assassination of the heir apparent. The report had just been dispatched to Vienna, and for the first time since he'd learnt of the plot, Breitner felt as though everything was now out of his hands.

He had arrived in Sarajevo with von Wiesner three days previously and had done his best to assist the industrious lawyer, but his presence had been largely resented by both von Wiesner, who quite rightly saw him as a mole for Count Tisza, and General Potiorek, who was determined that the report should prove the Serbian government's guilt.

Von Wiesner had carried out a speedy, two-day investigation into the assassination and the circumstances around it. Working in his hotel room until four in the morning each day, he waded through the mountain of paperwork produced by the civil and military authorities. Von Wiesner also held a number of conferences with General Potiorek, his chief advisors and the lead investigators. Potiorek did his best to shut Breitner out of these meetings, but credentials from the Hungarian prime minister were hard to ignore.

In any event, there was little Breitner could add to what was said. The main focus was on the extent to which the Serbian government had been involved in the outrage in Sarajevo, and that proved to be impossible to determine with the information at hand.

Breitner was inclined to believe that the assassins had been acting independently of both the Serbian government and the Black Hand, although the assassination was certainly supported and approved by officers within the Serbian Army. Whether or not these officers were acting officially or had gone rogue, he doubted anyone would ever know for sure.

Breitner felt the assassins and their confederates might have been able to spread some light on the mystery. Apart from Mehmed Mehmedbasic, all of them had been arrested, including members of Narodna Odbrana, which ran the underground route into Bosnia.

The most senior member of Narodna Odbrana to have been caught was Veljko Cubrilovic, who was the brother of one of the assassins, Vaso Cubrilovic. They'd both taken part in the conspiracy without the knowledge of the other. Veljko was a teacher, with a family, who'd helped Princip and Grabez during their journey to Sarajevo and had directed them on to his friend, Misko Jovanovic, a rich and very nervous merchant from Tuzla. The assassins had been given Jovanovic's name by their contact in Belgrade before they left, as someone who could help them once they'd crossed the border.

Breitner had thought it might have been possible for von Wiesner to do a deal or to apply pressure to get more information about Belgrade's involvement, as had been done in the case of Danilo Ilic. Ilic, Veljko Cubrilovic and Jovanovic were over twenty and would hang, and Breitner had felt that this fact could have been used to pry more information out of them. Veljko Cubrilovic and Jovanovic certainly had a lot to lose; they might have been persuaded to cooperate in return for a lighter sentence. By the terms of Austro-Hungarian law, people under twenty could not be executed. However, Princip and his accomplices would be sentenced to twenty years in prison, an intimidating prospect for teenagers, even assuming they survived the sentence.

Von Wiesner evidently felt that the conspirators had said all that they were going to say to the police and he had declined to interview them, which was largely why Breitner had accompanied him to Sarajevo, to provide insight into their motives.

If Johnny had been there he might have made a difference, but Breitner doubted it. Everything Johnny knew had been fully documented and passed on to von Wiesner, under Breitner's name, so he'd let Johnny disappear in Vienna. They'd both got what they wanted and Breitner knew that if Johnny's role in the assassination ever came to light it would cause embarrassment to both Breitner and the authorities. Consequently, Breitner had spent much of his time purging any record of Johnny's presence in Sarajevo from the official files.

Under the circumstances, Breitner felt that the report von Wiesner had written was remarkably fair. He hadn't found any evidence of the Serbian government's complicity in ordering the assassination of the heir, in training the assassins or providing them with weapons – quite the reverse, in fact.

He did suggest that there was actual proof that the plan to carry out the assassination originated in Belgrade and that elements within the Serbian government should be held accountable for their role in the assassination. He named Milan Ciganovic, an employee of the Serbian state railway and Tankosic, a major in the Serbian Army, as the people who'd assisted the assassins and used Serbian frontier guards to smuggle the conspirators across the border.

Von Wiesner suggested that three demands should be added to any ultimatum sent to Belgrade. Firstly, the Serbian government must end any official involvement in smuggling persons and material across the frontier. Secondly, the dismissal of Serbian frontier officers implicated in the smuggling of the assassins and thirdly, the arrest and prosecution of Ciganovic and Tankosic, by the Serbian government.

Breitner knew that von Wiesner's report was too meek to pacify the hawks. General Potiorek had already added a paragraph to it stating that there was an 'alternative government' in Belgrade that must be held responsible for the assassinations.

When an ultimatum was finally put to Belgrade, Breitner had no doubt that its terms would be a lot stronger than the ones suggested by von Wiesner. Even Count Tisza had been convinced of the inevitability of a war with Serbia; the only question that remained was on what scale that war would be fought.

Breitner had already started packing up what possessions he had in Sarajevo – it was unlikely that Count Tisza would still be in need of his services if there was going to be a war in the Balkans. However, Breitner was still a reserve officer and was expecting his call-up papers shortly. After everything he'd done, it would be the war he couldn't prevent that was going to give him back his career, he realised grimly.

*

Johnny gazed at the vaulted ceiling of Sir George's Swiss bank. This was where everything had all begun. He looked back to the cashier on the other side of the counter; it was the same sober man who'd passed Johnny the recall telegraph from Sir George, triggering the first in his series of rash and cataclysmic decisions.

Johnny smiled and signed the last slip that paid the money back into Sir George's account. It was a lot easier to put money in than to take it out.

'Do stop dawdling, Johnny, we'll be late for lunch. Humpty's expecting us.' Libby had escorted Johnny to the bank, to keep a watchful eye on him and to wire the rest of the money they owed to their creditors.

Johnny shrugged stoically. 'I hope I've put everything right, now.'

'That's the spirit. Don't worry, we still have enough left for a half decent holiday.' Libby led him to a cab and they took the long scenic drive back to their hotel, which was set on a mountain overlooking Zurich, its spires and turrets giving it the look of a fairy-tale castle. Libby snuggled up to him on the back seat of the taxi and whispered the rewards she planned to bestow on him for having paid the money back without any fuss.

They had an excellent lunch with Humpty, Libby's nickname for the retired general she'd met at the Ilidza spa. He'd been in Switzerland as part of his tour of European spas, taking mud baths with innocent chambermaids in the guise of finding the cure for all his worldly ailments. Libby had cabled Humpty to join them, as she felt it only right and proper for him to have a share in the spoils. Part of Johnny had hoped the general would turn out to be his 'uncle'; he could have touched him for a few hundred. He should have known that the old duffer would never have gone to any trouble to keep an eye on him. Johnny was, as always, very much on his own.

'Whole thing's a lot of stuff and nonsense, Swift.' Humpty had decided to share his incisive analysis of the Balkans crisis over lunch. 'Great Britain will place indirect pressure on Austria through Berlin, as they did during the last bloody mess in the Balkans. Berlin will put pressure on Austria to reduce their demands, and Britain will refuse to support Russia should they intervene. The great powers will then come together and settle things like gentlemen, in another Conference of London.'

Johnny grinned. He liked Humpty and as a former member of the Committee of Imperial Defence, he might be able to further his career. 'The problem is, Humpty, the Germans have given the Austrians a blank cheque to deal with Serbia. The Austrians are bound to launch some kind of attack.'

Humpty snorted and finished his Riesling. 'So what if they do? Whatever happens on the continent, we're under no written obligation to go to war for our colleagues in the Triple Entente.

Johnny hoped Humpty was right. He knew from the endless dispatches he spent his days copying out that this was a precarious time for British foreign policy, which had traditionally been used to maintaining the balance of power, thus protecting commerce and the sprawling British Empire. Over the past few decades there'd been seismic changes to the traditional order of things as Great Britain's rivals industrialised and rearmed, threatening her global interests.

To safeguard the empire, Britain had negotiated agreements with France and Russia, known as the Triple Entente, while the Germans formed their own Triple Alliance with Austro-Hungary and Italy.

The British Empire continued a delicate relationship with its new allies and had been obliged to support France as her enmity with Germany developed into rivalry for imperial possessions. Helped along by the kaiser's expansion of the High Seas Fleet, Britain had become increasingly drawn into conflict with Germany.

'Even if we did go to war, Great Britain would never deploy an expeditionary force on mainland Europe – not after the hash we made of it in the Crimea. No, all our fighting will be done through a naval blockade, you mark my words. We'll starve them into submission while the French attack in the West and the Russians come at them from the East. The whole thing will be over by Christmas,' Humpty stated confidently.

Johnny poured him another glass of wine and ordered a third bottle. This was going to be a good, long lunch and Humpty would insist on paying. If Humpty understood the intricate workings of Whitehall as well as he did those of a roulette wheel, Johnny didn't think he'd have anything to fear from a war. It would just be a spot of local difficulty; the antagonism between Serb nationalism and Austrian imperialism reaching its final and inevitable conclusion. Nothing at all for Johnny to worry about, and along with everything he'd found out recently, it might even help him, he decided.

*

Major Tankosic found Apis in his office incinerating files. Belgrade was evacuating and Apis was one of the last officials left in the capital. The Austrians were expected and he evidently wanted to ensure that no sensitive information fell into their hands.

Apis acknowledged Tankosic with a nod, his huge bald head glinting in the firelight, making him look like a giant Mongol chieftain. He signalled for Tankosic to prepare some drinks.

'Who would have thought that little pipsqueak Princip could have caused all this trouble?' The major said as he poured out two generous measures of plum brandy. 'Kicking Princip out of the partisans must have inspired our young revolutionary to do something so heroic.' They raised their glasses and threw down the brandy.

'It's a shame he couldn't keep his mouth shut,' Apis said. 'Or take his life.' He let the implied criticism hang in the air – Tankosic had after all, interviewed and supplied the conspirators. It was still a mystery why the potassium cyanide they took hadn't worked; either it hadn't been a strong enough dose or it had been defective. Whatever the reason, the major reflected, he'd been dropped right in it.

He'd just been released from custody and had come straight to see Apis, before he rejoined his unit. The Austro-Hungarian ultimatum had been sent the previous day, 24 July. It demanded the arrest of both Tankosic and Ciganovic. The major was picked up and then let go. He knew the Serbian government was concerned that any investigation might reveal their collusion in, or at least knowledge of, the plot.

'What of Ciganovic?' the major asked.

'Can't be found. He's gone off, "on leave",' Apis replied solemnly.

'He was warned?' Tankosic asked.

'If Ciganovic was an agent for the government, our glorious Prime Minister Pasic certainly wouldn't want him interrogated,' Apis replied.

'You think Cigo's a spy? Tankosic asked.

'It would also explain how he managed to clean himself up and get a job with the railway. Not to mention how the government found out about the plot,' Apis said.

'Ciganovic was born in Bosnia – maybe he was tipped off by a friend in the police and fled to avoid possible extradition as an Austrian citizen,' Tankosic said, pouring them another drink. 'In any case, he'd better report for duty. He's one of my best men.'

Apis shrugged. 'Did they interrogate you, Major?' he asked, accepting the brandy.

'I told them I did it all to spite Pasic and they left it at that.' Tankosic raised his glass and gulped the brandy down.

Apis smiled faintly. Their intention had partly been to spite Pasic, Tankosic mused, while undermining the prime minister's treacherous foreign policy and ultimately weakening Pasic's position in the power struggle they were having – a power struggle in which the prime minister had started to get the upper hand.

Pasic had been out of Belgrade electioneering when the Austro-Hungarian ultimatum was delivered. He'd rushed back to Belgrade and had done a good job in answering the demands, Apis conceded, as he went through the events Tankosic had missed while he'd been detained. The prime minster conducted a wonderful exercise in diplomatic tap dancing, accommodating the Austrians without losing too much face. He'd carefully drafted his reply to give the impression that Serbia accepted all of the demands, except point six, which required that Austrian officials be allowed to participate in the Serbian investigation of the assassination.

'Not even Pasic would have allowed that,' Apis said. 'He could never justify such a grievous violation of our constitution and law.'

'Plus, who knows what the Austrians might find out about the old devil,' Tankosic added and they both roared with laughter. 'If Cigo was actually the prime minister's spy, he helped and trained the assassins.'

The major raised his glass again. 'Well, we've certainly strained relations between Pasic and his Austrian friends.'

Apis grimaced and Tankosic realised that it wasn't a topic for levity. They hadn't planned on provoking a reaction on this scale. In the past the Austrians had settled for, or been forced into, a diplomatic solution that had humiliated Serbia, weakening Apis's political enemies and raising his stock amongst the nationalists. A full-scale war was a different proposition all together.

However, the ultimatum had clearly been a clumsy attempt by Austro-Hungary to provoke a war and was bound to incite their Russian cousins to take action. The rejection of the ultimatum had been delivered to the Austro-Hungarian legation at 5:55 p.m. Serbia was now preparing to receive a declaration of war and the inevitable attack that would follow.

Apis poured his brandy onto his burning files, and a huge flame jumped out of the smouldering fire. 'If the Russians stand with us, this will be the start of an all-out fight to the death which can only end in our victory and the destruction of the Austro-Hungarian Empire. Even if it results in my losing the struggle with Pasic, even if we both die, we will finally get back what we have been dreaming of since Kosovo.'

Chapter 44

Johnny arrived at Paris's Gare de l'Est to the sensational news that Madame Caillaux had been acquitted of murdering the newspaper editor, Gaston Calmette. The story appeared to be on the front page of every Parisian paper.

Johnny turned away from the headlines to catch a last fleeting glimpse of Libby, as a swarm of porters and embassy officials escorted her through a group of French soldiers. They'd travelled back to Paris separately, for the sake of discretion, with Johnny safely secured in second class.

Johnny waited at the newsstand until the last embassy flunky cleared off. He couldn't see anything about the Balkans crisis in the papers: obviously nothing critical had happened during his glorious three-week sabbatical with Libby.

He smiled contentedly to himself. Libby had bestowed every possible reward on him that her mischievous and creative mind could devise. A pretty brunette behind the counter saw the look on Johnny's face and grinned back coyly.

At nine o'clock the following morning, fully reacquainted with the hurly-burly of Parisian life, Johnny presented himself to Sir George Smyth in the imperial finery of his chancery office.

Sir George was too incensed to speak for a moment, his face flushing with rage. The undertone was clear – how dare Johnny have the barefaced cheek not to get his bloody head blown off when a better man had been killed.

'If you haven't got anything tangible to report, God help you, Swift,' Sir George managed to say at last. Without going into the whys and hows, Johnny explained that he'd liaised with the Austro-Hungarian joint ministry of finance to investigate the Young Bosnia Movement, which he felt was the main threat to the Austro-Hungarian rule in Bosnia, its aim being to unite the South Slav people through a revolution that would overthrow its imperial masters. They believed, Johnny continued, that such a revolution would be sparked by the assassination of a leading Austro-Hungarian personage. It was this belief that led to the outrage in Sarajevo.

The Assassins

Johnny was about to explain his role in foiling Nedjo's attempt to throw a bomb into the archduke's car, when Sir George interrupted him.

'Yes, that's all rather by-the-by now. The Austrians have already given us the findings of their police investigation, in German. I believe it's still in the basement of the Foreign Office, unread. Did you actually manage to find out anything useful?'

Johnny's stomach clenched in frustration. 'With respect, Sir George, you sent me to Bosnia to investigate the nationalist question.'

'Did I indeed? Was that really the reason?' Sir George let that dangle, like a noose around Johnny's neck.

'I have paid off all the debts ...' Johnny said, taking the wire receipts out of his pocket. Sir George went red and got up from behind his desk to properly express his indignation.

'Don't be so damned vulgar, boy!' Sir George shouted and then, regaining his composure, he sat down and in the correct manner of a British gentleman addressing his staff, asked, 'What were your exact instructions, Swift?'

'I believe my exact instructions were to "ferret about a bit",' Johnny replied as tonelessly as possible.

Sir George smashed his fist onto his desk. 'I believe you were instructed to make yourself useful to the Viennese embassy, with a view to understanding the spread of Pan-Slavic nationalism in the Austro-Hungarian monarchy – not to charge about the Balkans swilling wine and chasing women!' Johnny tried to maintain a straight face, but he could tell Sir George knew his assumption was correct. Johnny may have been able to pass himself off as a Bosnian revolutionary, but one whiff of moral indignation from his betters and he went to pieces.

'I did report to our Viennese embassy, but they didn't know anything about me, or why I had been sent there.'

'Are you contradicting me, Swift?' There was nothing Johnny could say; Sir George was leading him into a trap. Johnny could continue to disagree with him and Sir George would get one of his cronies in Vienna to say that Johnny hadn't been within a hundred miles of the place, and God help him then.

He looked around the office for something that might help him, but all of the scandal in the papers had played itself out.

'Well, have you got anything to say for yourself, before I initiate a formal disciplinary?' Sir George asked mockingly.

Johnny remembered his letter of commendation from Count Tisza. 'Well, there is this.'

Sir George snatched the letter out of Johnny's hand and scanned through the few lines that thanked Johnny for making himself useful in the general investigation around the murder of the heir apparent to the Austro-Hungarian throne. It was the last part that Johnny hoped might turn things around for him. No one was more conscious of royalty, even foreign royalty, than a minor aristocrat trying to further his power and influence.

Sir George looked at Johnny steadily as he carefully folded the letter and passed it back. 'A letter of commendation from a country with whom our allies could well be at war in a couple of days doesn't really hold much sway.'

Johnny coughed – he should have thought of that. It was practically high treason, aiding and abetting a hostile power. 'I'm sorry, but at the time I was doing my best to assist a sovereign nation we were on good terms with.' His mind scrambled like a rat in a trap as he tried to think of the correct phrasing.

Sir George's eyes flickered with opportunity, 'You're not holding something back are you? Something you think will get you up the greasy pole? I know you, Swift; you have the back-alley cunning of a guttersnipe. What else have you found out, moving around in the exalted circles of your country's enemies? Any little snippet might help us form a coherent foreign policy. The foreign secretary and the cabinet are split over the possibility of war and what our involvement should be.'

'War, Sir George? You mean us – Great Britain, at war?' Johnny had allowed himself to be distracted at the newsstand and must have missed something important.

'My God, do you really have no idea why I sent you to the Balkans?' Sir George looked dubious. 'You are aware that the foreign secretary believes that making concessions to Serbia is vital to sustaining the Entente with France and Russia? Didn't you notice that he championed Serbian territorial claims over Albania's at the Treaty of London?'

Johnny shrugged, 'It was before I joined the service.'

Sir George sighed impatiently. 'The point is, Swift, there is a policy of increasing the security of the Entente Cordial through Serbia. I believe it was von Bismarck who said that the next war in Europe will come out of some damned foolish thing in the Balkans. It's vital to know what the state of play is down there, so that any potential threat to peace can be mitigated.'

'You mean, to prevent a clash between Serb nationalism and Austrian imperialism,' Johnny said – that much he'd worked out for himself.

'I'm more concerned about the Russians. They're the real problem here. They've turned Serbia into a client state to act as a barrier against Austro-Hungarian expansion into the Balkans, safeguarding Russia's own plans in that ghastly peninsula. In a potential diplomatic crisis the Russians won't care what the rights and wrongs are and they will act to protect their interests. They'll have the full backing of the French, who are desperate to ensure the Russians fulfil their treaty obligations and attack the Germans if a war breaks out. They've been pouring money into Russian train lines for years, to speed up their mobilisation.'

'I don't understand why Serbia and the Balkans are so important,' Johnny said. None of this had been in any of the dispatches or minutes that he'd copied out during his year of clerical servitude.

Sir George picked up a bust of Napoleon as he patiently explained the finer points of France's diplomatic strategy. 'Serbia and the Balkans are important, Swift, because to the French way of thinking the Russians are most likely to participate in a war against Germany if it begins in the Balkans against Austria-Hungary. The Serbians will absorb large numbers of Austrian troops, allowing the Russians to unleash even larger numbers of Cossacks against Eastern Prussia, thus reducing the burden on the French Army in the most critical period of any future war.'

He paused to put the bust down. 'In short, France and Russia have fixed their defence policy on Europe's most violent and unstable region. Which, Master Swift, was why I sent you there – not necessarily to get killed, although that would have been amusing, or to pay back the money you stole, but to be my eyes and ears, using that guttersnipe cunning of yours to keep me one step ahead of the competition.' Libby had told him as much, but Johnny didn't think that would have been tactful to mention.

'Unfortunately, you have failed, spectacularly, to provide me with one shred of useful information,' Sir George continued. 'The Austro-Hungarian government has declared war on Serbia, Russia has begun part-mobilisation, and it's only a matter of time before the French drag us into things.'

'But that's not possible!' Johnny couldn't believe it; his world was coming unstuck.

'It's the very thing I sent you down there to prevent – Austro-Hungary's growing disputes with Serbia have escalated into war. The Russians will take the opportunity to further their influence in the region and maybe even get a port in the Mediterranean under the guise of helping their Slavic brothers. Germany, Austria's ally, will see an opportunity to smash the growing power of Russia and declare war. France, not wanting to see its key strategic ally beaten and hoping to right the wrongs of 1870, will attack Germany. And then Great Britain will inevitably have to step in and restore the balance of power and safeguard its interests.' Sir George spoke with an accusatory tone, as if somehow, this was all Johnny's fault.

'But we're under no written obligation,' Johnny managed to say. Humpty had told him so.

'Semantics – we still have an understanding. The French may not have learnt anything militarily from the Franco-Prussian war and can't wait to go haring off into Germany in a glorious Napoleonic cavalry charge, but they've certainly learned diplomatically. They've made sure that the Russians are able to mobilise and are insisting on our support by every possible means.'

Johnny took a moment to absorb this and he wondered if the grand idea he'd had could still work with that level of escalation.

'The problem is, France views the Entente as a means of keeping Germany in check. For His Majesty's government it has been a way of protecting our empire. The assassination you failed to prevent has exposed the inherent contradiction of being allies with our closest imperial rivals. Whitehall's policy is now somewhat garbled and can be interpreted as either pro- or anti-war. Currently, the British government is calling for a conference to solve the crisis. If you know anything that could help bring about a diplomatic solution, I might overlook your collaborating with a foreign power, but otherwise ...'

Sir George let his voice trail off and Johnny knew that he'd make it his personal business to use the letter of commendation from Count Tisza to destroy him. As much as Johnny disliked Sir George, there was clearly a lot he could learn from him – maybe not as much as he'd learnt from his wife, but even so, he was the person to latch on to and whose coat-tails Johnny could ride to success. Johnny saw no other option than to tell Sir George everything he knew and hope it would work to his advantage. He did his best to describe what he felt should be done to prevent a war, based on what he'd seen and heard in Bosnia and Vienna, meeting everyone from

Breitner and Princip to Count Tisza and the Russian imperial ambassador to Vienna. When he finished, to his amazement, Sir George was dazzled.

'Come on, we're clearing out of here.' Sir George started shuffling papers into his briefcase.

'Where to?'

'London, of course – can't keep something like that to ourselves.'

'Shouldn't we see the ambassador?'

'The French are expected to begin mobilisation at any moment. Now is not a good time to be in Paris – we're right in the firing line here. In 1870 the Hun was knocking at the door in no time.' Sir George rang for his assistant and turned back to Johnny.

'I'll send a telegram to Sir Edward requesting a meeting. In the meantime, you can spend the August Bank Holiday weekend in London with your family.'

Johnny was astonished – Sir George was actually going to take him along. People of Johnny's grade weren't received by Sir Edward Grey, the foreign secretary. Nevertheless, the idea of spending a bank holiday weekend with his parents didn't thrill him.

'Will Lady Smyth be joining us?' Johnny asked.

'No, she'll be staying here.' Sir George was too busy packing to notice Johnny's disappointment.

*

London was filled with bank holiday sightseers drawn to the metropolis by the sunny weather and the pending conflict. Johnny was back among the privet hedges of his parents' South Ealing home, enjoying a cauliflower cheese supper.

W. G. Swift, Johnny's stepfather, a bull-necked ex-hooker famous throughout Wales for his brutality on and off the rugby pitch, was sitting at the family dinner table in a stiff winged collar. 'Swift, The Language' looked more like a Prussian diplomat than the learned schoolmaster who'd taught Johnny everything he knew.

Johnny's mother, Grace, smiled at him affectionately, pleased to have her boy back. Grace had been a wayward young governess, forever destined to pay for her mistake in having Johnny out of wedlock. Yet the light hadn't faded from her eyes and her charisma had been sufficient to catch a man willing to take on as precocious and troublesome a brat as her son.

'I hope you've kept up your studies while you've been away,' W.G. Swift said.

'Yes, I have,' Johnny replied in Serbo-Croat.

'That's something, I suppose,' his stepfather said begrudgingly.

'As a matter of fact, my language skills are in great demand. I was even called upon to translate for the imperial Russian ambassador in Vienna,' Johnny said, pleased with himself.

'"Called upon" were you? Like some fetch and carry servant!' The words stung, but Johnny knew that he meant well. His stepfather was a strict adherent to the values of Prince Albert, believing that a person's character could be moulded through discipline, hard work, and moral and intellectual guidance – certainly not by showing off at the dinner table.

'Do you suppose you might be "called upon" to sit out the war, with your language skills?' his stepfather asked derisively.

'Well, yes, as a matter of fact, one has made oneself indispensable. That is to say, if there is war, which one rather suspects there won't be.' Johnny winked at his mother who turned away to hide her smile.

'Oh, you think that's funny do you? You'll be laughing on the other side of your face soon enough, boy. The Russians have begun full mobilisation, Germany has answered by declaring war on them and now France has begun to mobilise. What do you think about that?'

'Yes, that does sound bad, but I'm sure it can all be stopped. If there is a war Great Britain may not necessarily be involved, and if we are it's highly unlikely that we'll send an expeditionary force.'

'I see – heard that from one of your colleagues in the diplomatic service?'

'It was a former member of the committee for imperial defence, actually.'

'You mark my words, you'll be getting your call-up papers soon enough. You're in the reserves aren't you?'

There it was, the real reason for this tirade, Johnny realised. His stepfather still hadn't forgiven him for getting expelled from school and joining the army to keep his 'uncle' happy.

'I am a special reserve officer, but I'm sure I can get some kind of deferment, as I'm involved in quite high-level work,' Johnny said, hoping that would show he hadn't wasted the time W.G. Swift had invested in him. He wanted him to know that he was making good on the opportunities given to him – opportunities his stepfather had never had.

'My God! Where are your guts? If your country needs you to fight, boy – you fight. I didn't bring you up to be a shirker!'

The Assassins

Johnny recoiled. He'd completely misjudged his stepfather's mood. 'I'll do my bit for king and country in the diplomatic service, where my skills will be of most value,' Johnny said firmly, sticking to his guns. If Nedjo Cabrinovic could face the fury and disappointment of his father, then so could he.

'Thank you for the postcard you sent by the way, Johnny,' his mother said, cutting the tension. She got up and took the postcard down from the mantelpiece and passed it to her husband, who avidly studied the gothic spires of Vienna's City Hall.

'Wonderful draftsmanship,' his stepfather said and then gave Johnny an approving look for the first time since his return from the continent.

'Did you buy it from the painter, in person?' his mother asked.

'No'. Johnny couldn't tell them he'd brought the postcard from a down-and-out, desperate for a drink. 'No, from a friend of his; they lived in the same pension, I believe. They have since fallen out, but he believed the painter moved to Munich.' The front doorbell sounded before his parents could ask any more questions. The outline of a telegraph boy could be seen through the frosted window of the front door.

'It's just a shame you can't see the faces of the people,' his mother said, before going to answer the front door.

'That will be your call-up,' his stepfather said with glee as his mother came back with a worried expression and a telegram.

Johnny opened it and smiled smugly. 'I've been summoned by the foreign secretary.'

*

The light was starting to fade over the crowded streets of Whitehall. Johnny could hear the mumble from the waves of people as he sat inside Sir Edward Grey's office.

Johnny revelled in his new-found glory; he'd left his stepfather speechless for the first time in his life and was now sitting in one of the key centres of power in the world, watching Sir George present his big idea to the austere foreign secretary and Sir Arthur Nicolson, the senior Foreign Office mandarin.

'I anticipated a Balkan crisis at the end of May when I learned of the archduke's visit to Sarajevo and so I dispatched young Swift here, to see what could be done. I'm sensible of the fact that you place some importance on the region for the security of the Entente, Foreign Secretary,' Sir George said.

Grey gave Johnny a weary glance. 'Very commendable. A first-hand account of events would have been most interesting I'm sure, were we not in the presence of a European conflagration,' the foreign secretary said dryly. He was famously mistrustful of foreign travel, feeling anything worth knowing could be gleaned from his official papers.

Johnny knew that Sir George had pulled every string he could to get this interview and he wasn't going to be made to look an ass. 'The situation over there is very clear, Foreign Secretary. Austro-Hungary intends to punish Serbia for the assassination – nothing will pacify them,' Sir George insisted.

Grey was doing his best to appear interested, but Johnny thought he looked wrung out; by all accounts he'd had a very trying day. Sir George persevered, desperate to keep his audience.

'What I suggest, drawing from my sources in Vienna, the Balkans and the Russian diplomatic corps, is that Great Britain and the rest of Europe be persuaded to stay out of any conflict and let Serbia and Austro-Hungary fight it out. I'm told that Count Tisza, the Hungarian prime minster, doesn't think the Austro-Hungarian Army will stand a chance. Serbia will beat them off. The Austrians are unprepared, ill-equipped and badly led.'

Grey and Nicolson looked astonished. 'That is simply incredible,' Grey said. 'How can such a small country possibly beat one of the world's great powers?'

'Serbia has been hardened by two recent bitter wars, both of which it won. It's a new, resurgent country, and deeply patriotic, even more so now it has recaptured Kosovo, its spiritual home. The Serbs are willing to go to extraordinary lengths to unite the South Slav people, as I believe, Gavrilo Princip, the assassin, has demonstrated. The Austrians on the other hand, haven't been in a major conflict since they pacified Bosnia and Herzegovina over thirty years ago, and they made very hard work of that against irregular troops, armed largely with obsolete weapons.' Sir George smiled. 'Imagine how they would stand up against a veteran army with modern arms.'

Nicolson and Grey didn't respond to Sir George's attempt at levity, but they weren't looking at him as if he was insane anymore. Johnny wondered if they were remembering the trouble Great Britain had had beating the Boers in South Africa.

'However, the key piece of information I received from a former Austrian intelligence officer is that the Serbs are familiar with the Austrian plan of attack, which the Russians obtained from a mole in Austrian intelligence. Although the Austrian general staff may have now amended the plan, the Serbians will have a good crib to guess where the Austrians are likely to attack. We can be sure the Serbs will be ready and waiting for them.'

Nicolson spoke for the first time. 'Surely, the Austrians will beat Serbia through overwhelming firepower and sheer weight of numbers?'

'Eventually, yes, but Serbia will win the opening bouts, by which time we can intercede to set up a peace conference, as we are trying to do now. The Austrians are convinced that they'll have an easy victory; when they see that is unlikely the hawks in the Austro-Hungarian council of joint ministers will be more receptive to negotiation. If Russia doesn't get involved, neither will Germany, and then France won't have any reason for declaring war. The whole thing can be resolved as a local squabble,' Sir George replied.

'And how can we prevail upon Russia and Germany to mind their own business?' Grey asked.

'We assure the Russians that we won't allow Serbia to be overrun by Austro-Hungary and we give the Russians the key to their own backdoor – a free hand in the Bosporus. I know we've traditionally tried to avoid that, but it's better than letting Austro-Hungary and Germany have a bigger influence in the Balkans.'

'Germany won't allow themselves to be sidelined,' Grey said. 'They want total hegemony in Europe and to have that they need a war to humble France and Russia.'

'If the Russians stop their mobilisation then the Germans will have no reason to go to war and they will leave the Austrians to chastise Serbia on their own. Once the Austro-Hungarian invasion fails, the different nationalities within the monarchy will see how weak it is and start to pull the whole crumbling edifice down. The Germans won't wish to be shackled to a corpse and face total encirclement, so they will either have to support a peace conference to save their ally, or bail the Austrians out militarily and be labelled as the aggressor in a war, with the negative effect that will have on world opinion.'

'You're forgetting Germany and Austria's other partner in the triple Alliance – Italy,' Grey remarked.

'Italy will take the opportunity to seize the Austrian territory they covet and leave the Triple Alliance,' Sir George said.

'You make some interesting points, Smyth, and if you'd come to me a week earlier, I may even have been able to make something of this rather eccentric notion of yours. Events have rather stolen a march on you, I'm afraid,' Grey said wearily.

'War became inevitable when Russia started full mobilisation, commencing the timetable. We fully expect Germany to attack France through Belgium in a matter of hours; their troops have already entered Luxembourg,' Nicolson said.

'And that, gentlemen, has decided the waverers in the cabinet and will bring us to war,' Grey added.

'Will we be sending troops to help the Belgians?' Sir George asked. 'Or will our involvement be purely to blockade Germany, as some have suggested?'

Johnny didn't like where this was heading. He wasn't planning on spending the next few months standing around in squares while German Uhlans charged at him with bloody-great lances – he'd seen enough death recently. However, he felt fairly confident that after this meeting Sir George would get him an exemption from his call-up.

'A British expeditionary force will be dispatched to Northern Europe. If the Germans take the Belgian ports they'll be practically sitting on our front lawn and if they win another European war, it will change the balance of power dramatically in their favour,' Nicolson stated.

'We must also support our allies – the empire can't be held without the goodwill of France and Russia,' Grey added as he looked out of the window, towards the Admiralty building. The daylight had turned to dusk, and he watched as the street lamps were lit. After days of indecision and intrigue he had the look of a man who'd finally come to a resolution.

'The lamps are going out all over Europe. We shall not see them lit again in our time.' Grey turned back from the window, 'That was an extremely unconventional analysis you presented, Smyth. You're just the sort of chap Winston wants at the Admiralty. I'll get someone to make enquiries.'

Johnny followed Sir George down the Foreign Office grand staircase, with mixed feelings of elation and guilt. If he'd come back earlier rather than frolicking about in Switzerland with Sir George's wife, he might well have been able to prevent a war. At least he'd provided Sir George with something with which to dazzle his superiors. Johnny hoped that there would be a post in it for him as well, and that it could put him in a position to help shorten the war.

The Assassins

Sir George stopped on the central landing. 'Well, I wasn't expecting them to implement your idea, but at least it got me out of Paris. What are your plans now, Swift? There's obviously no point in you going back to your old billet at the embassy. Actually, I filled it, come to think of it.'

'Well, I believe I'd be of best service to the country if I come with you when you take up your new placement in the Admiralty – maybe at a slightly higher grade. I think I've earned it.'

'Nonsense, a young man like you obviously wants to be at the front, having a lark!'

'No, I'd be perfectly happy working with you, Sir George.' Johnny thought that with a war, the Admiralty would be at the centre of things and there were bound to be chances for rapid advancement.

'You'd rather be in an office? How extraordinary. You may not like this, then.' Sir George opened his briefcase and handed Johnny a small beige envelope.

'What is it?' Johnny asked. 'Is it my next posting?'

Sir George smiled, 'In a way. It's your call-up notice. They'll be going out in the next day or two, I wanted to make sure you got yours first. You're to report to your regiment, forthwith.'

'What?' The suddenness of it struck Johnny like a blow.

'I didn't want you malingering, so I brought you back to England personally to make sure you joined up. Can't have a slippery character like you in Paris left to your own devices – no telling where you might slope off to.'

Sir George made a signal with his hand, and two stocky soldiers came out of the shadows at the bottom of the stairs. 'I took the liberty of arranging your transport to camp. Really, no need to thank me.'

'But I gave you my idea. You've landed a plum job because of it,' Johnny said.

'Some might say you're getting your just desserts. You don't honestly think I'd forget about you sleeping with my wife, running up gambling debts against my name and then blackmailing me?'

'Why all this? Why did you bring me here?' Johnny found it impossible not to sound whiny.

'To meet the gods?' Sir George laughed, Johnny was giving him exactly what he wanted, but he couldn't help himself. Johnny understood now how Ilic must be feeling as he faced the gallows.

'I wanted you to see me take your idea and make it my own, then send you off to war.'

'You bastard! I could get killed.'

'Yes, rather a fait accompli I'm afraid,' Sir George grinned. 'Now take your medicine like a man. You know what happens to mortals who fly too close to the sun.'

Sir George gave Johnny a dismissive wave and continued down the stairs. Johnny looked up at the domed ceiling; it reminded him of City Hall in Sarajevo and the last time he'd seen Kati Weiz. He grinned – he had wanted a Belgium posting, after all. He followed Sir George down the stairs with a renewed swagger in his stride. He thought a few medals wouldn't hurt his prospects and he remembered that Libby was still in Paris.

Sir George stopped at the bottom of the great staircase, glorying at being at the heart of the British Empire, thanks to Johnny. 'Cheer up – you'll be home by Christmas.'

Johnny shrugged, 'I'll be glad to pay my respects to your wife on the way back and convey your regrets for leaving her in Paris.'

'You really are contemptible!' Sir George flushed with anger and pushed his way out onto the street, the open doors filling the hall with the sound of singing and cheering from the people outside.

Johnny walked over to the waiting soldiers – it was time to take his medicine, once again.

Historical Notes

Following the trial of the conspirators in 1914, Danilo Ilic, Misko Jovanovic and his friend, Veljko Cubrilovic were hanged.

Gavrilo Princip, Trifko Grabez and Nedeljko Cabrinovic were each sentenced to twenty years. All three died in Terezin's small fortress – Nedeljko Cabrinovic and Trifko Grabez in 1916, and Gavrilo Princip in April 1918. Most accounts agree that they died of tuberculosis and malnutrition.

Cvjetko Popovic was sentenced to thirteen years. He was released after the First World War and became a teacher. Vaso Cubrilovic was sentenced to sixteen years; he was also released after the war and became a history professor.

Milan Ciganovic joined up with Major Tankosic's company at the outbreak of the war, but was later sent to the USA by his government. He returned to Bosnia in 1919 and died in 1927.

Major Tankosic returned to active service and was mortally wounded in October 1915.

Colonel Dragutin 'Apis' Dimitrijevic finally lost his power struggle with Pasic, the Serbian prime minister, in 1917. He was accused of plotting to kill the Serbian regent and after a show trial in Salonika was executed alongside Rade Malobabic.

Mehmed Mehmedbasic escaped the Austro-Hungarian authorities after the assassination, but was put on trial with Apis and was sentenced to six years. He later returned to Sarajevo and was killed during the Second World War.

Franz Janaczek remained with Sophie and Franz Ferdinand's children until his retirement. One of Sophie's sister's, Henriette, brought the children up and did her best to help them overcome the trauma of losing both their parents and the turbulent years of the First World War and its aftermath. The two boys, Ernst and Max, opposed the Nazis and were put in concentration camps – both survived. *The Assassination of the Archduke*, by Greg King & Sue Woolmans, has a particularly good account of what happened to the children.

The assassination of Archduke Franz Ferdinand was the pivotal event of the twentieth century. It led to the war which formed the modern world and resulted, as the assassins had hoped, in the end of the Habsburg monarchy and for a period the creation of a South Slav state. However, there is still a certain amount of mystery around the events that led up to the assassination. This is largely a result of the clandestine nature of the people involved in the assassination, the conspirators' attempts to mislead the investigation and the Austro-Hungarian government's determination to prove Serbia's involvement in the assassination, while downplaying its own negligence.

Consequently, there are a number of grey areas in the history of the assassination, so I've used a certain amount of artistic licence to fill in the gaps while trying to remain as historically accurate as possible with regards to the actions of the conspirators and the failure of the authorities to stop them.

There are two basic schools of thought about the origins of the assassination plot. Firstly, that it was Colonel 'Apis' Dimitrijevic's idea and that he planned it and recruited the assassins, through Major Tankosic. Secondly, that the assassination was purely the idea of the assassins and that Apis gave his support on a whim. There is however, no evidence to prove either case conclusively. What is known for sure is that the assassins were supported by Apis and his associates. Whether Apis conceived the plot or just approved it, he made it possible for Gavrilo Princip to carry out the assassination.

The version of events depicted in this novel is an amalgam of the two perspectives, with the assassination conceived by the assassins as an act of 'tyrannicide', but with them lacking the means to change it from coffee shop talk into action. At the same time, Apis was looking to recruit people through Major Tankosic in order to carry out similar operations, and agreed to help.

There is also some debate as to whether or not Apis tried to stop the assassination, either when his government found out about the plan, or when he'd had a chance to reconsider his decision. Djuro Sarac was sent to Bosnia and met Danilo Ilic in mid June 1914. It isn't known for sure where they met, or what they discussed, but Ilic's doubts about the assassination seem to have increased after the meeting, and he spent the second half of June 1914 trying to persuade Gavrilo Princip not to carry out the act. It is possible that if a cancellation order was sent, it could have been an act of subterfuge, to fool the Serbian prime minister.

Following on from this, there is also a lot of speculation as to why Apis's master spy, Rade Malobabic, went to Sarajevo during the archduke's visit, if indeed Apis had ordered the cancellation of the assassination. Ilic's mother is reported to have said that a man with big feet came to see her son on the eve of the assassination, but the reason for his visit is unknown. Apparently, Malobabic had big feet, so it could have been him. There are many theories about Malobabic's presence in Sarajevo, but I've tied it into Johnny's story, having him there to warn Ilic of a possible attempt to foil the assassination.

No explanation has ever been put forward as to why Danilo Ilic was late meeting Misko Jovanovic to collect the weapons, putting the whole plot in danger, so it seemed fitting to me that Johnny should have kept him out drinking the night before (from the accounts I've read I think that the Semiz wine shop, where Gavrilo used to go, was on the opposite bank of the river to Franz Ferdinand Street, overlooking Lateiner Bridge).

The assassination itself happened as a result of a whole series of mistakes and missed opportunities. Nedjo Cabrinovic met Detective Vila on the way to Sarajevo; Vila was a friend of his father's, whom he'd recently seen. Vila saw Trifko Grabez and Gavrilo Princip sitting in the same train carriage and asked who Gavrilo was, but his suspicions were not raised. A simple request to see his papers would have revealed that he was travelling illegally.

There was no centrally coordinated intelligence to counter the activities of the nationalist movements in Austro-Hungary's Balkan provinces; the conspirators' letters were not intercepted or deciphered. The repeated warnings of a possible assassination were ignored by General Potiorek, the archduke and the Austro-Hungarian government. *The Archduke and the Assassin*, by Lavender Cassels, is particularly interesting on this point. If Bogdan Zerajic had been identified as a nationalist after his assassination attempt on General Varesanin, the authorities may have been more aware of the growing militancy of the Young Bosnians and reconsidered the archduke's visit, or at the very least increased the security around it. Viktor Ivasjuk, the Chief of Detectives, was said to have been a student of Lombroso's theory of criminology and to have kept the skull of Bogdan Zerajic on his desk, which he used as an inkpot (see Vadmire Dedijer and David James Smith).

All the accounts that I've read agree that Nedjo Cubrilovic threw his bomb at the archduke's car from the river-side of Appel Quay, just before Cumurija Bridge, but there is some inconsistency as to where exactly he, Ilic, Mehmedbasic, Cvjetko Popovic and Vaso Cubrilovic stood at the junction when this happened. Some accounts have the plotters lined up along the river side of the embankment in the open, with Nedjo. Some suggest they were on the city side, in the shade. This is largely because the assassins themselves gave varying accounts and changed positions from the ones Ilic gave them when he led them down the quay the day before the assassination. The lengthiest investigations of where they stood are given in *One Morning in Sarajevo*, by David James Smith and *The Road To Sarajevo*, by Vadmire Dedijer, which I've tried to follow in this book.

I've made an educated guess as to what the surrounding buildings were at the junction, having studied maps, old postcards and photographs of the time. The wooden picket fence where I think Mehmed Mehmedbasic stood and the place where I think the Mostar Cafe was, at the bottom of Cumurija Street, have long gone, (along with the trees). A road now goes through the place where I've depicted them. I know that there was a doctor's surgery where the injured from Nedjo's bomb were treated and a tobacconist's where Cvjetko Popovic stood, but not exactly which buildings they were. The Girls' High School and the bank were in the places described in the book and the Prosvjeta building is still there and is now a hostel. Gavrilo Princip worked for Prosvjeta prior to the assassination, so I'm assuming it was in this building. Popovic also hid his weapons in its basement after Nedjo threw his bomb.

There was a great deal of confusion in City Hall after Nedjo's attempt and the decision to change the route added to the complications. Dr Grade, Sarajevo's chief of police, who was riding in the first car of the motorcade, was apparently told to repeat the instruction that the route had changed, but whether he understood what he was being asked to repeat as he hurried to join the motorcade, or that he was supposed to inform the drivers, doesn't appear to have ever been fully established. If the archduke's motorcade had carried on down Appel Quay after leaving the reception in City Hall then the whole catastrophe would have been prevented. No one investigated the reason why the car went the wrong way and followed the original route, probably either to save face or because the authorities didn't want to be distracted from the real issue of blaming Serbia for the assassination.

The Assassins

Lastly and perhaps most poignantly, the archduke's car stopped in front of Gavrilo Princip after it had made the wrong turning. A policeman saw Gavrilo Princip point his gun at the archduke's car and ran to intercept him, but a spectator stopped him with a kick. Many people have attributed this action to Mihajlo Pusara, the actor who worked as a clerk in Sarajevo's City Hall and who had sent Nedjo the newspaper cutting announcing the archduke's visit. However, there is another account of a policeman trying to stop Princip after he'd fired the first shot, but it states that he was punched in the stomach by someone in the crowd.

If you would like to read more about the assassins and what motivated them I'd strongly recommend David James Smith's *One Morning in Sarajevo*, Vadmire Dedijer's *The Road To Sarajevo*, or *The Desperate Act*, by Roberta Strauss Feuerlicht. If you're more interested in Franz Ferdinand and Sophie's story I'd suggest *Archduke of Sarajevo: The Romance & Tragedy of Franz Ferdinand of Austria*, by Gordon Brook-Shepherd and *The Assassination of the Archduke*, by Greg King & Sue Woolmans. *The Archduke and the Assassin*, by Lavender Cassels, covers both sides of the story fairly equally.

Other books I found useful in trying to understand the assassination and the history of Bosnia were: *Sarajevo* by Joachim Remak; *Black Lamb and Grey Falcon* by Rebecca West; *The Secret of Sarajevo: the story of Franz Ferdinand and Sophie* by Hertha Pauli; *Sarajevo, A Biography* by Robert J. Donia; *The Bridge Over The Drina*, by Ivo Andric; Borivoje Jevtic quoted in *We Were There: An Eyewitness History of the Twentieth Century* by Robert Fox; *The Balkan Wars: Conquest, Revolution, and Retribution from the Ottoman Era to the Twentieth Century and Beyond* by Andre Gerolymatos and *Bosnia: A Short History* by Noel Malcolm.

I found the following books useful for the history of diplomacy, and the background and events that led to the outbreak of the First World War: *Thirteen Days: The Road to the First World War* by Clive Ponting; *August Guns* by Barbara Tuchman; *The Sleepwalkers: How Europe went to war in 1914* by Christopher Clark; *The War that Ended Peace: How Europe abandoned peace for the First World War* by Margaret MacMillan; *The Three Emperors: Three Cousins, Three Empires and the Road to World War One* by Miranda Carter; *The British diplomatic service 1815-1914* by Raymond A. Jones and *The Origins of the War of 1914 volume 2* by Luigi Albertini.

Books I enjoyed with reference to Vienna and the Habsburgs were: *Emperor Francis Joseph, Life Death and the Fall of the Habsburg Empire* by John Van der Kiste; *The Dissolution of the Austro-Hungarian Empire 1867-1918* by John W. Mason; *The Radetzky March* by Joseph Roth; *Last Waltz in Vienna* by George Clare and Count Miklós Bánffy's wonderful *Transylvania Trilogy*. Also *Thunder at Twilight: Vienna 1913/1914* by Frederic Morton, which in addition has a good account of the death of Colonel Redl, as has, *The Second Oldest Profession: Spies and Spying in the Twentieth Century* by Phillip Knightley.

I'd also strongly recommend a trip to Sarajevo. It is an amazing place, still rich with the fusion of Western and Eastern cultures of a bygone age, with the addition of communist-era tower blocks. It isn't hard to imagine how it would have felt to be there in 1914, despite the traffic and the damage caused by the siege of the 1990s. The 103 trolley bus from the airport drops you off at the gardens where Gavrilo Princip sat on the morning of the assassination. These gardens are opposite Appel Quay (now called Obala Kulina Bana), Lateiner Bridge and the corner of Franz Joseph Street (now called Zelenih Beretki), where the assassination took place. There is a plaque on Schiller's delicatessen commemorating the assassination. The building is now the Museum of the History of Sarajevo 1878-1918, and contains a small display about the assassination. (Directions to the 103 bus stop can be found in Lonely Planet's guide to the *Western Balkans*).

The Museum of Military History in Vienna houses the Gräf & Stift car in which Franz Ferdinand and Sophie were travelling when they were shot, as part of an exhibit about the assassination which includes three of the assassins' guns, some of the bombs recovered after their arrest, the chaise longue Franz Ferdinand died on and his blood-stained uniform.

Artstetten Castle where Sophie and Franz Ferdinand are buried, is an incredible place to see. It has a museum established by Sophie and Franz Ferdinand's great-granddaughter, Princess Anita of Hohenberg, and has the feel of walking through a family scrapbook. It has a very good display on the assassination, including the all-important official programme of events for the archduke's visit to Sarajevo and many photographs that I hadn't seen before.

Sophie and Franz Ferdinand's favourite country seat, Konopiste Castle, is also a beguiling place to visit. All three tours of the castle are very good, but tour three is the best, as it takes in Sophie and Franz Ferdinand's private apartments. I tried to identify which bathroom gave the best view of the rose gardens (see: Cassels and King & Woolmans), however the trees now obscure everything. Tour three also features a few artefacts from the assassination, including the ermine stole and bodice that Sophie was wearing on 28 June 1914. The bullet that killed Sophie is also displayed.

If you enjoyed *The Assassins*, please share your thoughts on Amazon by leaving a review.

For more free and discounted eBooks every week, sign up to our newsletter.

Follow us on Twitter, Facebook and Instagram.

Printed in Great Britain
by Amazon